APRIL

a Homeless Story

APRIL

a Homeless Story

BY

T. RANDALL

FOREWORD

Homelessness to us, living in a modern society, seems unlikely or at least improbable. To the concerned, it brings up the question: "Why is there homelessness?" With a country economically prospering, on top of having the affluence to benefit its people and industries thriving on international trade, how could there be people, though a minority, living homeless and in destitution? Yes, poverty has been with mankind since the beginning of time and will be with us into the future. It seems illogical to the realistically minded living in a democratically-oriented society with all of its social provisions applied to the people. Where did society go wrong? The answer can be found in the past.

Though homelessness has been around for thousands of years, it is an issue that has yet to be resolved. Since it is considered a stigma by many, I used to be very critical of the homeless society myself. From having been born into the remnants of a WWII-devastated country, Germany, and witnessing destruction and devastation, homelessness to me was widespread but understandable. It only lasted until people rebuilt cities and towns. In today's prosperous society it seems illogical. However, is it possible that tax payers are overburdened with too great of financial commitments to accommodate humanly underprivileged shortcomings in our nation?

It was not until I researched, investigated, and observed the homeless society that I began to understand the dilemma. It is a two-sided sword hanging over civilization. On the one side we have sufficient social programs to take care of the homeless. But on the other there is a culture insisting on adequate living conditions at ever increasing demands.

Where will it all end?

There is no end to it in the near future.

From the onlooker's perspective, homelessness seems a creation of a segment of society that is unwilling to conform to the social standards stating that every abled body should work and contribute to society to allow it to grow and flourish. It would seem logical that everybody in the country would have enough pride and responsibility to follow the rules of the majority population. However, this is not the case. The sentiments of the citizens are as diverse as the rules and regulations set forth by the government.

From the homeless point of view, their plight, whether voluntary or caused through poverty or otherwise, deserves an equally important consideration, many times ignored by local authorities.

But why is it mostly ignored?

Because homeless people come from a wide variety of backgrounds and conditions. In today's society, one would think the government and social services provide enough incentives to be able to take care of the homeless predicament but this is not always the case because the majority of homeless refuse to be confined within four walls. Shelters are only used for food and, in extreme cases, as sleeping quarters to keep from freezing in cold months and baking during the summer. For the self-imposed homeless, the preference is to sleep in the open under a starry sky no matter how many shelters are built and how much money is made available.

AUTHOR NOTE

I feel obligated to explain my reasons for writing this book in first place. Yes, there was one time I had also been homeless. It was at the onset of my life's journey. At 21 years of age, after graduating, I left Germany to seek opportunities in Switzerland. Arriving in Zurich after a two-hour train ride, with only 50 DM in my pocket and checking hostels for temporary quarters, I could not secure a room for several days. Homelessness was not prevalent at that time because city ordinances were still strictly enforced. I decided to seek shelter at the only place I could think of, by sleeping in an uncovered rowboat tied at the shores of Lake Zurich. It was only until I could find an empty room to rent that I spent my time in the open. And yes, watching the brilliance of a starry sky with shooting stars cutting across my vision is a spectacular view not easily forgotten.

There were other occasions I found myself in similar situations. During my 30-year career working as a defense contractor for the U.S. government, there were a number of times I felt homeless when arriving in a foreign country without prior reservations or local connections. Where the difficulty comes into play is the language barrier and unfamiliarity of the place. Regardless of the stated incidents, it does not make me an expert on the homeless style of living. What it provided me was a sense of understanding situations a homeless person could encounter.

For this reason, though I was very critical of their homelessness and living conditions, I was not judgmental and accepted their choices, no matter what the circumstances were.

After a successful and rewarding career that began in Philadelphia in 1962, and subsequently migrating to a new home base, San Francisco, in 1977, with a final move in 2008 to Colorado Springs, I have had ample opportunities to observe several cultural changes within the country so dear to me, the United Stated of America.

Unfortunately for the wellbeing of its citizens, not all of the changes have been encouraging for maintaining the solid foundation the country was built on. Many nations experience political and economic fluctuations with the periodic election of new leadership, and so does the United States.

Fortunately, citizens of this country uphold a strong bond to the democratic constitution the nation was built on. Being a relative newcomer as a nation back then, largely populated from well-established European cultures, it was the pioneering spirit that created the New World quickly, followed by an industrial revolution unlike any other on the planet.

At one time this New World was successfully managed for over two centuries, but as a result of gradual growth and development from its seemingly unlimited resources, it did not remain this way forever. Changes were about to take hold, not only economically, but culturally and socially as well. Within this book, I will describe and illustrate one such change, the addition of a homeless culture destined to remain with us into the future.

I perceived the idea for writing this book from a homeless person I met in 2019 while living in Colorado. I had her approval to illustrate her life in homelessness since her childhood. Unfortunately, events took over our lives that very year, eventually breaking our connection. The world was taken hostage by COVID-19, the worldwide epidemic, which we are still plagued with to this day, in 2021. As a result, the homeless, in many instances, were transported off to shelters and places outside of cities and towns without keeping track of the individuals.

A TRIBUTE TO THE HOMELESS

This tribute is written and dedicated to both my reading audience and the homeless people who provided much material, not so much through individual accounts of their own lives, but more so through my personal observations over several decades.

I have had the good fortune, provided by the U.S. government, to travel extensively not only within the country, but also outside of its borders, and in the process have had the opportunity to gauge foreign cultures against our own. It was this platform that provided me with great insight into other country's problems, as well as with homelessness, not only inherent to the United States but worldwide.

Other countries have the same or similar issues with diverse social behavior not being easily managed. It seems that money does not matter much to the self-imposed homeless. Their objective for a successful life is geared towards a freedom of movement and social independence. I realize that there are three factions when addressing homelessness. One, there are the unfortunate ones landing on the streets who have lost a job, home, family, or income, become too ill to work, or felt culturally deprived of equality. Two, there are the disabled American war veterans, drug and alcohol addicts that cannot perform their jobs, and many other related social victims. Three, there are the nomadic hippies, preppers and survivalists seeking independence from government subjection and social responsibility.

PERSONAL DEDICATION

I have given the subject of Homelessness much thought and consideration over the past year. Since the book is about the fragile life of a homeless woman, I needed a clear understanding for the psychological makeup of the woman. From a male perspective, my dilemma was not to fully understand feelings and emotions taking place within the woman's mind. It was a personal notion that surfaced not only recently. I already noticed the differences from childhood on when quietly observing women behavior, especially entrapped within the close confinements of air raid shelters. I needed a full understanding and it came in the form of my dear neighbor friend, Lyn Reeder.

When discussing my recent work, "April – a Homeless Story" with her, I offered her a copy.

She readily accepted.

I willingly complied.

It'd turned out she was an avid reader. Days later I had her response on the concerns I had with woman's emotional perspectives and interests. Her view set me straight to organize my work into a comprehensive and meaningful novel. I am grateful and thankful for it.

"Thank you Lyn."

SPECIAL DEDICATION

This book is dedicated to all the homeless people in this country struggling to make a living, a living based on freedom and prosperity most enjoy but also take for granted. All may be well, we think, as long as we can enjoy freedom from oppression with liberty provided for all as stated in the Constitution, but this is not the case. The preamble may work for the greater majority of the country's people, but there are cultural and economic exceptions not readily accepted to understand and resolve. It is the exceptions to a people that society has created, whether it evolved by chance or was shaped intentionally, that need our serious consideration. To the majority of citizens living within the parameters of organized society, it may not make much sense to ever consider a life lived in poverty and destitution. It only makes sense when one understands the reasons behind the diversity of social rejections in the society branded as homelessness.

Notwithstanding individual justifications by some homeless people, the underlying reasons for their plight are not simple. Government agencies and social organizations have been trying to solve the homeless issue for many decades without much progress, costing billions of dollars annually, and deprived of a workable solution.

To justify the problem and to be fair to both sides, the government and public making attempts to resolve the growing issue of homelessness, much of the burden is carried by organized society, but it should be carried equally by the homeless themselves, especially when the economy is thriving. It may not be as easy or may even become impossible during severe recession periods as we are presently experiencing during the COVID-19 pandemic. Homelessness, regardless of its apparent hardships, is here to stay.

TABLE OF CONTENTS

PART ONE | CALIFORNIA '70s ——————

California, as a state, was divided into two major parts of attractions: the northern region with its tempered climate and rugged cliff line spread out along the ocean front, and the southern region, known for its pristine beaches populated mostly by wave surfers and sun worshippers. But those pleasures were mostly reserved for the local population. Visitors from out of state and tourists from abroad had not yet taken off en masse. That would come with the introduction of Boeing's 747 aircraft, specifically designed to carry large numbers of passengers. However, designs were on the drawing board to implement changes to a leisurely travel existence reserved mostly for the privileged and wealthy. It would take several more years before California would become a Mecca for world travelers.

For one, while America was the leader in industrial evolution following WWII, it took the development of technology to kickstart the new age. Entrepreneurs from other states were seeking out and securing affordable real estate and low cost wage earners to create numerous business parks. One such park became Silicon Valley, to this day, still a major hub of the business world.

Where until such time, San Francisco was a sparsely-visited place reserved mostly for the locals, to leisurely stroll along Beach Street lined with a variety of stores and shops quietly offering their wares, to eventually land on Pier 39 with its prolific barking from sea lions. Seated in the serenity of the place while watching the sunset within the sea breeze, one could already make out a variety of different languages, mostly of Chinese and European origin. In later years, after the Cold War, Russians would become prominent visitors, but that was still fifteen years into the future, following the collapse of the Soviet Union in 1991.

For now, in 1977, there were a number of other attractions for the local strollers. To get there, one would head in the direction of Columbus Avenue to reach Chinatown, passing numerous Italian restaurants extending their space onto the sidewalk. Regardless of the season, people preferred to be seated outside amidst the bustle of city traffic and pedestrians when taking in the dining flavors served. It was a rare spot in the city, providing a small slice of Italian culture. It's an ancient, inherited custom to share leisure time with neighbors and to keep connected with nature.

Despite the continuous stream of automobiles and busses passing by, it was still quieter out there than the indoor seating, with waiters calling out orders, dishes being served, TVs mounted against walls broadcasting sports shows or news, and patrons trying to converse in elevated voices.

Then, there was the Embarcadero with its ferry building facing Market Street. Fortunately for the commuters, some were able to have the luxury of daily travel to and from work across the Bay, while the majority of the workforce was stuck in traffic, at times for hours, taking the bridges to their workplaces.

These would be popular attraction spots, but the City had much more to offer, from Union Square to Pacific Heights and beyond. Along the route one could stop to take in scenes at Ft. Mason, the Marina, the Presidio, and Crissy Field before circling back through Lombard Street or Broadway, or stopping at the Coit Tower, Levi Strauss Campus, or Ghirardelli Square, and finishing off the evening at one of the many quaint restaurants one could find on many city blocks. Where other sectors such as the Mission and Market Districts had their special offerings, it was streets like Geary, Grant, Sansome, Mason, Powell, and Battery that attracted attention. This was where the city blossomed.

To finish off the city journey, many would seek out Chinatown to stop for dinner before ending the day. Chinese cuisine was too inviting, with the rich menus offered by the many restaurants along the way, to not take advantage. There is one thing that can be said about Chinese food: no matter what dish one selects for a meal, their hunger will be satisfied and they'll be able to walk out without feeling stuffed. I suppose it was the six thousand years of perfecting their cuisine.

There was one more special place for the city adventurer; hidden away within the complexity of the Cannery was Jack Quinn. What attracted one to the place was the European atmosphere one sensed when taking the first step across the threshold. It was a popular place, which, in time, would attract many tourists. One could detect numerous foreign tongues being spoken. But that was not the aim for the evening. One had the luxury to choose from one of seventy-five brands of selected imports. One could savor beer from a number of countries around the world, from a British Stout or Italian Peroni to a Singha from Thailand or Asahi beer from Japan.

What a place for a thirsty traveler amid a pleasantly amiable environment, hearing the ringing of bells from the ever-fashionable streetcars at the next intersection over, alerting prospective passengers of their arrival. Aside from being a novelty providing a panoramic view in motion into the Bay, despite being crowded at times, tickets were cheap and affordable for anybody, though locals preferred to hop on and off for a short ride without purchasing the fare before the ticket agent arrived. It was all fun and games for the cunning.

What made San Francisco special was the cleanliness it prided itself in. For the most part, cleaning began even before dawn with an army of broom-carrying sweepers attacking the many streets and sidewalks, primarily in and around places tourists frequented. City administration did its best to keep the city clean. After all, it was this attraction that brought first-time visitors and repeaters back. Though there was one exception: Chinatown. The many trash collection containers discarded by kitchens after closing were tolerated, permeating the alleyways alongside shops and restaurants, now closed for the night, with the intense odors of food waste. An attraction in itself, this delineated Chinatown from the rest of the City.

DAYS OF INNOCENCE

"What a beautiful day," April, a child ten years of age, thought in the quiet of the morning, pulling the drapes open. The window from her tiny room located on the first floor did not give her much of a view other than of a blue sky overhead, for which she had to crane her head out the window. The horizon was blocked by gray building walls all around her vision. She checked her mom's room but only heard heavy breathing interrupted by laborious coughs.

"Good," she muttered, giving her mom the liberty she sought on this brisk but sunny morning. With Mom still asleep, school was not on her mind on this spring day. Though the climate in San Francisco does not vary much through the year, everyone seemed to sense and feel the changes in seasons. It is the steady ocean temperature that keeps the climate stable in the area. While most nights are foggy year around, daytime clears up as soon as the sun makes its appearance.

For April, it would be a day of leisure and exploration. She contemplated walking to Pier 39, the most popular on the wharf, but it would take her forty minutes to cross the city on foot from where she lived, at Mission and 4th Street. It was either the Embarcadero or the south side along the Bay. Today, she decided on the Bay, the closest point. It was only a short distance, within a ten-minute walk. In past years she had made it her mission to explore the once-thriving South Park and Mission Bay, long-deserted places along the East Bay shores, aside from frequently-played baseball games taking place at Oracle Park located at the China Basin.

The way the piers were constructed were that passenger ships docked from Embarcadero Pier 1 to Pier 39 headed west, and cargo ships docked to unload at Pier 2 through Pier 40, separated by the Marina and which continued on to Pier 96. It was there April headed this morning. Her exploration may have seemed like a fruitless effort, but this was not the case. While Pier 1 through 39, due to their clean and organized environment, may have been an attraction for most travelers and local pleasure walks, the even-numbered piers had much more character to them. It was here where the City's life thrived. It was here where money changed hands between merchants, dealers, gamblers, and whatever illicit bets could be placed.

Chinatown may have been the heart of the city, but this part was the cauldron, boiling with not-so-visible activities. April could spend all day here and never get tired of watching ardent people of different races and cultures bustling their wares. It was here where she found the adventure to satisfy her innocent and curious mind. Though not inclined to classroom discipline and learning, here was a place to satisfy and saturate her mind with the curiosities life harbored. It was here where she learned to become street smart, a trait not yet realized, directing her future life and survivability out under an open sky.

For now, she enjoyed the world observed through the innocence only an uncluttered mind could have. Not having had breakfast this morning, she could feel her stomach growl. With merchant ships flying foreign flags unloading cargo vans lifted by enormous cranes, there was plenty of food to be snatched after crates were opened within the many warehouses. Since she was a child, innocent in appearance, looking through beautifully-shaped eyes though unkempt in appearance, nobody paid her much attention. People assessed what she was, a street urchin begging for morsels.

Watching activities nearby, her eyes were focused on a sidewalk vendor grilling some meat and vegetable dishes in a Chinese fashion. The aroma was too appealing to ignore. Striding up next to the vendor, her pleading gesture was quickly rewarded with a couple of spring rolls wrapped around stir-fry. She was happy, and the vendor was happy, knowing he'd done his Samaritan deed for the day. It was all April needed to continue on her day's journey.

She found a quiet spot on the pier nearby and lingered there for some time in thoughts focused on her life. At her age all she knew was the limited means provided by her mom. Saddened by this, wishing for a better life than her mom provided, she longed for companionship as well as the toys she'd never had. April quickly learned that she did not fit in with the other children she met in school. She could sense the aura of aversion from other children in classes and at play. Rarely invited to participate in games, she avoided going to school as much as she could get away with by cutting classes.

In first grade she had already gotten in trouble for not showing up, but it was not her fault back then. Her mom had overslept or was still too drunk to see her off to school, resulting in her oversleeping as well. It did not matter how much the teachers reprimanded her and complained to her mom to take action or have April be expelled from school. The idea was welcome to both of them, but the law dictated otherwise. Every child in this nation was obligated by civic law to attend grade school. Threats like this were disregarded by her mom even though child welfare agencies came frequently knocking at their door. All it took was for her mom to speak with one or another client of hers, the city mayor or a council member, to pacify the school's head teacher into ignoring mother and child.

It was this simple if you had the sound connections her mom had with city officials. It might have resolved the immediate situation for her mom, the irresponsible person that she was, but it did nothing for April's future, leaving her seemingly trapped in a life of destitution and poverty.

For now, April enjoyed her freedom with its abundant variety in values and culture provided by the nation's most beautiful city by the Bay, San Francisco.

NATIONAL CRISIS

Though April, living in poverty, was not aware of the nation's economic crisis periodically appearing and being resolved by state authorities, she was indirectly involved with the lack of proper housing and food with the shortages her mom would or could not provide. The following statistics are brief excerpts from the "Ending Homelessness in Los Angeles" (January 2007) report through the Inter-University Consortium Against Homelessness and authored by Jennifer Wolch, Michael Dear, Gary Blasi, Dan Flaming, Paul Tepper, and Paul Koegel, with Daniel Warshawsky.

Economical

Between 1950 and 1970, during a period of post-war prosperity, the gap between the incomes of rich and poor narrowed. But this trend was reversed in the 1970s, and became entrenched during the '80s in what economists describe as the Great Turnaround. The national economy shifted from manufacturing to service industries, where wages were lowered due to deindustrialization. Over three-quarters of the new jobs created during the 1980s were at minimum-wage levels. By 1983, over 15 percent of Americans were living below the poverty level, even though half of them lived in households with at least one person working.

Housing

In the decade following 1973, 4.5 million units were removed from the nation's housing inventory, primarily occupied by low-income households. In the same period, in contrast, the rise in single-person households dramatically increased the demand for housing across the nation, creating a crisis of unprecedented proportions. The number of poor renter households grew by tens of thousands but the number of affordable units fell dramatically. Virtually no new public housing units were constructed during the 1980s, leaving the low-income earners desperately searching for shelter.

It was at this time that the general public began to notice, forcing the government into action to help the homeless.

Welfare

The Nixon era ushered in a restructuring of the welfare state that has been continued by all subsequent Republican and Democratic administrations. Driven by ideological commitments to privatization and decentralizing welfare to states and localities, the erosion of public welfare took many forms, but two changes stood out in terms of the 1980s crisis.

The first of these was deinstitutionalization, a plan to empty the asylums treating and housing mentally-disabled individuals, which was promoted by both civil libertarians and cost-conscious policy makers. In the two decades after 1950, the inmate population of national state and county psychiatric institutions was reduced from over 1 million, to just over 100,000. The plan was that deinstitutionalized people would be served by community mental health centers funded by the federal government, but these never materialized in sufficient numbers to address the growing needs. The promise of deinstitutionalization remained unfulfilled. Many former patients ended up on the sidewalks of America, homeless and without care. Today, many of them are in county jails, where they have been joined by people who would have been institutionalized in previous eras.

The second key event was the cut in welfare. Nationwide, between 1982 and 1985, federal programs targeted to the poor were reduced by $57 billion. Because of adjustments to the eligibility requirements, over half the working families on federal aid were removed from welfare. There was little comfort for families who sought help at the state level, where many states had cut their assistance payments in half, with some states lacking such programs altogether. In post-Proposition 13 California, welfare payments were effectively cut by repeatedly eliminating cost-of-living adjustments, including Medi-Cal coverage. Health and mental health funding were cut as well, along with funding for substance abuse treatment, forcing the homeless to live on public sidewalks.

Vulnerabilities
Later on, during the 1980s and 1990s, additional factors worked to increase personal vulnerability and expose more people to the risk of homelessness. One was the explosion of crack cocaine usage that created an epidemic of drug abuse and addiction, and unraveled the lives of countless people who became caught up in the drug market either as users, suppliers, or distributors. Later, other drugs such as methamphetamines became widespread and were no less destructive to human lives. While demand for treatment and care of addicts skyrocketed, the number of public treatment facilities drastically fell across the country.

At this time, attitudes toward criminal justice turned away from rehabilitation to punishment. The rise of stricter sentencing and three-strikes laws dramatically increased the number of incarcerated people, causing the prison population to triple, rapidly worsening the trends for California. The result was a growing population of ex-offenders with little or no rehabilitation or job prospects.

Lastly, the rising cost of health care and rapid growth of the uninsured population meant that many people with medical problems had no recourse for affordable health care. People often faced a choice between paying for health care or for housing, and as a result frequently found themselves homeless.

The decline in personal incomes and the squeeze on affordable housing, along with rising rates of personal vulnerability, created, in America, a broad class of precariously-housed families and individuals who were only a paycheck or two away from eviction. With diminishing prospects of help from cash-starved public welfare agencies, many people lived on the edge, knowing that one more personal setback would precipitate a crisis that could cause the descent into homelessness.

It was this situation that caused April and her mom to live on the edge of poverty. Since April was born out of wedlock, she accepted her status since she was not aware of any other family condition. When she questioned her mom about her dad, she was brushed off with one or another excuse. She never got to meet or know her dad.

THE UNFORTUNATE

"Can I get you something, Mama?" April asked her mother who, like most days, came home, took off her dated coat, threw it carelessly into the corner next to the entrance, and, on unsteady legs, headed in the direction of the bedroom. She could have just hung the coat on the hooked board mounted to the wall next to the door, but that would have been an added chore to a person under physical strain.

"Don't bother me, child," she replied between coughs and puffs from a crumpled cigarette clutched between her lips.

It saddened the child to watch her mom in agony day in and day out, suffering from what doctors would describe as withdrawal symptoms. "I wish I could help you," the child muttered, lost on deaf ears. She lingered by the bedroom door as usual, hoping Mom would emerge to join her company, but, as usual, this was wishful thinking.

The child retreated into the only other room in the apartment, the living room. Propped on the sofa, she scanned channels for a children's program on the small-screen television. Luckily, PBS televised Sesame Street, her favorite show. It always perked up her mood, but not enough to be happy and cheery. Where other children would laugh, expressing emotions while watching a program, the gesture of a loud laugh did not come naturally living in the drab shadows in San Francisco's Mission District. The Mission was her world, a world filled with misery and poverty. While she saw the city swept clean by municipal workers in other areas, the Mission District appeared to be neglected. She, too, would rather be strolling along Pier 39, watching the impatient sea lions barking for food. She could relate to that, as hungry as she was most days.

The very thought saddened her even more. Only on rare occasions did her mom take her to the piers, usually on a holiday to beg for money. It was always a happy time, standing next to Mom, holding out her little hand while watching a visitor rummage through pockets or purse to hand over a few coins. "Thank you," she would reply while her mom sat smoking on the bench nearby. "Look," she would proudly proclaim, "Quarter," while handing the meager alms over. It usually earned her a casual shrug of the shoulders but otherwise did not seem to produce an emotion in her mom.

The child stood patiently waiting for the next handout while taking in the beautiful scene near the bay. Four hours later, her mom stood up, indicating she had enough earned for the day. It was a good thing because hunger pangs emanated from the child's stomach. Pangs were nothing new. As a matter of fact, she was used to it. Most days she would anxiously wait for Mom to come home carrying a bag containing a piece of bread or some fruit someone discarded in a trash can near the park.

While her mom would sometimes make a measly earning on a day job, most days she came home empty handed. "Where is the money?" the child would unhappily demand, realizing it would be another hungry evening, night, and next day, but she was used to it. Food, to her, seemed a luxury. When hunger took over her body it also affected her mind. Her thoughts began to drift for something to do. Unfortunately, living in a small, cramped one-bedroom apartment amidst other apartment dwellers did not leave much space in the living room for recreation and decoration. When she looked around the room, there was only one space of interest: the bedroom. She headed there as quietly as possible so as not to wake up Mom. Her hands reached for the only treasure, placed on the top shelf, hoping Mom had left the box unlocked. Like many times before, today was no different; it was locked. "Maybe someday," she said in the quiet of the room. She had yet to find out its contents.

Hours passed before she was shaken from the TV. "April!" the voice shouted from the bedroom.

It stirred the child into action, and she urgently rushed for the bedroom. "What, Mama?"

"Bring me the bottle," Mom demanded.

As usual, there was an opened bottle of whiskey or other distilled grain waiting in the cupboard below the sink. April rushed to retrieve the bottle. Her mom had no patience and would get angry at her if the bottle was empty or slow at being delivered. It still puzzled her why her mom would drink such ghastly brew. One day she stole a sip from the bottle to taste it but cried out in pain, thinking her mouth and throat were on fire. It would be the only time she would ever try an opened bottle again. Just the thought of it brought on repulsion.

April was too young to realize that her mom was addicted to alcohol and smoking pot. Her mom was not the only one with these habits. Other people living in the neighborhood displayed the same habits. For this time, those were the accepted practices by many of the poor in the country. Ecstasy was just emerging and hard drugs had not yet spread to the general population. Sure, people were aware of drug addictions, but those were isolated cases mostly practiced by frustrated artisans and entertainers who had fallen prey to heroin, a hard-core substance leading, ultimately, to a life cut short.

In the limited sphere of April's existence, at her age, her immediate neighborhood was the only world she knew. It was a world of struggle for a meager existence carved out by the poor and desolate, forsaken into lifelong poverty created by society. There were the wealthy blessed by the inheritance of an industrial revolution, thrifty shop owners with a sense of diligence catering to their neighboring customers, skilled workers holding part-time jobs awaiting the next technological revolution, and professionals making a living at various laboratories and hospitals, with the rest watching the dwindling of the American Dream. Once the essence of prosperity, the good old days were far from April's concerns. Hers was a struggle for survival repeated each day from waking to sleep, a life created by her mom through prevalent conditions in a city subjected to economic changes.

"April," her mom's voice reverberated from the bedroom, "get me another bottle."

"Uh-oh," she muttered, knowing that it would cause trouble. Rushing to the cupboard did not solve the problem. There was no bottle left. What made it worse was that she had no money to quickly fetch another at the liquor store down the street. Rummaging through her mom's purse did not raise enough cash for the purchase. She had to face her mom. On wavering strides, she opened the door and went in, only to see her mom sprawled across the bed and, as usual, puffing away. "Sorry, Mom." She whimpered. "No bottles left."

"Then go and get some," her mom shouted.

"But, Mama, there is no money." This brought silence but only for a few seconds.

"Go begging. Now!" Mom ordered. "And don't come back empty handed."

April knew the routine. As much as she disliked crouching by the sidewalk holding out her tiny hand, watching passing pedestrians sneering at her, it was an order with which she had to comply. Depending on the day of the week and sidewalk traffic, when luck was on her side it would be minutes, or it could take hours to accumulate enough coins to buy the bottle. It was her responsibility. It was her job, the only one she knew aside from homework. Homework for April was not the ordinary schoolwork assigned daily to the students. Homework for her was much like a slave that used to be hired by a rancher. It meant getting up at dawn's early light, preparing breakfast for Mom with whatever stale bread and spread was left in the cupboard, washing whatever clothing was tossed into the hamper, doing the dishes, making their beds, cleaning rooms, vacuuming floors, shaking out rugs when the weather was nice, and taking a shower to clean her own body.

"What about school and homework?" one might ask.

School was not considered an important task by her mom. Most days April skipped school. Though it reflected on her grades at the end of the school year, her mom did not seem to care much, so neither did she. Many children her age living in the inner city missed a day or more. Teachers were used to it and so were the parents. Education was not that important. "What do you need to be educated for?" grownups would reflect when the subject came up. "There are no jobs anyway."

The country had just emerged from a decade of riots and cultural clashes that were not yet over. These grossly affected the economy, stagnant to begin with, which mostly affected the poor. For April, it was nothing new. She was born into it and did not know anything else. Sure, grownups talked about better days and reminisced on more glorious times, but that was an era she did not know and couldn't imagine.

Reading for her was still difficult and so was carrying on a conversation, things necessary for a productive life and meaningful career, but to acquire both she had to go to school. She did not know the importance, a responsibility usually instilled by parents.

And so, this morning, she hurriedly trotted down the street to a nearby store front, a grocery she knew would be the best spot for today's emergency. Despondently, crouching on her haunches with her head facing the ground, she waited. It helped, avoiding eye contact with people passing by. To her, they were all strangers. She had picked up the trade from grownup beggars. This encouraged passing pedestrians to stop and drop a coin or two into the cup clutched between her hands. As time passed by, her mind usually wandered from the immediate chore. Even though her education was close to nothing she was street smart, a trait much more suitable for her position. Today, her mind played out images about people she did not know.

First and foremost, images of a dad appeared in her mind like so many times before. Though not real, it was an image she had made up years ago after asking her mom about her dad, but all she learned was that he was a Bum and No-good Bastard not living up to his promises. Her mom had had plans to get married, coming from a family having kids, but he had skipped out on the day of the wedding. He just did not show up at the church, standing up family and friends, who waited patiently for an hour before the ceremony was adjourned by the priest.

Today, this early morning, April lucked out. The stars or whatever spirit was guiding her miserable life had mercy on her. She earned enough money for a cheap bottle of whiskey, loaf of bread, carton of milk and a quarter pound of cheese, the daily essential items for the two. Money to buy meat was a rare occasion, usually reserved for the holidays when people were more apt to feel sorry for the poor.

Back home, her mom had been waiting for her to reappear. "What took you so long?" were words thrown at her entrance.

"Sorry, Mama, but I have good news," April announced with a victorious smile. "Look." She handed over the grocery bag.

It pacified her mom.

Ten minutes later April was alone once more for the day. She never knew where her mom went or what she was doing at the places April was not allowed. For the most part, she had no idea about her mom's activities, but there were times she would sneak along at a distance to find out. It appeared that her mom knew quite a few people not far off, with whom she would meet. It was mostly neatly-dressed men apparently from a better level of society. She envied her mom for it but did not dare to reveal her stealthy presence on her scouting. Her spying on Mom would reveal times when her mom and a stranger would drive off in a posh vehicle to places unknown. At other times they would walk to a nearby hotel only to reappear an hour or so later, departing with a hug accompanied by words too far off for her to hear.

What April did not know at the time was that her mom was earning a living, not by ideal means, but a living nevertheless. Unfortunately, she never learned how much her mom was earning. It was a secret never revealed. It was money the two could have used to live in comfort, but it was squandered daily by her mom on booze and drugs, essential necessities for facing repeat customers and new clients with each day.

Her mom was enslaved in a cycle of alcohol and drug use not easily broken. A victim of society, like most users, April's mother's use had begun gradually with an initial sample handed out at no charge at a party. Unbeknownst to most adolescents, it's to get one hooked by a dealer. At that age, a dealer is not a hard-core user and pusher. It likely is a popular school pal, making an earning beyond that usual for a boy his age. The sampling quickly turns into a habit. Daily school routines become bearable with occasional stops to the restroom to replenish the habit. Life turns into pleasure but things don't remain this way. Drugs have a means of sneaking up on one's wellbeing, slowly at first, then gradually taking over the innocent's being, directing and enslaving every waking moment and ending in eventual premature death. A life cut short by overdosing on heavy drugs or a chemically-poisoned substance concocted in some illegal laboratory.

It was a state April's mom had not yet reached, but eventually she would be consumed by and succumb to it unless a rehab clinic got their hands on her first. It was an unfortunate destiny April might face as well, brought on by an adult who had an opportunity at a potentially productive life turned immoral.

"What's wrong with drugs and alcohol use?" the question may be asked. "They've been around for centuries."

"It's immoral," the logical response should be, but is generally not the case. They provide a service and way of living to the pusher and grower. Somebody other than the user always benefits. Drugs and prostitution have followed man for thousands of years. They will follow man into the future and into space as well. Most prevalent in wartime situations, the provider of sex meets the needy male in all sorts of situations and levels of society.

For April, though used to the meager living her mom provided, it was good enough since she did not know any different. Unfortunately, the city's educational system thought otherwise. With her frequent absences and missing classes, the law finally caught up. Child services was instructed to take action that would take April from her mom and put her up in foster care until she reached the age of sixteen. Where she was terrified at the very thought of being torn from her mom, the only person she knew, Mom, on the other hand, seemed somewhat relieved from the burden of caring for her child shifting to the city's social system.

A HOMELESS CULTURE

April, at age ten, knew today was the day Child Services would come and take her away. It was not a comforting thought after the stories her mom had told her. As she was too young to effectively comprehend, these stories had projected images on her mind more like a horror story than a fairytale. Having just awoken from a troublesome sleep, April saw it was still dark outside. Darkness did not scare her much since she was used to begging into the night. What scared her more was the clinical environment of an institution she was about to face. The thought sickened her so much it forced her into making a decision. So as not to disturb Mom still sleeping, she quietly entered the bedroom, rummaged through the space they had lived in for the past ten years, and found that, aside from adult clothes, there was not much left.

Next, she inspected the closet. Straining to reach the upper shelf, her hand touched on a solid object beneath some hats her mom had used to wear. Pulling it down, she saw it was a small wooden box people use to save valuable items. Clutching the box under one arm, April took one of her mom's belts from the closet hook and hurried for the exit. On the way out of the bedroom she grabbed the blanket and pillow from her bed and pushed the door shut. The blanket and pillow would prove to be two valuable items in the years ahead. On unsteady legs she stood in the darkness of the hallway, taking in a few deep breaths that calmed her jittery nerves, thinking what would be ahead.

For her, it would mean begging from morning to evening, hoping to earn enough for another day's livelihood. She was jolted from her troublesome thoughts by the sound of the doorbell. April was devastated and shouted, "Mom!"

"What?" the voice came from the bedroom.

Trembling in the dark hallway, April ignored the bell but seconds later it was followed by a repeated knocking. "Please go away," she whispered.

Both knew the day had come to vacate the apartment but they refused to open the door despite multiple shouts from the outside: "Police! Open up."

April hastily retreated into the bedroom to be by the side of her mom. They had hoped to get another reprieve when things suddenly quieted down for a minute, but they were jolted into reality when the landlord and police stepped into the room in which they were hiding. They had forced their way into the building with the landlord's passkey. The eviction process did not take long. It was over in minutes. The only things April and her mom were allowed to take were the only suitcase in their possession and what they could carry.

Fortunately, April was allowed to remain with her mom since Mom still had personal connections with some city officials, who, after some pleading, extended both their liberty to move freely with a promise from her mom to move into a shelter. But these promises proved to be empty. Both would spend most nights tucked under a blanket listening to the quiet of night while watching the starry sky overhead until both succumbed to restless dreaming.

Two years had passed since they lost their home. At age twelve, April had learned the cruelty of life. Ever since, they had been on the move from shelter to shelter and, when all were filled at the end of the day, they moved on to city parks, hoping for her mom to find a bench to rest on for the night while April slept on the bare ground, covered by frayed blankets to keep rain, frost, and fog off of their haggard bodies.

Their life of begging, as it had turned out, was tolerable for most of the year, but when the winter months set in, it could become miserable even in a relatively temperate city such as San Francisco. Until now, April had never experienced the cold of winter. She had never touched or played in snow. The city was located near ocean currents drifting up from the equator, which influenced the ambient temperatures in the region. Aside from the nightly fog, the climate held steady through the year. It might have snowed at some time in the past but, for April, she had not yet experienced it.

"Mama," April would ask the first few months they were homeless, "why can't we get another apartment?"

"Can't afford it," would be her ready reply. "Everything is getting too expensive here."

It was a chilling revelation. Not only did it mean a life permanently deprived of a permanent dwelling, but it could mean moving from the city into the country where things would be more affordable. It was the competition against other homeless who were less impoverished, fending for a spot on a storefront or hallway that, unfortunately, kept increasing by the numbers with each month.

Even the homeless had a code of conduct. They were judged by their immediate environment and the number of belongings piled into a shopping cart. A tent was not an easy acquisition, but it elevated one from living on bare ground into a semi-permanent dwelling. It was a sought-out commodity April and her mom had not acquired yet, and were consequently forced to move on to another empty spot, which were becoming scarcer with each year. It was a constant migration for the poorest of the poor to stake out their next living space. No matter how much they tried to protect an acquired space, the male species still dominated the homeless. On the brink of starving, April would witness her mom disappear with some homeless man, to return with a few dollars she'd earned. For April, it was a gesture of mercy by the individual, or so she reasoned.

Ever since her mom had developed pneumonia a few months ago, they had been penniless for the most part. People kept their distance from anyone having such an affliction, visible mostly due to the constant coughing up of mucus in-between uncontrollable hacking spells. This also held true with her mom's personal customers, who had avoided close contact at first, then broke connections altogether, denying them their only source of income.

They were both subjected to these stringent but survivable conditions until the day her mom would not wake up. Not knowing what steps to take next, April cried out to a nearby homeless person who had enough sense to wave down a passing patrol car. When the ambulance arrived, April knew she would be alone from here on.

Several days later, her mom was cremated, with her ashes contained within a modest urn, handed over to April for safekeeping. The only item she inherited from her mom was the wooden box, once filled with bracelets, necklaces, jewels and trinkets, now empty. Poverty stricken to the extreme after her mom's illness, since every valuable item her mom had owned had been turned in at the pawnshop, April only had the urn to remind her of her mom. Although her mom had not been the best child caretaker, April treasured the urn with fond memories. She had been a mom, the only living relative April had had. For a child who had lived a sheltered life, the current environment was the only condition she knew. Everything else was hearsay and susceptible to dreams and imagination.

From here on, April had to fend for herself. In a way, she was relieved of the one responsibility she knew, taking care of her mom, but it did not lift her spirits. She was penniless without shelter, facing an uncertain future.

SAN FRANCISCO – '90s

It all began in the early '90s, with local governments throughout the nation desiring some of the $3 billion dollars appropriated to the budget the U.S. Department of Housing and Urban Development (HUD) annually spent on homeless services. To get a better account on future budgeting, cities were to count the unhoused and unsheltered population. Shelters usually full to the bursting with waitlists hundreds to thousands of applicants long, and county health or human services agencies, in addition to nonprofit organizations burdened by the task, often resorted to the simplest method of enumeration known. Organizers and citizen volunteers went into the night with flashlights, clipboards, and pencils and literally counted heads they located curled-up on sidewalks, in tents, and in RVs.

How many people were assessed using this method only came close to be an educated estimation. True numbers were not available and counted data could only be estimated into 500,000 homeless throughout the States, with approximately 8,000 homeless people residing in San Francisco alone.

Investigative agencies among homeless experts explained that census figures collected when using untrained volunteers in the dark were inaccurate and flawed and probably an under-exaggeration. Whenever one asked, "How many homeless people are there?" one could take the official number and, depending on city location and size, add thirty to fifty and perhaps one hundred percent more. Anyone who spent some time in San Francisco or Oakland gained a painful awareness that the region's homeless problem had evolved from being a novelty in the '80s, attracting tourists, to an international embarrassment, and, of late, into a humanitarian crisis.

Not localized to only the Bay Area, similar situations also evolved in Los Angeles and Orange County as well. Tents on streets or poor people living in RVs, with human misery filling in the landscape of wealth and human prosperity. It had become a California-wide concern and did not stop there.

"What are the causes for such trends?" local citizens and visitors would ask. It could easily be explained with the following rationale: too high of rent, a lack of affordable housing, an increase in prosperity for the work force, and incurring affluence for the already wealthy. According to San Francisco city consensus, "For every person escaping homelessness, three more people take their space."

Blaming all of it on California or Californians would be a wrong assumption. The U.S. once had a national, federally-funded budget for the destitute under then-president Ronald Reagan. Today, homelessness has become particularly bad in California because housing prices and the cost of living are out of proportion, primarily due to restrictive growth and zoning laws. If anybody could afford to pay $1 million for a 950-square-foot bungalow in Palo Alto, it was only the Silicon Valley wealthy.

It may come as a surprise to the nation and the rest of the world, but a recent poll taken by the state proves one point: California was "Okay with all of this."

It could be because the state has become liberal under its prevalent democratic sentiment or because the citizens of the state are accepting the homeless situation without penitence. The homeless are here to stay.

Where the homeless at one time had been regarded as impoverished individuals void of opportunities, today, in the fast-paced world we live in, though reluctantly in most cases, homelessness has become an emerging culture accepted and tolerated by citizens and neighbors.

THE MISSION

For April, more time had passed, and she'd grown from a child into puberty. Crouched on her haunches by necessity, as she had done for most of her life, she watched seagulls drifting in and out of her sight. As was the case on sunny days in San Francisco, she would spend most of the day at her favorite spot on Pier 39.

The morning chilled her body so she wrapped the blanket around her shoulders. "Cozy," she muttered, embracing the warming effects of the wool. Being left to her own demise after her mom's death, she was subject to fending for herself. At first, she struggled to find daily food and shelter. But over time, being the street smart girl she was, she adjusted to a life of permanent homelessness, mostly played out on the open, absorbing daytime sun with starry skies at night, thinking of her mom and a better life.

"Now what?" her mind prodded after waking up to a new day, bringing the lonesome child into the present. Reality set in once more. "Where should I go?" These were the two most important questions in her life. Having grown up within a limited and defined space, there was only one answer: "The Mission." She headed there.

The Mission, in today's world, her world now, was one of San Francisco's poorer sections, extending out from Market Street, the city's prosperous business district. The transition from one sector to the next became obvious after crossing Van Ness Avenue.

The Mission was a district April could relate with. She and her mom would seek out dinner here when there was money left. Lunches were always quick snack items bought at a grocery store near the apartment. While the Mission today had degraded into a poverty-prone part of the city, it had a rich heritage of which most dwellers were unaware.

The Mission District, commonly known as "The Mission," is a neighborhood in San Francisco, California, originally known as

"The Mission Lands," meaning the lands belonging to the sixth Alta California mission, Mission San Francisco de Asis. This mission, San Francisco's oldest standing building, is located in the northwest area of the neighborhood.

The Mission is often warmer and sunnier than other parts of San Francisco. The microclimates of San Francisco create a system by which each neighborhood can have different weather at any given time, although this phenomenon tends to be less pronounced during the winter months. The Mission's geographical location insulates it from the fog and wind from the western part of the city. This climatic phenomenon becomes apparent to visitors who walk downhill from 24th Street in the west on foggy days towards Mission Street in the east.

Prior to the arrival of Spanish missionaries, the area which now includes the Mission District was inhabited by the Ohlone people, who populated much of the San Francisco Bay area. Spanish missionaries arrived in the area during the late 18th century. Franciscan friars were reported to have used Ohlone slave labor to complete the mission in 1791.

Around 1900, the Mission District was still one of San Francisco's least densely populated areas, with most of the inhabitants being white families from the working class and lower middle class who lived in single-family houses and two-family flats. Development and settlement intensified after the 1906 earthquake, as many displaced businesses and residents moved into the area, making Mission Street a major commercial thoroughfare. In 1926, the Polish community of San Francisco converted a church at 22nd and Shotwell Street and opened its doors as the Polish Club of San Francisco, referred to today as the "Dom Polski," or Polish Home.

The Irish American community made its mark on the area during this time, with notable residents such as etymologist Peter Tamony calling the Mission home. During the 1940-1960s, a large number of Mexican immigrants moved into the area—displaced from an earlier "Mexican Barrio" located on Rincon Hill in order to create the western landing of the Bay Bridge—initiating white flight, giving the Mission a heavily Chicano/Latino character for which it continues to be known today.

In the 1960s and 1970s, the Chicano/Latino population in the western part of the Mission declined somewhat and more middle-class young people moved in, including gay and lesbian people (alongside the existing LGBTQ Latino population).

In the 1980s and 1990s, the neighborhood received a higher influx of immigrants and refugees from Central America, South America, the Middle East and even the Philippines and former Yugoslavia as people fled civil wars and political instability at the time. These immigrants brought in many Central American banks and companies, establishing branches, offices, and regional headquarters on Mission Street.

From the late 1990s through the 2010s, and especially during the dot-com boom, young urban professionals moved into the area. It is widely believed that their movement initiated gentrification, raising rent and housing prices. A number of Latino American middle-class families, as well as artists, moved to the Outer Mission area, or out of the city entirely to the suburbs of the East Bay and South Bay areas.

However, in 2008 the Mission still had a reputation of being artist-friendly. The Mission remains the cultural nexus and epicenter of San Francisco's Mexican/Chicano and, to a lesser extent, the Bay Area's Nicaraguan, Salvadoran and Guatemalan communities.

EMERGING APRIL

When April emerged from puberty into adulthood, homelessness was on an increase through parts of the City. Still sparse in the early '90s, isolated cases were seen at popular spots along Market Street but were still considered more of a vagrancy trend. Beggars and drifters made their appearances. Crime in the city was almost nonexistent even though tourism had been on the increase during the past decade. Not even petty theft, usually targeted at the tourist, existed. This elevated the city of San Francisco into the nation's most popular tourist spot. For the time being, beggars were considered a novelty to vacationers and treated without prejudice. Most people handed over donations to the seemingly destitute who quickly became part of the city's culture, and over time this attracted more and more destitute.

It was not until mental institutions were permanently closed by the state that homelessness took possession of many sidewalks and, as a result, became a stigma for local dwellers. This influx caused a shift from the inner city to suburban developments in the southern, northern and eastern parts of the Bay.

For April, the first few days were difficult while she explored her new neighborhood. Looking at the Mission District from her new vantage point of being homeless, her life took on a new turn. Whereas in the past years it used to be the place to shop and dine inexpensively compared to most other parts of the city, it had now become the place for survival with three objectives: eating, sleeping, and keeping clean. Since she had no obligations anymore, such as tending to her mom when she was alive, there was plenty of time in a day to explore.

The most pressing item on her mind was locating a restroom facility. This did not present much of a problem since there were many restaurants in the area. All she had to do was walk into the place, head for the toilet, splash some water on her face, run her fingers through her unkempt hair, and exit. It was that simple. Nobody bothered her. She was just another patron in a hurry. This would become the first routine in her daily personal regiment. Eating was a bit more involved. Since she was penniless, begging would be required. Having many years' experience in that skill, the only one she had acquired, all that was required was for her to seek out an ideal spot with an abundance of foot traffic. It proved to be an effortless solution to set up temporary camp with her miserly belongings. Camp, in April's vocabulary at this time, was one pillow and blanket bundled around her mom's urn, folded into a cushion to sit on.

Since there was hardly any competition, begging for a day's eating expense was accomplished within a couple of hours if she was at the right spot. It did not take long for her to realize that she lacked a number of personal items she'd have to acquire. There was the need for a comb, hygienic pads, a toothbrush and toothpaste. That was all she could think of this first day, looking over the counter in the pharmacy she was standing in, waiting for the cashier to ring up her items.

Finding a sleeping space turned out to be more of a challenge. Asking around the neighborhood, she could not get any information about a homeless shelter. There were none since homelessness had not yet been common. The only option was a flophouse or an inn, both scarce in this part of the city since much of the population were families living in single homes.

She ended her search by tossing her package next to a row of hedges on a quiet street, hoping to get a few hours of sleep. Sleep did not come easy that first night, wrapped in her blanket in the open. She did not care. The scene was too spectacular. "My god," she muttered. "What have I been missing?"

Being mostly residential, the Mission became quiet as soon as the last restaurants closed at midnight. Though there were lights to illuminate the streets, it was nothing like in the city. It was dark enough to reveal a completely new world to April: the overhead starry sky. Overwhelmed by such beauty, "Splendor," she thought, was an understatement. "It's more like brilliance." Like many people looking into a night sky, she was overcome by the sheer beauty of the Milky Way with its bountiful cosmic display. Though silence and the infinite were embracing her vision, a new experience was cutting across her vision: shooting stars.

She laid there for hours in a restful state without worrying about sleep. It was a new world to enjoy.

Shaken from a wonderful world of dreams early in the morning, April felt something prodding her body. "Must have fallen asleep," she muttered, turning on her back. Looking straight up, expecting a starry sky, she found it had become daytime. She was staring into the questioning eyes of a uniformed officer, peering down at her and demanding, "Police. Get up. This is not a public park."

Somewhat surprised at the rude awakening, she stammered, "Sorry, officer. Won't happen again." Jumping to her feet, she quickly gathered her belongings and was about to leave.

"Not so fast, lady," he said, stern faced, taking hold of her arm. "What are you doing here?"

Still drowsy from sleep and not quick to respond, she hesitatingly explained, "I was watching the sky and must have fallen asleep," hoping he would let her go. But he didn't.

"How old are you, anyway?" he asked, assessing her.

"I'm twelve."

"You should be home with your mom. Where do you live?"

"In the city," she said in a wavering voice. It must have triggered a sense of alertness in the uniformed law officer.

"Okay," the officer replied. "Let's go." He promptly took her to the police station a few blocks away. After arriving, trying to get more information from her proved ineffective. All he could get from her was, "I don't know." The result was April getting fingerprinted and cited with a warning. "Don't stay out at night. You could get in trouble."

Though it was a sincere warning to a young girl who appeared innocent, at the moment trouble was the least of her worries. Prying further would not reveal any information at the station and, since there was no crime committed other than a city ordinance infraction, they let her go.

"Better find some sleeping quarters," she muttered. "But where?" Since it was still early in the day, she had plenty of time to find some suitable place, she hoped. With her belongings slung over one shoulder she marched on, up one street, down the next. Since it was spring time, not having sleeping accommodations did not worry her much. She had enough confidence in herself to secure a place before the cold set in, many months away.

"Room for rent," a sign proclaimed, posted on a door. April suspected what money was in her pocket might not be enough for a night, but had to find out the cost of the room. "Six dollars a night," she was told by the woman who lived in the apartment. "Why, you are so young. How old are you? You're not a runaway or in trouble?" the woman prodded.

"Thirteen," she lied, not feeling guilty despite only being a few weeks short of twelve. "How much a week?" April needed an idea for how much money she had to beg.

"$42, but I'll let you have it for $40 if you stay longer.

"Okay, I'll take it," she said. "I'll be back later."

"Wait," the woman brusquely demanded. "I'll need it now or I can't hold the room."

"I'll take the chance," April replied. "Don't have it now." She could sense the woman's change in mood at the empty promise and assured her once more, "I'll be back," then turned on her heels and walked off. Two things were gnawing at her: her stomach and where to go to work. She could still not grasp the fact that she was penniless and bound to be a beggar. Referring to her trade as work at least gave her a sense of direction into the future, whatever it may hold. She sought out a promising store front to start with.

She soon found out that people in this part of town were not apt to easily part with their hard-earned money, even if it were only a few pennies. As always when begging, her mind wandered to fill the emptiness in her life. Tears came into her eyes as she thought about her mom. Though sharing a poverty-stricken life, taking care of her mom had not been an ideal situation, but it was her mom's company she so dearly missed. "Mom," silently, she pleaded, "why did you have to die?"

Born into an empty life without much education, she had never learned to pray. There was no heaven and salvation in her mind because most of her brain was empty space, yet to be filled with knowledge. She realized her shortcomings when listening to people talk. There were many words she did not understand, and she could not grasp the meaning of the exchange. In the case of April and her mom, she'd mostly learned orders and commands. "Another thing I have to learn," she thought, watching people huddle together while talking, "how to converse."

It was already getting late in the afternoon and she had not earned enough to pay for the room. As it'd turned out, it had been a long and not-rewarding day for her. The coins she'd earned were hardly enough to buy a hamburger and fries, her favorite treat. At least she could satisfy her hunger pangs for the day. Eating only one meal a day was nothing new for April. No matter what the night might hold in store for her, sitting by the window at the local McDonalds, watching passersby rushing home after a day at work, she completely enjoyed the special treat.

Two hours she lingered at the place. It was getting dark and her need to find a place for the night was pressing. "But first," she thought, and promptly headed for the toilet. Checking herself over in the mirror, she saw there was the need to wash her body, hair, and find a change of clothes, but that had to wait for another day. For now, she squeezed some soap from the container, turned on the water faucet, washed her hair using the soap, and scrubbed her face, neck and upper body as much as the space allowed. Drying up under the blower, she exited into the cooling air with her bundle slung over one shoulder. "Guess the park will have to do," she decided, heading in the direction she had passed earlier in the day, hoping it would not attract the police again.

Cuddled under a tree within the warmth of her pillow and blanket, she enjoyed another night in splendor, observing the starry sky. While a life without social responsibilities had not yet entered her innocence, in the recesses of her mind she knew that living under the stars would be her destiny, if there was a means where she would not be pestered by the police. She could not tear her eyes from the grandeur of the night.

April was surprised at the bustling traffic on the street as soon as she opened her eyes. She had slept many hours and felt invigorated. Despite facing another day in uncertainty, at the moment she did not care. She was ready to explore her new world. She had to seek out and move on to a different section of town if she wanted to earn some money. Applying for a job was impossible because of her being underage. Child labor had been banned in this country decades ago. She suddenly realized her predicament. "I'm enslaved into begging forever." It urged her into action, at least for the moment.

Striding onto the sidewalk along the street once more, after some time her eyes caught a familiar building in the distance. Speeding up her stride, minutes later she confronted the entrance of the popular supermarket, Safeway. She decided to make it her spot for the day. Several hours into the day, she realized that it had paid off. She was dollars ahead. "Now we are talking," she said out loud, delighted at the earnings. It was the most she had earned in a long time. It gave her a sense of power she had not previously felt. She'd had to turn over her earnings to her mom in the past, but now it was hers, all hers. She was elated and called it quits for the day, deciding to be back the next day.

Trotting her way back, she hoped the room from the previous day was still available. Elated by the "Room for Rent" sign still up, she rang the doorbell.

"It's you again," the woman declared, somewhat surprised, checking April over. "What happened to you yesterday?"

"I was visiting some friends. It was getting too late and I stayed over." It may have been a lie but to her it was a necessity; fabricating an excuse had become a way of life. It was better than outright lying. She always felt guilty, but not with an explainable excuse. "But today I'm ready to rent the room," she declared.

"You have the money?"

"I'll pay for a week. Is that okay?"

"It's your money, as long as you can pay. You ready to move in?"

April handed the woman the $40 and received the key. "One week?"

"One week. It's what we agreed."

"Thanks," she said, following the woman down the hallway.

"That all you have?" the woman said, checking her into the room.

"For now," April said.

The woman left a joyful April to take possession of the room. Upon inspection, the place was clean and spacious enough for one person. For the first time in weeks she was content, but not for long. After it turned dark, she realized there was one thing missing: the starry sky. Disappointed, she realized she'd made a big mistake by being enclosed within four walls. It troubled her to the point of questioning her decision. "It's only one week," she placated herself. It turned out to be a long week for her. She could not wait to get it over with. In the meantime, she returned to the supermarket daily, earning more money than she had expected, until the day uniformed security showed up, demanding, "Get out of here. Go away. This is no place for beggars." She was promptly led away from the premises.

Her windfall sadly ended. She had to seek out a new place to earn a living. While she had longed to sleep in the open again, her joy was clouded over for a couple of nights when it rained. Having not considered such a possibility, she had to re-evaluate her lifestyle. "I know," she came to the conclusion, "I'll compromise."

The word 'compromise' was not part of April's vocabulary, but she understood what it meant. It had been readily used by her mom. The thought of her mom clouded April's mind once again. She dearly wished for her presence, or anybody's presence. "Strange," she muttered after realizing that she had not yet made a single friend, and she wondered what it would take. Sadly, she already knew the answer. People keep their distance from beggars. She was destined for a life in solitude.

In the loneliness of night, she contemplated, many times, her present and how she could fit into society. Unfortunately, there was no solution unless somebody would be willing to guide and educate her so she could get a job. But that seemed out of her reach since everybody she met was in a hurry, tossing a few coins into her hand only to rush off. She realized it would be a despairing life, feeling hopeless and trapped without an end in sight. "There is always hope," she pacified herself, and would have prayed if she knew how.

Consequently, days went by, then weeks, followed by months when she sadly realized nothing had changed in her life. The cold had settled in at the end of the year without any change for her in sight. The year following was a repeat and, before she knew it, another year had passed with her living under the sky. From the initial monetary windfall she had experienced that first week, she contemplated, "How long has it been?" That turned out to be the exception for her earnings.

And so, it appeared, one day felt like the next and the next, while time marched on. It seemed that there was no chance for April to change direction or improve on her life. What made it worse was her frequent run-ins with the law. It was always the same. In the darkness of night a uniformed shadow would appear out of nowhere while April was asleep, prod her in the back with the tip of a boot, and demand an ID only to drag

April to the precinct and book her, followed with being locked up for the night then released the following morning. Not having committed a crime, there were no charges other than an ordinance violation[1] to justify spending one night in jail.

The unfortunate thing for April was that she felt trapped in a lifecycle beyond her control. No matter how hard she tried, she could not figure out a solution to her dilemma. It would be a struggle without an end, living in poverty. More time had passed by her when she realized another birthday was only days away. She would be fifteen years old without having anybody to celebrate with.

---

[1] Ordinance violations used to be enforced in those days, but in today's world of a homeless culture, an ordinance will only be acted on by authorities if a crime is committed.

UNION SQUARE

At age 15, April was cautious with strangers but experienced a new sensation and the knowledge that came with it. Contemplating the reason, she remembered something her mom would say: "Be careful of men when you grow up." When April asked for the reason, her mom's reply would be brisk and secretive. "All they want is to get in your pants." The first time she'd heard the expression it did not make much sense. *Why would a boy or man want to wear my pants?* Having grown up, she knew better now. There were other times when she questioned the insanity of life. After waking up one morning, she felt wet. Thinking she had wet her pants, she checked, but was shocked when her hand came up bloody. She let out a scream. "Mama!" But there was no answer. Still drowsy from sleep, upon spotting the urn, she was reminded that Mom had passed years before. Frightened beyond comprehension, she tried to run away from herself, leaving the mess behind.

Not realizing how long she had run and how far she had come, exhausted and breathless, she collapsed on the sidewalk sobbing. It was not long after when a voice entered her senses. "What's the matter, girl?"

She realized then that a woman was crouching beside her, gently stroking her hair. "Who did that to you?" the woman demanded with a stern gesture at April's legs. The running had aggravated her plight with even more blood trickling along her skinny legs down to her feet.

"I don't know. I was asleep and woke up bloody."

"Come." The woman beckoned her to a nearby park bench. "I will explain."

"Explain what?"

"Your mess. You see," she began, "there comes a time in every girl's life when her body goes through changes. Didn't your mom tell you?"

"Tell me what?"

The woman believed the girl's ignorance as April stared back at her through innocent eyes.

"You are becoming a woman," she explained while April patiently sat on the bench next to her, somewhat calmed by her soothing voice. "Don't be frightened about the blood. It'll happen to you each month."

"Every month! Why?" It was still inconceivable to April to have such a frightening experience once, but every month? "For how long?"

"Many years. For as long as you are healthy and can bear children."

"Children? I don't want kids." The thought alone made her shiver. She could not imagine how and why she would ever want to bring a child into this world, a world filled with pain and misery.

It was a reflection instilled by her mom who had always complained about April being born. "You are the reason I have to prostitute myself."

Back then it did not make much sense to April to be accused of something that was not her fault. Her sense of reality dictated that Mom must have been wrong about some things but she could do nothing about that. Though Mom was the only person she depended and relied on, April respected her for raising her as best as she could within the means she had. April did not feel guilty about it since her mom was the one that spent all of their earnings.

"Let's get some ice cream," the woman suggested. While April normally would have refused such offer from a stranger, today it was a welcome gesture. Ten minutes later they entered an ice cream shop, a rare occasion for April.

"Can I have one of those?" She pointed at a fruit shake picture on the counter. She was thirsty and had always wanted to try one of those big drinks she'd watched people order. When asking her mom, the answer was always, "Not healthy for you."

While April openly respected her mom in everything she did and was told, at times she did question the adult's wisdom. "Other people do it."

"Other people are stupid. They believe everything they read and hear."

"I believe you," April objected.

"I know best. Besides, you don't read."

"I can read," April protested. The problem she had with the language was with spelling from a lack of writing.

"I'm talking about books."

"Not my fault," she stated. "We never have money to buy any." That would end their verbal exchange. Short comments like this was the extent of their conversations. No matter how much she would beg growing up, her mom never read to her from a storybook or made up a fairytale like other moms did. The consequences were visible. She grew up into a stern and questioning person. Recollecting her mother and daughter relationship, she could never remember having a happy and joyful moment. Nobody ever heard her laugh.

It was minutes later before April became aware again of her company. "Sorry," she said. "My mind was on my mom."

"Where is your mom?"

"She died a few years ago."

"I'm sorry."

"Not your fault," she managed to say, almost in tears. Her mom was strict with her most of the time, but she still loved her. She was the only person in her life that had shared the limited and restricted space of her world. April and the woman spent another hour at the park before the woman finally bade her goodbye.

"I have to go now," she said. "Are you going to be okay?"

"I've managed so far," April promised. "Thank you for explaining the facts of life."

The woman turned and was out of her sight seconds later. It was here when April realized how much she missed talking with people. It was a trait she'd never expected or wanted before. "You can't trust anybody," her mom would say. This laid the ground rule for her future life. April returned to the place she had slept the previous night. Expecting her pillow, blanket, and—

"Mom's Urn!" she yelled out in anguish, as she found the spot empty. Thinking she had made a mistake in location, she stood there a minute, recollecting last night's events. Theft was not an option to consider. The destitute might be a poor and deprived lot but they live within a strict code of honor. They were honest people. That was what turned them to a life of poverty to begin with, getting away from a society mostly out for material gain.

Feeling dejected about having lost her items, especially the urn, which was irreplaceable, she decided to relocate to a more promising place. The Mission had become a part of the past, she decided.

"Time to move on," she said to herself. It was not her choice, but due to the conditions she'd found herself in lately. She'd had too many run-ins with the police to come up with constant excuses for illegally sleeping out in open parks, private properties, backyards, doorways, and other less clean places. There was one thing she would never give up, sleeping under the sky, no matter how often she would have to move. Watching day turn into night was the only entertainment she could call her own. It was the only treasure, though distant and out of reach, with which she was left. Relocating would be easy without any objects to carry but the challenge was where she would go.

Moving on empty handed may sound like an easy task, but ask anybody: it takes preparation time, if only mentally. From a realistic point of view, it is dependent on the things one owns within the acquired comfort zone. From a psychological perspective, some will always resist. Today, it was April's second turn to face reality. There was one place she remembered where her mom had taken her. It was a better district than the Mission, not only for affluence but, more importantly, it was within the city and close to people and traffic, the two necessities for a beggar to effectively survive.[2]

And that's what she did, turning her back on the Mission and heading straight for Union Square. At the pace she was walking it would take her only a couple of hours, in time for the evening crowd. Her path was direct and pretty level as she strode along Van Ness Avenue, taking a right turn on Geary Boulevard, and four blocks later she arrived at her destination.

"Wow." She had not expected this many people at the park. "I'm home," she muttered, happy with her choice of location. While Union Square[3] was a well-known landmark among tourists, it was also the place to go for local and visiting shoppers alike. "I'm gonna like it here." It might have been an easy spot to fall in love with, but making it a living quarters for April proved to be a new challenge.

Only a few years earlier, around the time she had become homeless, the city center had been a leisurely-paced area, but the environment since had drastically changed. Trolleys stopped almost constantly from both directions, dislodging their loads. People of all languages, it seemed, were targeting the Square for their personal pleasures. The first thing April did after arriving was seek out a place to rest in the park.

Swiftly stepping up the spacious stairways built to enter the square from every direction, she arrived on top of the platform topped with palm trees, exotic shrubs, and other trees in a setting much like a tropical garden. It was exhilarating just to be here at this unexpected metropolitan paradise. The square

---

[2] There are other terms for beggar. There is the drifter, panhandler, vagabond, penniless, indigent, and more, but for April at this time it was beggar.

[3] Union Square is a 2.6-acre public plaza bordered by Geary, Powell, Post and Stockton Streets in downtown San Francisco, California. "Union Square" also refers to the central shopping, hotel, and theater district that surrounds the plaza for several blocks.

might have been a local attraction only a few years earlier, but today, seated on a comfortable, clean bench, April found a peace of mind she had never experienced before.

To others nearby she might have looked just like any other visitor enjoying the day. Not burdened with pillow, blanket, and urn… "The Urn," she silently cried out, wondering again why she had lost the precious item.

It took some minutes to calm her nerves. In her feeble state of mind she had already taken possession of the bench and did not want to lose the spot, silently replacing the lost urn with the bench. It was the first time she thought in terms like that and would claim this very spot tonight and in the nights ahead. Somewhat calmed, her physical needs took over. She had to seek out a public toilet facility. She lucked out. There was not only one restroom nearby, but several to accommodate the influx of daily visitors.

On entering she could see the cleanliness of the well kept up facility. It was pure pleasure for April and her free spirited lifestyle to have access to it. She made ready use of it, not only to cleanse her body but to also wash and comb her tousled hair. Luckily, she'd had the foresight to keep her intimate belongings in one of her inner zipped-up jacket pockets. It reminded her of something she had been meaning to do. "It's time to get another jacket." She'd realized some time ago that she had outgrown the well-worn overcoat someone had given her years ago. All she had to do was earn enough to purchase another at one of the many nearby clothing outlets. It would not present a problem. As was the case with most cities, there was always the Salvation Army in addition to Goodwill stores.

Feeling clean and invigorated, April took an exit from the public restroom but halted after a few steps. "Where to?" The answer came in the form of a rumbling stomach. Undecided on what direction to take, she spotted a display case at one end of the Square and headed for it. As expected, her eyes captured a city map showing the immediate district she was presently in. Aside from projecting local streets and alleys, it also listed shops and restaurants in the area. "But first," her mind prompted her, "I need money." Penniless like most mornings, she headed in the most likely direction toward the BART Powell Station.

She remembered her mom's advice from years ago: "You'll always find some eateries near BART." She proved to be right. Every street April entered was a goldmine for the stomach. All she needed was money that she didn't have at the moment, leaving her with two choices: go begging now, or wait until evening when shops and restaurants closed. Looking herself over, the first choice was out of the question. With the loss of her trademark as a beggar, the soiled pillow and blanket, nobody would take her seriously begging for money. The problem was that she was famished now. She did not want to wait many hours to satisfy her hunger.

A thought came to her mind. "Why not?" She headed for the most likely spots, sidewalk restaurants and cafes. Since it was already lunchtime it would be easy pickings, as she had done on numerous times before, living by the motto, "Where there's a need there's a solution." In practicality, the process went like this: enter the shop and beg at the counter for a leftover, or snatch a plate when the waitress was preoccupied, or grab some leftover morsel from an eater that had just left the store. It was this simple but did not always go as smoothly as expected. There was always a do-gooder or well-meaning citizen calling for the attendant, reporting the misdeed she had just committed. When caught, after she explained that she was homeless and famished, the business owner usually just released her and let her go.

Today's plan went as smoothly as she'd expected. In the flurry of eaters, nobody paid her any attention when she took a piece of bread and some cheese, along a half-empty cup of soda, off a table a patron had just vacated. Seconds later she was on her way, munching on the easily-acquired sandwich and sipping her way back to the Square, happy with the involuntary decision forced onto her at the Mission. "Life's good. Think I'll stay."

Her next needs, getting a pillow and blanket, turned out to be more of a challenge. Like earlier, she trotted back to the display case. "There it is," she muttered, her eyes homing in on the Salvation Army[4] depot located not far off. She spotted the place after a ten-minute walk and briskly entered. Stopped by the desk clerk, she explained her situation to the attendant. "I'm homeless and just arrived this morning." It was enough information, after signing in, to gain her access to the place.

To a homeless person, the place was much like a candy store to a child. All one had to do was select the item dearly needed. Today it was a pillow and blanket. Nothing more, nothing less. This was the trademark she had decided on years ago. Any more would burden her freedom of movement, any less would expose her to the elements. Today she lucked out. Looking around the store, her eyes caught additional items such as racks of clothing that seemed to be plentiful. She asked the clerk if she could exchange her well-worn overcoat for one that would fit. "Of course," was the ready reply. Since it was so easy, she asked for grownup clothes as well since she had outgrown her shirts and jeans. There was even a personal dressing room to try on the clothes.

"A place to remember," she thought on the way out, with a promise to the custodian to attend the weekly sermons[5] the

---

[4] The Salvation Army is well known for its network of thrift stores or charity shops, which raise money for its rehabilitation programs by selling donated used items such as clothing, housewares, and toys. Clothing collected by Salvation Army stores that is not sold on location is often sold wholesale on the global second-hand clothing market.

[5] In addition, the Salvation Army is a Protestant Christian church and an international charitable organization, reporting a worldwide membership of over 1.7 million, consisting of soldiers, officers, and adherents collectively known as Salvationists. Its founders sought to bring salvation to the poor, destitute, and hungry by meeting both their "physical and spiritual needs."

Salvation Army offered, feeling slightly guilty since she was not a religious person. It was an empty promise. With her shopping over, a new bundle slung over her shoulder, April felt exuberant. Energized once again, the previous night was all but forgotten. Today would be a new chapter in her life, that of a grown-up woman.

ADULT APRIL

April, clad in new attire, felt like a newborn open to adventure. Until now, her life had been nothing but a struggle for survival. Not only had she transformed, but the environment had changed as well. Returning to the spot she had arrived at in the morning, she sought out her bench once more. Slightly saddened, she realized that it was occupied and took a seat on the containment barrier encircling the Square. With feet propped onto the bundle of new clothes, she waited for her bench to be free. In her mind she had already taken possession while watching the local scene. In contrast to the Mission, her life played out completely differently. People were rushing from one place to another as soon as they stepped from a trolley.

Though free to move at any moment she still felt somewhat restricted from just getting up and leaving her place because of the bundle. Not knowing anybody to watch her things, for fear of losing it, she had to take it everywhere she went. It presented a problem with most places around the Square. Identified as vagrant as soon as she stepped into a store, most places would not permit her entrance, saying, "We don't want your kind here."

Banned entry was nothing new to April, but with so many places geared for shoppers, though she rarely spent money other than for personal necessities, given the opportunity she was curious. Safekeeping her effects was an issue she still had to solve but, at the moment, no solution came to her mind. Watching people enter and depart the Square, she was able to reclaim her bench. The couple that had occupied it had just left.

Though happy with her relocation, wholly content for the moment, she felt her day had been unproductive. She realized the cause. She had not spent the time begging.

"I'll make up for it tomorrow," she decided and remained withdrawn in thought. "What is this?" she pondered after an idea encroached on her mind. She could not erase the thought. It kept popping up despite her discounting it. It was an element she had never considered in the past. "No," she shouted silently. "I could never do it."

The thought that kept entering her mind was something she had pushed from her life years ago. It would be the ultimate challenge, rejoining society. For her, living in an organized society ended with her mom's death. Ever since, her life had been driven solely by survival from one day to the next. Though difficult at first, once she had figured out the trade and how to avoid the law it had become routine. It became her lifestyle, a life free from obligations.

Like many vagrants before her, it was a situation brought on by some unfortunate event. Until homelessness became a trend, there usually had been some external force and justifiable reason for it. In most cases living in destitution was not a voluntary act; it was forced onto the individual. One had to learn to live with it day and night through all seasons.

Seated on her comfortable bench, April considered the alternative but disbanded the thought for one reason: "I could not and would not live confined by four walls." It brought a shudder to her body, thinking about her earlier life with her mom. Returning to the same living conditions would be intolerable now. She needed the freedom of being beneath the stars. While submitting to a life of sustained deprivation, it was complete freedom from obligation she and some other homeless people sought out.

There were other reasons as well. She realized that in order to survive in a modern society, food production was of foremost importance. The task force for preparing the ever-increasing demand came from an army of dedicated citizens much like her. There were many other services as well, demanding just as much devotion. There were occasions when she'd wondered and asked herself, "What could I do?"

She did not know because she'd never learned a trade nor was she guided by her mom or in public schools to the responsibilities of contributing to society. Most people have an instinct for duties inherited from parents but, in her case, the discipline was missing. Unaware of the consequences, she grew up without a sense of self preservation. Directed by her mom, it was always, "April, get me this or get me that," without her ever explaining the reasons. April grew up much like a slave.

For now, having settled on Union Square, April was relatively content. The begging was easier than in her past. She learned that the location was perfect. Not demanding much at her age, whatever she earned in a day was adequate to support her lifestyle. Spending mostly the coins, she was able to save the bills handed to her. It was a new experience supplemented by a feeling of prosperity. Because of it, she was able to purchase items she had never tried or tasted. "Life is good," she decided, with a promise to make the Square her home.

Unfortunately, prosperity did not last for her. Disaster came in the form of the law. Sleeping under the stars each night, in the eyes of the public she was viewed as a vagrant. Sooner or later someone will report the person. That's what happened to her. Gaining competence and feeling comfortable at the Square, earning more than she ever had, she became complacent. Staking claim of the bench, her nightly home, must have upset someone, because late one evening she had a visitor. Like many times before, it was a uniformed officer demanding her ID. Since she had never acquired one, she knew the penalties only too well: getting booked with one night in jail and an added police record in the local precinct. It was nothing new and did not bother her much at first, but after repeated visits by the law, she had to consider moving on. At least she'd had a good run for almost a year.

What April did not anticipate but became aware of was the influx of other beggars encroaching on her territory. Annoyed at first, she became concerned at the growing competition. Though begging was a trait with an open season for all, it severely impacted her earnings. Suddenly, she was forced to fend for herself. Her savings were rapidly dwindling. With the law bearing down on her almost nightly and having to deal with competition during the daytime, she was forced to explore new territories.

At first, because it was within easy walking distance, she headed for Market Street. Spending her first day on the sidewalk begging for a few hours, she decided it was sufficient for an evening meal. Her living expenses and demands were minimal and at the moment did not greatly impact her present life, but things were about to change.

Market Street, the hub of San Francisco for Fortune-500 corporate headquarters, was bustling with commerce. People generally arrived on location by 9:00 am. After spending eight hours in an office with one hour reserved for lunch, they would depart the office by 6:00 pm, five days a week. A different crowd arrived on weekends. It was vacationers on Saturdays and families from the peninsula on Sundays. It was mostly those the beggars depended on. Enthusiastic and happy from being in the nation's number one tourist city, people readily supported the vagrants.

Changes to vagrancy were about to take place. It began innocently enough over a couple of years. At first, the jobless musicians appeared, trying to earn a living by playing an instrument, generally a flute, trumpet, or harmonica, easy items to carry. Next were magicians and jugglers displaying their skills, quickly followed by palm readers and story tellers. Powell Street Station became the focal point for open entertainment. Visitors and performers alike were enthusiastic for the opportunity to perform, a situation readily tolerated by the city council. It appeared that the problem with vagrancy was solved. Unfortunately, happiness was mostly a front for the daytime display and to earn money. The real reason was a means to sustain individual lives after the dark that followed.

April's first journey here was a joyous one. Being entertained was a new pleasure for her. It was something she could live with and decided to relocate from Union Square. Although there was ready competition for begging, it was acceptable because of the pleasure the location provided. The first night did not prove much of a problem as she bunked on Powell Station grounds. The weather was warm with the night cooling to a comfortable temperature if one had a blanket. What was important was that she continued to sleep under the stars. She was not the only homeless. Others shared her space. She had her entertainment for the day with the sound of musical instruments lulling her into the world of sleep and dreams. She became oblivious to what went on around her and in neighboring alleys.

April awoke early the next morning with sun rays warming her face. Propping up on her elbow, she assessed her situation. With an approving nod, she cheered, "Going to be a beautiful day," and rolled up her blanket and pillow into a bundle as she did each morning. The present location could not have been more ideal. Right away she spotted the prominent sign located at the restroom facility next to the BART subway entrance. On entering a just-vacated ladies restroom, April arrived prepared with soap, toothbrush and toothpaste, as well as with her comb and hairbrush. She spent some leisurely time grooming herself.

Thirty minutes later she stepped outside feeling fresh and invigorated to face what looked like another promising day. She decided to check out the immediate neighborhood. About to cross the sidewalk in the direction of Ellis Street, headed for the Mason District, her immediate goal, she collided with a young man on a bicycle rushing to beat the traffic light. Her clash with him was easier than the young man's fall. While she was cushioned by her bundle of clothes, he landed on the concrete, scraping up knees and elbows.

Angered at first at the unexpected collision, after examining his bloody knees, he apologized to her. Her anger immediately turned to compassion.

"You're hurt," she declared, bending down to him, still sprawled on the street. Reaching out, her hand grabbed him by the arm, helping him on his feet.

"Nothing a bandage can't heal," he replied with a forced smile, inspecting his elbows.

The bicycle did not escape the collision undamaged. The front wheel was bent. He would not be able to continue riding the bike. From here on out it was walking until he had it fixed.

"What are you going to do?" April said, casually inspecting him. *Young, good looking, inches taller than her, neatly dressed beneath a blond set of hair, nice,* she decided, reaching for the set of fashion shades laying in the gutter that he had dropped.

"Don't know at the moment," he said, taking back the shades. "Get the bike fixed, I guess." It was here when he took notice of her. Much like her, he was measuring her presence and offered, "You visiting?"

"The blanket and pillow," she acknowledged with an ardent smile.

The recognition was mutual when he offered his hand. "I'm Eric. What's your name?"

"April," she responded with hesitation, questioning if giving out her name was a wise decision. Trouble always followed, usually with the law.

"How about a latte?" he suggested with an inviting smile.

"What about the bike?"

"I'll take care of it right now," he said, unclipping the front wheel from the frame.

"That easy," she said, marveling at the mechanics. She had never paid much attention to transportation designs. To her, it had always been something others owned.

"Nothing to it," he said, leading. While she was burdened with her bundle, he was with carrying the front wheel slung over one shoulder, and with the other hand clutching the frame. His focus was a Starbucks one block over on Market & 4th Streets.

It was only a couple of minutes' walk. Seated comfortably inside while keeping an eye on his dismantled bike leaning against the outdoor bike rack through the window, he prodded, "You must be visiting. It's not easy to find an affordable place in this city. Right?"

April, it being her first encounter with the opposite sex, considered an excuse but quickly changed her mind. Sooner or later, most likely sooner, he would find out her true status anyway. Consequently, she decided on telling him the truth while watching his response. "I'm homeless."

"What a coincidence," he said, his face set in a broad grin. "So am I."

"What?" She did not believe his words. "You don't look even close to being a homeless."

"It's true," he repeated. "I'm homeless. Been here for over a year. How about you?"

"I was born and grew up here."

"You must be kidding," he said, shaking his head in disbelief. "Homeless aren't born here."

"This one is," she emphasized by taking a sip from the latte.

HOMELESS TOGETHER

After the initial revelation and surprise Eric had laid on her, April was still watchful about him. She had grown cautious over the years living fancy free in a homeless world mostly populated by men. She had yet to meet a homeless woman. In her mind, he was only being friendly to get what most men want from a woman, sex and gratification like her mom had warned: "All they want is to get in your pants."

"I may not appear like the typical homeless," he volunteered, "but I am. You see, I live this way by choice. I choose this lifestyle."

Her eyes widened in surprise. Other than herself, it was the first time anybody else had ever stated so. Still doubtful, she tested him. "You're lying."

"No, I'm not," he fired back at her. "Why would I lie to you? I don't even know you. I am an honorable person looking for adventure."

"Everybody lies," she replied, shaking her head. She remained silent. Her thoughts wandered back to living with her mom, a life prone to cheating and lying. Acquired through their environment, those were two traits she had learned early on in life, enforced by her mom: "It's a means of self-preservation."

"What does preservation mean?" she had asked.

"To protect yourself," her mom replied with an all-encompassing wisdom. From that moment on, it became April's gospel to protect her belongings and secrets at all cost, as modest as they were. At this time, she had not acquired a homeless person's mode of mobility, a shopping cart. All her miserly possessions were wrapped up in a small bundle she could easily carry and protect. It was her choice. It gave her the mobility she desired where others, in possession of a shopping cart, were in constant fear of losing their belongings to others.

April savored her latte to its last drop, "This is great," she admitted. "Never had it before."

"Want a refill?"

"No. I better get going. Have to earn money," she explained with a smile. He paid the bill on the way out while she took the time to watch the cashier adding up the total, questioning if she could perform the function. "No," she decided. It would mean giving up her freedom.

"Now what?" Eric said on the way out, looking over the damages.

"Guess you'll have to get bandaged up and get the bike fixed."

"Why don't you come with me?" he offered. "We can talk on the way."

"I don't follow strangers." It was a strict rule, her rule she had decided when mom had died. Rumors were always circulating about some poor person disappearing. Maybe they were legitimate rumors, or they might have only been conjecture, but the facts were never known because nobody ever returned.

"I'm not a stranger anymore. You know my name."

"I don't want to get hurt. There are evil people in the world."

"I know, but this city is safe. What shelter are you in?" Eric asked, genuinely interested.

"None," April replied. "I don't like shelters. They have rules." As usual, she was short with words. She had learned early on in life that the fewer words she used, the more discouraged anybody would be from prying further. Besides, skipping most of her classes did not help with her limited vocabulary range. "I sleep out in the open."

"You are homeless," he admitted with a grin.

"Told you already."

"Come." Eric gestured for her to follow.

"Where're we going?"

"I know a place you'll like."

They walked along Market Street headed towards the piers. Three blocks later they passed Montgomery Station. "This is where I usually hang out," he said with a gesture towards the square. Much like Powell Station, the place was filled with entertainers earning money.

"Why here?"

"It's closer to where we are going." Walking three more blocks brought them to the Ferry building at the Embarcadero. April had never been here and, stepping out on the docks, she realized why it could be one's favorite spot. The view was breathtaking. She'd had no real idea of how large the bay actually was. It extended all the way to Sausalito in one direction and Oakland in the other. In wonder, her eyes scanned the panorama reaching from Golden Gate Bridge in the west to the Bay Bridge east with Alcatraz and Angel Islands in-between and ships traversing the view.

Pulling his bike along by the frame, Eric headed straight for the Ferry landing's edge, stating, "My favorite spot."

"I can see why," she admitted. "It is pretty. But what about the bike?" She could not imagine him dragging the damaged bike along the rest of the day.

"I'll fix it later," he explained.

Her interest piqued. "How can you fix the wheel? It's all warped."

"Don't worry about it. I have the tools."

They sat for hours talking, with him mostly explaining and her interrupting to clarify. It did not take her long to realize that he was pretty bright. She also learned that he was born and raised in Iowa by affluent parents, and had been sent to Yale for his education, where he dropped out after the second semester. "All I could think of was California: ocean, sunshine and surfing." he explained. "So I landed in L.A."

"What brought you to San Francisco?"

"Ten years surfing at Laguna Beach was enough. I wanted to see the rest of the country. What attracted me here were cultural places I've heard of."

"And?"

"Silicon Valley. I might try to land a job there one of these days."

"Then," she contemplated, "you're not actually homeless."

"Yes, I am. I need the freedom and flexibility just like you and every other homeless. If I can land a job that provides flex hours without an office environment, I might consider it."

"What about school, the training for a job? Doesn't it require great knowledge?"

"Not for me," he assured her. "I can pick up any trade and profession without them."

"Are you a genius?" She was genuinely impressed. To her it was unthinkable to ever meet anyone with that kind of intelligence.

"If you want to call it that, with an IQ of 165."

"What's an IQ?" She'd never heard of that and felt completely inadequate, especially when he shot a quick glance at her.

"The scale to measure people's knowledge capacity." From here, Eric spent a lot of time explaining things to her, but did not seem to mind. He must have realized that she had qualities of her own. For one, her practical approach to things. "Why don't you talk while I fix the wheel."

She looked at him, dumbfounded. "Here? What about tools?"

"Got them right here," he said, pulling a couple of items from the saddle pouch.

"Can I watch?"

"Suit yourself."

She sat quietly while watching him straighten out one spoke at a time using tiny wrenches, wondering if there was anything he did not know. "What about your family?" he asked while diligently at work.

"My mom died a few years ago. I never knew my dad. I've been alone and homeless ever since."

"Tragic," he admitted with a hint of compassion. "That drove you into homelessness?"

"That, and the begging Mom taught me."

"Sorry," he said, genuinely regretful. As expert as he was, it still took close to an hour to adjust the wheel to perfection, but the tire was still flat. He pulled out another couple of tools. "Miniature irons," he explained while April watched, again impressed at his skills as he removed the valve and pried the tire from its rim. A quick patch slapped on the leak, tube and tire mounted back on the rim, air pumped into the tube, and the bike was fixed.

"You are a genius."

"This," he said with a gesture at the job just finished, "is called knowhow, practical skills applied."

"I want to learn," she said, hoping he would stay with her. In only a few hours she had become so impressed and enchanted with him she wanted to know more. *I am such a fool,* she thought, recalling her excuses for skipping classes. "Can you teach me?"

"It depends," he said, leaving it up to her.

"Depends on what?"

"Whether you have the patience."

"Patience is not my problem," she said, then explained. "I spend most of the day daydreaming without a goal. My problem is trusting people."

"I'm not just anybody," he assured her. "My word is my honor."

"I'm happy to hear that. What do you have in mind?"

"I'd like to learn how and where you spend the day."

"Really?" she expressed in astonishment.

He was slightly surprised at her response. He briskly got up and patted the headlamp, talking to the bike like it was a horse. "Today, you'll get a break." He walked, with April keeping pace.

Striding north on Embarcadero they cut west at Pier 33 onto Bay Street. An hour later, they arrived at "My Place," as Eric called Russian Hill. She could already guess why he had selected this prime real estate spot. Arriving at the top, she could see forever. The 360-panoramic sight was spectacular. Looking out west, the Pacific horizon appeared like a mirror with a blue sky merging into an limitless ocean.

"Wow," she exhaled, taking in all of the beauty. "Where have I been?"

"I thought you'd like it here."

It was then that she spotted a few tents staked to the ground against one end of the hill. He headed for the one with the best view, parked the bike, and invited her into the tent. "Here we are. My abode."

"You must really like your space," she said, admiring the size of the tent.

"Don't we all," he replied with a grin.

"Well, yeah," she admitted. "But not everybody has the money for a tent this size." There were even a couple of folding chairs propped against one side. "A TV?"

"I get bored at night only watching the stars," he admitted.

"I thought freedom provided all that."

"A bit of entertainment doesn't hurt, especially with the new channel networks."

"You mean cable?"

"Yes, cable."

"I've heard of it but never watched any." She stepped outside to absorb more of the view while he rummaged around the place. The sun was just setting. She put on her overcoat to keep away the evening chill. San Francisco might be warm during the day, but after sunset the air turned chilly. The reason why many people were attracted to this city was its temperate climate. With fog drifting in from the ocean most nights, people even turned on their heaters at home, but as soon as the sun came up, it did not take long for the temperature to warm the day.

Thirty minutes later Eric joined her. "You feel up to a party?"

"A party here?"

"Not here. A friend's home. We are invited."

"I've never been to a party."

"You must be joking."

"I'm serious."

"Parties are the things to do in this day and age."

She only took a second to reply. "Of course I want to go. What time?"

He checked his watch and said, "We'll leave in a couple of hours."

"What can I expect?" she asked, anxiously anticipating the event.

"Nothing but fun," he said. "You'll see."

"What should I wear?" she said with heightened excitement.

"Let's see what you've got," he said, looking her over. "You can't go like this."

"Why not?"

"You look like a homeless."

"But I am a homeless."

"Yeah. But you don't want to advertise it. Not while you're with me."

"You're ashamed of me?" She threw him a defiant look. "I won't go."

"People will snob you. They'll avoid you."

"I don't care," she said with finality.

"Look," Eric reasoned with her. "On your own you can do whatever you like, but while in my company I want you to look pretty."

"I'm not pretty."

"Are you kidding?" Not believing her he shook his head. "You are a pretty girl. All we have to do is fix you up a little."

"What do you mean, fixing up?"

"You know. A little makeup."

"I don't wear makeup."

"We'll see. Let's go."

"I thought we'd leave later."

"Come." He beckoned her along. "I'll take you to a couple of places first."

"What about my things?"

"Leave them in the tent."

He led her down the hill towards North Beach. North Point Street was only a six-block walk where all the shops were. It was the busiest area in the city. Tourists sought the place out not only for souvenirs, but attire as well. Passing a hair salon, he pulled her to the entrance. "Let's stop here."

April resisted. "I won't feel comfortable in there."

"Why not?"

"People don't look real. They all look artificial."

"It's the trend with parties. You'll see." Eric practically had to pull her into the salon, where they headed for the counter. Despite April's disheveled appearance the attendant was very courteous. "How can I help you?"

"Can you do something about her hair and face?" Eric said with a gesture at April.

The attendant led her to a vacant chair. "Make yourself comfortable," she said, and disappeared. Seconds later she emerged with a hairstylist and makeup artist. Both went to work on April, who just sat in the spacious chair not completely understanding what was transpiring. She felt her hair getting washed, dried, pulled and clipped, fingernails being cut and painted, and final touches of makeup being applied to her face.

The entire process took less than an hour while she caught brief peeks at her face, her chair being swiveled in all directions. Once finished, she was spun to face the mirror straight on. Mesmerized by the person staring back, all she could stammer was, "Who am I?"

Eric was standing by her side in admiration. "You'll be the prettiest girl at the party." He paid the bill and off they were to the next stop. It turned out to be several shops, one after the other, trying on an assortment of different dresses. "I like this one" or "that's definitely you," he would comment as she exited the dressing room.

The end result was enforced with his comment: "You look stunning."

"I never knew what that meant," she commented and did not mind his eyes caressing her body. He realized that she had the potential for having a well-toned body, but did not comment on her figure. It would require working out at the gym, an activity she was probably ignorant of, he suspected. For the time being, on the way to the party, he was extremely supportive of the way she had turned out. Money well spent. People would definitely take note of her, and they did the second they entered the party room. Room was an understatement. It was more like a hall, filled with dozens of party seekers.

"And who is this fine lady?" the host asked Eric. They had been friends ever since he had landed in the city.

"Somebody I picked up this morning," Eric offered. "Actually, she picked me up off the ground after colliding with my bike."

"Anybody get hurt?" the host asked, checking them both over for scrapes.

"Only the bike and a few skin scrapes," Eric said with a concerned look at April. "Did you?"

"Not a scratch," she said with a smile.

"Come," the host invited her along, "I'll introduce you to my friends." He then turned to Eric. "You go fix her a drink."

"I don't drink," April, embarrassed at the attention, shouted after Eric, who turned and came back.

"What are you saying?" He seemed surprised, and rightly so. Who in his right mind would turn down an offer like a drink? Definitely not a homeless. He was about to object but kept quiet. He realized April's innocence and would not have appreciated additional attractions beyond what she had already endured. He remembered her reaction after giving her body earlier a once over.

"I don't want to talk about it. Not here."

"Then," he prodded, "what can I get you?"

"A bottle of water," she said.

It brought a grin to his face, suggesting he knew what she was up to. "Ecstasy?"

That was what all the parties were about. This was an era when Ecstasy was the most desired drug on the market, with hardly anyone not being a user, especially the young and the party crowd. While he cherished the thought, she had no clue, but was about to find out.

It did not take long before she was approached by a fashionably-dressed woman with an open hand, asking, "How many?"

April started to count the pills, but was interrupted by the woman. "How many do you want?"

Eric was nearby and overheard their exchange. He quickly rushed to her rescue. "I'll take care of it." She watched as he exchanged money for several pills, putting most of them in his pocket. "Here," he said with an invitational smile. "Take one."

"What is it?"

"Come on," he said, slightly taken aback at her displaying such ignorance. "Ecstasy," he insisted. "It's what everybody here wants."

"I'm sorry," she pleaded, accompanied by a genuine innocence in her eyes. "I don't know."

It suddenly dawned on him that she really did not know. It explained the reactions she'd displayed during the day, not only once, but several times during their conversations. He had shrugged it off as shyness on her part, but it all made sense now. He did not know whether to be happy or sad about meeting her. On the one hand, he appreciated her innocence but, on the other, he wondered if he had the patience to educate her. "We'll see," he muttered. His words were drowned by the increase in sound coming from the DJ booth. To Eric, the setting would have been complete if April would have been willing to try the substance.

"I thought the water bottle was for the pills." His assumption went unheard. She had turned towards the exit door, ready to depart. He was highly disappointed at her spoiling a fun evening and rushed after her. "Wait. Let me explain." He pulled her into a quiet corner to enlighten her about what the party was all about. "You see…" He talked while she listened.

Partying was the pulse of the city. Everybody came to town on weekends to celebrate. People arrived from the South Bay, the Tri-valley, Oakland, and as far as Stockton and Sacramento. On any given weekend night, dozens of parties were held at various halls rented for the occasion. They were not just privately-held parties; they were organized affairs sanctioned by the city and tolerated by the law. At other times police cruisers would flag you down for a sobriety test, but in San Francisco this was not the case, due to the reasons stated by the host. "We don't sell alcohol."

"What about people staggering in and out of the place?"

"They bring their own booze but most come here to experience the drug effects. It's the pulse of the party."

"What drug?"

"Ecstasy."

What Ecstasy did to the body was dry it up, forcing a person to consistently drink water. It suited everybody just fine. Then one might ask, "How did a host cover for the expenses of the party?"

"By charging anywhere from $5 on up," was the answer, people soon learned. The result was a relatively inexpensive evening out when considering the cost of a drink at a bar or club. As for the cost of Ecstasy, it might have been the most inexpensive drug ever on the marketplace, even though one pill only provided a high for a couple of hours. That was the reason why people bought several pills throughout the evening and night. An Ecstasy party usually lasted into the morning hours, with sexual benefits dished out in private spaces and rooms reserved for these pleasures.

April was finally educated about the pleasures of drugs and sex when Eric insisted, "You've got to try some. You'll be bored otherwise."

"I don't know." She wavered. "How does it feel?"

There's still hope, Eric thought. *At least she's interested.* Handing her a colored pill, he insisted, "Take one. Try it. It won't hurt. You won't be sorry."

Observing other guests being happy and having fun, laughing and swaying with the rhythms of in-vogue soundtracks, April said, "What the hell," and popped one, though reluctantly.

Unaware about what to expect after taking the pill, April was handed off by Eric to several of his friends while he enjoyed the lively party activities himself. She was slowly losing the anxiety she had felt all day since meeting Eric. The world he had introduced to her, a world of personal risks and emotions, took ten minutes for the drug to take effect, opening a door to a world April had never anticipated would exist.

INNOCENCE LOST

April, responding normally to questions raised by Eric's party friends, gradually succumbed to the effects of the drug. Consciously unaware that her personal responses were becoming friendlier and more alluring by the minute, her mind opened up to emotions she had never felt. "What am I doing?" she questioned her unfamiliar behavior, "I can't stop giggling." There were other effects she had never experienced; an emergence of sexual feelings were taking hold of her body and her mind.

Where, in the past, she would have slapped the woman touching her body in the face, this evening, in the midst of a crowded dance floor, her mind objected to the notion but her body did not. For the first time in her life, she thought in wonder, "It feels nice to be touched."

"Having fun?" a familiar voice asked from behind her. She turned away from her current dance partner, to realize Eric had sidled up to her.

"I don't know what I'm doing," she responded with a broad smile, "but I feel great." She suddenly felt attracted to him. Reaching out to cradle his head, she planted a kiss on his lips, her first kiss ever in her life. It felt wonderful. She wanted more. Eric realized she was under the effects of the Ecstasy.[6]

"Come," he said, pulling her from the floor in the direction of a secluded space. Since most of the weekly metropolitan parties were held in sanctioned places with ample space, mostly rented and vacant warehouses, privacy was not an issue. Organizers made sure that patrons were accommodated in secluded rooms reserved for their personal pleasures. Eric pulled her through a door identified by a sign, "Private."

————————

[6] Ecstasy, popular at the time, is a stimulant drug that can cause hallucinations. It is known as a designer drug because it was created for the purpose of making someone feel high.

What transpired next was completely alien to April. Eric placed his hands on her body, which felt extremely pleasurable. Striking and exotic, his touching her elevated her feelings to a level she did not know how to handle or what to expect next. She completely submitted herself to him, not caring about potential consequences. Whatever he did to her body felt great. She was euphoric, demanding more of him. Although he was only superficially caressing her body while kissing her, her body was longing for more from him.

April was not totally ignorant of people's behavior when desiring a sex act. Curious while growing from child to adulthood, she had learned about it by secretly snatching up an occasional magazine from a street vendor's shelf while they were busy with customers. Though they did not explain emotions or personal feelings, they illustrated the act between two people having sex. When she asked her mom to explain, she was rebuffed with, "You are too young. Don't ask." April had never learned the intricacies of foreplay, its potential consequences, and what usually ended in euphoria.

Minutes into their embrace, April was highly disappointed when Eric stopped his amorous advances by whispering in her ear, "Let's take a break." She watched him rummage through his pockets, pulling out a small metal box that contained more pills. He, as well as most partygoers, were familiar with symptoms of Ecstasy[7] and its limited duration.

"What?" April stammered, unhappy with the unexpected turn.

"Here," he said, offering another dosage. "Have some more."

---

[7] The effects of any drug (including Ecstasy) vary from person to person. How Ecstasy affects a person depends on many things including their size, weight, and health, and also whether the person is used to taking it and whether other drugs are taken around the same time. The effects of any drug mainly depends on the amount taken.

She had sensed that her initial exhilaration had somewhat waned during her time on the dance floor and with him in the private room, but had not paid much attention to it since she was taken over by the effects of her present environment.

"I'd better not," she gently refused. "I don't know what I'm doing."

"You do just fine. As a matter of fact, my friends tell me you are great. They all like you."

"Really? Nobody's ever said that."

"Then," he said, with an offer from the small container, "have another pill." In the state April was currently in, it did not take much persuasion. It was a state almost everybody attending the party was in. Offers of pills between couples, and strangers as well, could be observed through the night. Much as with alcohol, taking another pill was considered a refill to sustain the euphoric high, quickly dissolved and activated with a swig from a water bottle.

"Let's dance some more." She beckoned, left the room, and headed for the dance floor. Eric followed closely behind, mixing in with his friends.

Dancing was a new experience for her, but Eric was not much of a dancer. He preferred the company of friends, exchanging ideas in between telling jokes.

About four hours into the night, April came rushing up to Eric, urgently demanding, "I want to go."

It was a bit unusual since she had been having such a good time. "Why? What's the matter?"

"I don't want to talk about it," she said and was adamant that he take her home.

"Let's stay for a while longer," he suggested, but was pulled in the direction of the exit. "Are you alright?" he said, trying to figure out her plight. Nothing seemed to be out of place.

"No. I'm not alright." Both left the hall, with him still trying to persuade her and her urging him on to leave.

They headed back to the camp in silence, with him anxious to find out what'd been troubling her. It was useless to get an answer from her as upset as she was. It was still early for him to turn in, especially since it was warm outside and the place was illuminated by the brilliance of a clear night sky. Besides, not used to her unpredictable and disappointing display earlier, he wanted to find out what was troubling her.

"Let's stay out here," he suggested. "We can talk in the sleeping bags."

"Fine with me," she agreed, waiting for him to retrieve and prepare the bags.

"Are you comfortable?" She was stretched out comfortably lying next to him. He was still concerned, but waited patiently. "What happened to you back there?"

She took her time, then explained. "I was on the dance floor having fun with your friends, when this stranger came up and suddenly kissed me. Not only that, he started fondling my breasts and groping my backside. He smelled of alcohol. I almost got sick. I couldn't stand to be at the place any longer," she said, close to tears.

Eric lay there in silence for a minute, then burst out laughing. "Is that what happened?"

"What? Why are you laughing?"

"Because you are silly. It's what people do at parties. Especially when they are drunk."

"I thought alcohol wasn't allowed."

"Well," he explained, "many people have a drink before they show up. It's accepted as long as they don't cause trouble. That's what security is for. By the way," he said, taking the moment, "what do you have against alcohol?"

It took her a while to loosen up, but she then explained her plight with her mom being an alcoholic for as long as she could remember. "I could not talk to her when she was sober, but after she had a drink," she muttered, "Mom became impossible to be around. She would shout and slap me around without a reason. I loved her but could not stand it when she was drunk. I would run away but always came back home because I didn't know anybody and had nowhere else to go."

She began to sob like Eric had not seen before. All her pent-up emotions from a life of desolation and hardship came flowing at him. He felt so sorry for her that he cradled her head in his arms, trying to pacify her. "You don't have to worry anymore. I'm here for you. I'll protect you. You come to me anytime somebody bothers you or is mean."

By now, both had sobered up from the effects of the drugs. He was stroking her hair. It must have had a soothing effect, since she calmed down to where he could talk. "Look," he said. "You are still young and don't have much experience in life, or in people, for that matter. But you have to understand that when people are under the influence, they behave differently. You can't get upset at someone not in control of their emotions."

"But a stranger…" she objected.

"Especially a stranger," he cut in. "They go around trying to find a date. Some are polite while others can be rough. All you have to do is say NO. Most will respect your response and move on. May I ask you a personal question?"

She kept quiet for some time, then said, "What do you want to know?"

"You are still a virgin?"

"I have never been with a man. Does that answer that?"

"It sure does. How about with a woman?"

"What do you mean?"

"Have you ever slept with a woman?"

"Well yeah. Mom."

That was all it took for Eric to break into laughter. "You are too funny," he managed to say while watching her reaction.

"What's so funny?"

"You are precious. I am so happy we met."

"Let's go inside," she said. "It's getting chilly." He agreed, even though he preferred to sleep under the sky. With both of them getting undressed, him boldly naked as usual and her as bashful as ever, he was surprised at her pristinely-shaped form and apparently well-toned body. Her naked presence and bashfulness turned him on.

Shy as always, April slid into the comfort of the quilt, expecting sleep but, to her surprise, sleep did not set in. Her mind wandered through the turn of events of the day. It was the first time that she had experienced a feeling strange and unfamiliar to her. It started in the lower abdomen, gradually traveling upward towards her breasts and on into her brain. She did not understand why her nipples became hard nor had she expected the wetness between her legs. Alerted, she tried to get up.

"Where're you going?"

"I think I have to go to the bathroom." Though there was a public lavatory facility in the area, hardly anybody used it during night time when people slept.

"You want me to go with you?"

"I don't think I have to pee but I feel wet," she said, slightly embarrassed.

This brought on another laughing spell from Eric. "That's normal." He got up, reached for her hand and pulled her under his cover, and gently reached for her body.

She could feel his hand caressing her breasts. She liked it this time. Taking his hand into hers, she slowly moved it across her body. "This feels so good," she whispered into the quiet of the tent.

"Want more?" he prayed, moving his body closer to hers.

"Yes," she whispered again, not knowing what to expect. Being with him this night made her feel like she had never felt before. She felt glorious and wanted more of him. Eric exercised restrained patience, letting her drive all of the advances she desired. Their lovemaking, his experience in years, hers the innocent she was, felt thrilling and exuberant to both, and eventually ended in complete satisfaction and collapse, with both extremely gratified. April fell asleep, oblivious to the world.

Eric felt more content as he had in a long time. He lay awake for most of the night, contemplating what to do with the girl who had so unexpectedly entered his life. Her presence surely would change the goals he had set for his future.

CITY COUNCIL

The city mayor stormed into the assembly hall, shouting, "All right! All right everybody, quiet down." Pleased to see this many attendants, he headed straight for the podium. Taking hold of a water bottle propped in the cup holder, he unscrewed it to take a sip. Moistening his throat always helped with the speech, especially since today was no ordinary report on city issues. He had called this special meeting to solve an encroaching problem his city had not seen since the last earthquake. *How many years ago?* he tried to recollect. He could not remember the year. *Doesn't matter anyway,* he muttered to himself, *it wasn't on my shift.* Today's issue was on his shift and he had to solve it, but how was the question. While taking a few seconds to gather his thoughts, he let his eyes wander around the hall. They were all there: the board of supervisors amidst elected officers, seated among numerous other representatives from each district in northern California, in addition to the public sector, mostly store and shop owners. He was pleased. *At least I don't have to face the issue alone.*

"As you all know," the mayor began, "the city is dealing with an issue that has gone from bad to worse, namely, the growing reality of the homeless problem. As an example," he stated, "a recent surveillance taken by a shop owner in the Union Square district reports a homeless person undressing himself just steps from the store's front door and defecating right there."

"This is getting out of control," another shop owner complained, "and it's not an uncommon scene." He also stated that people were turning away from entering his and neighboring stores. "When I complain to the police," he added, "the response is always the same. 'There's nothing we can do.'"

The store owner went on to explain that when he had moved to San Francisco three decades ago, "Union Square felt magical then. It was the center of San Francisco. Now it has become a place nobody wants to come to anymore." He continued, "I feel like the city center is dying and I want you, Mayor," he boldly emphasized, "to do something to bring back Union Square like it used to be, prospering."

"I totally understand why you are unhappy," the mayor responded. "That's why we are here today."

He then turned to the assembly members. "Does San Francisco need a systemic change to address the homeless problem?" Watching most members' heads nodding, he agreed, "Damn right."

Directly addressing the assembly, he stated, "We need to do better and we need to do more. But I can't do it alone.

"To let you know," he said, turning to the public section to assure the store owners in the area, "I have already taken steps to alleviate some of the problem by setting aside rooms at shelters primarily for people with psychiatric challenges and I promise to get 1,000 people off the streets this winter."

"We appreciate it, but what about next spring?" one voice from the public sector called out.

"What about vagrants and beggars moving here from other areas?" another voice asked. "What about them?"

"We'll just have to address the issue then," the mayor replied, with a promise to personally address the individual complaints from establishments in Union Square.

"I beg you once more to do something," the shop owner with the first complaint called out. "I don't know how long my business can keep its doors open in the present situation."

And so, public complaints went on throughout the day, to be recorded by the assembly administrator for future reference, an important function for keeping track of public complaints.

Where the mayor and his city functionaries were satisfied about taking the first steps, the public, staring back at them, was not. They had heard it many times before. "Nothing but empty words."

The mayor adjourned the assembly for the day with one last promise. "I can assure you that I and my associates are on top of the situation."

A NEW BEGINNING

April woke up in the morning, surprised that she had slept so late. The sun was already high on the horizon, warming the inside of the tent. She was used to sleeping under the stars and waking up at the dawn of light. Her eyes touched on Eric who was huddled under the blanket asleep. "I've got to go," she whispered into his ear. He awoke. "What happened last night?" she finally brought herself to say.

"You were magnificent," he replied.

"Is that what sex is all about?" She could not help but grin at him.

"Yes, it is. Did you enjoy it?"

"Enjoy? I loved every bit of it. What about you?"

"You are the sweetest woman I've ever had sex with."

"Really? Me, a virgin without experience?"

"You don't need much experience if you let your feelings drive you."

"I'll have to remember." Both got up, collected toothpaste and brushes along a set of clean clothes they had decided to wear for the day, and headed for the public lavatory, her on shaky legs, hanging onto his arm and giggling.

"What's so funny?" he said.

"I can hardly walk."

"You'll get used to it."

Twenty minutes later both emerged refreshed and dressed in clean clothes, Eric clean and shaven with April soapy and having washed hair, facing their first day together. Eager for adventure, they thought it promised to be a beautiful day.

"By the way," Eric said. "You can stay here with me if you want."

"Really?" It had not occurred to her. She was about to ready herself to find a place in the city and claim her stake. "Can I think about it?"

"Take all day if that's what you want. I'm here to stay. I like my spot. You hungry?"

"I'm famished," she said. "I could eat a horse."

"Let's not go there. But if you want to try it sometime," he offered, "I'll take you to a place."

"You mean to eat horse meat?" She had never heard of this.

"Yes, horse meat and dog, cat, and rat too."

"You can't be serious. There are no such places."

"I assure you there are. It's called Chinatown."

"That I've got to see. I've heard of Chinatown but have not been there."

"You were born here and don't know Chinatown?"

"Seriously. Mom never took me anywhere."

"Well then, let's go there." It would take them forty minutes to cross the city from here on foot, and she forgot about her hunger in anticipation. As usual, he took off at a fast clip when going places. Normally on his bike, today on foot felt strange.

"Slow down," April said.

"Sorry. I'm not used to strolling the streets."

"We're not in a hurry," she said, reaching for his hand and forcing him to slow his pace. "I'd like to get to know the city."

"Okay. If you insist," he said with a chuckle.

Trotting along Bay Street for a couple of blocks at a more comfortable pace, she pointed at a tall building ahead, protruding above the city skyline.

"Transamerica building."

"What do they do?"

"It's an insurance company," he said, cutting a right on Columbus Avenue. "Washington Square," he gestured in the direction she pointed, and farther up, "Saints Peter and Paul church."

"Can we go there? Please," she beckoned, pulling him by his hand in the direction. "I've never been inside a church."

"Sure. If you insist."

"I insist." Her marveling began at the entrance doors at their sheer size and continued with him explaining the interior as much as he could remember from his high school trip to Italy.

"I want to attend a Mass," she said on the way out.

"Here's the schedule," he said, handing her a brochure on the way out.

"Thank you for being so patient putting up with me."

"Don't mention it. I enjoy your company."

"I'm glad you do," she said, planting a hasty kiss on his cheek, back on Columbus Avenue once more. The next object that caught her eyes and stopped April was a place where most tourists did the same. "The Stinking Rose?"

"You may be surprised at the name, but they serve the best rib roast in town."

"Can we go there?"

"Maybe later. They don't open until dinner time."

Marching on, her eyes caught some of the remarkable places along their walk: Mona Lisa, Trattoria Pinocchio, Calzone's, Piazza Pellegrini, Michelangelo Ristorante & Caffee, and more along their walk.

Intrigued by such diversity in foreign names, she could not contain her curiosity any longer. "Why the strange names?"

"It's Columbus Avenue."

"So?"

"It's Little Italy, right here in San Francisco."

"Now I understand," she said with a peek at his face, but he kept on walking. With her mind set on the cultural display of Italy, a place Mom used to talk about, and how much she wanted to visit there, April barely noticed that the scene changed as soon as they crossed Broadway. Streets and homes seem to shrink in size, sidewalks appeared dirtier, but what fascinated her most were the many shops along the sidewalks, one store after the other, displaying their services and wares with foreign-sounding names.

"Here we are," Eric announced, waving his hand across their path. "Chinatown."

Looking up to catch the street sign, April saw it said, "Grant Avenue." Eric did not pay much attention to her outbursts about the foreign-sounding names and kept marching on to his favorite place, knowing she would enjoy it.

"Cathay House," the sign indicated at the corner of Grant and California Streets. Enthralled as soon as they entered the restaurant, April found herself in the strangest world she could have ever imagined. Though modern in decor, there was a huge contrast in culture. Where she'd expected a semi-darkened and stuffy place like many of the places they had just passed, this place appeared super clean and well organized, and was populated mostly by non-Asian patrons. "Where are all the Chinese?"

"This place is geared to cater to foreign and non-Chinese visitors."

"But you promised an authentic Chinese place."

"I did, but you would not like it. You'll have to get familiar with the food first before I can introduce you to an authentic place."

"But why?"

"Chinese culture as lived here in Chinatown will take some getting used to. The cooking is different, the host and servants are alien, and the food is even stranger."

"If you say so, but I still want to see and experience."

"We will. I promise."

The dishes served looked exquisite, not only on the plate but when tasted as well. There were flavors and textures she had never experienced before served in a variety of dishes with names she'd try to remember: egg rolls, hot and sour soup, sweet and sour pork, sesame chicken, pot stickers, wontons, fried rice, chop suey. The dessert impressed her the most—mango pudding. She sampled and tried it all.

She groaned. "I'm stuffed."

"Me too," Eric agreed.

"You always eat like this?"

"Every time I come here."

April had never eaten until she was completely filled. The feeling was new to her. Though completely satisfied, she felt uncomfortable. "I ate too much."

"That will teach you to pace yourself."

"The food looked so inviting I had to taste it."

"Most people do."

"Now what?" she said, wondering what else he had in mind for the day. They had spent three hours at this place.

"Anything else?" the waiter checked in with April.

"How about baijiu?" Eric cut in. "It'll soothe your stomach."

"I'll try anything you recommend. So far there is nothing I haven't liked."

"Including sex," he said, accompanied by a sly grin.

"Especially sex."

"Hot baijiu it is," he ordered, with a nod at the waiter, who returned ten seconds later.

"That was quick," she said, getting ready to take a sip.

"Careful," Eric warned. "It's hot."

Expecting some hot tea, April took a sip. "Phew," she spat out. "It's alcohol."

"I'm sorry, I forgot," Eric apologized. "You don't drink."

"I hate the smell of it more than the taste."

"Won't happen again," he promised.

"Not your fault. It's Mom's. She was always drunk. I hated it. That's the reason I wound up homeless."

"I'll make it up to you."

"You will?" April was thankful for Eric's kindness and the sensitivity he had displayed so far. It was something new after years of unfriendly stares from pedestrians and shopkeepers, where emotional displays were either pity towards her, or empathy, with neither one being encouraging. She was hoping he would let her share his domain, and, more importantly, accept her into his heart.

"Have you decided what you want to do?" Eric said.

The last time the topic came up was the previous day. She was uncertain then. Today, after a night of passion and compassion, things had changed for her. She did not have to think much. "I'd like to stay with you if you'll take me in."

"I was hoping you would. My offer still stands."

"I'm so grateful. You won't regret it." For the first time in her life, she felt like a heavy load had been lifted from her shoulders.

"First thing we'll do is get you a bike."

"I've never been on a bike. I'll fall off. Besides," she wavered, "I don't have the money."

"No problem. I'll get it for you and teach you."

"Promise?"

"Promise. Let's get out of here," he suggested, and paid the bill. They took a different route back. "I want to show you something," he said when she asked him why. After leaving Chinatown behind he cut a right on Broadway, followed by a left on Battery Street. Three blocks later they entered Levi's Plaza.

"This is a beautiful place. I had no idea. What is it?"

"Levi Plaza."

"Jeans?"

"Yes. The original."

"If I worked, I would wish it could be here."

"Nothing can stop you," he said, but also understood the lifestyle both of them had chosen.

"The stars in the Milky Way will." They remained quiet for some time, each reminiscing in their own thoughts.

"Let's go," he urged after checking his watch. "I want you to see something." Leading her through the courtyard, they exited at the opposing street, Sansome Street. Cutting a right and striding ahead to the next block, she was about to pass an entrance leading upward. "Not so fast." He gestured. "We go up here."

"What's up there?"

"Coit Tower."

He let her climb first. After a couple dozen steps she halted. There seemed to be no end ahead. "How many steps?"

"290."

"You sure?"

"Yes, but you can count them. I've done it a number of times."

"Is it worth it?" she asked, with him trying to keep up.

"The view is spectacular once you get there."

"You lead," she huffed a dozen steps later, following closely.

"You're right. 290," she said after taking the last step. The view from Coit Tower, straddling Telegraph Hill, was as spectacular as he had promised. They had full view over San Francisco Bay, stretching from the Golden Gate Bridge to the Bay Bridge and places in-between. "Straight out in the middle of the bay," he explained, "you can see the island of Alcatraz with Angel Island not far off." With another gesture he indicated, "Tiburon and Sausalito in Marin County and beyond." They spent an hour on top of the tower platform with Eric pointing out the various landmarks in and around North Beach.

"I could live here," April said with a smile. "It's much like looking up at a starry sky. Endless. I feel at home here."

"We are two fortunate people," Eric agreed.

"Why?"

"I don't have to work and you don't want to work." Both laughed at his remark. It was so true. Having a choice to plan your life was more than most people could claim.

Being together was a new life experience for the both of them. It taught them a sense of responsibility they'd been unfamiliar with before. Although their lifestyle together was a pleasure for both, they respected each other's privacy when desired. There were times when he would take off on his bike without telling her, and she did the same, generally on foot. There were so many places for her to explore that her mom had never mentioned or taken her to. When together, they enjoyed each other's company to the fullest of which they were capable.

The time and seasons passed from one to the next, then a third, without any personal incidents or mishaps. April completely accepted Eric's dominance while he totally appreciated her willingness to learn and share their adventures.

While Eric provided for the cost of living, April passed her 18th birthday, totally devoting her time to him. And time went on, fulfilling both their needs.

CITY COUNCIL

Three years had passed since the San Francisco City Council had seriously addressed the homeless problem. Where, in the past, the homeless situation had just been emerging from individual beggars and vagrants without putting much of a burden on the city budget, things had taken a drastic turn only recently. It caught city administrators by surprise. It was as if everybody had been asleep at the wheel, but that was not the case. With a new mayor at the helm, supported by newly-elected council members, budget priorities had been with other, more pressing issues, such as prisoners fighting for more liberties and a vast increase in drug users creating enormous legal issues with international tourism, and the social breakdown as a result. Topped by a rapid rise in homelessness, it all added a drain on city and county budgets. Preventing a city bankruptcy had been the mayor's primary agenda and it had completely taken over his and the administration's time.

"Order. Order please," Thomas Allen, the mayor, yelled at the arguing assembly. It took several more warnings for the noise to diminish. "I have called this meeting as an emergency measure since we all have to work together. We have a number of issues to address." He started several times before he managed some sort of respect. He knew it would not be an easy task, taking control of a city that had deteriorated so rapidly in only a couple of years.

"We have more pressing problems to solve," one of the attendees called out.

"You are right," Allen said. "I have to restate the urgency once more. About today's meeting, I will only focus on one item, the homeless problem. Nothing else. Is that understood?"

When nobody protested he continued. "If you cannot comply, or think you are more important, please excuse yourself from the assembly." He took a few moments to let his words sink in. *Good.* He sighed in relief when nobody left the hall. *I've established my position.*

He waited another moment in silence, while scanning the many faces staring back at him, in anticipation for what many already considered to be an impossible problem to resolve. Other cities had tried and failed.

He took the assumption he read from the faces when he continued, "I will not let this beautiful city be destroyed because of the homeless." He took a deep breath to place importance. "I am sure some of you may remember a song specifically created for our city."

He was interrupted by a caller. "Tony Bennett."

"That's right, but more importantly, does anybody remember the words to his most famous song?"

"I left my heart in San Francisco, high on a hill, it calls to me. To be where little cable cars..." the same caller replied, humming.

"Thank you," Allen said, cutting in, underscored by clapping his hands. "I wanted to bring it up to remind everybody how valuable our city is, not only to us, but to the rest of the world, and it is the world that has supported our city for many decades. Unfortunately," he went on, "that has changed. I don't have to explain the reasons. You can all see the results each and every day walking along sidewalks. It's atrocious to let something like this happen."

"We are not the only ones," another caller interrupted, trying to justify his department, the Office of Economic & Workforce Development (OEWD).[8]

"That's true," the mayor acknowledged, "but we are different."

"How so?" one caller objected.

---

[8] Office of Economic & Workforce Development (OEWD), supporting tourism and other hospitality sectors, such as: Convention Facilities Department, San Francisco International Airport, the Port of SF, Department of Public Works, and SF Municipal Transportation.

"We care and we will solve the problem." Cheering applause followed, indicating his status with the city was secure. He was satisfied with the direction the assembly was taking. "Now," he said, "let's get to work."

It took all day just to hash out and read city complaints issued against the homeless. Addressing each and every item would take much longer to evaluate. There was much cleaning to do in and around the city. Sidewalks, curbs, shop entrances, walls, benches, and more needed to be scrubbed, cleaned, and painted to cover feces and urine stains. The same held true for streets, public restrooms, parks, and recreational facilities soiled by the homeless. It was this negligence and carelessness that had caused the city's deterioration in past years. While the public took great offense to the neglect, nobody in the administration wanted to address the problem and take ownership over the task of cleaning up the city.

"But first," the mayor directed, "we will have to get the homeless off the streets."

The meeting was adjourned, with numerous tasks delegated to the various departments responsible for city sectors. The homelessness initiative had started.

BROKEN BOND

Everything April and Eric had planned seemed to turn out in favor of both. April had finally found a permanent home, if only living in a tent with Eric. They experienced some sort of responsibility for a possible future together. Their current existence was mostly directed by spontaneous action, and, for the time being, they lived a carefree life hoping it would go on forever. One day, after contemplating her windfall in meeting Eric, April asked him, "How do you support yourself?"

He was honest with her. "Dad left me and my mom a pension after he died."

"When did he pass on?"

"A few years ago. He had a climbing accident on Mt. Shasta, fell several hundred feet to his death."

"Sorry to hear that. Do you climb?" The very thought of height and falling chilled her to the bone.

"I used to. Dad taught me. It's why I love freedom and the outdoors so much. I used to spend most weekends camping, but felt like something was missing. That's when I started traveling down the coast to explore other places."

"I'm glad you did. That's when I met you."

"To answer your question, I invested the lump sum insurance payout in long-term index funds. I draw the dividends monthly to pay for my living."

"Clever," she said. "I wish I could understand Wall Street and all that."

"Don't feel bad," he pacified her. "Most people don't. They are just happy to have the money."

"Am I a drain on your living expenses?" she asked, showing concern.

"Not at all. Don't worry about it. There is money for both of us. What do you want to do today?"

"Can we look for a bike? It doesn't have to be fancy, just as long as it will take us places quicker. There are so many places I want to explore."

Eric understood. "Bike store it is." They walked on foot with him pushing his bike and her striding along. They purchased a Schwinn model made for a woman. Following their exit from the store, Eric led the way to a field, not far off. "Where are we going?" she said.

"Crissy Field," he said. "There're some empty roads for you to practice on."

"Today? Now?" April said, not very comfortable with the thought of learning to ride.

"There's no better time." Ten minutes later, she experienced for the first time what balance was all about. Following several jump starts with her yelling, "Hold me," followed with "Catch me, Eeerrriiiccc," and more calls for help, April finally managed to stay on the bike without falling off. While learning to ride was a natural thing for youngsters, for an adult, it was something that required much more practice. "Let's bandage the scrapes," Eric said at the end of the practice session.

"Good. I need a break." They spent the rest of the day back at the tent, her recuperating from falls and him from catching her worst falls.

The following morning, revitalized and ready to go, April demanded, "I want to ride the bike."

"Where do you want to go?"

"Fisherman's Wharf. There is a French bakery. It smells so good every time we pass by."

"The piers it is." They arrived there without incidence, though he had to caution her several times to slow down. As was the case with most beginners, she started out too aggressive to be safe. He had to throttle her speed when on sidewalks and intersections.

The bakery was only their first stop. "You're right," Eric agreed after they took a seat inside with her ordering sourdough bread served with butter and honey. "This tastes wonderful." What he had planned for the day would take them across the Golden Gate Bridge. Taking in the aroma of baking bread in the oven, with patrons coming and going, they sat mostly in silence for the next thirty minutes, fully savoring the baking.

"What do you want to do next?" Eric said. "The day is yours."

"What do you suggest?"

"Muir Woods."

"What's that?"

"You'll see." 15 miles and an hour and a half later, they turned into what could only be described as "a Fairyland." Awestruck, April had yelled out.

"Thought you'd like this place," he confirmed after her expected reaction.

"You were right," she readily agreed. "It's wonderful. I never expected such a place existed outside of fairytales."

Unless one has experienced the mysterious silence of the darkened forest filled with redwood trees reaching a hundred and more feet up into the sky, there are no words to describe the event. One is completely dwarfed by the sight. It's something that will stay in your mind for the rest of your life.

After securing and locking their bikes on provided racks, April took the lead in their daily exploration. She could not restrain herself any longer. Leading on, hop-skipping ahead, she joyfully jumped over fallen branches, embracing moss-covered tree trunks, brushing up against dried bark, and taking in fresh smells and sights provided by the pristine environment. Every direction she turned brought on a new scene she was anxious to explore, with Eric following closely, trying to keep up with her pace.

"Yippee!" April, filled with boundless energy, repeatedly shouted into the forest in between brief stops to wait for her echo and to feel the different textures in her new environment. She yelled at Eric, "I wish I could live here."

"You can't. Nobody does," he replied.

"Why not? There's so much open space." She had stopped to catch her breath. Eric joined by pulling her near a tree trunk to rest.

"Wildlife protection."

"I'm wildlife," she joked.

"That's not the wildlife Teddy Roosevelt had in mind."

"Who's he?" This had another sobering effect on her.

"Former president. You should have learned about him in school."

"Sorry. I skipped classes that day."

"How come? Teachers let you?"

"Mom's fault. She didn't take me." There were many such days where her mom was either too drunk or too tired to get up.

"What about the bus?"

"Never had enough money."

"I meant a school bus."

"They got tired of waiting for me."

"What a shame. You missed out on much of history."

"Why?"

"It's from history one learns about life."

"Maybe you can teach me."

"I'll do my best." April remained silent for some time while enjoying the walk through the woods. Eric seemed to appreciate the serenity as well.

"Can I ask you something?" April said.

"Sure. You can ask me anything at any time."

"If you had a choice of where to build a home," she asked, "where would you go?"

"Washington state."

"I hear it's beautiful there, attracting many homeless." It was a place she'd overheard other homeless mention quite frequently. While curious about it, she never thought to find out more. Moving from the City was never a consideration in her life.

"The state and local citizens don't like all the influx."

"Why not? We don't cause any harm."

"Not everybody is as clean and health conscious as us."

"I know but I've had my share of filth and dirt."

"As long as you keep your space clean, it's not a problem."

"Then," she wavered, "why is there so much controversy?"

"It's a matter of support and burden to the local government."

"I don't cause any problems. And, by the way," she protested, "I pay for my living."

"You and I do, but not everybody does. Most homeless don't care about keeping public places clean and orderly. They don't clean up after themselves. That's where the problem starts."

"I'm beginning to understand." It was the first time someone had explained the facts of homelessness to her.

"Promise me one thing," Eric demanded. "It's very important to me. You'll always keep clean and clean up after yourself."

"I promise. I always hated the mess Mom left for me to clean up."

"Then you know how I feel. I don't like dirt and disorder either. It drives me to look for pristine places."

"Can I come with you?"

"I couldn't think of a better partner," he said without fully committing to a long-term relationship. He had learned that relationships were fragile and too vulnerable, easily influenced by personal differences.

"You getting hungry yet?" he said, checking his watch.

She'd noticed he did not carry the iPhone many people did. Though not popular with the homeless because of the cost, not just the purchase price but mostly the monthly service fees, he should be able to afford it, and she said so.

"I don't like the attachment," he said.

"What attachment?"

"People calling and demanding things."

"What demands?"

"Where are you? What are you doing? When are you coming home?"

"I understand. I wouldn't like it either," she agreed. "But what if I get lost and you couldn't find me?"

"You can find your way back," he stated, shrugging his shoulders.

"Not very thoughtful," she replied.

It was these kinds of stressed demands that he knew, from experience, could break up an otherwise loving and sound relationship, and kept quiet.

"What's the matter?" April said, wondering why he had gone silent.

"What'd you feel like having for dinner?" he said, diverting the subject.

"I am open for anything." Ignoring her growling stomach, she realized they had spent hours in this wooded paradise. "On second thought, let's try the Stinking Rose. You up for it?"

"Good choice." He had made peace with himself.

They arrived at this world-famous restaurant at the right time; one outdoor table was still available without having made prior reservations. "We lucked out," Eric remarked. Unlike most homeless, both carried themselves as expectedly-dressed patrons, casual but neatly dressed. It was the one thing Eric insisted on, blending in with the environment without offending anybody or advertising his status as a homeless. While he befitted the carefree status of the culture, he also appreciated the discipline society placed on people and the environment, when required. It might have appeared like a hypocritical notion to the general homeless, but, then, he was not the average vagrant off the street.

"Wow," April exclaimed, ready to leave after the waiter delivered the menu. "Let's go. This is crazy." She had taken one look at the menu prices: $49 for prime rib, the selection the house recommended.

"Not so fast," Eric insisted, reaching for the menu. "Let's take a look."

He had known what to expect, but agreed with her about the inflated prices. "Getting more expensive by the year."

"How can you stand it? I used to live an entire month on this. It's made me lose my appetite."

"Okay then," he suggested. "Let's look at the menu together." Minutes later, they'd decided on a lite cut for her at $36.99, and regular cut for him at $41.99.

"Can you really afford these prices?" she asked, concerned.

"Not every day. But today is a special day, don't you think? Let's celebrate." He had already selected a brand of wine, hoping she might like it. "Beringer, white zinfandel." He placed the order for two glasses accordingly when the waiter showed up, but was immediately rejected by her.

"You know I don't drink alcohol."

"Give it a try. Just sample it. Think of it like grape juice. It's the lightest and best on the market. You may just like it."

"Okay, I guess," she decided, with a wrinkled nose. "One sip." The drinks were served minutes later. After her first tiny sip she took a second, then a third. "I didn't think alcohol could smell and taste so sweet."

"It's the grapes and process best known for German wine."

"Do all taste this sweet?"

"Not by all means. Take Italy for example. Their wines are pretty gruff."

"What about ours?" April took interest for the first time in drinks. She still shuddered, thinking of the booze mom used to drink by the bottle, or inhaled, to be more correct.

"Our winegrowers learned to compromise."

"What do you mean?"

"They develop brands to our taste, rich but mellow." He watched her sip frequently and liked the results. *At least*, he silently reckoned, *I finally have pleasant company, and a pretty one to show off.* He was pleased with the direction their relationship was taking.

PERSONAL CONCERNS

Life for April turned out to be far more than she could have ever hoped. Each day turned out to be another adventure, lived in a different setting. When in Eric's company she felt secure and euphoric, rejuvenated each day in anticipation of another day's experience, reading much like in a perpetually-revolving novel. There was no end in his suggested plans for the day, with her adding her wishes and desires to learn and experience more with each sunup. After spending years burdened within a poverty-stricken disciplined society, living side-by-side with Eric turned out to be the happiest days of her life, and she hoped it would never end. While he had his personal demands at times, she did not. No matter what he'd decide for the day, she accepted it with veneration bordering on worship for him. Her every minute of the day was dedicated to him and their time together. They became inseparable.

Their day usually began at sunup, starting with their daily morning ritual at the public restroom facility nearby. Since he had grown up in an orderly environment structured by educated parents, hygiene and cleanliness were an important concept to Eric. He insisted on the daily cleansing, which April did not mind after spending much of her recent life associated with grime and dirt. It did not take long for April to develop a loving feeling at first, followed quickly by a sense of deep devotion for him. Eric, while keeping a sober state of mind most of the time, accepted her attention wholeheartedly. Life for both, after years of drifting aimlessly through individual space and time, seemed to have taken a turn for a solid bond spent together forever.

Of course, there were minor ups and down, as was the case with most relationships. But they were quickly disbanded and resolved with agreed satisfaction without lingering consequences. Their future seemed solidly bound, living together in harmony. Following their morning cleansing ritual in a somewhat crammed public space, the rest of the day was exploration and play. Unless April had a destination in mind to discover, he would usually take the lead, with both strapped to their bikes headed around town or along more distant paths leading across one of the bridges, with Mill Valley being their favorite destination. With both being young and full of energy, their touring kept them in excellent physical shape, complemented by keen minds and individual spirits.

Following a day's journey, spent on energy, hours later they would return to his tent to rest for a couple of hours. Then they would get ready for the evening and night's exploration as a couple or spent in the company of friends. Eric favored company, though April preferred the setting of Fisherman's Wharf with its boundless offerings in entertainment amid its cultural diversities in wares. She never got tired of listening to the chatter from a stream of foreign visitors bartering for trinkets or souvenirs to take home to family and friends. At times, she envisioned herself as a tourist, haggling to purchase a vendor's ware on display, waiting for her to take possession. Not having a personal income any more through begging, she was dependent on Eric for her wishes, though he did not mind as long as their monthly spending was within his invested dividend allocation.

"What do you feel like doing?" he asked as he usually did after sundown. April had developed a liking to light wine during their nightly escapades, but she felt like she needed a break from alcohol and crowded places. The drugs Eric would generally provide to supplement their euphoric high, purchased from friends or sellers at places, enforced her decision.

"Why don't we stay home?" she suggested.

"What's the matter?" he wondered, slightly concerned. "You don't feel well?"

"It's not that," she assured him. "I'm not used to all the alcohol and drugs. I'm afraid of turning into an alcoholic like Mom."

"Is that what's bothering you?"

"It's on my mind when I'm sober."

"Come here," he said, inviting her into his arms. He understood her worries and wanted to address her concerns, but did not want to have her turn against their social life. For him, their nightly outing was an important part. Without it, he'd decided years ago, life without friends and fun would be a grind. It was the grind part he had escaped years ago into his carefree existence of today. As for April, he was concerned about losing her if he wasn't careful. She might have been hardened against the demands government and society put on her, but when it came to relationships, he realized that she was still fragile.

He gave her a gentle kiss on the cheek and said, while stroking her hair, "Let me ask you a question to determine your condition." She eyed him expectantly as he continued. "Do you feel a strong urge to have a drink or drug?"

"You mean right now?" She did not quite understand the question.

"Yes. This very moment."

"Of course not. I still feel last night's effects," she replied in a challenging gesture. "Why do you ask?"

"To determine your mental state," he said. "And, based on your response, you have nothing to worry about."

"How can you be so sure?"

"Alcoholics and drug addicts desire or demand a fix every waking moment. If you were in that category," he assured her, "your body would be quivering and shaking by now, not to mention having stomach cramps."

"You sure?" She was not quite convinced.

"You've come across enough addicts in your past, haven't you?"

"Yeah, but I thought it was from hunger."

"Not a chance. Eating is far from their minds."

"I'll take your word for it," she finally accepted. "I don't want to end up like Mom. You're such as smart person," she said in genuine admiration.

"That I am," he agreed, smug-faced. Eric knew he was smart and well read, enough to impress many of his friends on any topic on which anyone decided to challenge him. Aside from qualified social skills, this was the reason he'd been so popular.

As for April, she was pacified for the moment, accepting any social challenges he'd decided for her. "After all," she contemplated, "I do enjoy the company of his friends."

ESCAPADES THROUGH CITY LIGHTS

It was Eric's assurance that essentially released April from her past bondage she'd had with her mom's life and plight. From here on, she enjoyed every moment with Eric's, as well as newly-made, friends with unrestrained enthusiasm. Though fully aware of her actions between the highs or lows within her state of mind, her past life of hardship under the control of her mom faded with time. However, there was one concern that surfaced at times that scared her: "What if something happened to Eric?" The thought alone was frightening enough to jolt her into reality. Those were the times she needed reassurance from him.

"Please," she would say amid a trembling mind. "Promise you'll never leave me."

It always caught him off-guard and he would give her his full attention. "I promise." His assurance would calm her for a time to completely enjoy her existence and dependence on him.

Some time had passed when, one day, April beckoned, with imploring eye, "Let's do something different today."

This slightly startled him. He thought she was okay with their routine of gathering with friends. It was friends he felt most comfortable with, rather than the pleasures of bar-hopping some people desired.

"What do you have in mind?"

"I want to visit some of the places I used to live."

"But why?" he said, not understanding her rationale. "I thought you left that life behind."

She took some time to respond, for she did not have a meaningful answer. It was more of a notion or internal urge she felt.

"I don't know. I feel compelled to remind myself of the unfortunate living on the streets. I think I need some assurance about never having to go back to that life of poverty."

"If that's what you want," he said in agreement, "it's what we'll do." He was not at all against her notion to revisit her former home. He was just surprised that he didn't think of it.

On second thought, he invited the opportunity, since it would provide a sense of adventure he had almost forgotten. Most homeless wound up living on the streets either through self-imposed means such as drug and alcohol use, or by economical depravation enforced by society, but with him it was self-imposed freedom from social obligations. Not many had the choice of being supported through the foresight of parents.

The spot he had claimed on top of the present hill was not an ideal place for mingling with homeless. For that they had to wander into town, to the busy metropolitan sectors, preferably with sidewalk traffic. "You ready?" Eric led on.

"What place do you have in mind?" April said.

"Let's check in on the place I used to hang my hat." This brought on a genuine giggle from her.

"Fine with me. But first, could we stop by I used to live?"

"Sure. I'd like to see the place." On bikes today, with April in the lead, they headed for the Mission District, surprised at the increase in street traffic. It took thirty minutes at a leisurely pace to get there. They were peddling against evening traffic arriving from across the Bay Bridge, weaving in and out of oncoming vehicles seeking out carports.[9]

As was the case with many places popular with foreign tourists, local living expenses seemed to increase with each year based on visitor mandate. Thoughts like this crossed April's mind as they headed to their destination. "How can anybody afford to live here? I sure couldn't." She felt fortunate to have Eric in her life, and she hoped they would always be together.

"Mission Street," the sign directed them as they peddled beneath the 101 overpass. This was the boundary of their destination. April had to stop momentarily to get her bearings.

---

[9] Parking in the city has been a challenge for many years and still has to be solved. Parking fees of $25 add another burden onto the cost of dining out, but is necessary when planning an evening in the City.

"What?" Eric said, slamming on his brake pedals.

Slightly out of breath, she replied, "I don't recognize the place. Things look different." Though it only had been a few years since she had departed her birthplace and where she'd grown up, her mind still needed time to assimilate her surroundings.

"It's usually like that, visiting home after some time," Eric agreed. He was quite familiar with the tricks the mind was capable of. "How far are we from the place?"

"A couple of blocks," she said, wondering what all the people were doing here. It was this view that kept her from getting her bearings. During her growing years the area had had a gray appearance, mostly drab looking, but as she faced the place now, it was filled with colors from green to yellow, blue, red, white and more. It suddenly struck her. "A tent city," she exclaimed, shaking her head in awe. "Where are all the people coming from?"

She had been aware of the homeless influx into the city over the years, but had never expected to see entire communities of homeless emerge. "I thought that the mayor and city council provided housing for the poor. Must not be the case."

"You should know better. What do many of these people have in common?" he tried to explain.

"Unrestricted freedom."

"You're right."

"Let's walk," he suggested, headed for some crosswalk banisters to lock up the bikes. After securing their wheels she led the way down Folsom Street towards 17th, their destination. As they crossed the street, her mind began to recognize some familiar places. "Look." She gestured in the direction of a grocery store. "That's where Mom used to send me to buy food. And here," she indicated with renewed exuberance, "is where I bought her booze." They were places she would always remember. Her whole life was practically lived between those two shops. While mostly filled with unpleasant memories, it was still the place that shaped the basis of her existence.

"What about your home?" he said, searching for an expression on her face.

"I don't know if we should stop there."

"Might as well. It's the reason we came here."

"Okay. See this place at the end of the street?" She gestured, already headed in that direction. He briskly followed towards a row of homes, which, based on their architecture, probably had been built seventy some years ago.

"Looks different from the rest of the City." It was not only the architectural changes he'd noticed, but the environmental as well. The Mission's geographical location insulated it from the fog and wind from the west. This climatic phenomenon became apparent to visitors who walked downhill from 24th Street in the west from Noe Valley (where clouds from Twin Peaks in the west tend to accumulate on foggy days) towards Mission Street in the east, partly because Noe Valley was on higher ground.

Where, in her past, the street had been a fairly quiet place, here and now, it seemed busy with tourists handing out money to the poor in between shopping for souvenir trinkets sold by street vendors. The place seemed to be thriving for the poor and travelers alike.

"Should I ring?" April asked with her finger poised near a set of doorbells after they had arrived at her former home. "I know the lady."

"Go ahead."

The shuffling of feet could be heard from the inside hallway. Seconds later an elderly woman appeared at the front door with a questioning look on her face that rapidly changed into a grin after she recognized her visitor.

"April!" the woman, haggard in appearance, blurted out in a raspy-sounding voice. "Girl, where have you been? Come on in. Who is this?"

"A friend," she replied. After she introduced Eric, both visitors were invited into the woman's home, which was located on the third floor above a narrow, winding staircase. Minutes later, they were seated and served tea and cookies, customary snacks for this time and location. "Tell me what happened to you after your mom died," she said with anticipation.

Surrounded by a friendly atmosphere, they spent two hours with her, with her and April doing most of the talking and Eric seated, quietly listening. April had a rich story to tell her, but the woman did not. Her life was as lonely as always after her husband had passed away. The only adventure for her was daily gossip with other lonely neighbors. Eric sat deeply in thought, having his own concerns, evaluating his and April's future together when life got to an old age. *Too far in the future to worry about,* he decided. Getting up to leave, they said goodbyes, with the woman insisting, "I've missed you. You come back soon, you hear."

April paid her lip service with a promise. "I'll come back." Headed back to fetch the bikes, April muttered, "I don't think so." Living with Eric in their present tent home in Great Meadow Park, the Mission was some place she had left behind years ago. With her mom gone it no longer had an attraction. She had satisfied her curiosity and made inner peace with herself, happy with the way her life had turned out. In spite of the fact that she had missed out on a proper education, orderly homelife and loving family, and had instead been raised in a poverty-stricken apartment in somewhat questionable surroundings, she had no regrets about her past.

From here on she could enjoy Eric's company no matter what the future presented. For now, their immediate destination was the Tenderloin District, Eric's former turf. They were not sure what to expect.

Heading north on Folsom Street on their bikes took them to 5th Street. A left turn brought them right into the center of the

Tenderloin, the Powel Street cable car terminal station. Securing their bikes at a nearby rack for cyclers, provided by the city since bikes were allowed on cable cars, gave them room to freely move about.

"Feels like home," Eric remarked, pulling her hand in the direction of Union Square. It was a place attracting both local and visiting shoppers from all directions. While they had frequented this place in the past, it was at different times before they had ever met. He had left already for the hill, their present home, when she arrived on the scene.

Presently, seated on a vacant bench within the square, they wholly enjoyed the place. All the other benches were occupied by homeless who had staked out their individual spots weeks and months ago, much like April had when she'd arrived only a couple of years back.

"Feels nice to be among your own kind, doesn't it?" April asked in serenity. Union Square, being an elevated park, distant from immediate trolley, automobile, and pedestrian traffic, was relatively quiet, filled with ample trees and colorful gardens.

"I can't make out any familiar faces," Eric said, searching around the dozen or so park benches. "I used to have many friends here."

"Do you miss them?"

"Yes. Most of them were decent people. Smelly but honest."

"Your place is much nicer."

"That's true, but no friends."

"You have me," April said with an anticipating smile.

"I'm happy about that," he replied, planting a kiss on her cheek.

"I'm hungry," she said. "How about you?"

"Let's go. I know a nice place."

"Where?"

"Embarcadero. The Docks."

"Oh yes. I like it there." They covered the six blocks distance on their bikes in ten minutes, weaving in and out of pedestrian and street traffic. Though inconvenient to shoppers at most times, bicycle riders were an accepted utility in San Francisco. It was transportation to take you places, at times faster than trolleys could.

They had arrived at Pier 1, the Ferry Building and farmers' market specifically. In addition to goods and wares sold at a dozen places, specialty shops and restaurants were abundant. One only had to select the cuisine of choice to enjoy a variety of cultural eateries. Pulling April through the building, Eric picked a French outdoors cafeteria facing the bay with its nearby islands in full view. Having skipped breakfast, both were hungry for a solid meal.

"What will it be?" the waiter asked, assessing his patrons.

"Fish and chips," April ordered, since it was the only fare on the menu she recognized.

"Try something authentic," Eric suggested.

Feeling inadequate about the foreign-sounding items and not wanting to sound ignorant, she stayed with her choice. "Fish and chips it is," Eric agreed, and placed the orders, his being a French dish. The waiter left with a shrug of his shoulders, indicating his state of mind about not expecting much of a gratuity.

"I was here once before," she said, starting off the topic.

"Only once?"

"Homeless are not allowed on the piers."

"I know. It's a shame," he agreed. "The newly-elected mayor and city administration might change that."

"I'm afraid of that," she admitted, evading the fact that they were homeless as well.

"Are you changing your mind about your life?" he said, squinting his eyes.

The bare mention of giving up a carefree lifestyle brought on hostility among the homeless. The reason was always the same: local administrations enforcing disciplined social rules and regulations on the homeless. To the observer, it might appear to be a life spent in carefree encirclements, but a closer look revealed a set of problems to which most citizens would not want to be subjected.

"No. Not at all," April vehemently objected, throwing him an angry look at the very suggestion.

"Don't get angry," he pacified her. "Just checking."

"I love living with you. You should know that by now. Wouldn't want to change it one bit."

"What do you want to do for the rest of the day?" After him enjoying the fine French cuisine and her British-style fish and chips, they had been sitting at the pier for two hours, watching ferry boats come and go shuttling passengers between the City to Tiburon, Sausalito and on to Richmond. While Eric was ready to venture on, April felt like spending the remainder of the day in the serenity of their present setting.

"It's your choice," she said with a sigh, getting off the bench. Back on the street again, they headed north on Bay street, back towards The Hill. Passing Crissy Field, Eric was spotted by a couple of familiar faces, yelling at him. "Hey, buddy!"

This brought on astonishing reactions from several homeless lingering in the shadows nearby. "Look what the waves washed up!" and "Eric, you hound, where've you been hiding?"

"Up on The Hill," he cheerfully responded at the grinning faces.

"That you up there?" one said with a gesture at The Hill. The Hill was a favorite spot for people strolling and jogging along the shoreline. The problem was, you had to have a city permit to set up a tent at the pristine location. Eric had no problem getting permission since he was considered a touring visitor. He had extended the permit a couple of times without any rejections after assuring the authorities of his honorable intention. That was the reason he was not part of any tent city, as administration officials labeled the rapidly-growing homeless communities on every available space. He achieved his desire over the average citizens not so much through cunning, but more from being street smart.

From April's observations, while most homeless were aware of their environment, many did not care how much they damaged it. All they cared about was being among like-minded drifters with an urge to make the outdoors their home. To them it did not matter how much filth their presence created as long as they earned enough change to survive another day filled with drugs and alcohol abuse. Their entire life was centered on substances and the subsequent euphoric high. The problem was, when asked, none would ever admit their addiction to themselves nor anybody else. Their entire lives were lived in denial.

Holding her hand, Eric pulled April along the rows of tents, being welcomed by drifters he knew. Strolling along, they stopped next to a large tent amid a heap of bicycles, scavenged office furniture, and a shopping cart full of food. Every few minutes, someone emerged from one of the tents to fetch something to eat or share a smoke. While there, both perceived the smells of weed and urine punctuating the air. Situations like this could be observed all around the city, since hundreds of homeless encampments had cropped up across San Francisco in only a couple of years, permanently changing the landscape in residential neighborhoods and other highly-visible areas.

While homelessness had been a feature of life in San Francisco ever since the city was built, the concentrations of used needles, feces, and urine that came with the current influx was new. In spite of an ordinance authorizing city councils to clear out drifters and clean up their mess, more tent camps lined freeway underpasses and sidewalks throughout the city.

Over the years, since their appearance, numerous attempts had been made to rid the city of homelessness without making any progress. Demanding a homeless person vacate the premises by closing one spot only moved the problem to another location, then another, and so on. It was a never-ending imposition on both the drifters and law enforcement with nobody ever winning. And so, life went on, with the homeless displaced without an end in sight. The homeless culture was here to stay and had become a permanent feature of many places. It was not only popular cities having to deal with the issue; authorities in charge of towns, parks, lakes, river embankments, urban expansions, suburbs, bridges, forests, and many pristine spots were confronted and challenged by the constant influx of drifters.

"Hear ye, hear ye," Harry, one of Eric's former buddies, yelled out, with a gesture at Eric. "King of The Hill has made his entrance." This attracted the attention from homeless up and down the street. Most gathered to see what the yelling was about. It was not customary for the homeless to attract attention. They were a quiet bunch, trying to blend in with the terrain, obscured from city officials to hide their presence. Everybody in the city knew about the increase in drifters each year. The city government was suppressing the conditions the drifters created, but concerned citizens made every effort to alert the public.

Eric, heralded for his cunningness in gaining control of The Hill, for all practical purposes became a hero. Word spread quickly through every cluster of tent dwellings in town, inspiring many to become his followers. One thing was certain. They knew, the comprehending ones anyway, that in order to grow their homeless culture, their chances for a lasting existence would cause a never-ending problem with city administrations. Based on this principle, word was spread to follow Eric to The Hill to decide on a plan that would force city policies into accepting the homeless cause.

"Why didn't I think of it?" Eric proclaimed after accepting becoming their leader. Unbeknownst to him, many had been impatiently waiting for a leader to emerge. Now, it seemed that they had found one. Though he was more of a loner in his quest to tour the country, the thought of being their leader was alluring.

"I accept the nomination," he confirmed, following a few moment's hesitation, with Harry.

"Meet our leader!" Harry's voice roared above the crowd's cheering while he held up Eric's right hand.

Even April, who took in everything quietly, was captivated by the monumental turn of events that had just taken place. She could immediately sense a change in their attitudes. It would assure her a secure place by Eric's side for the things ahead. She was also aware that there would be many changes taking place for them, for the good as well as the bad. Complacently, she handed over her future into his capable hands, with the immediate thought: *My future is secure.*

CALL TO ACTION

"Notify council members about an emergency assembly," Thomas Allen ordered when word spread about the leadership election for the homeless. His initial reaction to his deputy was, "We're in trouble. This could turn into a civil war if we allow it. Also alert city law enforcement to report for duty."

"It may not be that bad," the deputy cautioned. "At least we have a face to negotiate with. It could be a good thing."

Regardless of potential consequences, the mayor anticipated a confrontation to be not far off.

It did not take long for the city council to be called into action. Following a weekend of widespread celebration, the homeless showed up in force, marching in the direction of the city's capitol. Homeless members from the Crissy Field area had observed a massive gathering earlier that day. There was great anticipation for protest directions. Debating what action to take, Eric and Harry, his first elected officer as his deputy, decided on converging on City Hall with an agenda still up in the air. It would be discussed during their march, which took them east on Marina Boulevard, headed for Van Ness Avenue, and eventually turned south in the direction of City Hall.

"What's our agenda?" Harry asked..

"Let's talk it over," Eric suggested. It would take four hours of marching to cover the 8-mile distance. What amazed Eric the most was the number of homeless joining in along the way. Groups and singles emerged from many alleys and backstreets, cheerfully accepted by the growing mass.

"What do we want?" Harry started with a grin. "I had no idea how popular you were." He had to shout to be heard. The march was not a quiet affair. Many had showed up carrying makeshift flags torn from bedsheets and blankets tied to canes and sticks hastily painted in many colors amid shouts and cheers, escalating the level of noise as they marched along.

"I didn't have any idea either. Hell," Eric said. "This has turned out much bigger than I ever expected."

"Me too," Harry agreed, showing concern. "We need to organize this bunch quickly before it turns into a mob. That would defeat our entire principle and purpose."

"That'll be your job," Eric said with a sly grin he could not suppress.

"Thanks for a task I could have done without," Harry shot back not happy. "There goes my leisure time."

"Okay," Eric suggested. "Here are our immediate demands." He then called out the initial agenda for meeting with the city council:

1. Legalized settlements in the city and county
2. Freedom from harassment and persecution
3. Dedicated restrooms, canteens, and shower facilities
4. Ready access to public transportation and services
5. Free health care support, medical and emergency care.

Harry kept track of Eric's list of demands by making notes on a piece of paper. "Is that it?" he said, looking over the list.

"Not yet," Eric insisted. "We need at least ten points to make it a meaningful declaration. I don't know how many the city council will honor, if any at all."

"What's our reaction if we're shut down on all demands?"

"We have no choice but to negotiate," Eric said.

"What about demonstrations?"

"The council won't take us seriously."

"Why not?"

"Just look at this bunch. Would you?"

"What about protests? We have the masses."

"We have no money for weapons, no training in combat, and no commanding force. We are subject to their will or we'll wind up in federal prisons. We are no match against national guardsmen and especially the military."

"That means," Harry postulated, "our cause is in vain?"

"Not necessarily," Eric replied with a sense of optimism. "If we remain calm and play it smart, we can achieve much of our agenda."

"How so?"

"Liberals listen. They like to talk. They have the compulsion to help anybody and everybody through the eyes of humanitarian justice. Hell," Eric explained, "in this state, as long as they can show progress to the taxpayers, they'll readily appropriate the necessary budget we already require. Let's work on the remainder of our demands:

6. Jurisdiction for equal protection from the law
7. Abolish discrimination against the homeless
8. Rights to the homeless freedom of movement
9. Rights and freedom of unrestricted expression
10. Rights to free education and choice of school."

"Not bad," Harry muttered when reading their demands. "Not bad at all, but why schools? There are no children."

"Wait and see. They'll come as soon as schools accept homeless children."

"If you say so," Harry said, though still in doubt.

"But," Eric interjected. "If all fails, I'm gonna give them my solution to homelessness."

"Wow," Harry could not restrain his enthusiasm. "I didn't know you had any."

"Nothing firm. Just a thought," Eric hinted. "Let's get back to the agenda."

Eric recapped his suggested list, then stated, "At least they'll have to listen. We might even make amendments to the constitution."

"Wouldn't that be a feat? Homeless forcing a political change in the government. I can already read tomorrow's headlines." He beamed. "Homeless forces on the move to challenge the government."

"We'll find out soon enough," Eric said with a concerned look on his face. Their effort could lead in either direction:

gaining some recognition for the homeless, or being disbanded and incarcerated for political insurgency.[10]

Their effort could be successful or end in complete failure. It was the chance they'd have to take. Hours already into the march and well on the way to City Hall, Eric's mind was torn between doubts and beliefs of this one-time opportunity they had chosen.

---

[10] An insurgency is a movement within a country dedicated to overthrowing the government. An insurgency is a rebellion. Insurgency is also used for less serious situations: for example, a rebellious group within a company, political party, or school could be called an insurgency. All insurgencies are made up of rebels.

CITY COUNCIL

As forewarned and anticipated, alarming reports arrived almost by the minute, called in by alert citizens, about the approaching homeless force. Much of the city assembly had been ordered to the office. City Hall was buzzing with calls and commands to prepare for action and counter measures, if it came to that. Much of the police force had been called up for duty and staged to protect all entrance points. "How much longer before they arrive?" the mayor checked with his deputy again and again. He, as well as all law enforcement command and council executives, were kept informed of the homeless' progress, closing in within the hour.

"Twenty minutes," the deputy said, being informed once more by calls from a news media reporter following the homeless' progress.

"You've got the action list?" The so-called action list were excerpts from constitutional articles the council staff had extracted in haste over the weekend. It provided discussion points the council expected from the advancing force. At this stage of emergency, none of the council members knew what to expect and how much of a threat the homeless posed. It all depended on their leadership and their intentions, which were, at this time, still unknown. Rumors had it that they meant business in spite of the threat of being detained by law enforcement or incarcerated for an illegally-organized protest. The minimum the mayor and his staff could hope for was that the protesters would listen to reasoning. It would not be an easy task, especially since the city assembly had tried it on numerous occasions over the past decades, only to see unrelenting homeless growth.

They all heard it now, yelling and shouting from the mob getting close. Minutes later, the force arrived at the grounds.[11] Thomas Allen took one last glance at the action list, ready to face the homeless leader.

"Sir." Flanked and guarded by the police chief and accompanied by several law enforcement officers, the mayor's deputy gestured at the unwelcomed protesters. The homeless leader and his lieutenant were shoved into the room to be introduced. "This here homeless claims to be their elected leader," the mayor's deputy unceremoniously announced. The mayor made a quick assessment of his guests and decided, *They don't look anything like bums.* He quickly realized that the two were no ordinary drifters.

This could be dangerous, he decided silently, placing his senses on guard. Then, facing the leader, he said, "What's your name?"

"Call me Eric. I am the elected leader representing the homeless cause."

"How about you?" He'd turned to Eric's companion.

"Harry. I'm his lieutenant."

"Have a seat," the mayor said with a gesture, directing them to the conference table. While introductions in City Hall had been respectful and orderly, they could hear protesting shouts from the courtyard, demanding entrance. Tension-filled seconds passed before the mayor opened the session with, "State the intentions that bring you here." He'd decided to keep the confrontation strict. For the time being, there was no reason or protocol to be social, not with the homeless mob.

---

[11] The building's vast open space covers more than 500,000 square feet and occupies two full city blocks, located between Van Ness Avenue and Polk Street, bordered by Grove and McAllister Streets.

"With due respect," Eric offered with a forced smile, "I came here with peaceful intentions to negotiate for the plight of the homeless."

"Define plight," the mayor demanded.

"The hardship and restrictions you and the citizens place on us homeless."

"What I want to know is," Allen further demanded, "are you a bonafide homeless or are you a contracted activist?"

"I am a self-imposed homeless, I assure you. And so is Harry." Eric nodded at his lieutenant. Then, pulling the list from his pants pocket, he said, "I have a list of demands here I would like to present to the city." He handed the mayor the ten demands before leaning back in his chair to allow the mayor and council members to respond, watching their faces while the list was handed around the table. It did not take much time or expert psychology to anticipate their response. Regardless, he had taken on the role and responsibility for the homeless to represent their complaints. Eric was in no hurry and had no intention to leave. He had committed himself.

"Eric," the mayor addressed him after allowing his staff to read the demands. "Since it's already past noon, why don't you and Harry join me for lunch." One had to admire the mayor's gesture; in one swoop he defused the tension in the room.

Some of the mayor's trusted advisors joined in at a reserved section of the cafeteria. Conversations were limited to short queries and responses about today's confrontation and what led up to it, mostly presented by the mayor and his staff. Never having been this close to the homeless, all had their own personal agenda and curiosity. Eric responded to most questions:

"How long have you been a homeless?"

"Four years."

"Where're you from?"

"Wisconsin."

"What attracted you to this city?"

"It's the most beautiful city in the country." The reply seemed to startle some members. Eric could almost read their thoughts about the fact that a homeless would appreciate the values of a place.

"What made you decide to become a homeless?"

"There are several reasons."

"Give me one."

"Freedom from an enforced society."

"You realize there have to be rules and regulations."

"I had too much of those at home and in schools."

"Everybody needs a certain amount of discipline."

"It didn't fit with me."

"What makes you so special?"

"I can think for myself."

"Oh," the mayor interrupted. "You are a rebel."

"Not a rebel," Eric corrected him. "More of a leader."

"I guess that's why you are sitting at this table."

"Probably." Eric had tried to avoid every possible confrontation with City Hall, but had his personal agenda about leadership he wanted to voice. He had pondered about executive decisions many a time. "With due respect, Mayor," he said, "your council needs to be educated about our cause. You don't take the time to listen to us. We are tired of being patronized year after year without any visible results."

"Now we are talking," the mayor fired back. "And you people don't listen either. No matter what I do for you it's never enough. Am I right?"

"You only see our needs through your eyes. You don't listen to our plight."

"You are here now, aren't you?"

"Not by your invitation."

"Look at it from my perspective," the mayor replied. "How am I supposed to negotiate with thousands of individuals?"

"I am here now."

"That you are," the mayor replied. "Let's not start bickering. The situation you created is serious enough."

"Are you ready to address my agenda?"

"Okay. Let's get back to the office." Lunch was over, with the assembly moving back to the emergency at hand. They were well aware of the shouting coming from the mob gathered outside. More had joined in with the Crusade, as some had labeled the demonstration.

Seated in the conference room once more, the mayor pulled the list of demands from his jacket pocket to study it closely while the council waited impatiently. He then passed the list to his assembly members once more, facing Eric. "What's your most urgent priority?"

"Legalized settlements in the city and counties."

"You know," the mayor cautioned him, "that'll take time and may not be possible. We've tried numerous times to accommodate the demand. We even went as far as constructing new housing, but none of you ever took possession. What is it with you people?" the mayor exclaimed. "I spent millions of dollars accommodating you, and what do I get?"

Eric and Harry waited for the punchline.

"Bitching from both sides, with you people and taxed citizens screaming at me."

"We can put a stop to it if you are willing to negotiate," Eric suggested. He was well aware of the issues his people had forced on the political front.

"What is it you really want?" the mayor said, extending a personal courtesy.

"We want a plot of land we can call our own." There it was, out in the open. Eric's suggestion came on the fly. He and Harry had prepared the list, but they did not have the time to formulate the demands. Much like it had for the mayor's office, the protest had come on suddenly.

"What about the rest of your demands?" the mayor challenged.

"They will work out themselves."

"What assurance do I have that your people will respect my proposals?"

"I'll make sure of it," Eric replied. "I represent the demands for your council to evaluate. I want to settle the issue as much as you."

"I can't promise anything," the mayor said with a doubtful face. "But I assure you I'll make it my highest priority."

"That's all I ask," Eric said, getting up. He had nothing more to contribute for the moment, thinking in silence, *We'll see soon enough how high his priority values are.*

The mayor adjourned the meeting with a promise to address the agenda, afraid that the mainstream media would escalate the homeless agenda into a frenzied affair, as usual. His concerns were always the same: how will the public take the homeless demands? He did not want to think about it at the moment. He needed a drink. Dismissing Eric and Harry, "Join me at the club," he said to the council members, who wholeheartedly accepted. There was a lot to talk about that could not be accomplished in a sober state.

When Eric and Harry appeared at the entrance they were received with a suspended expectation. The courtyard had gone silent in anticipation, partially to hear the anticipated results and partially by the police force protecting city premises.

"Listen, all of you," Eric announced in an elevated tone of voice, raising his hand to silence the crowd. "We have the mayor's and city council's attention. I presented our agenda and they will give it their highest priority." Immediate cheers went up, overwhelming the City Hall space. Eric gave them a minute to express years of frustrations before he continued to speak. "Listen. I promise you that things will change. It may take some time, but they will change."

This brought on more cheering and applause. With that, Eric, rejoined by April and Harry, quickly left the demonstrators and headed back for The Hill. All three considered their effort a great accomplishment and there was much to discuss and celebrate. On the way back, Eric stopped at a local liquor store to purchase a case of Jack Daniels for the occasion. It was his favorite Bourbon, and he anticipated many guests stopping by his tent through the night.

Following a night of celebration with substances ranging from alcohol to drugs of all sorts, the next days were spent recovering from the effects. Hangovers and after-effects were prevalent throughout tent cities, but life did not return to "as usual." As expected, the news media had had a field day that lasted days, with so-called experts presenting ideas and demanding to be heard.

For Eric and April, life had changed as well. His time was on demand from dusk to dawn from both sides, the homeless and the city council as well. Her time was solely dedicated to Eric on his way to success and fame. Since his only transportation was the bicycle, whenever the mayor scheduled a meeting he would send his personal limousine to The Hill, causing heads to turn in wonder, speculating, "What's going on?"

Though both sides were making serious efforts to resolve the homeless pain, progress was slow. What took time was the council's demands in dealing with the citizens. After all, it was their money they spent, not only for the homeless cause, but to justify the mayor and council member's time and efforts. Consequently, money was being spent without much visible result. A vote was put to the citizens for a budget increase, but when the results were counted: not enough funding, an indication of the city's sentiments. Citizens had been overtaxed for years, mostly for liberal social needs, and there was little funding left to address the homeless plight. What made California more demanding than other states was that voters were overwhelmed from a social burden that was caused by the state itself and originated with uncounted influx from across Mexico and its southern borders, which had yet to be resolved.

It was not California's fault that the southern entry was so demanding; it was the economically inferior conditions prevalent over many years in Mexico and its Central American neighbors. Not all countries in the world were firmly directed by a set constitution governed by a humanitarian-minded democratic people, as in the U.S. It was this mentality that attracted many of the world's people.

Three months later, "Folks," Thomas Allen announced as soon as he stepped up onto the podium, after calling an emergency session. "We have a serious problem on our hands." Glancing around the room, he could see that the assembly's sentiments were clearly painted across their faces, since those sessions were seldom hosted with good news. He composed himself before going on. "We cannot expect any help from the federal government. We will have to solve the homeless crisis on our own." He paused to let the uproar that followed subside, then continued with his delivery. "It's going to be impossible to hold up our promises to the homeless, but there is no other way than to inform their leader." More shouting and cussing followed, directed mostly at the insensitivity of the federal government. It took several minutes again for the disorder to quiet down before the mayor could be heard.

"Order please." The bailiff stepped in with a threatening gesture.

"What I need from every one of you members is a list of suggestions for how to streamline our state budget to raise enough funding for the homeless cause," the mayor demanded from the assembly members. In their eyes, since every dollar from the state budget was already spent as soon as it was appropriated, any additional funding would have to come from the pool of state government members. All personal spending, as liberal as it was in the State of California, had to be curbed for months, and perhaps years to come.

Nobody was willing to give up an individual luxury for the benefit of homeless drifters and vagrants, no matter how much of a nuisance they had created. It would be much like asking any affluent family to give up their acquired wealth in favor of the poor. Their entire existence depended on controlling and managing deprived citizens. It had taken many decades for governments to eradicate many of the middle class citizens in order to become a dependency factor, the only means to govern the masses preferably kept poor.

"Cannot be done... We won't stand for it... Such an insult..." were some of the shouts directed at the mayor. The bailiff was forced to step in to restrain some of the members. Thomas Allen, once heralded for his successful official functions in governing the city, today was viewed as villain. There was nothing he could say to rectify the situation and so he turned and left without adjourning. He sought out his chambers, followed by the bailiff, who provided personal protection. It would be days before he was approached by the more tolerant members with suggestions about how to remedy the present dilemma and perhaps a means of settling the homeless issue.

"Eric!" April yelled, excitedly approached him. "There's a letter for you," she said, handing it to him. "It's personal."

"Who's it from?"

"The mayor himself."

This immediately caught his attention. "The mayor?" He practically tore the letter from her hands, anticipating good news.

"What does it say?" she asked, waiting for him to read.

"I don't know."

"What do you mean?" She was perplexed at his response since he was always spontaneous with answers.

"Could be good news or could be bad news," he said, handing her the letter.

She read: *Eric, I must appeal to your intellect and good nature. The news this letter carries is not good. To this day, I have not been able to raise any of the funds required to allocate a meaningful budget to your cause. What I ask from you is to work with me personally to come up with a temporary solution for your honorable initiative in resolving the state-*

wide homeless matter. I herewith extend my unofficial invitation to you at my private residency and am waiting for your acceptance.

"I can't believe it," April shouted out, rushing to embrace him. "You might even become a politician."

"You're not serious," he said with misgiving.

"You'll be famous," she said, astonished at the sudden turn of events. "We'll be famous."

"Now hold on," he said, calming her. "Nobody is promising anything. All the mayor has suggested is collaboration, an alliance. It's a friendly invitation."

"Friendly, my ass," she responded. "He's in trouble. What's your reply to him?"

"It doesn't matter what the reasons are, of course I'm accepting."

"Don't you see," she objected, trying to reason with him. "He's shifted the whole burden on you."

"I can handle it. Don't you believe in me?" Eric asked.

"Of course I do. I'll support you one hundred percent."

"Then, let's work out a response letter."

Honorable Mayor, the letter read.
I am honored at your suggested invitation. It is not every day to be invited to your esteemed residence. Of course I will accept. My time is flexible at your discretion. Your schedule permitting, I am dutifully awaiting date and time for your calling.
Respectfully yours,
Eric - Representative for the Homeless

"Nice work," April said in admiration. "I could not have written it better." They both laughed at her remark.

"I went to college, remember?"

"I'm proud of you," she said. giving him a hearty hug. "Let's celebrate."

"We haven't achieved anything yet," Eric protested, but headed for the cooler to follow her suggestion.

The mayor's reply arrived by official delivery within hours, with the invitation scheduled for the following morning. It was a reason to celebrate.

The mayor's limousine arrived at The Hill at 8:00 a.m., suggesting the meeting was for 9:00 a.m., the customary time for the mayor to conduct business. Sure enough, he was at his mansion when they showed up. "Eric," the mayor addressed him, with a courteous nod at April, who had accompanied him. Prior to leaving, after several objections, Eric had decided she should come along, reasoning, "It will keep the intensity of negotiations in check." She was thrilled. It would be the first time anybody would ever listen in case a question was directed at her. Doubtful, but possible.

Two of the mayor's staff were in attendance, his deputy and secretary. It appeared that he wanted to keep the meeting as private as possible. He had decided on that because of the lack of support he'd received from the assembly. "Eric," he began. "I invited you here for a private audience for one reason: to solve our differences in the homeless matter. Before we get into specifics," he stressed, "I want to recap the city's efforts on the matter. As you are probably aware, homelessness is not a recent occurrence. It has been around for several decades. For this city, I believe, it infiltrated in the '60s with the hippie[12] movement."

"You are absolutely right," Eric agreed. "We started it."

"You mean your predecessors?"

"Of course. I wasn't even born yet. It was my dad's culture."

---

[12] The noun "hippie" is the most common spelling for the 1960s youth-and-counterculture people. More specifically, a hippie is a usually-young person who rejects established social customs (such as by dressing in an unusual way or living in a commune) and who opposes violence and war, especially a young person of this kind in the 1960s and 1970s.

"You may accept homelessness from a cultural perspective," the mayor continued. "To me it is a burden I have to manage and have yet to solve."

"I understand."

"Do you?"

"I wasn't born into it. I elected to live within the culture not long ago."

"Oh," the mayor expressed with surprise.

"I had to get away from my dad as well as my teachers' dominance."

"I understand," the mayor said, underscored with a nod of his head. "There were times I felt like running away from home too, but also knew that it would destroy my heritage and chances for a political career. In time, I learned to accept the discipline instilled on the young."

"You are a better man," Eric said with a grin on his face. The mayor seemed to understand. "I want to explain something," Eric said. "I didn't chose to become a homeless. I just live this way because it provides the liberty I need. I still respect society with its rules and regulations, believe me. I just need the freedom to move around the country and the world, unrestricted to explore places I want to learn about."

"Such as?"

"Foreign customs and cultures."

"That's commendable. I envy you. What about you, April?"

Being addressed by the mayor directly took her by surprise, and with a question in top of it. All of her life she was used to being reprimanded and scolded. It was only in recent times with Eric that people had begun to respect her.

"I was born into poverty," she explained.

"I'm sorry to hear that," the mayor said. "Where are you from?"

"Right here in the city."

"What changed your life?"

"Eric here," she said, beaming at her savior, seated beside her.

"I'm happy for you," the mayor said in honesty. "Now," he turned to Eric, "let's move on. We have a lot of ground to cover. Before we address your list of demands, let's take a look and see what the city has accomplished for the homeless. For that, we'll have to go back a number of years. Specifically," he explained, "since the '80s, we've had to resolve a variety of migratory influxes such as drifters, vagrants, beggars, nomads, panhandlers, as well as migrants of recent years, to accommodate each and every one's demands for support, housing, and individual needs. While their demands were justified in many cases, others were not."

"Wow," April expressed in wonder, "I had no idea."

"Many people are not aware of the migratory influx," the mayor explained to her. "They only hear homeless. That's because the homeless have increased in numbers far beyond the initial tourist attraction. In case you didn't know," he said, addressing April directly, "not long ago, San Francisco was the world's most popular tourist attraction, and people visited specifically to see the homeless."

"I didn't know," April replied in amazement.

"Yes. They came from all corners of the globe, supporting the drifters who were not much of a burden to the city other than keeping track of their activities. There was not much crime involved. They were a peaceful lot."

"What made it change?" April said.

"Illegal substances," the mayor replied.

April avoided his gaze as much as possible. She knew well that it was true, if only from her own recent exploits into substances. Her excuse was, "I only do it for recreation."

"That's how it always starts," the mayor said, looking for collaboration from Eric, who agreed with a slight nod. "Am I correct?"

"You're right," Eric agreed.

"Sir." The mayor's public affairs officer popped her head into the room. "The press is demanding an update."

"No news today," he said, shaking his head. "And don't schedule anything with anybody."

"If you insist." She closed the door, shrugging her shoulders.

"Media," he muttered, indicating his dislike. "Can't live with them and can't live without them." It was understood that the media had its proper place. What he did not appreciate was the incessant pressure to sensationalize stories. "It's nothing but *Breaking News*, lately."

"That's one thing I don't have to worry about, living under the open skies," Eric agreed.

"I envy you," the mayor said. "Sometimes I wish I'd followed your dream."

"I know a beautiful place," Eric said with a smile. "I'll keep a spot open for you."

"It may come to that if we can't work things out," he agreed. "Let's get back to work."

Following another invitation to lunch, the group spent the rest of the day assessing the effort it would take to bring the homeless situation under control, with issues ranging from legal implications to taxation and provisions offered by the city in order to entice the homeless into the prevalent socio-oriented population desired by the majority of California's citizens.

The mayor's detailed explanation about the City's plight opened up Eric and April's perception about the other side of the homeless culture. It appeared that the City administration's effort in resolving the increasing influx with tent encampments had not been very successful.

They have become a permanent feature in the city, despite aggressive efforts to clear them out periodically. Municipal workers would clear out an encampment and confiscate tents and property, and the next day one would pop up elsewhere. Unfortunately, the city has run out of vacant spaces, with no place available to accommodate the homeless anymore. For now, they just camp out on the sidewalks and, for convenient reasons, near freeways, for ease of migration access. Other popular places to pitch tent are supermarkets and store and business fronts, in addition to claiming stakes at parking lots.

Not obvious to the eyes, but more importantly for the well-being of the city, the homeless encampments have made the poor more visible while the middle class has been quietly disappearing. Competition among the middle class for scarce housing in the once-pristine city is taking on a new housing profile. Many of the growing numbers of middle-class workers and professionals in San Francisco have been reduced to living in dorms with shared bathrooms and communal kitchens because they cannot afford to rent an apartment. Such ventures catching on in San Francisco simply reflect the stark reality for school teachers, mechanics, musicians, and anyone else in the non-technology sector. Homeownership has grown out of reach for the average wage earner.

The question of what to do with the homeless still remains unsolved. To better understand the plight of homelessness in the city, in places such as the Tenderloin, Mission, and many other neighborhoods on any given day, the streets are essentially an open-air drug and prostitution bazaar, all within easy walking distance of City Hall, with employees and major corporate headquarters having their drug supplies delivered on a daily basis.

As one can easily see by walking the streets during daytime, since sidewalks are occupied by the homeless with smelly filth splattered everywhere, it does not take much of an imagination to assess how prolific a nightlife was, with deals for drugs and sex being brokered.

While much of the homeless plight was largely being fueled by San Francisco's economic success, the resultant mess could easily be spotted in street gutters, with used needles and human feces so prevalent in San Francisco that even private citizens and visitors know to avoid certain areas.

What makes it more mysterious were assumptions that the homeless were increasing in numbers from migrations from out of state, but this was a mistaken perception. Most of the city's homeless were homegrown Californians. When asked, nearly every homeless person claimed they had lived in San Francisco for many years, but also expressed their distaste for staying at city-provided shelters or other prearranged dwellings, all for the same reasons: attached strings with meetings, prayer sessions and other mandatory demands to which nobody was willing to be subjected.

While city ordinance enforcement has become a notion of the past, the once-revered law enforcement arm has been reduced to begging vagrants to pack up and move, because nobody likes to deal with the problem. Since there was no strict law enforcement exerted on the homeless, they just relocated to another spot down the street, asking, "Where else can I go?"

The ultimate answer remained the same. "The shelters." Likewise, enticing the homeless to move into permanent housing by making drug use easier and safer did not seem to work either. Most of them reject it out of hand on the grounds of "infringing on their liberty rights and freedom of living."

DISRUPTED HARMONY

Dealing with the change in their lives, disrupted by a sudden prominence of Eric as leader for the state's homeless cause, came as a blessing for him but as a burden to April. Eric had hoped to gain some sort of individual notoriety with a sense of direction to his driftless life, but April, in contrast, preferred a more secluded existence. She had never developed an ambition towards fame and fortune even though she had grown up surrounded by poverty longing for a better life. One would think anybody would jump at such an opportunity. Eric could sense her inadequacy to effectively deal with it and kept her at a safe distance from public intrusions on her life. It did not take long for his fame to spread up and down the Pacific coast, rapidly expanding through the other states with similar homeless issues. April stayed home most of the time at The Hill, taking care of the household, if one could call a tent such, while Eric was rushed almost daily to one place or another to participate in public affairs such as TV and radio coverage, the mayor's office and other meetings. He completely enjoyed the sudden visibility he was receiving.

"When will you be back, Sweetie?" April asked just as he rushed to the mayor's private limousine, waiting to drive him to another early morning meeting.

"I don't know," he said with uncertainty, but took the time to plant a hasty kiss on her cheek on the way out. "I'll call you."

"Love you," she yelled after him, watching him disappear inside the limousine. Though considered a luxury among the homeless, Eric was dependent on the iPhone he was forced to acquire, paid for by the city, while she'd had a difficult time adjusting to the increasing pace of their lifestyle. Back in the tent, she felt a slight sense of sadness with him gone and her alone for another day. It gave her time to assess their relationship and the way it'd turned out in recent weeks.

Being a woman with an inherited instinct to nurture her man, including a strong drive for having an offspring since her life had taken on stability, her present situation did not satisfy her needs well. However, considering the recent changes in life from poverty to prosperity, it was not so much the monetary compensation but more so the celebrity status Eric seemed to thrive on. It was thoughts such as these she tried to cope with in the loneliness of the tent.

It would have been easier for her if she had a female friend close by to talk things out with, but with the homeless being mostly male, she lost out on companionship. And so, days turned into weeks, then months, pretty much a repeat of the previous day, with him gone and her alone at The Hill, dwelling on her private thoughts.

It was one of those days where April felt the loneliness and desertion in her relationship with Eric. Confined to inside the tent, pacing the cramped space did not help much since the customary morning fog still lingered in the outside air. While it was enjoyable to hear the foghorn blowing during the night, fog could last until noon and beyond. The City by the Bay had a famed reputation for sunny skies year-round, but that was a misconception. A heavy layer of fog, due to a rapid temperature swing, often developed during nighttime.[13]

"I've got to do something with my time," April muttered in the quiet of the tent. Contemplating how to make use of idle time, she had an idea. "I'm headed for the streets." Her mind was still foggy about what she wanted to do once she got there, but it came into focus when she spotted Eric's camera near the bedside. "Why don't I take photos?" she muttered. "I might even sell some." With this focus in mind she slung the camera over her shoulder, grabbed a water bottle on the way out, and

---

[13] Where the sun gradually heats up the atmosphere and land below during daytime, it rapidly cools after the sun disappears beneath the horizon, creating a temperature difference between land and sea. It is this temperature exchange that creates the nightly fog.

jumped on her bike. "Wait," she directed herself. "I need a notebook." It occurred to her that, in addition to taking pictures, she needed to take notes to remember. She turned around to fetch a notepad and pen and dropped it into a bag. Back on the street again, she headed for downtown.

With the fog dissipated on The Hill, she had clear visibility over the city. Golden Gate Bridge, in its splendid rustic red, as always, stuck out as the monumental landmark in the region. She was headed in the opposite direction, towards Market Street. The ride through the city was always pleasant outside commuter hours. People were less stressed and allowed cyclists the right of way most times. For visitors and locals alike, a trip through the city was more of a journey than anything else. Performers provided ample entertainment near popular street crossings.

The reason she headed for Market Street was simple. It was near her former territory, the Mission District, where she hoped to meet some familiar faces. Arriving at Powell Street Station, a popular subway entrance for shoppers, she hitched her bike onto the rails specifically for that purpose and took off on foot. It took her a few minutes to figure out how to operate the camera and was happy when she'd mastered focus, aim, and trigger. "That was simple," she said with an approving nod. The quality of photograph had to be proven yet. She took a couple of trial shots to check the viewer and was happy with the results, before striding towards Mission Street.

Already, as had been the case since drifters had arrived in the city, ample entertainment was provided on many intersections, from aspiring magicians, skilled jugglers, wannabe illusionists, musicians, poets, and other entertainers ready for a handout. Observing the life that she was familiar with and had once lived came from a completely different perspective through the eyes of the camera. It was more like watching a movie than being involved with the surrounding destitute. She then realized the desperation of being penniless without much hope for a better life.

Standing there in thought while taking in the busy scene, she suddenly felt sorry for the homeless. For now, penniless but in good spirits, she marched on.

Walking along, she came across a face she thought she recognized and headed for the person squatted on the sidewalk. Not expecting to be acknowledged, she brought up enough courage to approach him. "May I ask you a question?"

Lifting up his head, he studied her for a couple of seconds then, in a grumbling voice, said, "What'd you want?"

"I just want to talk to you."

"I don't talk to strangers," he said.

"I'm not a stranger," she corrected him. "I used to be homeless."

"So what?"

"I may be able to help."

"I don't want your help," he insisted, trying to shut her out. It appeared to April that he might have had a rough life with possible rejections by women. He appeared angry at her intrusion.

"Do you mind if I take your picture?" she conjured up the nerve to ask.

"Go ahead. Everybody does."

Despite his rejection she took several snapshots of him, prodding further. "Where're you from?"

"The city."

To encourage him more, she took up the space, squatting next to him. "What made you a homeless?"

"Lack of money?"

"Why don't you work?"

"I can't. Don't know anything."

"You could learn."

"Don't want to learn. Don't want any part of society."

It quieted April because she understood his rejection well and hoped she could prod him some more. What followed was her first interview with a homeless person, or any person, for that matter. At the end of the interview, April decided to return home to prepare a list of ideas to further question willing prospects ready to accommodate her.

Back at the tent she realized what she lacked was organized guidance to effectively pursue her interests. With Eric gone on his daily quest supporting the mayor, the tent became quiet as it usually did with only her at home. She called it home because that's what it was. She very much preferred the lofty tent over feeling trapped within solid walls as she had been living at the apartment with her mom.

Recalling the lonely days back then, the solution for her present shortcoming came with the thought of not having an organized life. With her mom gone most of the time, her mind used to drift aimlessly through the day without any meaning. "What I need is some direction," she contemplated. Looking around the tent, her eyes caught on a book propped next to Eric's pillow. She'd watched him read it many times but had never paid much attention. Reaching for it, she read the title: *European Travel Guide*.

Leafing through the pages, she was enthralled at the picturesque display in the guide. "That's it. This is what I need," she muttered. Striding over to one corner of the tent, she knew Eric kept some of his belongings in his suitcase. Rifling through the case she found what she was looking for: an empty journal.

It took some time for her mind to assimilate her thoughts into a meaningful list. But, to her surprise, once she got started, ideas kept flowing onto the pages. Not long after, she was impressed at herself for the bullet points she'd produced. It entailed highlights befitting any homeless.

In the days ahead, she developed enough courage to approach many more homeless. When back at the tent she would present her notes to Eric, detailing her daily progress while he told her of his achievements at the mayor's office.

With both of them occupied with meaningful tasks and discussing their daily accomplishments, time passed by quickly.

JOURNAL ACCOUNTS

April, with journal in hand, she knew that her quest would be challenging. Looking over her list of tasks, and they were numerous, she headed back to the most likely section in the City, Market Street, regardless of her personal concerns for success. This was the district where many homeless congregated who could provide her with plausible materials. She stood there some time, observing the current activities, with some homeless performing individual tricks and shows, while others watched the performances like her. Finally, she gathered up enough courage again to approach one person leaning against the building wall next to a business entrance. "Enjoy the performance?"

"I do," he said with a smile at her. "What about you?" She was not quite sure if he meant the performance or a query directed at her personally. *At least,* she thought, *he's not rejecting me,* and said, "Can I asked you a few questions?"

"What," he said, cautiously, "you a reporter?"

"No," she quickly replied, watching him backing away from her. Most homeless were weary of reading nothing but negative news about people like them in papers and magazines. "I'm writing a book." Though only wishful thinking at this time, a book was her ultimate goal. "I'm making notes in my journal and have some questions.

"What do you want to know?" Looking over her notes, she asked him what drove him into homelessness. Surprisingly, he was willing to explain much of his situation, where he was from, when he arrived here, how he landed in his present situation, and how he felt about it.

April was able to spent an hour with him until the information became somewhat overwhelming. She felt that she needed to digest most of it before going any further, and said, "I very much appreciate your time and patience with me. Do I have your permission to use it in the book?"

"You have. Look me up if you have any more questions. You know where to find me. I spend most days here."

Extremely satisfied at the initial response, she spent the coming weeks much like today, approaching idle homeless for more book material.

April had numerous troublesome, and at times harmful, experiences of her own living a homeless life within the homeless culture. In addition to many more interviews she conducted, some of the statistical data and reports listed in her journal were complemented from the San Francisco Chronicle News article "SF Homeless Project," providing current homeless coverage since 2016.

Homelessness Explained
Though April had been homeless for some time, she'd never felt comfortable mixing or sharing her plight with others. She mostly sought out a private spot to shelter for the night in the familiar range of her neighborhood. Today, with a meaningful purpose at hand, she ventured into uncomfortable and sometimes hostile territory she thought she could handle. The first and foremost question on her mind was, "What is it like, living on the streets?"

After gaining the trust of the homeless April interviewed, she quickly realized that everybody had a story, and some were willing to share. It was not just on a superficial level, but to a depth that even surprised her, explaining in detail how life actually turned out living on the street. Whether they were displaced or chose to leave the safety of their home or job and organized society, they willingly explained the specific personal plights that had forced them into this uncaring environment. Others were not so accommodating. With them it was mostly the distrust of talking to any stranger. Her journal was taking shape based on interviews with a variety of homeless.

While much of daily life can be coped with, as many have to accept after some time living on the streets, there were two things that could make you feel miserable: boredom and depression. April was no exception. Recalling much of her involuntary miseries, for which she still blamed her mom, "Being homeless is mostly scary for a few days until you fall into the beggar's routine." The homeless she interviewed expressed similar or even more dramatic experiences.

"In my world, it's up in late morning unless you're being evicted from a property or accosted by the law, mostly to move on."

"In the early days of homelessness, regardless of the excuse you might muster up, you landed in jail, if only for the night."

"Homelessness does not have to be boring. It can be exciting and even adventurous with the right spirit and attitude."

"Having a steady companion will also help ward off boredom. It's your choice and decision. But finding the right companion could take months or could never happen."

"Also, the territory you live in matters, whether it's a quiet neighborhood or thriving city metropolis."

"Any spot downtown is preferred for two reasons. First, you can catch many pedestrians to beg for money, and second, it provides for ample entertainment."

"Yes, it's our way of being entertained. It's depression and boredom that are our enemies. If exposed to boredom, your mind will tear down your wellbeing until you wind up in a mental institution, the worst place to be."

Looking over her list of talking points, April realized that she had covered quite a few topics in only a short two weeks. With many issues covered and many more items left in her journal, for the first time in her life she felt a great accomplishment. Proudly striding through the Tenderloin District, she knew just where to find more prospects, hopefully willing to cooperate and share their plight.

As expected, she found a somewhat older fellow who appeared seasoned enough to know life on both sides of society, affluent and poor. When she asked him about possible choices he may have had in life he readily replied.

Common Homeless Complaint
In the coming months, when prodding on, April learned that there were two kinds of people to avoid very quickly: groups of young men out to create trouble, and fellow homeless men out to hurt you. She learned just how little a homeless person mattered to anyone living in an organized society. When she approached strangers, with her camera slung across one shoulder and notepad in one hand, and asked about their wellbeing, many responses fell into one of these categories of complaints: a) strangers or groups of people presenting a personal threat, or b) messing with the homeless for the fun of it.

"What's unfortunate about it," April explained, "is that people nearby may be watching contemptuously but won't do anything to help you."

Safety for the homeless, in most cases, seemed less important to anyone watching a potential threat than for the unfortunate to be out of sight and not be seen. Most authorities, such as the police, who would normally show concern for the common citizen, shied away from getting involved with the homeless. It makes you think about organized society and safety.

Constant Fear of Assault and Robbery
"Walking the streets after dark is awful, especially when you're young," April was told by a young homeless woman. "People try to rob you, take advantage of you, sell you drugs then follow you for whatever evil reasons they have in mind. At times," she said, "I was chased on foot until I yelled for help. It's a terrible feeling not knowing the reasons for being pursued. There were times I was held up with a gun or a knife, not understanding why anybody would do that knowing I had

no possessions whatsoever, demanding that I hand over my jacket and pants. When I refused, they would kick and beat me to the ground just for the fun of it."

"Why didn't you defend yourself?" April asked.

"It's hard to do with a gun pointed at your face or a knife held against your throat."

"What about the authorities?"

"Depends on the severity of injuries," she explained. "Some may take action, getting the police department involved, but others don't seem to care much. It all depends on their criminal workload."

"I agree with you," April readily admitted. "I've experienced much the same."

Like so many times when walking the streets taking pictures of the homeless, April found herself wishing she could do something to help the poor. Today, strolling along shops and storefronts on Union Square, the place where she'd begun her homeless life, watching shoppers darting in and out of world-class brand name stores like Nordstrom, Target, and Zara, a light went on in her brain. "That's it. I'll create a picture album about the homeless to sell on the Internet." She was thrilled at the thought and couldn't wait to tell Eric. "Wonder what he's up to," she pondered.

She was proud of herself and of him for having found meaningful occupations after a life of nothing but vagrancy and aimlessly drifting through life.

Occupied with thoughts like this, she'd noticed someone following her a few paces back. To make sure, she stopped at a storefront to get a glimpse. It was the typical drifter, clad in heavy, dark, and tattered clothes, the signature of the destitute you found in any tent city in and around San Francisco. He also stopped in front of the showcase window, closely watching her.

Boldly, she turned and confronted him. "Can I help you?"

"No. I just like to watch pretty girls," he said with a grin on his face. "Does it bother you?"

"Yes. It bothers women to be stared at. You don't know?" She wanted to teach him a lesson in social behavior, although she clearly remembered her own inadequacy not long ago. She used to stare at men in the same manner and wanted to let him know that it was not a nice gesture.

"Sorry," he said with a shrug of his shoulders. "I didn't mean to bother you."

"Well, you do, but let's forget it."

"Fine."

"I'll make a deal with you. Let me take a couple of pictures of you and ask some questions about your life on the streets."

He hesitated for a moment, then said, "You an undercover cop?"

She laughed out loud at the very thought and assured him, "No. I'm a photographer."

"In that case," he offered, making an effort for a friendly pose, "go ahead."

She took the opportunity to snap a few shots while throwing some questions at him. "Where are you from?"

"Milwaukee."

"How long have you been homeless?"

"Going on five years."

"What brought you here?"

"Fame and fortune."

"What?" April shouted. "In the streets?"

"Not the streets." He couldn't help but laugh out loud. "My focus was on Hollywood. I wanted to get into movies. You know, Tom Cruise, Brad Pitt."

"What happened?"

"Couldn't make the right connections. Was turned down too many times. I got some bit parts but nothing big."

"Sometimes it takes time," April said with a hint of compassion. "What made you leave Hollywood?"

"Got involved in drugs and landed on the streets."

"What brought you to this city?"

"Got too crowded in L.A."

"I feel for you."

"Want to go out with me?" he ventured.

"I already have a boyfriend."

"Sorry. I guess I'll go on my way."

He made a gesture to leave, but she stopped him. "Wait. I wanted to ask you some more questions." It had just dawned on her that she should capture some life story to accompany each picture in her photo album.

He stopped. "What do you want to know?"

"For one thing," she said, "I used to be homeless." It was obvious by his reaction that this caught his attention.

"Really? What got you out of it?"

"The man I met."

"Your boyfriend?"

She nodded.

"You have any suggestions?" he asked, apparently uncertain where she was going.

"First," she suggested, a concerned look on her face, "you'll have to get off of drugs." It looked like he was going to object when she raised her hand. "Let me finish. Organized society doesn't like drug addicts on the loose. And it's society that has the job for you. The first step is a rehab center."

He was obviously paying attention to what she said, but from her experience with most homeless, something really drastic had to happen to make them take that step.

"I can try but won't promise anything." At least he was honest with himself.

"Glad you feel this way. Now," she prodded, getting back to the questions she wanted to ask, "how do you cope with being on the streets?"

"You can see for yourself." He gestured around the square. "The pain of carrying your life with you everywhere you go is real. You can see it on the faces. Just look around."

April was quite aware of it.

"There is no moment in a waking day where you can feel safe not losing your possessions, as measly as they are. It starts with the most precious item, your sleeping bag. The next item to lose is the suitcase. Once it fills up with your everyday supplies for making a living, it gets too heavy to carry around. Stealing a shopping cart solves the problem until it fills up too. That's when your realize you have reached the end point of your possessions."

"I know the burden well," she agreed.

"It's also the time when you realize how cumbersome your life has become by dragging the heavy cart around town to each place you have to visit. There's the public toilet first thing in the morning and several times during the day, followed with the canteen or charity place to eat every time you get hungry if you didn't earn enough from begging. By the time it gets dark, you are so tired that you stake out a spot to sleep as close as you can find a place."

"You always sleep out in the open?"

"I do," he said, underscored by a nod. "When night falls and you get tired of listening to the sounds of night and watching people passing on your sidewalk, usually too drunk to keep your eyes open, you can't sleep for fear of losing your belongings. If you are lucky, you'll wake up late morning, reaching for your shopping cart with foggy eyes, wondering where you are and not remembering how you got here."

April was checking the sun for time. It was getting late in the afternoon. "I appreciate your frankness and time spent with me," April finally said, "but now I must get back to my place. Thanks again and I wish you the best of luck in your future."

"Don't mention it," he replied. "I wish that you were single. We would make a nice couple." He abruptly turned and strode off.

Fear Living in Shelter
In the days ahead, when asking other homeless about their preference for living on the streets or seeking shelter, the response seemed to be unanimous.

"The scariest thing for me," one explained, "is spending the night in some homeless shelters, but it cannot be helped at times, especially on cold nights and winters."

"I am claustrophobic of confined spaces," another confessed. "I don't know where I got it from but remember as far back as my childhood."

"I go crazy being locked into the room in the dark with lights out and doors locked."

"As a young boy, I remember being examined for the cause, defined as an anxiety disorder prone to panic attacks. No matter how hard I try to lose it, I have not been successful and remain homeless out in the open, probably for the rest of my days."

Homeless Choices

"When people asked me whether homeless living was a personal choice or forced on me, I feel like slapping them in the face. There is no choice for homelessness. It's always forced on you through unfortunate circumstances," another homeless explained.

"Of course, everybody prefers an affordable life, but not everybody is destined for success. Much depends on your upbringing, family association, siblings, environment, income security, and other factors. But, between you and me," this homeless insisted, "it takes a willing disciple to fit into today's society."

"Why is that?" April knew it well, but wanted to hear him explain his side.

"Because there are too many rules and regulations that make you feel confined and restricted. If you have a free-spirited mind, it's something completely contradictory from what the constitution presents."

"Such as?"

"Freedom and a right to live freely."

"What else?"

"Good people with problems like drug addiction and mental disorders have been neglected from treatment.

"The shelters require that you work to help maintain the building and grounds as well as assisting in serving meals and cleaning up after. You get my drift?"

"I get it," April said, ready to move on. As she strode further up Powell Street, in spite of the mid-day sun burning down on the ground, there were homeless asleep, oblivious to the immediate environment. It was apparent that they were sleeping off drugs or alcohol. Some slept on brick walls with others on somebody's front yard, and more on the sidewalk, cowered against the foundation of a building. Unable to help, she suddenly felt pity for them but also knew that Eric was working towards some sort of salvation for the homeless.

It became obvious to April that a homeless' primary concern must be the lack of privacy. When asked, they were only too eager to share their predicament.

Homeless Sex

One day, strolling along on the sidewalk, April approached a self-assured appearing man. Since he was not clad in dirty, worn-out clothes he visibly did not fall into the homeless category. April had studied his behavior for some time when he approached her with an assuring smile on his face. "Can I be of help?" he offered.

"Not really," April replied. "I just want to study people living on the street."

"What are you?" he said. "A reporter?"

"No, just taking pictures."

"Want to take mine?" he offered, straightening out to full size, getting ready for a pose.

April had noticed one thing that many homeless had in common. As a general rule, most of their bodies were slightly stooped and hunched over.

"As a matter of fact," she believed, contemplating her own life as a homeless, "I used to do the same." In hindsight, she recalled her reasons for such poor posture. "I wanted to appear humble. It helps with the begging. People are more willing to part with a few coins or even an occasional dollar bill. I guess it makes them feel like a Samaritan."

April enticed him into telling her some of his personal experiences and interactions with common people. She wanted to dig deeper than just his daily routines. He seemed to be willing to share some more personal and intimate events.

"I hate to admit this for the shame of it, but I used to sell 'services' to guys to survive another day in the gutter."

April looked at him in surprise at such a bold statement, expecting more details. "Go ahead."

"I call it gutter because that's how I feel about the services I provided. Though I'm not gay," he explained, "I was desperate to get out of my predicament and did what I could to better my life. Unfortunately, when you are into drugs, there seems to be no way out of your dilemma. You feel trapped forever in a daily, immoral cycle with drugs, sex, and filth being the norm. I hate it but am helpless to break the cycle."

"You are not alone in this," April sympathized with him. "I used to be one of the homeless."

"Really?" he said, not totally convinced. "How did you get out of the streets?"

"I met the right guy. He helped get me on my own feet to stand up for my rights."

"We have no rights," he complained, shaking his head.

"We all have the same rights," she insisted. "It's called birthright. You, me, and everybody alive in this country."

"I understand the law but cops don't have much compassion for an unfortunate like me. Believe me. I tried to go straight but society kept beating me down. I flunked out of high school for missing my grades and ever since," he complained, "I've been in the dumpster."

"Don't give up," April pleaded with him, feeling his pain.

"As long as there are convenience stores and game rooms," he volunteered, "I can always find clients to pay for my services. I'm ashamed of what I do, but it's the only means for my survival."

April left in a depressed mood, feeling blessed at her good fortune for having been saved by Eric from a possible life in the gutter forever. Reading over her entries in the journal, in spite of mostly depressing accounts from the homeless, she was happy with the way it was taking shape but felt she needed a break from collecting nothing but gloom and despair.

"Hi, sweetie," she greeted Eric with an inviting hug when he arrived at the tent. "How was your day?"

"Hectic as usual," he said. "The mayor is dumping most of the homeless issues on my shoulders. Don't know if I can handle it all. I feel overburdened most days. Today was no different. I think I need a break. How about you?"

April wanted to share her journal experience with him but the way he looked, burdened and exhausted, she thought otherwise. "How about a drink?"

"That'd be great. You going to join me?"

"Of course," she said, mixing a Cuba Libra, popular at the time, served on ice. Both had acquired a taste for the drink for its uplifting and refreshing qualities. "Feel like fooling around?" she said, followed by an inviting smile.

"Not today, honey. I am beat."

"I understand. I feel that way most days lately myself."

"Let's just watch the stars. We haven't done that for some time."

Though slightly disappointed at being rejected, it was enough for April to just be stretched out next to him, cuddled in his arm. "Sure." *The journal can wait another day,* she thought. The evening and night turned out as she'd hoped. It ended with having sex, followed by a fulfilling sleep in the open, tucked in and warmed by their sleeping bags. [14]

---

[14] See Appendix C for more of April's homeless entries.

CITY CLEANUP

"I'm off," Eric said, rushing out the tent. He was running late this morning. Throwing a quick glance down the hill, he could see the mayor's limousine was already waiting alongside the curb.

"Wait," April called. "What time are you coming back?"

"Don't know. I may be late. Don't wait up."

"Okay," she managed to yell after him, saddened, watching him disappear down the hill. It had been like this almost every day since he had gotten involved with the mayor's office. At times she wished that they had not become involved with city politics. It was at a point where she felt remorseful about him on top of having feelings of resentment for herself. But she also realized that it was too late for Eric to just turn his back on the huge responsibility to which he had committed.

Fortunately, on what would otherwise have been lonely days, she was involved with preparing the text and pictures she had taken for the album. One problem surfaced almost from the beginning: how to process the material into a product to be sold on the Internet. She had discussed it with Eric on several occasions, but each time he put her off, saying, "Don't worry about it. We'll figure something out." That had been months ago.

Not wanting to waste more time, she had thought of several alternatives, but always came to the same conclusion: "I don't know anything." What that meant was that she had absolutely no skills to even attempt to process a document or format photos. Feeling rather inadequate, she felt a barrier growing between Eric and herself, separating them ever so slowly. She did not like the realization at all. When she brought this up with him, he would only shrug it off as temporary, stating, "Just be patient."

Most evenings when they were sitting out in the open, when she brought up the subject of her project, Eric would avoid it. "Look at the Milky Way," he'd say. "Doesn't it make you feel humble?" or something similar.

She realized that he might be too exhausted to talk about her tasks and deferred the discussion until later when they were tucked comfortably in their sleeping bags, but it did not help. He would just doze off or pretend to be asleep. The result was the same; she was getting frustrated with him and his postponements, but continued to grant him more time, hoping things would eventually work out for her like they had when they'd met.

Eric, on the other hand, had been so involved with the mayor's office that he did not have enough energy left at the end of the day to even discuss his day with April. Though he realized he was neglecting her, he hoped it would only be temporary. And so week after week slipped by, turning into months. What may have been a temporary commitment to the mayor's office had turned into an effort he had not expected. The mayor was piling more and more tasks onto his shoulders. By the time he'd realized the burden, it was too late to pull out from under his responsibilities. Because of his experience living on the streets, the mayor and his staff were heavily relying on his invaluable input to make political decisions.

In a way, it made him feel important, consulting and having been selected as an adviser. But when confronted by April, he felt guilty about neglecting her. He wished that he could divide his time more productively for her, but it did not seem possible at the moment, for tomorrow the mayor and his staff would execute the "City Cleanup Plan" that they had so diligently developed.

The Cleanup Plan included a list of proposed articles of ordinance extracted from years of citizen complaints and recommendations from the city council.

Prior to implementing the plan, the mayor's office released it into the morning news, causing much unwanted uproar amid the homeless, but it entailed essential measures to help clean up the city. Reading over the major points once more, the mayor realized that the city, over decades, had failed to enforce many ordinances.

"This'll shake up the legislators," all agreed when Eric voiced his opinion. At this point the mayor's assistant rushed in, waving a newsprint to capture everybody's attention. "Hot off the press," she announced.

Thomas Allen was the first to read, followed by Eric and the rest of the work group. "This is bull," the mayor shouted as the room fell silent. "All our work is for nothing?" Even Eric was stunned. What he read looked much like a declaration prepared and issued by the liberal branch of the government. It was something that went completely against the initiative they had been working on for months. Eric read the particular section headings once more to grasp it—the articles for an action plan that would take years, if not decades, to implement. It read, "Homeless Together - The Federal Strategic Plan to Prevent and End Homelessness."[15]

The mayor kept shaking his head while reading the particulars, making periodic comments such as, "This is insane," and "It'll never work."

Even Eric had negative opinions about it when he read the details. However, it did not appear as bad as the mayor had proclaimed. "Let's not be hasty. This plan might just work."

"What about my city?" the mayor, furious beyond reasoning, screamed at him, shaking the paper in front of Eric's eyes. "Who's going to clean it up?"

"We'll have to give it a chance," Eric suggested, trying to calm the city leader. "We have no choice."

"Choice, my ass," the mayor furiously responded. "We've tried the public housing approach a number of times in the past. It has always failed." He adjourned the meeting. "I'll use force if I have to."

---

[15] If interested, follow Internet link for Plan details:
https://www.usich.gov/resources/uploads/asset_library/Summary_of_Essent ial_Elements_of_the_Plan.pdf

Where Eric partially supported the Federal Strategic Plan to provide affordable housing to the needy, the mayor thought it a waste of money and time since similar plans had been instituted several times since the 1970s, with little success. He was more interested in cleaning his city of the "Homeless Plague," as he called it.

Sometime during the '70s the only newspaper articles that mentioned "homelessness" in San Francisco said that they were created from recent earthquakes. But by 1980, the city had realized it had a problem. 25 years of social experiments had failed. A local church pastor, Paul Boden, thought he had a solution.

"The rights of citizens with beds to sleep in have been mostly ignored. They are forced to wake up and smell the urine, step over bodies, dodge shopping carts and fend off in-your-face panhandlers," the pastor wrote more than a decade ago. "Nowhere in the country has the homeless population been as visible, or as tolerated, as in San Francisco."

In the 1980s, funding for homelessness programs across the nation was described as temporary. "They thought when the economy got better these guys would go home," said Paul Boden, advocate for the homeless at Western Regional Advocacy Center.

But the homeless problem had become a chronic one. The pastor blamed it on budget cuts to subsidized housing in the early '80s, funding that went away and never came back. "All these people from subsidized housing started hitting the streets in droves. People just started sleeping on the floor of churches and food programs," he said.

"People don't want to solve the homeless problem," Paul Boden suggested. "They just don't want to have to see it. Homeless people would have to simply disappear to appease them."

He thought the solution for homelessness was more federal funding, a bigger social safety net, and more community outreach programs. "From our perspective there's a real danger because the social safety nets are really tapped out right now," he was told.

Some of these solutions are ridiculous and some simplistic. However, an apartment is not going to end homelessness, as has been experienced many times, especially given the target population.

In 1984, homelessness, as a chronic problem nationally, was still a novelty. In a congressional hearing that year, city leaders from around the U.S. lamented about homeless people who "exist like the untouchables of Calcutta, sleeping in streets and alleys and abandoned automobiles," in the words of Chicago's then mayor, Harold Washington.

"Homelessness in the United States has quietly taken on crisis proportions," said New York's then-governor Mario Cuomo.

The feeling of the "worseness" of San Francisco's homeless problem was not a new feeling. People have been complaining for decades. "Take away the homeless," wrote *San Francisco Chronicle* columnist Arthur Hoppe in a 1990 editorial that used humor to mock those who were increasingly speaking out about San Francisco's homeless problem.

"We have created an economic system that produces $5 trillion worth of goods and services every year. Yet we can't find enough funds to provide for those unable to make the system work for them," Hoppe wrote. "I have no pet solutions to their problems. But I'm pretty sure that unless we accept our guilt for each of them individually and all of them collectively, their problems—and ours—will be with us for a long, long time."

THE 21TH CENTURY

San Francisco, is, as the *Chronicle* dubbed it in a series begun in 2003, "the shame of the city." So then the question is why a city of such concentrated wealth and modern ingenuity as San Francisco hasn't figured out how to solve a problem that has plagued it for decades.

There have been several attempts made by the city to organize and help its homeless. For instance: that same year a Methodist church bought a 50-by-100 foot lot on Sixth Street between Howard and Mission for $73,000 and spent $40,000 turning it into a park. "We saw hundreds of people standing around on the street in that area, drinking, talking, drifting," Rev. Cecil Williams of Glide Memorial Methodist Church told the New York Times. "So we got the property and asked them what they wanted us to do with it. They told us they wanted a place where they would not be intruded on from the outside, even by the police. They wanted places to sleep, to sit at tables and to cook."

The park had toilets, benches, a water fountain, a fire pit, greenery, shelter, and a basketball hoop. Initially it had big concrete pipes to use as sleeping tubes, but they were removed after people fought over who would sleep in them and women were raped in them. Williams called it People's Park, but it was more often referred to as Wino Park.

THE 2010s

When the homeless were asked in 2013 why they couldn't get a job, 28% of respondents said it was because they didn't have a phone, even though there was a federal program that gave out phones to low income people; it was sometimes derisively called the Obama phone program. In a city with one of the highest concentrations of billionaires in the world, it seems like there could be some better options.

In 2013, San Francisco did not have more homeless people than other cities. Relative to the cities' populations, the over 6,000 people that were homeless in San Francisco was a higher rate than in New York City, but lower than in Los Angeles, Seattle, and Washington, D.C. What was different in San Francisco was the space. The city is just under 50 square miles.

Based on 2014 data from the U.S. Department of Housing and Urban Development, San Francisco was second only to New York City for the densest homeless population by land mass. But in NYC, the homeless were "sheltered" at much higher numbers, meaning fewer people actually sleeping on the street.

San Francisco's 2016 budget proposal included $1.2 billion for "human welfare and neighborhood development," from which funding for homelessness programs came. Plans for 2016, according to the budget, included 500 new "supportive housing units" for the homeless, 7 mobile restrooms in the Tenderloin to cut back on the amount of defecation on the street, and $4.6 million to build a dedicated adult shelter with 30 beds, nurses, and counseling for homeless people with chronic medical conditions. The budget noted that San Francisco provided emergency shelter for over 2,000 homeless people, but that was only one third of the homeless population.

San Francisco gave tax breaks to companies, like Twitter, that were willing to headquarter themselves on Market Street in the area that was ground zero for the homeless population. The hope was for corporate gentrification of a pretty rough zone. Now called "Mid-Market," it has reportedly simply pushed the homeless into nearby areas.

San Francisco also had Project Homeless Connect, one-day events that sought to connect homeless and low-income people with essential services. And, of course, like most cities, San Francisco had a "Homeward Bound" program that promised to give people a one-way ticket out of the city. These programs did not seem to be putting a dent in the problem.

The only state that has dramatically solved its homeless problem is Utah. It did so by giving homeless people homes and providing them with counseling. Utah focused on its chronically homeless, cutting the size of that population by 91 percent over a decade. According to state officials, the solution has saved the state millions of dollars. It is cheaper to give someone an apartment than to deal with the costs incurred from their living on the street: police encounters, jail time, and emergency room visits.

As the chronically homeless are such a large percentage of San Francisco's population, that seemed like the best approach.

But in a city where the cost of living is skyrocketing and nuns who help the homeless were threatened with eviction because the rent was too high, that's not an easy task.

To the tech entrepreneurs who kept complaining about San Francisco's homeless problem, know this:

"At the end of the day, the only way to end the homeless problem is to give people homes or the funding and support they need to find affordable housing themselves. There is not an application that will fix it. It is the kind of problem onto which you simply have to pour time and money," as stated in the "United States Interagency Council On Homeless" (USICH).

HOME TOGETHER

"Wake up!" April stirred Eric into action. While she was an early riser from years past by habit, to get a head start begging on the streets, he was prone to sleep in.

"Please," he muttered into the pillow. "I need some sleep."

"Get up," she replied. "You've slept enough." She pulled the sleeping bag open.

"What time is it?" he said, turning the other way.

"Noon. I let you sleep."

"Okay," he said, rubbing his eyes.

"Here," April offered, handing him a mug of coffee. "That'll get you up."

The aroma was too enticing for him to ignore. "I'll be right back," he said, heading for the public restrooms.

I wonder, April had thought on more than one occasion, *how convenient life would be living in an apartment or, better yet, renting a house.* She'd never brought up the notion because she knew how strong-willed Eric was against living indoors. He would hold it against her since she also preferred to live outdoors, under the sky. *But that was before we were a couple,* she reasoned. *The situation changes things. Maybe someday,* she muttered, hoping to have the chance. It was one thing to live enslaved by an alcoholic mother in cramped quarters, but having a spacious place for yourself to walk in and out of as you pleased would be a luxury she'd never had. A thought had just occurred to her. *Why not bring it up today? At least I'll know how he feels about it.*

"What do you feel like doing?" Eric said on his return.

"Let's take a ride down the coast," she suggested. "We haven't done it in months."

"Half Moon Bay?"

"That'd be great." The ride, quite lengthy, would take up most of the day. She collected a blanket and cooler for the picnic while he shaved his face using a manual razor. Since there was no electric feed to the tent, he was forced to recharge the few appliance batteries he had at Starbucks or other cafés he frequented.

The day turned out just as they had anticipated: quiet, sunny, with a cool breeze drifting from the west. Both of them waded along the shoreline, kicking up water in light ocean swells splashing against their legs. It was sheer pleasure they hadn't felt all winter. Winter in San Francisco was different from what most people experience in cold climates. Arctic weather patterns didn't make it this far south. It might get as cool as 40 degrees at night but, once the fog burned off, the air warmed up even during the cold season. The warm water ocean kept the temperature balanced.

They were playing chase. Eric made another playful pass at her, pushing April into the deeper water, yelling, "Try to catch me!"

Getting her footing, she chased after him. The day was spent much like this in-between snacking, resting, and short naps. Stretched out on the blanket, staring at the sky, April mustered up enough courage late in the afternoon to approach Eric with her earlier thoughts. "Honey," she said. "Have you ever thought about renting your own place?"

"Renting my own place," he said with a hint of disgust. "It'd be like getting locked up in prison. Don't you think so?"

"I just wondered how it would feel to have a home." For better or for worse, there is was, out in the open. She did not have to probe any further. His response had said it.

"What's got into you?" he said, eyeing her with suspicion. "I thought we had settled this when I met you."

She propped on one elbow to fully face him. "I know. But don't you ever think about it?"

"Not as long as I'm alive," he said, accompanied by a brisk laugh. "It'd be a death sentence."

April gently stroked his hair. "There are times when the thought comes into my mind." She felt that she had overstepped her boundary and wanted to pacify him. "Never mind."

"You turncoat," he scolded her with a tease, thinking she was playing on his intellect, and pushed the thought from his mind. She followed his gesture with a smile, pondering in silence.

"It's time to get back," he suggested, glancing at his watch. Both gathered up their belongings, turning to get one last glimpse at the sunset with a promise: "We'll be back."

"How beautiful," April agreed.

Another morning, sunrise, and a promising day in what was once a beautiful, well-kept city. "The night wasn't bad," April muttered, while stretching her body by the tent entrance. "Makes life worth living." *As a matter of fact,* she thought, as her mind dwelled on the personal blessing, *it was a beautiful night.* After months of neglecting her passionate needs, Eric had made up for the many nights and weeks he had neglected. Sure, they'd had their periodic sex, as many couples do, but it was mostly performed out of habit or bodily needs without any romantic notions. While her body received gratification, her mind and emotions were neglected. "But," she realized, "it must be life after it becomes a routine." Though she accepted the facts, after discussing it with Eric, she did not necessarily like living indoors and did not dwell on the thought since this was magnitudes better than living in squalor.

"Five more minutes."

She was well aware of Eric's delay tactics and insisted, "I made coffee." The smell usually triggered him into the waking state.

"Fine brew. Thanks." As usual, it took him several minutes to clear the sleeping fog from his mind. "What do you want to do today?" Experience told him that on most mornings she had a plan for the day, ready to explore. While he was generally a drifter, tackling each day as it unfolded, April, in contrast, wanted things organized and planned out. He did not mind.

"I want you to look at the photos I took and help me develop a photobook."

The look he shot at her did not seem very happy. "I don't feel like working. I'd like to give my brain a break."

She fully understood the rejection since he had been under a lot of stress at the mayor's office. "Okay then. How about a stroll down Market Street?"

It was something he could handle. Talking, for him, would be easier than work. Especially after last night's love making. "What happened last night? You turned into a tiger."

"That's what happens when you've being neglected," she said, accompanying her words with a pleasing grin. "You made up for it."

"I liked it," he admitted, getting ready for the ride. As they usually did, they started out on bikes. She had become confident enough in her cycling skills to where she could jump curbs and dodge in and out of street traffic. She even got her kicks from cabbies yelling after her, mostly catcalls. "Yippee," she would yell after them.

"That's my girl," Eric muttered, delighted by the way she'd turned out. "Real buddy." That was what he'd always wanted, a dedicated lover but also a buddy. It was the buddy accompanying him today.

They stopped along major gathering places for the homeless while watching them display their personal skills of juggling, magic, and card tricks, seemingly necessary for collecting enough money to enjoy another night of drug and alcohol-dazed existence. This was the life most of them chose and lived. Society had shut them out years ago, but friendship bonds among the homeless seemed to prevail.

"Everybody look," a face familiar to Eric and April from prior visits yelled out. "The Homeless King and his queen." It took both by surprise but it was not altogether unexpected. They instantly realized that over the past months they had gained celebrity status by having been projected on TV shows as well as newscasts. "What brings you here?" Harry, his homeless friend, said, sidling up to Eric. "Got any money for me?"

"Here." April jumped in and handed him a ten dollar note, not knowing what his intentions might be. If it was a semi-hostile act it should pacify him and, if not, they would find out soon enough.

Fortunately, it was a friendly gesture. "What brings you into this neighborhood?" he said with a grin on his face. "Thought you might be the vice-mayor by now."

"You've got the wrong idea," Eric said, giving him a friendly pat on the shoulder. "I haven't turned political. I just give advice." He explained further. "The mayor wanted our opinions about life on the streets. That's all."

"Don't be modest," was the reply. "You deserve it. We've been watching your success on the Starbucks TV monitor."

"What did you think?" Eric said, truly interested.

"You got it right, man. We liked what you said."

"What about you personally?" Eric asked.

"You know me," was Harry's quick response. "I'm the Bitching King."

"We know that already, but I want your personal feedback. The mayor wants to know."

"Fuck the mayor. All he's interested in is getting our votes."

"I don't think so. He seems really concerned."

"Yeah, right. They all do, but when it comes to keeping promises, they fail miserably. You know it and everybody else does too."

"It's different this time."

"Why? Give me a valid reason."

"We have federal government support. It's a solution for all states."

"I don't trust the gov," Harry proclaimed. "It's the same people ruining our lives."

"Nobody is ruining anything," Eric said, trying to appease his friend. "They are serious this time. They mean well."

"Maybe this mayor, but I still don't trust them."

"Think about it," Eric insisted as April quietly stood by his side. "What is the most important thing the city wants from us?"

"To disappear," Harry offered. "To just pack up and leave. That's what they all want."

"Right."

"So what's new? What's the solution you've been working on?"

"Tell you what," Eric suggested. "This isn't the place to talk politics. Why don't we meet at the piers later on and talk it over?"

"Pier One?"

"Pier One."

"What time?"

"How about five o'clock? Think you can make it?"

"I'll be there. Count on it."

"So much for trust," April said, not convinced that he'd keep the date. She knew the thinking process of the homeless too well. Schedules meant nothing, especially when they involved their personal livelihood.

"He'll be there," Eric said. They stopped along their path several more times with similar results. Some listened while others objected.

"What do you think?" April asked. "Will they come?"

"Some will."

"You sure you want to get involved?"

"I'm already involved knee deep. You should know. I've hardly had time for you."

"We'll see. Let's get a bite to eat." 'Bite' in the minds of the homeless meant a sandwich. They ate on the way to the pier, pushing their bikes along the sidewalk.

"I told you so," Eric said, when they approached Pier One. The homeless had showed up in numbers, the people they'd talked with and more. He must have struck a note with them. They were leaned along the safety railing and seated on the ground close to the water's edge. For a moment after driving up, there was a halting suspense signifying everybody's expectations.

"Harry," Eric called out. "I'm surprised. Where did you locate them all?"

"Told you," he replied. "You can count on me."

Eric took the lead. "Hi, everybody. For those that don't know me," he acknowledged the gathered, "my name is Eric and this is April, my partner." His introduction was followed by the usual greetings among the homeless. "I want you to know that I'm not here to make speeches. We'll leave that to the politicians." This brought on smiles and a few laughs from the crowd.

Great, April thought, *starting out with a joke's always a good ice breaker.*

Aside from a few snorting sounds to clear throats and lungs amidst a few grunts, the place went quiet. The only sounds present were distant foghorns from passing ferries. Eric noticed right away that they were interested in what he might have to say. "Everybody gather around," he said with a gesture at the bench where he and April were seated.

"You may have heard the mayor's announcement about 'Home Together,'[16] a plan the government is instituting." He gave them a few seconds to acknowledge each other with a nod. "That's what we are here for." Another few grunts followed. "I want to hear from every one of you what you think about it. It's important that you voice your concerns." As expected, the crowd immediately stirred into action. They voiced prolific opinions among themselves.

---

[16] If interested, follow Internet link for Plan details:
www.usich.gov/resources/uploads/asset_library/Summary_of_Essential_Ele
ments_of_the_Plan.pdf

"Listen up, everybody," Eric broke in. "I need you to behave orderly. If we want to get anywhere, it is going to be in an organized fashion." They understood. His immediate problem was instructing the crowd about organization even though the word itself had negative connotations among the homeless. In their minds "organization" means "social constraints," which in turn spelled "government control," the nastiest phrase in many of their vocabularies. Eric realized that he had to educate these people who've had been told what to do for most of their lives.

The homeless were eager to hear what he had to say. "Listen," he said, throttling their haste. "This is not some passing idea the government has concocted; it is a long-term plan. There are many elements to it so," he paused to let that sink in, "I need you to pay attention."

He pulled the list from his jacket pocket and gave them a minute to quiet down. "Here are the major highlights for every one of you to consider. Please don't interrupt until I have presented all articles. Understood?" There were nods of acknowledgment. He continued, "Okay. Here are the basic elements:

"One, ensure that homelessness is a rare experience. What this means is, collaboratively build lasting systems that end homelessness and increase capacity and prevent housing crises and homelessness.

"Two, ensure homelessness is a brief experience. What this means is, identify and engage people experiencing homelessness as quickly as possible to provide immediate access to low-barrier emergency shelter or other temporary accommodations to all who need it. But, more importantly, implement coordinated entry to standardize assessment and prioritization to housing and services. It will assist people to move swiftly into permanent housing with appropriate person-centered services.

"Three, ensure homelessness is a one-time experience. What this means is, prevent returns to homelessness through connections to adequate services and opportunities to sustain an end to homelessness in addition to sustain practices and systems at a scale necessary to respond to future needs.

"Listen, listen!" He had to interrupt their shouts after each article he read. There was resistance to every proposed objective on the list. "If you give me a chance I'll explain." This quieted their uproar enough for him to continue. "I heard you and understand your objections. Remember," he stated, "I'm on your side. I will address each item so that you can understand and think about it. It's something that'll affect the future for every one of you. I want you to know that it is the first time the government is listening to your plight."

"Yeah, right. It's always the same," one homeless man complained. "All they ever do is promise, but nothing ever gets solved."

"You have to understand," Eric said, directly addressing the caller, "we are a problem not only to the government but, more importantly, to the tax payers who support our lives."

"Screw them," one readily objected, "if they're stupid enough to pay taxes."

"Yeah," another followed. "Taxes for everybody and everything. That's why many of us are homeless."

"Don't want any of it," another chimed in. Interruptions continued with each article Eric presented, especially when he explained the specific items of their concerns.

"Collaborative. What does it mean?"

"Let me explain the meaning. Okay?[17]

After the initial interruptions from the crowd, Eric ignored all further questions until he had finished reading the articles. "Are there any questions?" This was the wrong thing to do. Eric was blasted with questions.

"End homelessness? They've gone crazy."

"Never. It's who we are."

"Not me. This is the life I chose."

---

[17] See Appendix A, for Eric's Collaborate Objectives articles.

"Communities? Are they out of their minds?"
"Affordable housing? I've heard that before."
"Consensus? Tagging? - Never!"
"Emergency shelter? Never again."
"Unique needs? We're all unique."
"End homelessness? They're trying to get rid of us for good."
"Give up homelessness? Not this guy. Never."
"Count and monitor us? Not very likely."

In view of the articles on a cursory examination, they all seemed legitimate responses. There was one flaw federal policy makers had overlooked: the individual aspects of the articles. Homelessness has developed into a culture created out of a common bond, either by having lost job, home, and family, being rejected by society or chosen as a lifestyle. There will not be an easy solution by any means, no matter how accommodating the government and policies were.

Eric could not let the federal plan fail. He had to try and make it work, as outlined in "Home Together." His failure would reflect on the future of the homeless as well as the homeless culture. The culture was here to stay, but the federal plan might not. Eric had made his decision, supporting the mayor in cleaning up the city, even if it meant using force, something the homeless would not like, but had to conform to. Much like with wars, it was necessary, at times, for conflict to be resolved through an otherwise impossible solution. "War it shall be," Eric determined.

HAPPY TIMES

Today, like most days, was another armistice mission to pacify the homeless. For several months already Eric had been working with the homeless, trying to convince them to clean up after themselves. While it had never been in his plans to manage a project to this extent, solving a homeless crisis eventually on a national scale, he felt that the effort was lending meaning to his life. Fortunately, he was not alone with his quest. He had received support from every sector of the streets, mostly from store and shop owners finally seeing some results. While the mayor was heavily depending on Eric to achieve results, he himself dedicated his time to the federal "Home Together" plan.

As anticipated, there was pushback from the federal government in getting budgets released for his effort. While the Democratic party kept pushing for it, the conservatives, the majority at this time, kept turning it down. When confronted by the news media, the mayor's response was ultimately the same: "I can't wait years for something to happen. I won't live that long."

With each occasion, more uproar came from the liberals. As was the case with most government projects in recent years, it had become a political issue. It would have been alright if both parties would have worked together, but that must not have occurred to the inflexible minds on both sides. Consequently, it was up to him and Eric, the mayor determined, to pacify the homeless communities. The federal planners had envisioned one consolidated neighborhood, but it had not materialized. With each city clean-up effort, the homeless just packed up and moved their tents to another vacant spot. And so, the clean-up effort kept shifting to a time where both entities, the city council and homeless, became entangled in a no-win situation that common sense was unable to break, resulting in a perpetual migration, not only in San Francisco, but in other cities as well.

Right from the start of his effort, Eric realized that one solution would not fit all homeless situations. What many politicians did not realize was the diverse backgrounds and rejections that drove destitute people into migrating. There were three types of homeless to disperse: drug addicts, outdoor preppers, and economically deprived.

The first category among the homeless, the drug addicts, were the most difficult to deal with; nobody could effectively manage them. Their minds had been so polluted from drug use that reasoning proved ineffective. They could not be managed other than to provide temporary shelter until drugs wore off, a cycle to be repeated the next day, and the next, until a time when the body gave out. It was the decision point to sink or swim, live or die. Some would recover in rehab centers or hospitals, while others relapsed shortly after again into the same useless addiction cycle, until one day they would be absolved from a troubled and worthless life, released through death.

The second category were the preppers. These were individuals using the homeless facilities and community as a temporary measure to hook up with likeminded pioneers to eventually find a suitable space or location distant from civilization. To them, homelessness was only a means to an end, to achieve the goal of living in isolation from organized society. Although their goal was much like living in an orderly fashion, it was on a much smaller scale, more or less managed by a few.

The third category, the economically deprived, was the largest group by far. These were people from all sectors of society that had wound up living on the streets. They might come voluntarily from affluence, like Eric, or have been kicked out of the family for one reason or another, evicted from an apartment for owing back rent, lost family and home from gambling away possessions and savings, released from a job due to an economic recession, or have medical problems they could not afford to fix. Sometimes entire families were put out on the streets due to economic deprivations, mostly afflicting minority groups.

It took Eric and April many months of talking to and convincing this diverse group to understand the city's plight for them to eventually cooperate, suitable to the individual. It was difficult in many instances to satisfy everybody's needs in a way everybody, government as well as citizens, could live with. However, it would not be without a struggle on both sides for years to come before unity could be achieved.

There was one thing Eric had accomplished; he was able to convince the homeless to clean up after themselves by using portable restrooms provided by the city to take care of personal business, or else they were banned from loitering in the city forever.

It must have driven the point home since tourism began to return once more, with many homeless migrating to sparsely populated places in the northern states as well as Canada. Unfortunately, it was not a unilateral migration. The homeless notion about the resettlement remained split into three factions: addicts, preppers, and economically deprived. It seemed that the pioneering-minded, the minority, welcomed the opportunity to create settlements at their location of choice, while addicts, the majority, kept clinging to dependent habits for easy drug access.

Eric realized that most addicts were hardcore and unwilling to giving up their doping habits. Smoking pot did not seem to affect the willing homeless because it was a legal substance, easily obtained anywhere in the country, whereas hard drugs were linked to the inner city. The initial effort for the clean-up was not easy. It took a tactical police force to move in and sweep the specific sections clean by hauling off offenders who were unwilling to move into city-provided housing as provisioned by the Home Together plan.

Being removed through force did not sit well with the homeless. In response, they moved from the provided housing complex just as quick into another location of their preference.

There was one thing in the mayor's favor: homelessness shrank to a size the city was able to manage. Much like in the old days, vagrants consisting of drifters, beggars, and panhandlers once more became a part of the city's skyline.

Where the drifters eventually settled into a semi-accepted existence between the city council and the remaining homeless, it was not without problems altogether. It was here where Eric, with April by his side, was dispatched into action to negotiate a workable solution. The mayor was grateful to Eric for his effort. This way, he had an emissary who would get things done and resolve issues without the city council spending additional funding and manpower, since Eric did not accept payment for his dedicated services. To him, it was a worthy cause and an opportunity to serve his country and still maintain the independence he so dearly desired. The same was true for April, who cherished their time together, hoping it would last a lifetime.

But then, as was the case with dreams, they don't last forever.

"Where're we headed today?" Eric asked on the way out. He had offered April the task of getting the daily schedule from the mayor's office, who usually received complaints reported to the police the previous day. She had readily accepted. It offered her an opportunity to get involved as a team, with her providing the target location and him resolving the local issue, whatever it would turn out to be, usually a shop owner who had a difficult time removing a homeless from his storefront. There were numerous other reasons as well, such as getting a drifter to clean up the mess he had caused during the night. It was mostly men leaving behind a mess, while a woman was more prone to making a conscious effort to clean up after herself. And yes. Women, as well as entire families, had recently appeared in greater numbers at homeless camps, which Eric and April had noticed.

Today's first call was Pier 39, the city's most popular tourist spot. The caller was furious about a family of four having pitched tent right outside his store refusing to pack up and leave. He'd repeatedly threatened them to leave or else he would call the police. Like numerous times before, they pleaded ignorant of understanding English. To the store owner, they appeared to be from Central America, Honduras or Ecuador, popular migration places.

When Eric and April approached the family, they were preparing a meal cooked on a portable kerosene stove. "Want eat?" the man offered them with a smiling gesture at the steaming dish, arranged on a blanket. Eric noted that he spoke some English, which he could use for negotiating, in case the man played ignorant, then said, with a friendly smile, "Where're you all from?"

"Peru," the man replied with a gesture at an array of flutes propped against the tent.

Eric understood as soon as he spotted the musical instruments. "Peruvian flutes?"

"We will play," the man offered by getting to his feet.

"No," Eric said. "You finish eating." He then spotted the shop owner waving to get his attention. Getting up from their squatting positions, he and April headed in that direction.

"Well?" the shop owner demanded. "Are they moving? I want to open the store."

"Now wait a minute," Eric pacified the man. "We just got here. Give us a chance to find out."

"Don't take long or I'll call the police." He was furious at Eric now, unwavering in his decision. He had a right to do so, but also knew that the city council backed law enforcement over his complaint, as he had been told in the past. He had no bargaining power with the city other than to rely on Eric's skills in negotiating with the drifters.

Eric, on the other hand, was reluctant to haul the family off by force since he truly enjoyed the sound of Peruvian flutes played by musicians daily along Bay Street. His problem was in finding a suitable place for the family to set up residence. He knew how important the musicians were in maintaining a friendly ambience at Fisherman's Wharf.

Back at the tent, Eric was all business now. "Listen," he said. "You have to leave here but I will help to get you a place."

"No place to go. No money for rent," was the reply.

"I know," Eric said, feeling some compassion. "In this country, you cannot live on the street. You have to move into a house."

"But others live in tents," the man protested.

"Not for long. New city ordinance."

"City ordinance I understand, but still have no money."

"Don't need money. Place for free."

"Where?" The family must have understood as well as they showed interest.

"Over there," Eric said, pointing in the direction. "Very close."

"Can I see?" the man asked.

"I will take you there."

Eric, with the head of the household, got up and left in that direction while April remained with the family. It turned out that the wife spoke some English and communicated to April their plight back home, telling about the oppressed life the natives of their country had to endure. Entering into the U.S. illegally, as many do, did not solve the problem like most migrants envisioned. Without legal immigration papers it only shifted their troubled lives to another location, hoping eventually to be accepted into American society, every foreign immigrant's dream.

Thirty minutes later they returned, Eric with a nod at April and the man with a wide grin at his wife, stating, "We move. Big place. No money."

Within minutes they had packed up and left, with a satisfied shop owner thanking Eric and April for their effort. "Come by my store anytime, please."

"We will," April promised, before heading to the next trouble spot.

"Where to next?" Eric asked.

"Washington Square."

"Washington Square," Eric said, not quite believing her. "Place's been cleared months ago."

"Appears that some homeless decided to make it their place. Several tents went up last night."

"We'll see about that," he promised, looking forward to the challenge.

"What a mess," April said. Even Eric was shocked at the scene. The place, an expertly-groomed park in the middle of the city, was reserved for artists to display their works on weekends.

"Can't wait to hear their complaint."

Usually expecting an explanation when following a complaint, as was the case with the citizens after causing a legal infraction, with the homeless, it's always a complaint on their behalf. They never considered the issues they caused and only saw things to suit their way.

"Who's in charge?" Eric approached one tenant getting ready to hop on his bike.

"Guy over there," he was told. "Red tent." Not only had they staked their claim in this pristine city spot, but they had advertised their presence with brightly-painted colors on tent poles tipped with black flags.

"What's with the flags?" Eric demanded, approaching the man in charge. Easy to spot, he wore a black outfit from top to bottom, ready to fight at a moment's notice.

"It's the name for my society," the man proclaimed. "Independent Preppers." As expected from a challenging brute, with arms crossed depicting arrogance, he stepped in front of Eric on spread legs. "What's it to you?"

"The mayor sent us to have a talk with you," Eric stated.

"Who are you?"

"I'm his emissary."

"Who's she?"

"My assistant."

"Why didn't the mayor come himself?"

"He is busy with city ordinances. Can't be everywhere at the same time. Besides," Eric said, self-assured, "I'm his representative."

"So then," the brute challenged, "what do you want?"

"Let's go," April urged. "This guy's dangerous." Eric was undecisive for a moment while the brute stepped around, blocking their way.

"Go where?" he challenged.

"I don't have any gripes with you personally. I just want to talk."

"Talk about what?"

"You taking over city property."

"I'm a tax payer," he said. "I have a right to be here."

"You do but not to stake claim."

"I pick my place wherever I like. Besides," he claimed, "I chose here."

"If you don't pack up and leave you'll get evicted," Eric said, firm but not intimidating. He did not want to start the fight. Fearless, especially of late, he was beginning to get annoyed and the brute sensed it. Like many of his breed, his challenge was a show of dominance. The numbers worked in their favor most of the time. Numbers meaning the size of his society, if one could call the group of raggedy-looking mix such. From the looks of it, the gathered presented a likeness to Hell's Angels, only on bicycles. Their leader, apparently enjoying the challenge, took his time. He was prancing in front of his flock to encourage more cheering.

"Please don't mess with them," April said. "They mean business."

"So do I," Eric responded. "I won't get pushed around. It's bad for business."

"You think you can handle them all?"

"It won't come to that," he assured her.

"How do you know?"

"All the work we did over the past months—this is the test."

Right from the start of their eviction process both realized that it would present challenges, not only verbally but physically as well. To gain individual confidence, as part of Eric and April's daily routine, they rose by sun-up, exercised to develop strength and agility, practiced judo katas as he'd remembered from his college days, and sparred karate-style, in case they ever needed to defend themselves.

The sparring was not always easy since Eric was more powerful than April, but she made up for it through her cunning skills, side stepping him and retreating into the safety zone, out of his immediate reach, faking and dodging in front of him, daring, "Come on, honey. You can do better than that."

Up until this time, the image Eric harbored of April was the timid and fearful girl he had first met. Though only a couple inches shorter than him, Eric being 6 feet, 2 inches, both were relatively tall individuals. The rigorous exercises shaped both into capable opponents though Eric had to remind April on many occasions to straighten up to her full size. Slouching was still a remnant of her begging days, making her appear inches shorter.

Today, her appearance was somewhat different. Lately, on Eric's insistence, whenever they went on a homeless complaint, he made her wear tailor-made boots, Levi jeans, tightly-fitted sweaters and even a leather cap similar to a Marlo Brando style.

"But why?" she would ask when he insisted she wear the outfit.

"You're my backup. Look presentable." And that was it, her transformation into a fighter.

Eric's thoughts were interrupted by a call to action. The brute approached him once more. "Made up your mind?"

"My orders still stand. Pack up and leave these grounds."

"That'll be the day. Make me." The challenge was out in the open, followed by a broad grin on the brute's face. Both opponents were about evenly matched, with one exception. Where Eric was lean and trim, the brute was overweight and sluggish to move. It would be to Eric's great advantage as long as he could keep from being punched in the head. One such punch might jar his brain and put him out altogether.

"Look," Eric offered one more time. "Let's not fight over it. Use your common sense and just find another location where you're welcome. You and your derelict cohorts don't really want to go to jail, do you?"

"What did you call us?"

Eric had deliberately used the derogatory remark to drive his message home. Everybody nearby could feel the tension build. "It's what you are," he underscored the label, "derelict."

It was enough to drive the brute into action. He stepped up in front of Eric and delivered the first punch. Eric side stepped the punch, pulled the brute by his extended arm, and pushed him to the ground. There was a momentary silence from the crowd who had gathered into a closed circle to prevent Eric from possible escape. Surprised at the quick reaction by Eric, with their leader landing on the ground, they cheered their leader into action. "Get serious… don't play around… take him out."

They were well aware that if their leader lost this fight it would be "pack up and move out" once more. It was not the first time they had been forced to move on. Losing the fight was not an option. They were tired of being pushed around the country by the law. After claiming their stake in this city, it was their time for a last stand, no matter what. They liked this place and did everything to protect their acquired turf.

Since the initial exchange had gone wild, as the brute had quickly learned, he'd lost some of his initiative to his opponent.

Eric, on the other hand, played a cautious defense and came out ahead using his initial mental judgement of his opponent, *this guy's gonna be slow,* as was every fighter's assessment seconds from the exchange. He was right. No matter what force the brute was about to unleash on Eric, it was a futile effort. The fight did not last long. Two minutes into it, once again on the ground, the brute was out of breath, rendered defenseless even though Eric did not get a chance to show off his karate skills.

With the brute on his back, staring up at his challenger, he gave up with a shrug. "You're the better man."

Eric knew that the brute would lose his superior standing amidst his followers and did the gallant thing to save his fate. He reached to the ground and, with an outstretched arm, offered his hand to the beaten leader, who accepted without reservation. Up on his feet again, there was cheering from the crowd to acknowledge his regained leadership. It was the code of ethics that any fighter may lose by default, if the opponent was "the better man" at the time of battle. It might diminish some of the prestige of the leader as a fighter, but the state of respect would still remain.

To preserve the brute's honor, Eric gave them one week to enjoy their stay, then watched them move out with April by his side, proud that he was her hero. It only took hours for word of the battle to make the news, with Eric being heralded as a hero by the mayor and his staff, as well as by the citizens of San Francisco.

Washington Square was liberated and returned to the artists for their exhibitions once more. April was thrilled at the outcome and visited the square often.

The battle at Washington Square, as people remembered the fight, was not the last battle between the homeless and the city mayor. Eric and April were called upon many more times, but mostly for appeasing individuals and small groups refusing to comply with newly-enforced city ordinances.

April and Eric formed a perfect match for their effort, with her hoping the city was a future for both.

CHALLENGES

"What's the matter?" April said. It was later than usual in the morning, and Eric was still under the cover of his sleeping bag.

"I don't feel like getting up," he said. "I'm taking a break."

"What about the list?" she said, waving today's task schedule in front of his face.

"Tell the city council to shove it."

"That's no way to treat them. They've been very good to us."

"I know, but it's getting to be too much of a routine. I need time off."

"What do you mean?" April said, somewhat worried by his negative attitude. "All day?"

"More time than just one day. I feel trapped in something I can't break away from."

"It's called a job," April said, trying to humor him, but he refused to accept it.

"That's exactly what it is. I didn't plan it. It's taking away my independence. It's affecting my mood."

"Go ahead," she suggested. "Take the day off. I'll go myself."

"No. It's too dangerous on your own. Someone will take advantage of you."

"I can take care of myself. You know that."

"Let's do something else today," he suggested.

"What do you have in mind?"

"Something special."

"Like what?"

"A bike ride. We haven't done it in months."

"You're right. Let's do it."

It was an enjoyable day, freewheeling along. Crossing the Golden Gate Bridge alone was worth the trip. They were in no hurry, leaving Highway 101 in their wake. The rest of the way was easy riding. From their present vantage point they could easily make out the San Francisco skyline in the distance with Angel Island not far off. One could dwell on the view forever;

some people did, such as the ones living in Tiburon, where they now were. April had no idea about this place and how Mediterranean the village appeared. She vaguely recalled her mom talking about it and how she'd wished to live there or at least visit. They'd never had a chance with her mom drinking herself into a stupor day and night. It seemed so long ago.

"Just look at this place," she said, overwhelmed by such beauty. "Why don't we move here?"

"It's not that simple," Eric stated. "It's very expensive now if you can find a place to buy."

"What about your inheritance? Wouldn't it cover it?"

"It could."

"Then," she replied, "why don't we?"

"Something to think about," he agreed.

"Let's do it," she said once more, hoping he would agree.

"We can talk about it over lunch," he suggested.

"Fine. What about this place?" They had arrived at Tiburon's water's edge, the harbor jammed with yachts and pleasure cruisers. "Wouldn't it be great to live on one of these?" April marveled with a gesture at one of the craft.

"I thought about it," Eric said.

"Just look at the place," she said, pointing at the hills. The view into the terraced hills was spectacular, with single dwellings clustered along the shoreline and apartment buildings sprouting up everywhere amidst lush green trees and flora, providing everybody with a view into the city skyline and farther south. Even Eric marveled at the view. It reminded him of Viareggio, a village near Pisa, Italy, that he'd visited during his college days. "You're right," he said. "I could live here."

They propped their bikes against the breaker wall rail, secured them with locks, and took an outside table at one of many restaurants along the shore front. The Italian-style cuisine, accompanied by a bottle of chianti, was as excellent as it could get.

Taking their time enjoying meal and wine, April kept on prodding him, "Isn't it marvelous?" and "I love it here."

Eric's depressing mood from the morning had waned. He was enjoying everything around, including her company. He silently evaluated his life and the way it had turned out since arriving in San Francisco. He should have had no complaints whatsoever about his life but, for some reason, he felt that there was something missing. A self-analysis did not reveal the answer. Watching April savor every bite she took, in between the light conversation, did not ease his concerns. What saved the day were the two bottles of wine they imbibed while spending the rest of the day at this charming place.

Their ride back to the city was a bit more challenging. It was already dark by the time they left, with their vision slightly impaired from alcohol, so they took their time in-between several stops. He had to step off a couple of times, relieving himself; she had to hop off the saddle a couple of times when traffic cut too close into her path, but they made it back without any incidents.

Tucked securely into their sleeping bags, both recollected the day's impressions, with him looking forward to more outings and her hoping he would take her inspirations and desires about buying a place there seriously, before slumbering into the world of dreams, and dream April did.

Eric woke up several times during the night, calming April from what appeared to be restless sleep. When he asked her in the morning, all she could remember was getting drawn into confrontations she could not solve. Her self-analysis later in the day did not resolve the reason for such violence. She kept thinking that it was the result of Eric's peculiar behavior earlier the previous morning that must have triggered her female intuition.

Eric decided not to report to the mayor's office for the next couple of weeks. He wanted to dedicate his time solely to April, who he thought might need his full support. He still reprimanded himself for his peculiar behavior the day before.

He also realized how fragile she might be as a result of her wasted childhood. He called the mayor's office and let his assistant know about his decision.

"I'll tell him," and "keep in touch," he was told.

Weeks later, they were reminded of their duties by the mayor's office manager, who let them know that her boss had been looking for them. After they connected with City Hall, the mayor insisted that Eric and April report to the office.

"What's up?" Eric asked upon entering the mayor's office.

"I need your true assessment," Thomas Allen threw at Eric as soon as they stepped into his office. "I'm getting conflicting reports."

"Reports about what?" Both Eric and April were baffled at the unexpected outburst.

"Reports about your progress, or the lack of it," the mayor fumed.

It was a revelation Eric had not expected. "I don't know what you are talking about. Please explain. I'm surprised as much as you, Mayor."

"Yes, Mayor," April chimed in. She was more surprised than Eric since she was able to analyze his progress from her unbiased perspective.

"I'm getting reports from all parts of the city about the homeless. From what I gather," he said, gazing at Eric for a plausible explanation, "they are getting more aggressive by the month."

"I can't believe what you are saying," Eric said.

"It's getting to where the police are called almost every day."

"What are the complaints?"

"Fights," the mayor, red faced, yelled at him. "That's what."

"I... I..." Eric stuttered. He was at a loss. After all the months they had spent educating the homeless, the implicated behavior was a mystery. His mind kept churning for answers about where he had gone wrong.

The mayor came to his rescue. "I want you back on my team to get to the bottom of it. Is that understood?"

"Of course. I am as much interested as you in what's going on."

"You do that," were the mayor's trailing words on their way out.

"Can you believe it?" Eric muttered, shaking his head at April.

"Where do you want to start?" she said.

"Let's get the lists and start from there," he suggested.

"Maybe the mayor is right," April said. Right from the top of the list they sensed that something had changed with the homeless' behavior and conduct. Throughout the sectors they visited, the homeless seemed to have become aggressive, some even hostile.

"What are you doing to me?" Eric challenged the offenders. "Your behavior is unacceptable after all I've done for you."

For the next few days, making their rounds down the list, they kept track of all the complaints. Analyzing the trends, a pattern emerged. "This is interesting," Eric muttered while studying the offenses they had recorded.

"What?"

"Listen to some of the complaints," he offered, reading the itemized trends: "Government is taking my freedom; I don't have a chance to earn a buck; Police are too brutal with us minorities; I won't be corralled, counted, and tagged; Too many conditions attached to us homeless."

"Wait," April stopped him. "It doesn't make sense. We've heard all this before."

"That's just it," Eric said in agreement. "I wonder what could be the problem. We'd better visit the places and take a closer look."

After making rounds on their bikes, they learned the facts. It was a revelation that probably made sense to the complainants but less to the city council. "What's the verdict?" April asked.

"You won't believe it."

"What?"

"It's a new generation taking to the streets."

"Mayor won't like having to deal with the same issues over and over."

"I know," he agreed. "Same goes for us."

"Well," April said. "It'll keep us busy for the years ahead." She waited for his response, but he remained silent. *Odd,* she thought, somewhat surprised and not quite understanding his silence, *he's usually so verbal about issues.*

"Let's drop it off and let the mayor decide."

April sensed a certain reluctance about Eric. It appeared that his thoughts were on other things. *I wonder what's on his mind?* She decided to hold off until evening to bother him with her concerns.

MORE CHALLENGES

Eric called the mayor's office to give him the results of his preliminary findings. "Damn them! There's no end to people's complaints." Seemingly enraged, he followed with a series of profanities Eric did not want to repeat to April, who was by his side. "No matter what I do, nothing seems to please them. I wish the homeless would just disappear, go away. What do you suggest?" he asked Eric.

"Let the federal government solve it," Eric suggested. "They started the whole mess."

"I want to see the full report in the morning," Thomas Allen demanded. "9:00 a.m. sharp, and don't be late." Both spent the rest of the day at Starbucks, Eric typing up his report with April discussing her ideas and supporting him.

As the mayor ordered, Eric and April reported on time the following morning. "Not gonna be a pleasant meeting," Eric mentioned on their way into the mayor's conference room.

"Not our fault," she replied, taking a seat at one end of the table. Surprisingly, neither Eric nor April recognized most of the faces gathered around. Waiting for the mayor to show, April was able to study those attending. "All young faces," she muttered to Eric, who agreed.

Seconds later, Thomas Allen made his entrance. "Let's get right to the point. As you can see," he informed Eric, "I have brought in a new team. When I received Eric's report yesterday, I realized what I had to do." All in attendance seemed to perk up, wondering why they had been selected on a moment's notice. "Where's the list?" he demanded of Eric, who handed it over. After a brief glance, the mayor passed it on to the table for everybody to read. In the meantime, he paced the floor for a few minutes, then addressed the assembly.

"As you can see, we have a challenge on our hands. I brought you in to get a new perspective on the problem all of you are familiar with." He paused to allow for responses, but nobody said anything. "Eric here," he continued, with a gesture, "had a great idea."

April was proud that her partner was finally getting some recognition. The mayor continued, "He proposed to let the federal government solve it. They started the whole mess and I could not agree more. But knowing the Feds," he explained, "they would only reject the idea and turn it back to us. That's the reason I selected you young folks to come up with a new idea."

At this point, everybody perked up at the mayor's directives. It would give all of them the opportunity to shine if anyone could come up with a solution to the homeless problem. "Anybody?" He waited for the council to chime in, but they maintained their silence. "What about you, Eric? What's your best guess?"

"Will somebody please explain what the 'Home Together Plan' really means?" one council member asked.

At least they're not completely asleep, April thought. *There might still be hope of getting something done.* She said, "It's not a complicated plan. Even I studied it and understood."

"Let's share it with everybody," the mayor directed at Eric.

Glad the mayor had addressed him, Eric stood up to earn some recognition for the time and effort he had expended on the cause.

"It's a plan that was implemented in the '80s," he started, but was immediately interrupted by one member.

"'80s? Hell, that's decades ago. What have they been doing?" Individual outbursts like this followed from other members.

"As I said," Eric went on, picking up the thread, "the plan was put into action by the Interagency Council on Homelessness, an independent federal agency to prevent and end homelessness."

Additional council outbursts continued with, "Who are the agencies?"

Eric waited for the room to quiet, then went on. "There are more than a dozen agencies involved within the executive branch with an annual budget of $3.5 million."

The mayor reminded the council not to keep interrupting. The topic was too important in order for him to continue on his quest to solve the city's homelessness problem. Turning back to Eric, he demanded, "What's the current status with the plan?"

"It's obvious, isn't it?" Eric said. "The plan's not working for everybody but there is some progress being made."

"Explain," the mayor directed.

"The plan seems to work for families and minority groups, but not for individuals. There have been positive strides made toward getting mostly the economically deprived into homes. Furthermore, there have been a number of amendments since then to include specifically addressed categories such as 'End Youths' and 'Veteran Homelessness' that actually seem to work, but the problem is still and always will be affordable housing."

"I can relate to that," the mayor said, shaking his head. "Just look at the rise in real estate prices in the city. I feel for the poor not being able to get a job in Silicon Valley. But then," he continued, "it takes an education to get hired by companies like Microsoft and Facebook."

"That's where the problem comes in," Eric said in agreement. "What does it take for minorities and the deprived to get educated?" His remark inspired suggestions, but nobody came up with a viable solution.

"Discipline," Eric boldly stated. "It's discipline along with confidence, and self-esteem, that's missing."

"What about being economically disadvantaged?" one member asked. "What about them?"

"Let me tell you something," Eric said, anger welling up. "In this country, we all have the same opportunities. All it takes is discipline and the will to try. I'm talking about self-discipline."

"That's a pretty bold statement," the mayor cut in. "Where do you get this?"

"From my parents."

"Care to explain?" somebody asked.

"It all begins at parenthood and teacher education. It has to be taught as a child. It's not something new I am telling you. The signs have been visible for many decades."

"What's the answer, wise guy?" Eric must have struck a chord affecting the young caller's dignity.

"Correction," Eric insisted. "It's 'wise man,' and I am trying to educate you." His comeback quieted the room.

"Do you have any suggestions?" the mayor politely asked.

"I do, but there is nothing I can do. It's up to people in government to get the country back on track. People like you," Eric said, indicating the protester.

"I want to hear them anyway," the mayor demanded.

"Okay. Here are the facts. It all began seventy some years ago when parents were forced to turn over home training responsibilities to school teachers. It worked well for a short while until legal suits against schools were brought on by parents protesting teachers disciplining their children. Consequently, teachers backed off from further disciplinary actions."

"Are you serious?" one young council member demanded.

"Yes. It was before your time. Anyway," Eric went on. "You can easily see the consequences it has brought to the American culture. The system is broken."

"What happened in the 1950s," the young member called out, "to cause this mess?"

"It's when both parents were required in the work force. Moms that used to stay home and educate their children were forced to give it up to teachers."

"But why?"

"It was the government way to obtain additional revenue for their ever-increasing budget demands that almost doubled as the result."

"That's right." Allen sided with Eric. "How did you know?"

"I read a lot," he said, "especially history."

"What can be done? What do you suggest," the mayor asked in earnestness, addressing Eric.

"There are two ways to get back on track. One," Eric stated, "for parents to take back control, and two, for the government to act. There is still hope to get the fundamental morals reinstated."

"Yeah?" An attending woman had taken Eric's lesson on morality personally.

"It's called discipline."

"Then," somebody else lashed out at him, "you are homeless. How do you explain that?" There was anger growing all around him.

Even April sensed the tension. "Let's get out of here," she whispered to him.

"Not just yet," Eric responded to her plea. "If we ever want to get anywhere, I need to drive the facts home."

She reluctantly succumbed to his appeal.

"Getting back to the question, why I am homeless? I'll tell you why. Because I chose it as my lifestyle. It's called free will." He could have spent much more time arguing about the merits of life but it would not have served any purpose. He could not have been more expressive and realized that people just don't like to accept the facts. This became obvious when somebody yelled out, "You're a bigot."

"That's it," Eric said, turning to April. "They don't appreciate what we've done for the city. Let's get out of here." Both briskly left. He'd come to the conclusion that nobody liked to be criticized, not the homeless and certainly not politicians.

"You were brutal back there," April said, beaming at him. "Did you really mean all you said?"

"Every word of it."

"I'm so proud of you," she said, reaching up for his face and planting a kiss on his lips. "You are not angry?"

"Not in the least. Knowing what you and I accomplished is good enough for me."

On the way home, April confronted Eric. "What's next?"

"I'm through with politics."

"What about the homeless? You through with them as well?"

"You see what has happened. The mayor pulled my power base."

"We can start out fresh," April suggested. "If not here, then someplace else."

"I'm tired of it. I need to get my life back."

"What do you mean?" April had not expected him to quit and throw in the towel so easily. Sure, it had been a sacrifice, but also a fair fight for the both of them, nevertheless. *What will I do?* she silently asked herself, then remembered her quest to publish her photobook. She found solace in the thought for her immediate future.

SHATTERED DREAMS

"Eric, wake up. You're wasting another beautiful day." Trying to get him up had become a daily routine for April. What was more, he had taken to smoking pot on a regular basis. Drinks, drugs, and pot had been reserved for special occasions like parties or gatherings with friends. Taken habitually, it seemed to change his mood; worse yet, it affected his mental ability. She did not like it and wanted to find out his reasons. "Here," she said, handing him a mug of freshly-brewed coffee. "This'll wake you up. We need to talk."

"What about?" He was still groggy from sleep.

"You."

"What's the matter with me?"

"You're not the same person I met. You've changed ever since we left City Hall."

"You're imagining things," he said, trying to pacify her. "I'm still the same Eric."

"I don't want to start an argument," she said. "But ever since the day we left the mayor's office you've been absentminded. All you want to do is sleep and smoke pot. Care to talk about it?"

"What's wrong with that?" he said, trying to excuse his mood change. "I've smoked pot since my college days. It got me through curriculums I didn't like and teachers I despised."

"That's what I mean. Are you tired of me like you were of boring curriculums? Is it me?"

"Of course not. Nothing you did."

"Then," she said, "why haven't you touched me? We haven't had sex in weeks."

That must have driven her message home. Gently, he reached out to embrace her. "You know I love you."

"How should I know? You never tell me."

Holding her hands, he took the time to caress her face. "I'm telling you now."

"Then say it." She was adamant. She wanted to hear the words. Up until now, it had only been implicit. Hearing the words would seal their bond. Bonding was something every woman wanted. With most men, it was only words exchanged in passionate embrace. They did not have the same emotional impact that they do on women. *It's probably why men do not need the periodic verbal reinforcement we do*, she thought.

"I love you," he said as emotionally as he could manage. "See?"

"Yeah," she replied, partially objecting. "It's because I made you."

"I love you… I love you…"

"That's enough," she said, bursting out laughing. "I believe you." She had regained her trust in him once more. To seal their bond, what followed was a long overdue exchange of pent-up emotions and passion. Her doubts in him would have been part of the past if he hadn't fallen into the same routine again, sleeping in late and smoking pot more than he had before. It began to trouble her more, but she held her tongue for the time being and distracted herself with the picture album.

She spent her time almost daily at Starbucks to recharge batteries. While April was dedicated with her work, her journal and populating the picture album, Eric seemed to have lost interest in everything. Time passed quickly for April, with Eric being somewhat responsive whenever she faced a challenge with her project. On his laptop computer, he showed her how to use Photoshop and other necessary applications to produce her photographic artwork, though he was neglecting his duties for her passionate needs. When April confronted him, he made up for his neglect, but only until the next time she had to remind him. *Must be part of a relationship,* she thought, *having to remind the man of his promised responsibilities.*

She came to accept the fact that men had different needs, until the day Eric confronted her with the shock of a lifetime.

"I'm leaving."

Innocently, not suspecting anything unusual, April put her work aside. "Wait up!" April yelled. "Where're we going? I'll come with you."

"Not we," he corrected her. "I'm going."

"You going to visit your parents? Please let me come with you," she pleaded. "I could use a break."

"You don't understand," he said, stepping up to confront her directly. "I'm leaving here."

It took April several seconds to interpret his meaning. Once she realized the severity of his planned action she was completely petrified. She put one hand over her mouth to keep from screaming out.

"But why?" she managed to whisper in denial. "What about me?" She had a difficult time keeping from crying. Still thinking he was joking, she needed clarification. "Is it something I did?"

She sought his face for an emotion, any emotion. She found only one, pity.

Eric did not expect such a great reaction and realized that he might have damaged her emotional limits. Years ago, when he had made up his mind to pursue exploring the country, he had not expected to meet a woman like April and establish a solid relationship along the way. Suddenly, after watching her intense reaction, he found himself in a quandary about how to proceed in the immediate future.

"Let's talk," he offered by gently pulling her onto the sleeping bag. He even made an effort to gently wipe the tears from her eyes, but she angrily slapped his hands. She had every right to do so after what he'd just said. "Look," he said, trying to appease her. "This doesn't have to be the end. You could come with me."

"Really?" It instantly cheered her up. *There is hope after all,* her mind acknowledged. "Where're we going?" she said, wiping her face dry. Beaming with joy, she thought that she might have misunderstood his intentions.

"Not so fast," he said, throttling her enthusiasm. "You may not like the places I intend to visit."

"I don't care as long as I am with you. I'll follow you to the end of the world. You know that."

"It may be just that for some people," he stated in a sobering tone of voice. "I want to explore the Canadian wilderness."

She reacted as he expected. Her face changed from being overjoyed to great disillusionment. "But," she protested, "there's nothing but wild animals. There's no culture. There're no people. There's no entertainment. Only nature."

"That's exactly what I need. I've had enough of people for a time. I need to find my calling."

"But completely isolated from life? I don't know if I can handle it."

For better or for worse, he had cast the die, shifting the responsibility onto her shoulders. It was up to April now to decide about her own future and if she would accompany him or step onto an unknown path on her own. She needed time to think. She got up, donned her jeans and blouse, reached for a pair of sandals and left the tent, ignoring the question he shouted after her.

"Where're you going?"

"It's your turn to worry," she muttered unhappily, jumping on her bike. She had to get away from him. Where? She didn't know, but headed for the Golden Gate Bridge.

April had no immediate destination in mind. Peddling rapidly with her eyes focused on the asphalt, her mind was churning with scenes from the past and images into the future. While her brain was trying to rationalize things out, her subconscious led her in the direction of Muir Woods, the place she so dearly treasured. It was a place untouched by human influence and life's miseries. She realized she had to make a monumental decision about her immediate future and could not cope with the thought of losing Eric. The implication of the wrong choice would be too great for her to bear. An hour later, almost in panic, she turned into her treasured place to seek an answer.

Dropping the bike to the ground, she rushed into her pristine world. As before, she was overwhelmed by its enormous beauty. There were no humanly sounds. *This must have been what Earth was like without technology,* she thought. The only sounds she perceived were the rustlings of treetops in the wind interlaced by the chirping of colorful native birds amidst the hollow hammering of woodpeckers echoing through the woods. It soothed her mind to where she could think once more. Somewhat calmed, the reality still gnawed on her mind. "What am I going to do?"

She already knew the answer. "It's up to me now," she muttered, knowing that she had nobody to blame other than herself by making the wrong choice. "Why," she wailed at Eric, "do you have to leave me?" There was no echo to offer her solace. Her mind remained an empty space without inspiration. She dropped onto the bare ground and whimpered herself to sleep.

Eric, the independent person that he was, had not realized the effect April had left on him until after she rushed from the tent. "What's happened to me? Am I getting soft?" he questioned the empty space April had vacated. Emotions had never been an issue with him. They were reserved for the young, the old, and married people, or so he thought. What he was experiencing was the feeling of guilt surface for the first time in his life, and he did not like it. When he tried to wipe it from his mind, it turned into remorse, another strange concept for him. "What am I doing," he muttered, shaking his head, "ruining somebody else's life?" Here he realized how precious April was to him.

"Damn," he silently cussed. "Why did I have to meet her?" He did not want it to happen, getting involved with someone. He always thought of himself as being an adventurer, an explorer without borders and bonds. This would change his whole life. What he had in mind for his future was to travel, not only in his own country, but to other places as well, across the world.

Left alone with his emotions, he had to do something to calm his nerves. He took a smoke. Several rollups later, dazed from the effects, he had not realized how much time had passed. "Six hours? I've got to find her," he decided, riddled with guilt. "Where would she have gone?" In this state of mind he was unsure where she could have gone or, worse yet, if she would come back. He knew how independent she used to be. His mind skimmed through familiar places he thought she might have gone: The Mission? No. Union Square? No. Embarcadero? No. Then it dawned on him, Pier 39. Yes, her favorite place, watching seals bark at her. He headed there.

Ten minutes later he was pushing his bike along the pier. It did not take long for Eric to realize that April wasn't there. While he normally enjoyed the place, watching tourists and listening to foreign languages, all that was on his mind now was finding her. Frustrated, he sat on an empty bench to think. "Where could she have gone?"

It then came to him. "Muir Woods. That's it." Newly energized with hope, he headed there next. It took him a little over an hour of heavy peddling to cover the 15 miles. On arriving, he locked the bike to the rail and went straight for the visitor center, interrupting the reception manager. "Have you seen a young woman about 6 foot tall, wearing jeans?"

"Mister," the lady said. "I don't know. We have many people fitting that description come by here." After a quick look around the center he stepped out again, when a thought hit him. "Bike." Sure enough, when he returned to the rail, he recognized her bike on the ground nearby. He checked his watch for time. It was already getting late in the day. Most people had already left the grounds. "Where could she be?"

He went to work, asking returning strollers, "Have you seen a lone woman?"

After several negative responses, one returning couple stopped. The wife mentioned, "There's one sleeping about half a mile up the path." She gestured in the direction they had come from. Eric headed that way.

"Where…?" April muttered, still drowsy from sleep when she recognized Eric's face. Thinking it was in her dream, she propped up on one elbow to get her bearings, then realized the place she had gone to sleep. Overflowing with emotions, she pulled his body close to hers and began to weep into his cradling arms. He gently stroked her hair while patiently waiting until she stopped crying.

With both in private thoughts, hers in contentment but his filled with remorse, it was a quiet ride home since neither of them talked much. Besides, they had to watch out for passing evening traffic. It was dark when they arrived at the tent.

The following few weeks worked out fine for April. Eric was attentive to her more than before the untimely revelation about his future. Their differences seemed to be something of the past. She went about working on her album. They enjoyed being with friends, once more having a good time in and around the city, until the morning his sleeping bag was empty. Thinking he had stepped out to use the public restroom, she began to worry when first ten minutes passed, then twenty, then half an hour. She really began to worry when faint thoughts popped into her mind. *He couldn't have, he didn't.* Rushing out, she headed for the public facilities but could not locate him. "Eric!" she shouted several times in vain with the faintly familiar feeling surfacing in her mind. She was petrified just thinking about. "Please," she called into the morning chill, "don't do this to me." There was no answer.

Deeply distressed, she slowly made her way back to the tent. It was then when she noticed the letter he'd left by the empty pillow. Her hands trembled trying to open the letter. April had to put it down several times before she found the courage to open it. Heavyhearted, feeling miserable, she began to read:

Dearest April.

It is with heavy heart that I write this letter. To start with, you have been the most beautiful gift to my life that I could ever have dreamed of and I did not deserve you. I want you to know that my leaving you has absolutely not been your fault. It was my solitary decision and there was nothing you or anybody else could have done to stop me. Although I brought up my choices in life as well as future plans with you on a number of occasions, you seem to have shut out the very thought of a possible separation. Let me explain.

Ever since growing up, I felt like I had a mission to fulfill. The urge, at times, became overwhelming to a point that it dominated everything else on my mind. What I am trying to tell you is, I feel like I was born an adventurer. It is this drive that kept me free and independent of the obligations others have to deal with. For this reason, I don't believe that I was cut out to be a family man or even deserving of a relationship. Let me assure you, if there is one person I tried to make it work with, it was with you.

I hope that with the passage of time the hatred you feel for me now will pass, and you'll forgive me for deserting you. Regardless of the direction destiny has in mind for me, I will always cherish our time together. You are a treasure among society despite the hardship that life dealt you at an early age. I tried to make up for the shortfalls that you had to endure since then but realized that it was not my mission to do so. You are a strong-willed woman and will survive without me. You have proven it to yourself several times over.

I wish that I could tell you the direction I am headed in, but not even I know my destination at this time. Headed north on I-101, I plan to drive on past Seattle, then on to Vancouver, the destination for my initial journey. At some point, if my bike holds up, I will head inland into the Canadian woods. I hope the isolation will give me the opportunity to sort things out. It is this uncertainty that keeps driving me on to explore and eventually find a purpose in my life.

I will probably hate myself for leaving you and hope that perhaps someday we may meet again. By the way, I left you the tent. Consider it yours. It'd be too bulky for the bike anyway.
Take care of yourself,
Love, Eric.

With every word she read her emotions transformed through all of her capable ranges. First it was a guilt complex she could not explain. "Why should I feel guilty?" she questioned herself, shaking her head. "It's he that should feel this way."

Placing the blame on him made her feel somewhat better when reading on. Next, it was not easy for her to suppress the tears seeping from her eyes when she read that he felt some guilt for leaving her.

Emotionally hardened by a mom's irrational demands, who had been stressed out most of the time through prostituting herself, traversing an emotional rollercoaster ride was a new experience for April. Though her mom rarely could display a kinder side, April dearly treasured those times. What she regretted most from reading Eric's letter was that he hardly showed any remorse for the destruction he had caused her. She burst out, in uncontrollable anger turning to hatred, "You son of a bitch. I trusted you. I gave you my life. You no-good traitor. Who do you think you are, you bastard? I hate you!"

April finally realized that she was out of control and hated herself for giving in to such vicious outbursts. Shaking her fist into the air while yelling out obscenity after obscenity, she eventually ran out of verbal energy and collapsed to the floor, sobbing. "Why did you do this to me? Why did you abandon me?" She then realized how much she loved him.

It took several days for April to get a hold of herself, during which time her feelings were torn between love and hate for most of her waking hours. Rambling around, mostly in dazed disorder, several days later, after catching her image in the mirror, April realized how much she had neglected herself and vowed to straighten up. She checked around the tent, which appeared empty since Eric had taken all of his belongings along, and rearranged some of her things into an orderly, easy-to-spot fashion. Though meager in personal treasure, every item she had served a specific purpose.

There was a fair-sized wooden table made from an empty cable spool used during someone's construction project. Eric must have taken it after the electrical cable was used up.

For seating, he had collected a couple of empty bottle crates someone had discarded. They had served them well during dinners cooked within the tent on a camping type kerosene stove. Since there was no running water in the tent, dishes and personal cleaning was performed at the public restroom facility. While it would have been an inconvenience to most people, for the both of them, it was part of their free-spirited lifestyle.

Ventilation was never a problem since the tent had mesh-protected window flaps on two sides of the tent aside from the main entrance, which opened and closed with a sturdy zipper. What served as a vanity desk was an extended cardboard box someone had discarded at a dumpster place. Their collection of furniture was meager, to say the least, but it served its purpose within the limited confinement of the tent.

For closet space, Eric had fashioned a rope strung between the pole and one edge of the tent, supplied with a few wire hangers for clothes. The makeshift closet presented not much of a problem since neither had much of a wardrobe other than what they wore. The few underthings usually found a place on the generally-empty vanity top.

Moving a few things around to her liking, April was satisfied with the decor. "What else can I do?" she muttered within the silent tent, trying to occupy her time. Not being able to think of anything else to do, she decided to take a ride. It had been some time since she visited the piers. So she headed to Pier 39, hoping to meet up with some friends.

Riding along at a leisurely pace, she took her time. Twenty minutes later she secured her bike at the rail provided. Her spirits were immediately uplifted as soon as she heard the happy barking of seals. As usual, she sought out a bench nearby to observe and take in the ozone-filled, sultry off-shore breeze caressing her face.

Since it was early springtime, travel had not yet picked up. *A few more weeks for tourists to arrive,* she thought while watching a couple of fishermen tossing out their fishing rods in the hope something would bite the lure. Occupied with thoughts about her personal trauma about Eric departing, April felt a sudden chill moving across her body. Somewhat bored by the lack of people on the pier, she decided to get going. *Maybe I'm catching a cold,* she thought on her ride home.

That was exactly what April had done; she'd caught a cold. She took refuge within her sleeping bag as soon as she arrived at the tent but her rest was interrupted frequently by coughing up mucus, in between rushing to the public restroom to throw up. Unable to get any sleep, her frustration built into a helpless reluctance about not having any cough medicine on hand. Her frustration grew even further at Eric not being at her side tending to her. He would know what to do, she thought, being reminded once more about her plight. She could not help but get angry every time her thoughts touched on him.

Getting up from the sleeping bag, in between hacking attacks, April rummaged around the few boxes of her belongings. She was looking for something, anything, to help relieve the cold and get some sleep. The search proved to be fruitless. No matter how miserable a sleepless night might be, it will eventually come to an end. Determined not to get caught up again without any sleep remedy, April headed for

Fisherman's Wharf, to the pharmacy she had been to on several other occasions.

"I can't go there," she yelled out, slamming on the brake pedals. She suddenly realized that she had no money. It was a revelation of how dependent she had become on Eric. "Damn," she yelled in frustration. "Is there no end?"

It was a brutal reminder of her current reality with all of its shortcomings. "Think, girl," she directed herself while waiting for inspiration. There was one thing she had promised herself after being together with Eric. "I will never go back to begging." She realized that she had a serious dilemma on her hands. There was only one alternative to begging on the streets; it was begging from friends.

Momentarily undecided on what direction to take, she kept searching for the most logical place to locate friends. While she had made a number of personal connections working at the mayor's office, they were mostly Eric's friends. "The Mission," she decided and that's where she headed.

Not long after riding past intersection I-80 and I-101, better known as the Central Freeway, she spotted familiar faces shuffling along the local tent city. "Hey," some called out. "Where's Eric?"

"Out of town," she would yell back.

"What brings you here?" one asked.

She stopped to confront the homeless. "I'm short on cash and need medicine."

"What's the matter, you've got a cold?" Her sore throat must have been the giveaway. "Here." He generously offered her a five-dollar bill.

"I'll pay you back," she said, thanking him.

"Don't worry about it," he replied, then added, "Tell Eric to stop by."

"Will do." Thankful for the money she headed back to the wharf, bought a bottle of cough syrup, rode back to the tent, and promptly went to sleep after finishing half the bottle. The following day was pretty much the same course: she begged for money from Eric's friends with a promise to pay it back. Though her cold was gone several days later, it did not stop her begging for more money. She tried to get some sleep without the medicine, but it did not work. In denial for days and weeks to follow, April developed an addiction to the codeine in the cough syrup.

And so, April made her rounds to different locations before she realized that she was addicted. The daily morning sickness from withdrawals came as a shock to her when she realized the symptoms. "What are you doing to me?" she whimpered into the empty tent space, with Eric's vision on her mind.

Some of Eric's friends would stop by the tent almost daily to inquire about his whereabouts, but hardly recognized her in the condition she was in, haggard looking, tattered in appearance, unkempt and unwashed. Soon people stopped coming. She felt deserted, a nameless person homeless again.

Weeks went by with April living from day to day begging money from friends. Although her plight severely affected her self-esteem, she could not break away and free herself from the bond of codeine addiction, as negligible as the substance was. As was the case with all drugs, the dosage had to be increased periodically to obtain the same drug effects, but that was not the worst of it. The duration of a "high" diminished at the same time, demanding ever increasing measures to be effective. On top of the discomfort withdrawals caused, her pain from missing Eric added to her misery.

Every time she encountered a new homeless face she asked for the direction they had come from. If it was from the north she would prod for personal information, trying to locate Eric's whereabouts. It seemed that Earth had swallowed him up since nobody ever had any information. April became depressed to a state where she had a difficult time coping with her involuntarily acquired life. The days when she was sober were especially hard for her.

Despite the promise she had made to herself about never going back to begging, there was no other choice with as penniless as she had become. After some time, friends stopped lending her money and even avoided her whenever she approached them. Before long, after recognizing her failure, she relapsed into a hopeless state of living once more. Without the slightest chance to ever get better, her emotions were torn between love and hate for her beloved Eric.

One evening, leaving the liquor store after the purchasing of a bottle of cheap whiskey, she was approached by two tall guys sporting seemingly friendly faces and wanting to know, "Where're you going with the bottle?"

"Home," she said.

"Where's home?"

"Not far," she said with a gesture up The Hill.

"Are you the one living on The Hill?"

"Yes. It's my tent."

"Would you like some company?" one of them asked with a grin at his partner.

She thought about it for a few seconds before responding. "Sure. Why not?" Usually drinking herself into a stupor followed with dreamless sleep, it had been ages since she'd had company, any company. She invited them along.

"Here we are," April said, pulling up the zipper on the entrance flap. "Home." It was already dark when they entered the tent.

"What a roomy place," one admired.

"I could live like this," the other agreed.

"Well," she said. "Find a spot to sit. I don't have chairs or anything like it."

"We understand. The floor's okay."

"Here's some cups," she offered. "Don't have any ice."

"That's okay. We're used to drinking straight up."

"Cheers." She offered her raised cup with a smile.

"Cheers to you too," were their replies. "Where're you from?" one of them asked.

"I was born in this city," she said. "What about you?"

"We're from Hawaii," one said.

"Samoan?"

"Yeah," he grinned.

"I wondered about your size and skin color."

"Ever been there?"

"In my dreams only. My mom used to talk about how beautiful the island was."

"It used to be pristine until settlers sold us out."

"What do you mean?" April was curious. She'd never heard the expression.

"Missionaries and landgrabbers from the mainland stole our land. They kept coming back each year in greater numbers. Before our tribes realized what was happening, our land was gone. Go there some time and see who else took their share."

"Hell," his buddy chimed in. "You can hardly find a beach front anymore. The Japs built their mega hotels right up on the waterfront."

"What about the lush hills, the palm trees, the pineapple fruits?" April recalled her mom talking about those.

Their conversations had begun in a friendly manner, but over the following hour the topics heated up into an unpleasant atmosphere, followed by swearing and cussing out the people responsible for the two fellows' plight. "That's why everybody is leaving the island. It's why we landed here."

April sympathized with them until all were drunk. It did not stop there. Conversations heated up and became belligerent, then aggressive, to where the two blamed even her for their miseries of unjust existence. When April recognized the danger, it was too late. Practically foaming from their mouths, both of them had zoomed in on her with unfriendly intentions.

Trapped between the two bullies, fearful at what was about to happen, she screamed out loud while trying to escape the tent. What ensued next was a petrifying but also sobering experience that would remain with her forever. One stepped up to block the tent exit. The other reached out with one hand to cover her mouth and wrapped his other arm around her body, while his buddy pulled up her legs, tossing her defenseless body onto the sleeping bag. She desperately struggled, trying to fend them off, but was overpowered. Both raped her, not only once, but several times over, until her body and mind slipped into unconsciousness.

Tattered, bruised over most of her body, and in pain, she regained consciousness hours later only to find the tent empty. Inspecting her body for damage, she blamed herself for inviting the brutes into her tent, outraged at the unjust means by which her hospitality had been repaid.

While rape was not an isolated act within the homeless, she had never thought it would happen to her. Outraged, she swore revenge on the two, screaming into the empty space of the tent, "I'll kill you both!"

April, at the time, did not realize the psychological damage the two had done to her. A trusting person until now, the event shaped her attitude towards men. Her mind became hardened, not only for warding off potential rapists, but also for getting even with the injustice inflicted on her and other defenseless women. She developed an aggressive attitude towards men, dwelling on the thought of retaliating someday. Her time for that would come soon enough.

Her thoughts touched on Eric frequently. She even blamed him for the rape and rightly so. It would have never happened with him by her side. It served her as warning to be careful and to have better awareness of her environment. It was also a time when she lost confidence in drifters, which was practically every homeless. "Who can I trust?" and "How do I protect myself?" became two important elements in her life.

As luck had it, one day, while strolling along the waterfront, she came across a few individuals seemingly behaving strangely on the beach. Fascinated, she watched them display their skills. It was not the ordinary calisthenics and gymnastics, the only form she knew. It was more of a fighting style unfamiliar to her. She had moved closer to get a better perspective when the one giving instructions walked up to her with a smile. "Why don't you join us?"

April hesitated, stuttering in her reply. "I can't do this."

"I'll teach you. See them?" he said, with a gesture at the group. "They are my students." He gave her a few seconds to make up her mind.

Hesitatingly, she finally said, "I'll do it." What made her decide were memories of the rape and her inability to ward off the aggressors. "How come you are practicing out in the open?" she asked. It seemed highly peculiar to her.

"Fresh air, open spaces, soft ground, beach to cool off. How can you beat that?"

"Clever."

"We are almost finished for today," he informed her. "Come back tomorrow morning and join the class, 8:00 a.m."

"I promise," she said, intrigued at the possibility of learning what he'd called martial arts, Taekwondo, specifically. Looking around to get her bearings, she recognized the beach as Crissy Fields. "By the way," she said before departing, "what's your name?"

"Hideyoshi. But you can call me Kendo."

"Kendo?"

"It's Japanese for 'sword fighter.'"

On joining the group, getting a taste for close combat, April was not much intrigued by the martial arts, but felt charmed by Kendo. It inspired her to keep coming back. Before long they started dating. Life, as difficult as it had been for her for many years, seemed to take on a more pleasant direction. Introverted since childhood, she took on a more assertive character, at times turning aggressive when called upon. It was a characteristic somewhat out of place within her community. It seemed that homeless people did not take to aggression. Their behavior was predominantly docile with a persistent characteristic when it came to begging. She kept her acquired skills to herself.

RESTLESS TIMES

More time passed without hearing from her beloved Eric. While the memories of the broken-up relationship faded with time, it still emerged as a vivid experience. Her friendship with Kendo slowly replaced the pain and emptiness she had felt after Eric's sudden departure. Unfortunately, there was one difference: Kendo did not offer a personal relationship and involvement. It may have been his upbringing in the Japanese culture that prevented the natural progression from friendship into intimacy. She struggled with it, but accepted the current distance in their relationship. The thing that bothered her was the homeless status Kendo categorized her as. "You are a homeless person," he would insist. She tried to understand but kept hoping he would someday adjust his attitude to eventually accept her as an equal partner.

The unfortunate part was, she had to revert to begging again. It was something that really bothered her after having experienced the taste of independence living with Eric. He had made her feel important regardless of her inadequacy in cultural aspects. While they lived out in the open by choice, protected only by the fabric of the tent, it was not the homeless state many drifters experienced. It was more of an adventure for them both. Unfortunately, it was part of the past for which she yearned.

Although she felt strong in body and mind after gaining a superior physical strength instilled through Kendo's training, her mind was struggling against a meaningful purpose. "Will I ever achieve a normal life?" she pondered. Having been accepted as bonafide homeless within her society, common citizen status might be something elusive forever. It bothered her like never before since she had acquired a taste for an orderly, accepted semi-social structure. It also confused her to the point of posing the question frequently: "What will become of me?"

"What's the matter?" Kendo said one day. He must have sensed her troubled state of mind. "Something bothering you?"

"May I be honest with you?" she said, but did not exactly know how to confront him.

"Of course. That's the basis for our relationship, isn't it?"

"Why don't you accept me into your heart?" It must have sparked an unexpected reaction. She could see his discomfort with it.

He remained silent for a minute then reluctantly answered her question. "You see," he offered hesitantly. "In my country, the homeless are outcasts from society."

That, she understood. "Same as in this country."

"But we are different. My family and friends will never accept you. You will always be a stranger, unworthy of society."

April was shocked. She did not expect his bold response. As a result, her mind kept churning with guilt. After composing herself, her thoughts went through an emotional rollercoaster ride from feeling inadequate as a person to anger at an unjust fate dealt to her at birth, and on to fury for being rejected as a wholesome person.

She brought up enough courage to ask, "Is it your whole country that feels this way?"

"Yes. Everybody. So you see," he explained, "you and I have no future together."

The revelation shattered her trust in humans along with tearing at the self-esteem she'd acquired through Kendo's training. What April did not know was the difference in cultural heritage between Japan and the U.S.[18] Kendo's revelation did not sit well with April. "But," she protested, "you live in this country."

---

[18] Whereas America is a fairly recent frontier country, Japan has a rich dynastic past based on Asian heritage. In addition, Japan, being a Pacific island, had itself completely isolated for thousands of years from the rest of the world. It is this isolation that not only formed the island's colorful culture with its disciplined customs, but also a strict conformance to its traditional laws, practiced unchallenged until well into the 1900s.

He seemed to consider her explanation, but still insisted, "We have strong family ties that cannot be broken. Sorry."

"Where does that leave us?" she demanded.

"You can always be my student," he offered, avoiding her stare.

"Not good enough," she said, then muttered, "I can't live through another rejection." It would be their last day together. She quit the club and bade him a final goodbye. "Men," she said, "just cannot commit to a relationship." It was another bitter breakup but she had initiated it this time. She did not feel as rejected and hurt as she had with Eric.

Back at her tent, though nothing had changed since she'd left earlier, it seemed empty to her. "I need a drink," she said, unsure if she would go through with the decision. Seeking out the cooler where Eric had kept his stash containing booze, drugs, and pot, she needed to test her strength. Removing the lid, she stared at the bottle of Bourbon, still unopened.

"Should I?" she asked herself, unable to make up her mind. It would be a test of courage for April over body and mind to determine if she had inherited her mom's alcohol-prone genes. "I've got to do something," she decided and opened the bottle. With her confidence in people pretty much gone, she poured herself a cup. April had tasted hard alcohol a couple of times but had rejected the liquid as revolting. Now, taking her first real sip felt different. It was a warming feeling. "Not bad," she determined. "Not bad at all." *No wonder people take to this stuff,* she thought, inspecting the label. "Jack Daniel – Black," it indicated. "Smooth as silk," she admitted.

April, as inexperienced as she was in alcoholic products, at this moment tasted one of the most refined and smoothest Kentucky bourbons produced.

Feeling the soothing warmth of alcohol running through her veins gave her an instant feeling of companionship. Minutes later she felt much better about the loneliness in the tent and herself as well. She poured another cup, then another, and did not remember when and how she passed out. The morning sun was shining into the opening of the tent entrance April had overlooked zipping close.

"Damn," April moaned as soon as she opened her eyes. Tossing and turning, it took her a minute to get her bearings. "Head feels like exploding. What happened?" It took another minute for her to put distorted fragments of time from the previous evening together before her memory was back. At first, she felt somewhat euphoric about having survived the test of drunkenness, but it did not last long. Putting two and two together, reality set in quick with an overwhelming feeling of guilt. She realized that she had broken her steadfast promise to never touch hard liquor. The feeling prevailed through the day, and she was not sure what to expect come evening. She was petrified at the thought of following in her mom's footsteps of becoming an alcoholic. She felt she needed to talk with someone if only to take her mind away from the thought, but realized that there was nobody she could consult with to share her deep concerns.

Finding herself without a trustworthy friend was a revelation that added to her frustration. Seeking out a psychologist never occurred to her since she was ignorant of their profession and to the extent of any benefit. Desperate for company, that evening she sought out her favorite place which she and Eric used to frequent with friends.

As soon as she entered the club, she was recognized. "Look who just walked in," someone shouted, waving her to the bar.

"Where have you been?" another said. "We missed you. Where's Eric?"

Smiling at the invitations to join, she quickly sobered when the name Eric was brought up. She did not know how to effectively respond and stammered, "He left me."

"What do you mean he left?" one said, shaking his head in disbelief. They all thought their relationship was as solid as any of them.

"He's gone and won't come back."

"But why?" another friend asked.

"He needed space." It sort of quieted the inquisition.

"Where're you staying?" another friend, a woman, reaching out for April, wanted to know. She warmed up to her since April had not spent any time in recent months in the company of a woman.

"He left me the tent."

"Come," the friend said, waving at the bartender. "I'll buy you a drink."

"I can't. I shouldn't," April protested.

"It'll make you feel better."

April had never shared her sworn secret with anyone and was not sure how a repeat of the night before would affect her. She refused, but the drink was already served in front of her. *Maybe one drink won't hurt,* she thought and took a sip. To her surprise, the headache she'd suffered all day dissolved within minutes. It gave her some confidence about accepting another drink when her friend offered.

"Feeling better?"

"I sure do."

"What are you going to do now since Eric is gone? By the way," her friend said, "where did he go?"

"Canadian wilderness."

"That explains it," she offered. "He seemed to be a loner. You know, independent."

"That he was," April agreed, saddened. "I'm glad you people are still here. Don't know what I'd do without you."

"You always know where to find us," her friend said and ordered another drink. The numbing effects of alcohol had already taken hold of April. She felt pretty much the same as the previous evening, inebriated after taking in several more drinks during the evening. It was close to midnight when the party broke up, with everybody bidding goodbye with promises to meet again soon.

"How can I get in touch with you?" April asked her friend. "I don't have a phone."

"I'll stop by your tent. Okay?"

"Anytime you feel like it," were April's departing words.

Feeling happy and drunk she staggered back towards The Hill, glad she'd left her bike at home. She would have been unable to ride or even push it back. In the old homeless days situations like this would have been handled differently. Decisions were made on the spot without considering personal implications and concerns. She would have dropped her body along one of the store fronts to sleep off the alcohol effects. In the morning, someone would have given her a slight kick in the side to wake her up and chase her off.

This evening, it would take April fifteen minutes to reach The Hill. Staggering drunk she arrived and could not remember where she'd left the tent. It was gone. All she found was a bare spot on the grass the size of the tent. "What…" she stammered, looking around the place for an answer, but there was only darkness pressing in on her.

It was such a shocking experience, she sobered up immediately. Disoriented with the tent gone, April found herself lost beyond comprehension. Her mind was racing for an answer that did not materialize. Flashes of the past were taking on shapes, switching between Eric and Kendo, homing in on her early years. Having lost everything she owned once again became a revelation she could not handle at this moment in time. "I've become Mom."

HOMELESS AGAIN

Trapped in the dark, penniless, destitute and impoverished with only the clothes she wore, April cussed out Eric for deserting her, Kendo for being a traditional egotist, Mom for giving birth to her, and society for rejecting the homeless. Her initial anger soon turned into pity for herself, seeking for answers. There were none. The night shadows remained silent. With the effects of the alcohol completely worn off by this time, she sat on the bare ground, huddled into a nameless being. She probably would have ended her misery if she'd had access to a weapon or enough drugs on hand to overdose.

Chilled to the bone, staring at the sky, hoping for an answer, April felt at a loss to take any action. She didn't know how much time had passed when a voice entered her mind. "What's the matter with you? Are you sick?"

At first she thought it was her mind responding to her silent prayers. She opened her eyes and stared at a person stooped low to the ground, inspecting her. Hearing the stranger's words triggered her pent-up emotions into action. April began to sob. Any homeless person that comes across the unexpected situation of a sobbing person can relate to the emotional pain. Unless the stranger has malicious intentions to begin with, they feel compassion. Such was the case here.

"What are you doing out in the night alone?" He patiently waited for an answer, reaching into his pocket and offering her a tissue. In between sniffling and wiping her eyes dry, she muttered, "Somebody took my home."

"Home?" He did not understand her. "Where's your home?"

"Here," she said, still sputtering. "It used to be here."

"The tent?" He, like other people passing The Hill, were well aware of the tent and its occupant. He began to understand her situation. "What happened?"

"Somebody stole it and all my things. There is nothing left. I am homeless and broke."

The night had turned silent once again when he said, "Why don't you come with me? I can put you up for the night."

He sounded sincere and she considered the offer. "Where're we going?"

"It looks like you could use a drink."

She immediately reacted. "No drink. I hate alcohol." Her current problem was directly connected to alcohol. "I don't drink. Not anymore."

"Okay. No drinks, but let me help you out anyway."

"That's what you guys always say but nobody ever means it."

He began to understand her plight. "Bitter," he muttered.

"What?" She did not understand his meaning.

"Nothing. What do you want to do? You can't stay here all night."

"It's not the first time I've slept out in the open."

"I just want to help," he said.

"I appreciate your offer but I don't know you. What's your name, anyway?"

"Greg. And yours?"

"April."

"Pretty name," he said with an outstretched hand. Shaking his hand she accepted. "You're freezing." He'd noticed her shaking body. "Let me take you someplace to warm up."

"Okay."

He checked his watch and suggested, "I know a place that's still open." He led her in the direction of Beach Street.

"Where're we going?"

"Jack's Place," he said. "It's open all night."

"I know. Everybody's favorite place." She was beginning to feel like a normal person again. Striding alongside Greg, she glanced at him, thinking, *He looks sincere.* Regardless of the current situation, April knew it would be some time before she would ever regain complete trust for any man.

Twenty minutes and ten blocks later, they stepped into Jack's[19] Place. As usual it was crowded with visitors, but they managed to find an empty spot at the bar. *Not an ideal place for a date*, Greg thought, getting seated, *if that's what it is.*

Taking in the warmth within the lively atmosphere of the place, April had similar thoughts. *Table would be better, but it'll do.* She did not have any future plan for them other than getting through the night and worrying about what place she would eventually wind up. To find out she'd have to get to know Greg and his intentions. For now, she enjoyed the tall glass of orange juice he'd ordered for her.

"So," Greg initiated the conversation, "how did you wind up living on The Hill?" He purposely did not mention the tent for it'd imply April was a homeless person.

"I inherited it from a friend." Watching Greg's inquisitive face, she explained further, "He left for the Canadian Wilderness."

"An adventurer?"

"You might call him that." April purposely stayed away from talking about her failed relationships because they were the reasons for her present situation. She shelved her past, for now happy to be in the company of a person, any person. Greg seemed to be a sincere person. *But they all are at first,* she thought, glancing at his profile seated next to her. Because of her unfortunate childhood, failed relationships, and relative inexperience with men, April decided to keep her distance from all further involvements. Although she sensed a certain interest

---

[19] Jack's Cannery Bar is the place to go, for tourists as well as locals. Conveniently located near Fisherman's Wharf, during daytime it offered the visitor an outdoor seating garden set within the Cannery complex. At night it is packed with visitors from all parts of the globe. A historic place established in 1863 during the Gold Rush, set in the decor of those days, it was unique in that it offered a rich veriety of beer brands from around the world ready to tap.

he had in her, she decided to enjoy life on her own for the moment, consequently keeping their conversation casual by avoiding personal questions. For now, she did not care much about his past and ignored any present intentions he might have had for her.

He must have sensed her frame of mind. "You don't talk much?"

Again, she avoided any specifics, and said, "It's been a rough night."

"I'm sorry. I forgot." He sounded sincere. "What do you want to talk about?"

"Anything. I am a great listener." She purposely put the burden of conversation on him. Hardly aware of his presence, she let him talk for much of the time while her mind was torn in different directions. She still grieved for Eric and many times wondered about him, hoping he would come back. Her friendship with Kendo was over. She'd stopped going to the dojo to attend his classes. She tried to continue but felt uncomfortable in his presence after receiving a taste of his prejudice. It was better this way. Working out in his class afterwards proved to be too distracting.

"You still awake?" she heard the voice penetrating her wandering mind. It reminded her that she was in Greg's company.

"Sorry," she said, excusing her indifference. "I have too much on my mind.

"I can understand that," Greg said attentively, "losing all of your belongings. What are you going to do?"

"I don't know yet. I can't think with the people around us." Although it was past midnight, the place was alive with conversations and laughter from inebriated guests.

"You want to leave?"

"I should, but don't know where to go," she said, seeking out his face.

"You can stay with me until we figure out something." It seemed he was sincere in his offer.

She accepted. "I appreciate it very much. I won't be a burden, I promise."

"I know," he replied. "I'll take care of the bill." She followed him to the register, where he promptly paid on the way out.

"Where do you live?"

"I'm renting a flat on Mason and Lombard. You'll like the view I have." Though he kept talking, she followed quietly on their way to his place. After stepping into his apartment, located on the top floor of a six-story building, as indicated, the view from his balcony was spectacular, and she said so.

"It's a small place but it's got the view to die for," he agreed.

"Is that Alcatraz Island straight out?" she said, pointing in that direction.

"It is. Over here is Treasure Island, and over there you can see Angel Island and Tiburon."

"Yeah. I recognize the shoreline. I envy people like you."

"The view?"

"It's something you don't see from the ground."

"Right. I don't have an extra room for you but you can bunk on the couch for the night," he offered.

She hesitated, then said, "If you don't mind, I'd rather stay out here."

"The balcony?"

"Yes. I like the outdoors and fresh air. Besides," she said, "I love to see the stars."

"No wonder you lived in a tent."

"I don't know what I'm gonna do without it yet."

"You can stay here as long as you like," he offered.

"I won't intrude into your life as long as you share the balcony with me. I promise."

"Friends?" he offered, extending his hand.

"Friends," she accepted, shaking it. She remained while he stepped inside the apartment. Minutes later he came back, loaded down with pillows and blankets, "Here," he offered. "Pillows and blanket, also got a sleeping bag for you."

"You are too much. I really appreciate you helping me out."

"I know you do. Anything else you may need?"

"Restroom."

"Of course," he offered, showing her the place. "Use it any time and the kitchen as well."

"Thanks. You're kind."

"I'm gonna turn in now," he said. "I'll make breakfast in the morning. Sleep tight."

"Night. Thank you so much." She was alone on the balcony. Bedding down in the open felt like old times to her, though there was one difference between the loft and the ground: she felt safe.

SHARED MISERY

"Good morning," April said, stretching her arms into the air as she stepped from the balcony into the kitchen. It seemed Greg was busy preparing breakfast, as promised.

"How do you feel?" he greeted her with a smile.

"Great. Just great. Haven't slept this late in ages."

"Have a seat." He gestured at the table. Though there were two chairs on the table she noticed only one serving plate.

"It'll be another minute," he said while she watched him by the stove. It gave her time to look around the room. The only thing she spotted was a clock prominently mounted against one wall. The rest of the walls were empty. "You just move here?"

"No. I've lived in this place for almost a year. I took over the lease from a buddy."

"He left town?"

"Not exactly," he stated. "San Quentin. It's his home for now."

April was taken by surprise. She had not expected to get involved with criminals, not now, not ever. It had always been her policy to maintain her freedom from social bonds whether voluntary or forced. Although she rejected government rules and regulations, aside from minor infractions for loitering, she'd always managed to stay clear of the law.

"What happened?"

"He got caught too many times selling drugs."

"How much time is he serving?"

"Three years, but he talked about the possibility of parole."

"He must be behaving. Do you ever see him?"

"Not lately. He doesn't like visitors." Greg changed the topic. "What are your immediate plans?"

"I haven't made any yet but will figure something out."

"Do you have any friends or family?"

"I used to, but my mom died years ago and the friends I had left town."

Greg stepped from the stove to serve her the breakfast plate containing hash browns topped with eggs and bacon on the side. "As I promised last night, you can stay here as long as you like."

"By the way," she said, slightly surprised at there being only one table service, "you're not eating?"

"I don't eat breakfast. I'm not hungry in the morning. Just have some coffee."

April thought it peculiar but did not reply. She enjoyed the freshly brewed mug of coffee he'd served. "Look," she said with sincerity, seeking out his face. "I really appreciate the offer but the place is kind of small for two people, don't you think? I don't want to cramp you."

"Did you sleep well out there?" he asked with a gesture at the balcony.

"Better than expected."

"Then you can stay. Are you working?"

"I'm not."

"Do you plan to get a job?"

"I was working on a book."

"You write?"

"Not exactly. I'm a photographer working on a photo album, but everything was lost—album, camera, and photos."

"What are you going to do?"

"I did some homeless work for City Hall."

"You think you'll get the job back?"

"I'll sure try. Don't have much job skills. What about you?"

"I'm a drifter. I promised to take care of this place for my buddy until he gets out. Don't know what will happen after."

"So," she surmised, "you are homeless."

"That's me."

They remained silent for a time before she said, "Me too."

"What. Homeless?"

"That's right. I used to live on the streets until my friend took me into his tent."

Greg had a spontaneous moment. He cracked up laughing, then chuckled. "Homelessness seems to be the trend."

It was not funny to her. "It may be trendy for some, but for me," she explained, "I was forced into when Mom died."

"I'm sorry to hear that."

To April's surprise, she and Greg had mostly pleasant times while she stayed with him. Sure, it was cramped in the flat, but each had their privacy when needed. April enjoyed her time on the balcony whenever they got tired of talking, sharing stories until overtaken with sleep. During waking hours, when she was tired of looking for work, both would stroll along sidewalks, with him stopping to chat with homeless friends and her quietly listening. There was not much she could contribute to any of Greg's conversations with his friends, spoken in the customary homeless lingo of short-sentenced dialogue. What she did notice was that he and his friends would frequently step into a quiet corner or seek privacy away from her.

She wondered about it but kept quiet until days later when he did not return. She kept waiting for an hour then decided to visit the piers on her own. Expecting the happy barking of seals, she was surprised when the place was quiet. It was the time of year seals spent out in the oceans, seeking a new mate, Eric had informed her years ago. They did not return for months, until the fall. She missed them, suddenly feeling deserted. It gave her time to assess her life. "What am I doing here, clinging to the past?"

It was not a joyful revelation. Saddened, it made her ponder the future. "What am I going to do?" She had no answer other than a distant yearning for Eric. "I wonder what he's doing?"

Life had become empty for April. Observing passing tourists did not cheer her up either. April realized that she needed someone by her side. It would have to be a permanent relationship. She had given up looking for a job days ago. She realized that without a skill it was a discouraging effort. "Nothing at the moment," and "We'll call you," were the customary replies she'd received, despite the job notices placed in storefront windows.

Her mind came up blank, searching for a solution. The only answer was going back to begging again since Greg did not have the means of supporting her. From what she saw, he could barely manage to support his own needs. She wondered about that, but did not press him since he had been kind enough to take her into his flat when she was desperate.

For now, April decided to just live for the moment, no matter how wasteful the day might turn out to be. With a reluctant sigh, she held out her hand, begging for money much like she had for most of her life. It did not take long before a passerby had pity on her and pressed a dollar bill into her empty hand. She was in business once more. From this day forward, she and Greg mostly went their own ways and only saw each other close to bed time. He was gracious enough to have a duplicate key made that allowed her to come and go without having to wait for him. For the time being, she managed, hoping for a better time.

April did not have to wait long. It came in the form of Greg's friend, who had been released early from San Quentin for good behavior. He showed up at the flat early in the morning, not very happy after he'd learned about April moving in. He pulled Greg aside into the bedroom for a private conversation. Minutes later, Greg emerged with bad news for April. "You cannot stay here any longer. He wants the apartment back. We have to move in the morning."

April was devastated, and Greg was not happy either. "Where do you want to go?" April asked him the following morning, undecided about what direction to take. While he was loaded down with a backpack filled with daily necessities from the earlier days, she stood there bare-handed and forlorn with only the clothes on her back.

"Let's try Castro. That's always been the nicest place in town."

Both agreed on the direction. It would take them close to an hour to walk across town. Quiet for most of the way, neither talked much other than about how nice of a view they'd lost and brief complaints about getting booted out from the flat. Though they could have begged Greg's friend to put them up, the place would have been too crowded for comfort all around. It would not have worked, and both were grateful for the time they had enjoyed the flat.

"Ever been to the Castro District?" April asked.

"Sure," Greg said. "A number of times, but not as a homeless."

"You didn't like it?"

"I liked it."

"You don't sound very optimistic," she remarked.

"It's not that. Castro is a nice part of town. The problem is that it's mostly residential and people don't like drifters."

"I heard different."

"Do tell," he said in anticipation.

"From what I've heard," she explained, "the whole district is nothing but drifters."

"It's true," he admitted. "But that was way back in the '60s, generations ago. Those are all retired baby boomers now. They don't want to deal with their own kind like when they were young. The Woodstock culture created the Castro."

"Then," she said, "why are we headed there?"

"To check it out. The Mission is getting too crowded, from what I've seen. Besides," he explained, "we can always move there if we get kicked out. It's right next to the Castro District."

Striding along Filmore Street for most of the trip, they walked mostly uphill until they reached Broadway. A couple of blocks later the path descended towards Market Street, making walking more enjoyable. As they got close to the Castro District, the scene drastically changed from business to residential.

Along the streets, brightly-colored rainbow banners fluttered from lamp posts and flagpoles, welcoming visitors to the Castro. The historic center of the LGBT (Lesbian, Gay, Bi-sexual, Transgender) community reflects a vibrant neighborhood popular with young families, tech workers, and the artist community, and is filled with popular boutiques, bars, and restaurants attracting a wide circle of patrons.

Greg kept elaborating on the district's high points while they were strolling along.

"As you can see," he went on, "vintage trolleys ply the F-Line all the way from Fisherman's Wharf." Passing by the intersection of Market and Castro Streets, they saw Twin Peaks Tavern, a historic landmark and symbolic gateway to this district, the first known gay bar to have floor-to-ceiling windows, indicating that the gay scene was now proudly connected to mainstream lifestyles.

Greg did his best to educate April about historic accounts in the city. "Near the geographical center of San Francisco's two hills, known as Twin Peaks and rising to 925 feet, Castro offers one of the city's best views. The windy summit is usually approached by car and those with hiking shoes." Visitors will learn that the undeveloped peaks are about appreciating native vegetation, hardy florals, sparrow, brush rabbits and the rare Mission butterfly. "There's one basic restroom up there, but no warming hut or coffee canteen. However, it is a spectacular view on a clear day and a treasure trove of nature.

"As the sun dips low, happy hour begins and the Castro comes alive. Among dozens of diverse spots are the city's first and only gay sports bar, Hi Tops; a famous karaoke piano lounge, The Mint; a neighborhood bar with a view, DJs; a drag queen show, The Lookout; a rocker bar with a jukebox, pinball machine and pool table, Lucky 13; and former speakeasy with nightly live music, Café du Nord.

"I could live here," April said, approving of the place.

"We'll find out come morning," Greg admitted somewhat reluctantly.

"You don't sound excited," April said.

"Look around. I haven't noticed any homeless and tents. They may not want us here," he replied.

"You saw the clubs we passed. We should spend the night."

"You're right. It's about the only place people have money. I didn't see many stores along the way."

"Castro it is," April agreed.

Since neither had any sleeping accommodations, propped against Greg's backpack next to the last night spot, the speakeasy, they put the place to the test. "Here we are," Greg said, "for better or for worse."

Surprisingly, considering the limited customer base the street provided, their first night begging went well. Patrons, though slightly surprised at the two beggars, came and went after hours of having fun at the place, dropping a few dollars into either April or Greg's outstretched hand. Both kept switching positions next to the exit door, with only one doing the begging. "Where're you from?" some exiting the place would enquire.

"Just passing through," April would reply. Though not exactly telling the truth, it would pacify the locals since neither Greg nor she were in a tattered condition.

Like most places in the city, the clubs closed by 2:00 am. There was always a last-minute rush to catch a cab, with many patrons signifying the end of a night filled with fun and pleasure. It also ended their unexpected windfall in earnings. "Let's see how much we made," Greg said, pulling his share from his pockets. When pooled together, surprisingly, their combined intake was well over one hundred dollars. "The most I've ever made," April cheered enthusiastically.

"Me too," Greg agreed. "Want to split?"

"Sounds good to me. Now where to?" April said, leaving Greg to decide.

"I'm hungry," he said, rubbing his belly. "Want to get something to eat?"

"I don't see any place open," April said, looking for store signs. The residential setting had become obvious. There were no fast food places in the area.

"We could go to the Mission," April suggested. Although it was only five blocks away, both were too tired. "Tell you what," he suggested. "Let's find a spot to settle for the night and have breakfast in the morning." April agreed. They picked the first dark space along one of the buildings to rest their bodies. "Here." He offered her a spare sweater from his backpack, then zipped up the jacket he wore.

Resting their heads on the backpack, despite the loss of the flat, both were content with the way things had turned out on their first day living in the open again. Both admired the familiar star formations clearly projected against the dark night. Within minutes both were sound asleep.

"April. April." The voice seeped into her dreams, accompanied by the image of Eric. "Eric!" She clung to the scene for some time, then realized it was only a dream when prodded in the ribs.

"You're dreaming." Greg was staring at her. "Who is Eric?"

Fully awake now, there was another pair of eyes staring at her. "Police," the uniformed woman proclaimed. She then demanded, "Get up, you can't sleep here. This is private property."

April stood upright to get her bearings, then remembered the place she and Greg had found refuge the night before. "Sorry," she apologized to the police captain. "It was dark."

The captain, though adamant but with an understanding smile, insisted that she and Greg vacate the spot. "You are homeless?"

"Yes. Since yesterday," April said. "We lost our apartment. It wasn't our fault."

"I've seen you before," the captain said, studying April's face. "At my precinct."

"I don't remember," April said in her defense.

"A couple of years ago. You spent the night in jail. Now I remember. Several times. You were homeless then. You're still homeless."

"I wasn't for two years. I had a home on The Hill."

"You're the one in the Tent?"

"That was me and my friend."

"What happened? Why did you leave? You were licensed to live there."

"The tent was stolen, but I met Greg here," she said with a gesture at him, who had been quietly listening.

"Now I remember," the captain said. "You and your friend worked with the mayor at City Hall. What ever happened? Why did you quit?"

"The mayor let us go. Didn't think he'd need us anymore."

"Well," the captain said. "I appreciated the work you did, but things didn't solve the homeless problem. As a matter of fact," she said, slightly scornful, "it got worse. They are much more aggressive now. My department has a difficult time controlling their influx. They seem to take over every district in the city."

"So we've heard," April agreed. "That's why we came to the Castro and not the Mission."

"You can't stay in this district. I got several calls this morning about you."

"But," April objected, "all the people living here were homeless."

"Yeah," the captain agreed. "But that was in the '60s. A long time ago. Now, most own a home and many have retired."

"We have no money and needed a place to stay," April said. "Where should we go?"

"A homeless shelter," was the reply. "At least you'll have a roof over your head at night. I've got to go." The captain took another call on her portable radio. "Bye now, and good luck to the both of you."

Both watched her drive off in a squad car.

"Wow," Greg said with an admiring grin on his face. "I've never seen such friendly contact with the police. I could use you as my personal negotiator." Both laughed at the thought.

"The San Francisco police have always been friendly with us," April explained. "They are good people."

"I can see that," Greg admitted. "So, we have nothing to be afraid of. Let's find a breakfast place. The Mission?"

"Lead on." April was highly disappointed about having to leave this place. "It's so quiet here," she remarked, "don't you think so?"

"Shame we got kicked out. I could live here," he agreed. "No wonder that the hippies took to this place."

"I agree." They left the same way they had arrived the day before, on foot, but encouraged once more for facing an uncertain future.

MORE HARDSHIP

April and Greg headed for the Mission District, her former homeless turf. Aside from the familiarity of the place, it provided access to shelters and stores for the homeless. Their first stop was the Salvation Army, a popular place for free clothes. If that did not have the right styles and sizes, an alternative would be the rescue mission or a specific homeless store. They visited all three places to pick up shoes, socks, underwear and shirts, a necessity both needed. Socks seemed to be a popular item among homeless. They wore out first from daily walking. Next was footwear.

They lucked out on this item. Both were able to pick out a fitting pair of Nikes, a coveted commodity. Regardless of a homeless' state of depravation, most embraced the sense of status above anything else. A substitute for a fashion brand might be an overcoat, needed for cold days. As long as it provided warmth, wear, size, and condition did not matter much.

"You ready to get out of here?" Greg said, sleeping bag and blanket slung over his shoulder.

"I've got everything I needed." April said, her purchase bundled up and ready for fighting off weather elements.

"Mission it is," Greg said, leading the way. Much like in recent years, Mission Street was as packed with homeless as ever.

"There are more people here than I remember," April said, shaking her head in wonder. "What do you think?"

"You're right. It looks that way." They walked past what appeared much like a metropolitan inner city, but this one was nothing but tents occupying every vacant spot on both sides of streets. City traffic was forced to share their space with pedestrians, indicated by the constant blasts of car horns expressing their dislike.

"I don't know," April said. "Should we find another place?"

Even Greg had his concerns. "Let's spend the day here. We can always find another location tomorrow. We might get some information."

"What about over there?" April suggested, indicating an empty spot.

"Public restroom," Greg objected. The vacant spot was right next to the public facility, obviously too busy for bunking comfort. "Guess one night will do." Since they did not have to set up a tent, he thought, *It'll be easy to get up and move.*

Gazing at the sky, trying to locate familiar star formations, both sought comfort in their sleeping bags. "I can hardly make out a zodiac," April complained. "Too much light."

"And too much noise," Greg agreed. Nightlife in the tent city was prolific. Occupants came and went for most of the night. It was not until dawn that the place somewhat calmed for a couple of hours. Early sleepers were ready to face a new day as soon as the sun came up. Late sleepers bunked until the effects of drugs and alcohol wore off. Despite the night's activity, both eventually dozed off.

"Hey, you." April was torn from sleep by a voice directed at her. She opened her eyes to stare at the stranger pushing her shoulder.

"What?" she said, rubbing her eyes.

"I know you," the stranger said. "You're the one who caused it all."

"What?" she repeated, not understanding.

"That," he said, waving his arm around the crowded area. "I remember you working with City Hall."

Greg was up by her side and said, "You can't blame her. She was only trying to help you people."

"What do you mean by 'you people,'" the homeless, slightly angered by the implication, objected. "You're homeless."

"That's true, but we don't cause problems. We are peace-loving folks."

April nodded at Greg in agreement, happy he had stood up for them. She did not like the present situation. "Let's get out of here." She sensed danger and feared that she might lose yesterday's acquired property again.

"Not so fast," the agitator said. "It's you that caused all this mess."

"You better explain," Greg said, confronting him. "I don't like being accused of wrongdoings."

"You'd better get used to it," the agitator insisted. "These people here don't like you being here," he shouted into the crowd gathering around, curious about the confrontation.

"Let's not fight," Greg insisted.

"Ever since your work at City Hall," he said with a gesture at April, "things have gotten worse. Hell," he insisted, "it's getting so packed you can't even find an empty space anymore. Just look around."

"And another thing," a bystander added. "All the soup kitchens are closing."

Greg took a step back, insisting, "You can't blame her. She tried her best to better homeless life."

"Just look what you did," the agitator insisted, closing in on them.

"Enough," Greg said, raising both of his hands, then stepped in front of April to protect her. He realized that they were not welcome here. "Let's go." Expecting more hostilities, he reached down to pick up his sleeping bag and blanket, ready to retreat when he received an unexpected blow to the head. Disoriented, rubbing his forehead, he'd been momentarily stunned.

April stepped in front of Greg, blocking any further advancement. "Don't do that again," she said with a threatening face. Though on the defense until now, anger had built when she realized that the homeless wanted blood. *They can have it,* she boldly thought, stepping in front of the agitator. The rest of the gathered were cheering at her.

A second later, she watched his body muscles react, indicating his intentions. Like in slow motion pictures, he stepped in to reach for her while she watched his right fist lunging at her face. To the amazement of the homeless, the aggressor landed on the ground on his back. Dumbfounded and dazed, he stared up at her in disbelief.

"Want more?" April hissed at him between clenched teeth, ready for another attack.

Sprawled on the ground, stunned and enraged at being punched by a woman, the agitator jumped to his legs and rushed at April again, yelling, "You dirty bitch."

Greg watched, shaking his head in wonder. He was as stunned as the homeless gathered around.

Five rushing steps later, the attacker was stopped short with a kick to his head, the preferred defense of a Taekwondo fighter.

Ready for a bout, April stood her ground, but there was no other attack. She had proven her point. "Don't mess with me."

That was the end of the fight. Rubbing his head, the attacker left the ground and so did Greg and April. Remaining here would have only agitated other homeless not sympathetic to their presence. "Sorry," April said to Greg in apology. "But he had it coming."

"Wow," Greg said in stunned admiration. "Where did you ever learn to fight?"

"I used to watch and take martial arts lessons years back."

"I'm glad you are on my side," he said. "That's all I have to say. You were terrific. Want to teach me some?"

"Any time. But not now. Let's find a better place." It took some thinking on both their parts to come up with an alternate location, hopefully not as hostile. "Can you think of another place?"

"No, but it has to be someplace they don't know you. I'd hate to have to protect you from attackers." Both cracked up laughing at his remark.

"Seriously," April said, somewhat sobering, "I can't figure out why they would hate me."

"I can only guess," Greg said with a chuckle. "You don't belong here."

What happened to the homeless culture she and Eric had so diligently tried to solve? It was a question both had on their minds. They had to figure it out. More pressing for now was finding a less hostile location. "What time do you think it is?" she asked.

Since neither of them had a watch, a quick glance at the sun was a general indicator. "I'm hungry," he said. Both realized how famished they were after skipping several meals. Headed towards Market Street, they knew where to find a place: Pier One, the Harborview.

The Harborview was a visitor's favorite eatery. With a spectacular view into the Bay and surrounding islands, the name justified the place. Although the place refused to serve the homeless, patrons dressed neatly with a clean appearance would be welcomed as long as they did not drive up in a shopping cart or unload large amounts of personal belongings. April and Greg spent several hours at the place without once being disturbed by patrons or management.

"The way I see it," April summed up their findings on the subject of the current 'homeless culture' they were trying to understand, "they're blaming me for failing to solve the problem."

"And the problem is?"

"Providing tax-free land for the homeless with easy access to public facilities. They don't want to be herded into a reservation, winding up in restricted living."

"That includes us, doesn't it?"

"I would think so. I wish it wasn't the case but the way my life has turned out, there is no alternative anymore." Although Greg and April had no firm attachment, they had become accustomed to each other, especially after today with her dishing out a lesson to remember.

"So," Greg said, to be clear, "we are back to join the homeless culture permanently?"

"I need a drink," April said, to the surprise of Greg.

"And I need a smoke," he suggested.

"We still need a place," April said.

"Let's try Forest Hill."

"Too residential. No tourists there. Besides, I prefer the shore."

"How about Crissy Fields?"

"We'll get chased off."

"What about The Hill?"

"Yeah." That was something for April to consider. "Let's check it out. We could get a tent if the spot's still available. The Hill it is." She led the way.

HOMELESS SOLUTION

In 1983 when homelessness became a social issue, cities and towns began to address proposed solutions. San Francisco was no exception. Whatever proposal and proposition was eventually implemented did not seem to work out. As time went by, decades, the problem escalated into a serious draw on city and county budgets. It became urgent that something be done. By the mid-'90s, numerous solutions were introduced and instituted. Some met with success with others (most) ended in failure. The following is an example account of San Francisco that every other city and major town has already experienced, or will face in the future.

In many neighborhoods in today's San Francisco, one can watch a new tent city being set up by the homeless. As of 2003, tent cities have been growing prolifically, having been given the term "shame of the city." Worse yet, where in past decades America's homeless had been counted every two years, the city stopped counting permanently. Also, where only a couple decades ago homelessness was a novelty, mostly to travelers, today, it is looked upon as a pest the city cannot manage anymore.

As you travel the country, it seems that homelessness in San Francisco appears worse than in other megacities. Perhaps due to the mild climate all year around, the homeless are "sheltered" at much lower numbers with more people sleeping on the street.

Another factor may contribute to the figures. According to 2013 reports by *The San Francisco Chronicle* on homelessness in San Francisco, almost 40% of homeless suffer from mental illness, with the majority having depression and disorders like bipolar or schizophrenia, mostly caused through drugs and alcohol addictions.

When analyzing consensus reports on the growth of homelessness, initial thoughts relate the issue to poor economy and funding problems, hoping the homeless would return to their hometowns when the economy improved, but such was not the case. The homeless problem has become a chronic one with budget cuts to subsidized housing resulting in a migration to sidewalks in hordes. When asked why the homeless move to the streets, the answers are many, with complaints ranging from: not enough experience for a Silicon Valley high-tech job; no incentives for a future career; too expensive to rent an apartment or flat; lack of affordable housing; and many more.

Furthermore, people can be homeless and not visually appear as such. They may have jobs, attend schools and college, attend church and social gatherings, and may even wear suits to work. Regardless of cause or appearance, they all lack a home. While some homeless are willing to work, others are not.

"Where does one draw the line on supporting homelessness?" April questioned on many occasions without a hint of a solution. Her only solace was, "If a mayor and city council cannot come up with a solution, I surely don't have the answer."

If municipal budgets are not enough, alternative resources may become necessary, such as provisions for homeless children to attend public schools, homeless with mental health issues, seniors stranded in a society without family ties, single parents divorced or separated, individuals with disabilities, and retired military with drug-induced habits creating mental issues, to mention some.

But that's not all. There are homeless that enjoy homelessness for many reasons. When asked, a response may be: freedom from government oppression, personal liberty for free living, prolific social interaction, no responsibility to anyone else, no recourse for one's own actions, no schedules to keep, no meetings to attend, no superior to boss you around, freedom from confinements such as work places, family obligations, relationship pressure, child care, and more.

The truth of the matter is, most homeless have adopted the free-spirited way of homeless living. Once accustomed to its lifestyle, giving it up to confined living, government rules, and social regulations is not considered an option because the consequences are too great to adapt to.

For the reasons stated, homelessness has developed into a culture and the culture is permanent. What remains is a means to accept and manage homelessness effectively to live alongside structured society without causing a major burden to the average tax payer. We are already overtaxed as it is.

There is one more element to consider, an important one. Homelessness has increased in past decades for many reasons as stated. Where the homeless come from all kinds of walks and places, there is one sentiment all have in common, easily equated with the following example. Life, in its simplicity as it can be observed in many third world countries, may be poor and destitute as lived by many people, much like the homeless culture in the U.S. But, there is one thing they have in common: they don't trust the government. For this reason, those countries have formed what is known as family governments. It's this bond that provides families, friends, relatives, and local society within a relatively secure safety zone.

It did not take much time and imagination for the homeless to recognize their shortcomings. They quickly figured out that safety was provided by numbers which, in turn, developed into the culture we see today.

For April and Greg, it was these failed conditions and hurdles they had to overcome. But to do so, they must first be confronted. The first such hurdle came in a form neither liked very much. Anxiously approaching the familiar tent site on The Hill, their hopeful anticipation was instantly shattered when they read the sign. It was a city-enforced ordinance, stating:

City Property - No Trespassing!
Offenders will be prosecuted.

Reading the proclamation came as a shock. It instantly changed her attitude towards the city April so dearly loved. "What now?"

"How much money do you have?" Greg had an idea, but it would cost them.

"I'm down to a couple of bucks," April said, inspecting the measly bills she pulled from her pocket.

"Not enough. We'll have to beg, but then it'll be too late."

"Too late for what?" Her curiosity was aroused. Greg was usually straight forward with his answers.

"To buy tools."

It took a minute for April to put things into perspective, hoping it was not with criminal intentions. "Tools for what?"

"To break in."

Her fear took on reality. "I don't want to get involved with any criminal act."

"Don't worry," he said to pacify her concerns. "It's only for cutting a lock. We won't steal anything. We just need a place to stay the night."

"What place?"

"The yacht harbor. I've used it before a couple of times."

"We won't take anything. Promise."

"I promise. Let's get a cutter. I know a place."

Relieved of her fears, it seemed simple enough for her to support the action. For April, the biggest fear she had would be spending time in jail, or worse yet, a prison like San Quentin. She thought she would not survive in disciplined confinement very long.

Ten minutes later they entered a hardware store on Bay Street. "Greg!" The store clerk, a former homeless, cheered upon spotting his friend. "How have you been?"

"Sorry I haven't stopped by, but things have been hectic lately."

"I've heard. City is getting tough on you guys. I'm glad I don't have to deal with it anymore."

"How are things working out living in controlled society?" Greg was well aware that his friend used to be a homeless. Years ago when they'd met on Market Street, their sentiments about life had been similar. What changed was his friend meeting a girl he fell in love with. The problem was, she did not want any part of his homelessness. Presenting an ultimatum shortly after was enough for his friend to look for employment.

"What brings you here? Showing off your friend? Ready for society?"

"Not by a longshot, but I need a favor."

"You name it, you've got it," his friend replied.

"I need to borrow a pair of pliers."

"Not the yacht harbor?"

"We don't have a choice. Got kicked out of our apartment." It was his friend that had come up with the idea years ago when they were in need of a place to stay.

Greg's friend came back with a brand new cutter. "Here," he said, "this'll cut through any lock, deadbolt and padlock. Nothing will keep you out." "Don't get caught," were his departing words, "and don't be a stranger."

With lodging taken care of, Greg led the way. "Let's get some money. What's the best place for begging these days?"

"Pier 39. It's closest to the Basin," April suggested.

"Good. Let's go. I'm hungry."

The remainder of the day past quickly. The begging was rewarding and so were a couple of hamburgers to silent stomach and hunger pangs. Hunger pangs were nothing new to homeless. They were part of their unrestricted lives. What was more important than food were addictive choices. For one, it was easy to walk into a liquor store to fetch a bottle of cheap booze. Not so easy was getting an affordable drug fix. The heydays for psychedelic drugs like LSD at $2.00 a cube were long gone. In today's market, you better had $50 in cash to get enough quantity to keep one high for the night.

"Keep your voice down," Greg cautioned April, who did her best to suppress her silly giggling. She was still inebriated from the alcohol she had consumed during their evening of celebration. Earlier, on arriving at the pier, April cheerfully mentioned that today was her birthday. She was slightly surprised to even remember the day. To her, it had never been a milestone like it was for most other people. Since her mom never initiated this special day with cake, presents, and inviting friends, birthday celebrations were never part of her childhood. Because of that, it was difficult for her to measure when another year had passed. As a result, one year after another went by her without so much as a physical or mental acknowledgement that she was getting older. In her awareness, each day was pretty much a repeat from the previous without visible changes, other than people's faces and an occasional change of venue. Since she did not know a lifestyle other than begging, with the exception of being supported by Eric, which seemed to be part of a distant past, she enjoyed the new experience in the company of Greg, both influenced by alcohol and drugs.

The mention of her birthday sparked a notion in Greg, who promptly drew April aside after earning a few dollars. "Follow me," he said, pulling her along the pier into a novelty shop nearby. She inspected the many items on display while he went to the sales counter.

Minutes later he joined her in the aisle to hand her the item he'd just bought. With eyes widened in surprise, she said, "What is this?"

"Happy birthday," he announced, clipping the bracelet on her wrist.

April was overcome with emotion. It was the first present anyone had ever bought her. Staring at her wrist in disbelief, she broke down into tears when reading the inscription: "To April with Love."

"I love it." She planted a kiss on his lips.

The emotional outbreak seemed to come as a surprise to him, especially after the kiss. He was unsure of how to deal with it at the moment, since they had agreed on being only friends. Putting the notion aside, he joined in with her happiness when leaving the shop, strolling along the pier, enjoying each other's company until dark.

Nighttime came, with darkness all around the yacht harbor when they arrived. While most boat owners accessed their vessels through the main gate during daytime hours, Greg led the way to the locked back gate boat owners used to gain entrance to their moored vessels after hours. "Hurry up," April urged, watching him cut the chain with the tool they'd gotten. She was not used to being an accomplice to a crime and felt highly uncomfortable in his presence now.

"Don't worry, I know what I'm doing. Just keep a lookout." It was the lookout part, her responsibility, that she did not like. She heard the chain fall to the ground and sighed in relief. "Let's go," he said, leading the way along the docks.

"What about the chain?"

"Don't worry," Greg said and tossed it into the water below. "Somebody will eventually report it and have it replaced."

"What about us?" April said, concerned about being locked out. "We cut it again?"

"No." Greg proclaimed. "From now on we'll exit and enter through the main gate once we know the name of the boat."

If it is good enough for him, she thought, *it's good enough for me.*

They guardedly passed dozens of anchored boats, some small, others large, with Greg looking for something specific she did not know.

"What are we looking for?" Since it was still early in the night they could spot the occupied boats being illuminated from within.

"Here," he gestured and promptly headed for an inconspicuous-looking craft, not very appealing to her. It appeared to be something that should belong to a junkyard. Her eyes had caught the crest of algae along the water mark. What appeared as dirt to her was an indication to him that the boat had been moored for some time without having been occupied.

"Why not select a better looking thing?" she said, her nose wrinkled at the craft.

"We don't want any visitors," he said, helping her across the narrow access plank. "Do we?" It became clear to her. He was looking for a permanent home for them. "Entre vous," Greg said, bidding her a grand entrance.

"What?"

"Home, sweet home. It's French." He beckoned her to step across the gang plank. Since they had no luggage, it was an easy entrance. Though the craft appeared small, Greg figured it was a 32-foot sailboat, and the interior opened up with enough space to accommodate four.

Pacing carefully within the strange environment, April inspected the inside, upper, and lower decks. "So this is how sailors live," she commented, unsure what steps to take next.

"Yes. That's how. See this?" He gestured at what seemed to be a dining area. "This is where we sleep."

"What? The table?"

"Look," he said, pulling her by the arm while lifting the tabletop. "It converts into a bed."

"Why," she exclaimed, "we have a complete home."

"This is what I was looking for." Both were satisfied with his selection. For whatever reasons the craft had been deserted, but it did not matter. What mattered was the home it would provide them for the times ahead.

"How did you know?"

"I was looking for barnacles along the watermark."

"Clever. What now?" April said while setting up the bed.

Though the outside was illuminated by the moon, it was dark inside the boat. Greg suggested, "I'll check on the water and electricity in the morning." As they stretched comfortably on the bed, the slight sway of the boat from the waves washing up against the hull put both to sleep within minutes.

HOME AGAIN

"Good morning." Greg's voice broke into her sleep. April opened her eyes into the strangeness of the immediate environment. The sun was shining through the portholes, illuminating the interior and promising a bright day. Getting out of bed, she took her time to inspect the galley. Unfamiliar with a boat, she sought out Greg to lead her. "Here's the kitchen," he pointed to the space on the far end. "And here is the head."

"Head?"

"Toilet," he explained.

"Can I use it?"

"Just a moment," he said, flushing the tank. "Good. We have water. Now you can use it."

April was surprised at the utilities of the interior. Though compact but functional, it provided all of the appliances found in an apartment including a refrigerator, stove, and pantry. She opened the pantry and to her surprise located a few cans of Spam in addition to several cans of potatoes and vegetables. While Greg was busy on the upper deck, she went to work preparing breakfast, happy to have a place once more.

They spent the next hour exploring every space the boat provided and decided to stake claim as their home. "What do you think happened to the owner?" she said, concerned that someone might show up.

"Could be a number of things," Greg offered. "He may have died without leaving descendants or else could be in the hospital or a nursing home, maybe a prison. Whatever place," he explained, "is good enough for me."

"You're not very compassionate," April said, hoping he had better feelings for her.

"But realistic, nevertheless."

From here on out, April put her fears aside with a final thought: *Whatever the reasons, I'm not going to worry anymore either.* She would have to deal with the owner's return, if it happened, like so many other times. Their daily chores became a routine, including begging for enough to sustain their lives another day. Though secure in the craft, both noticed that homeless competition was on the increase, affecting tourist's handouts, which resulted in a declining take. The outcome affected their lives as well by having to spend many more hours begging. The tradeoff became clearly visible by earning barely enough money to sustain another day.

"What do you think we should do?" April said one day, hoping the situation would change, but with the cold on its way to end the tourist season, the future did not look promising.

"You know what?" Greg proposed. "We could get a job just like my buddy did."

"But I don't know anything," April protested.

"You could learn. You are a bright girl."

"I'm scared."

Greg realized how vulnerable her existence must have been without a fallback to a learned trade. "You could try for a waitress. The only qualification you'll need is good looks. And you have that."

"What if I fail and break things?"

"Everybody does at first. You'll do just fine."

Hearing his encouraging words put her somewhat at ease. "You'll come with me?"

"I'll be by your side for any interview."

"Okay. We'll start tomorrow. What about you?"

"Don't worry about me," he said, assuring. "I can tackle many things."

The first day for April proved to be challenging. Not knowing what to expect with an interview, she was very nervous, with obvious consequences. Managers, sensing her discomfort, were quick to dismiss her. It took several more interviews for her to gain enough confidence to respond intelligently to questions. To her joy, she was able to land a job with a café at her favorite place, Pier 39. "I did it. I got the job," she announced with great enthusiasm, flying into Greg's outstretched arms, who'd been waiting by the exit. "I can start tomorrow."

"I told you," he said. "Let's celebrate."

The first day on the job was difficult for April. Extremely nervous at first, she missed a number of things the assistant manager explained. Sensing her discomfort and knowing she was a novice, he extended his personal patience regardless of several errors she incurred. First, she served dishes to the wrong patrons, who were not happy with the mistakes. Women patrons were more tolerant than men, especially when April explained it was her first day on the job, any job. Then, she served the wrong dishes and mixed up checks, billing the wrong people for their fare, each time profusely apologizing for her mistakes. It took several days for her to become experienced enough.

"How did it go?" Greg would ask. Each day he would diligently wait by the entrance for her to appear after a day's work at the café.

"Much better," she would say. "I made some tips."

"How much?"

"Enough to live another day."

"Want to celebrate?" he suggested.

"Sure. Where're we going?" He always had a place picked to spend the evening. "It's my day off tomorrow."

"Great," he said. "I've got a surprise for you."

"Oh?"

"We'll take the boat out."

"What do you mean?" The revelation came as a complete surprise especially since she did not think he would know how to navigate the sailboat.

"We'll go sailing in the Bay."

"You know how?"

"I've been on boats before. Not this big, but I can manage."

"Let's stay home then and get an early start." She could hardly wait for the morning.

Greg was already at work preparing the boat for the sea when she woke up. Following a quick breakfast he instructed her, "Untie the mooring lines." Over the past months April had become proficient, not only at her work, but with sailor terms as well. She followed his instructions and knew what to do.

The day was a thrill ride for April. To her surprise, Greg handled the craft skillfully on exiting the harbor as well as heading out to sea. There was not much for her to do other than enjoy the sailing.

"Where're we headed?"

"Checking out the territory," he said. "You'll see."

He took the boat east past the Oakland Bridge and further up the Bay. To her surprise, the Bay extended way past the horizon; she'd thought it ended at Oakland.

When they first started, they'd gradually exited the yacht harbor powered on the internal engine-driven propeller. Once out on the open bay, he hoisted both sails, catching the breeze headed north past Berkeley, Richmond, and San Quentin, and then changed into an easterly course crossing San Pablo Bay beneath both bridges into Benicia and Martinez. With sails partially hoisted, it took close to an hour before they arrived at Suisun Bay, their destination.

"I'm proud of you," she said, approving of his sailing skills.

He smiled in response.

"What else do you know that you haven't told me?"

"Quite a few things," he said, not volunteering more. She did not want to prod further and enjoyed the day to its fullest. Cruising along the shoreline, they gradually made it back to the yacht harbor just as the sun was setting.

"What a day," April said, audibly inhaling a deep breath of sea breeze. "I had no idea regular folks could have so much fun. I could get used to this life."

"It's all up to you," he agreed. "But you know," he cautioned, "it means holding a steady job and paying taxes."

"Don't remind me. You just spoiled my day."

"Sorry. Just wanted to point out the obligations that come with organized society."

"I know. Let's not think about it until tomorrow." Their adventurous day ended with both celebrating the success of her first day on the water with a few drinks and some pot. "When can we go again?" she said.

"Next time on your day off."

"Really?"

"We could go every day if you'd like."

"My job," she said, reminding him of her obligations. "By the way, how are you doing with finding a job?"

"I haven't given it much thought yet."

"Didn't you agree we'd both find work?"

"True. But with you working we could manage, couldn't we?"

His reply took her somewhat by surprise, but she remained quiet for the moment, hoping he would honor his promise.

Days later, after she finished work with the next day off, he suggested, "Want to go sailing?"

"Sure. Where're we going?"

"Fishing for dinner."

"Really?"

The day was another adventure for her. Considering possible fishing grounds, they anchored the craft near the Golden Gate Bridge. They had a successful catch, enough to last several meals. Fish, plentiful in the bay, would become their daily staple food.

Greg's idea about setting up a household on a boat, though illegal, turned out to be a great choice. Between her working and him navigating the craft, first one, then another year passed without major incidents or events. There were minor mishaps such as the day the engine quit. Greg had to use his sailing skills to navigate the craft into the basin. Though they bumped into a couple other boats along the path they made it back to their mooring spot without causing any damages.

Another time the craft lost the main sail during an unexpected storm that suddenly materialized. Trying to start the inboard engine had its own problems. The fuel tank was empty. Greg had forgotten to fill it up after the last trip. Drifting with the wind, they finally made it to shore to get some fuel. They begged for weeks just to get enough money together to purchase another sail, on the brink of starving.

All in all, after evaluating living on the craft, they decided it was still better than having to fend for a space amidst the homeless, who had increased in numbers even more, causing major sanitary issues for the city and county. Not only did it cut into each other's profits, but the upsurge brought along a multitude of diseases from severe virus strains to amoebic dysentery, and many more. As in times before, City Hall was in uproar once more.

Unable to stem the homeless influx into what used to be the nation's most desirable city, tourism, leisure, and entertainment took a severe hit on the city's already stressed budget. Unable to come up with a solution, numerous measures were tried but failed miserably. It seemed that the liberals had overextended their liberties with state and federal budget aid. Fortunately for the state, the economy in Silicon Valley was still sustained by its technological advantage over the rest of the country.

After analyzing the cause for such a lengthy demise in the state's declining prosperity, dated back to the '90s, blame fell to big businesses promoting the U.S. industry's most threatening buzzword, outsourcing. Needless to say that with each surfacing budget issue, business executives took the blame.

Fortunately for April and Greg, they were not much affected by the state's economic downturn other than having to deal with the increase in overcrowded conditions and filth when walking city sidewalks.

"Let's head for Columbus Avenue," Greg suggested. After weeks of surviving on their daily catch, they had decided to dine out for a change. Strolling along Bay Street, the nearest access to Marina Yacht Harbor, their current home, he led her in the direction of Columbus Avenue, a favorite place for diners, city residents and tourists alike. It was a section of town where homelessness had not yet taken root. Thanks to local shop and restaurant owners, the city ordinance against having vagrants and drifters bunking at their store entrances was strictly enforced. "What do you feel like having?"

"How about Italian?" April suggested. "Mom always talked about it but never took me. I wish I could take a trip to Italy someday, but that will probably remain a dream for the rest of my life."

"Italian it is," Greg agreed. "And about Italy, we could afford it and make plans someday if you keep on working."

While it sounded like something to work on, she was not very happy about the suggestion of only her keeping on working. Most days, too busy at the café and working many hours, she had not given it much of a thought, hoping Greg would step up some day to get a job himself. For now, without the burden of paying rent for an apartment, she made enough money to support their living expenses and the occasional dining out, like this evening. "For that to happen," she decided to bring up the topic of work again, "don't you think we need additional income?" At least her concerns about him not working was out in the open.

"We manage pretty well on your income, don't we?"

"Well, yes. But there are things I'd like to get."

"Like what?" In his mind, him taking care of their daily needs living on the craft should have been enough responsibility, and he had not considered taking on a job. After all, if it wasn't for his cunning, they would still be living on the street.

"Franchino Restaurant," the overhead sign proclaimed.

"Let's talk about it over dinner," he suggested, leading her through the entrance.

Like many restaurants along Columbus Avenue, this place also had an outdoor café style seating arrangement most visitors preferred. Where outdoor eating was not as common in the States, Europeans wouldn't have it any other way, especially during the warm season. Since it was still early in the day they were able to get a sidewalk table.

"Welcome to Franchino," the waiter announced, handing each a menu. "Anything to drink?"

"Yes. I'd like to order a bottle of Chianti."

"Chianti it is." The waiter, courteous as most are, disappeared as swiftly as he had appeared.

"What do you feel like having?" Greg asked, studying the menu.

"How about Traditional Italian Fare?" April suggested, as it stated on the menu.

Greg could not suppress a smile. "You'll have to be more specific."

"I'm not familiar with any of the dishes." April, uneducated for the most part, did not want to appear completely ignorant, but could not help it. "I'll let you decide."

"Good enough. Since you want to try a real traditional meal, let's start with antipasto insalata."

"What does that mean?" To her, the dish sounded as strange as the language.

"In plain English," he explained, "salad."

"What else do you suggest?"

"I'll come to that. How about a pasta dish?"

"Pasta?"

"Noodles. You like noodles?"

"I love noodles."

"Good."

The waiter made an appearance again, showing off the bottle brand. "Chianti – Italy's finest wines," the label stated. He poured a sample from the decanter into Greg's glass, patiently waiting for his approval.

"What are you doing?" April said, watching him take his time while tasting the sample.

"In Italy," the waiter explained to her, "it is customary to taste the wine before making the purchase."

"I approve," Greg said, nodding at the waiter before watching him fill their glasses.

"Have you decided?" With notepad in hand, the waiter was prepared to take their orders.

Studying the menu one more time, Greg gave him the order, "Spaghetti alla carbonara."

"Prosciutto, parmigiano cheese and eggs?" the waiter inquired.

"Yes please." With ordering out of the way, they could sit back and enjoy the passing scene in between taking sips of wine.

"Let's talk about it," Greg said, picking up her earlier concerns. "What is it that bothers you?"

"I like the taste," April said, stalling while raising her glass at him. She always felt uncomfortable initiating a conversation. Ever since childhood, she was so used to being ordered around and only answering questions others posed. She had never been given a chance and did not feel comfortable starting a discussion.

"You wanted to talk about me getting a job, wasn't it?"

April took her time before committing to the topic, as uncomfortable as she felt. "I thought we both agreed to build a future together."

"But we are," he assured her. "Aren't you happy?"

"I am," she assured him. "But there are many more things we could enjoy with both of us working."

He took his time to evaluate her suggestion before answering. "What is really bothering you?"

"I don't know where we stand in our relationship."

"What do you mean?" He wanted clarification before committing, especially to a long-term relationship. It was his way of not making another unfulfilled mistake. There had been several along the way where hasty promises had been made and been broken just as quick, ending in divorce.

"I want you to know that I am thankful to you for taking me into your life, but I don't know how you feel about me."

"I like to be with you very much," he said, reaching for her hands. "You should know that by now."

"We never talk about it," she complained. "You're always too busy with something when I bring up the subject."

And there it is, he quietly thought. *The first complaint.* He always wondered why the woman could not be content like most men. While he wanted peace and quiet for the most part, it was never enough for the woman. It's why he had stopped committing to a relationship. He'd always suspected that the woman needed a solid promise before totally committing, but he also knew that it would be a cause for bickering in the times ahead. He clearly remembered watching his parent's behaviors. That's when he'd decided to follow his own policy of "keep 'em guessing." It had worked in his favor for many years and would probably work many more.

"Like you," he said, assuming her past mistakes, "I want fulfillment in a relationship, but so far it's never worked out. Why can't we just be friends?"

"I don't know what it is," she explained. "But a woman needs more. She needs a bond."

"You feel strongly about it?"

"Yes," she said, hoping for a positive outcome to her concerns about men.

"So be it."

"So be it what?" she pressed on.

"So, I'll get a job."

"Really?" she said, overcome with joy. "It would mean so much."

"I promise." With the topic of commitments out of the way, both enjoyed the rest of the evening to its fullest, including a serving of dolce, a dish of homemade ice cream.

"This is delicious," April explained after tasting the dolce. "Why can't we make such delicious ice cream?"

"Too health conscious."

Although she'd never had a problem with obesity, she understood. April could have not been happier after discussing her relationship concerns. She felt that with his commitment, their bond would be for a life of joy and pleasure. She would be able to make plans for the both of them and, if by chance they would be blessed with a child, her dreams could finally be fulfilled. She was happier than ever before, planning to set events into motion after they got back to the boat by having passionate sex, the prerequisite for having a loving and healthy child, she'd read in some magazine. Reaching out for his hands, April leaned across the table and, for the first time in her life, uttered, "I love you."

With a satisfied smile on his face, Greg readily stated, "Your life as a homeless is over. That is my promise to you." It was a simple promise, but caused an emotional reaction in April. She broke out in tears and just wanted to go home.

Greg waved the waiter over for the bill, who promptly responded. Seconds later he handed it to Greg, who carefully looked it over. She noticed his gazing at the bill and became concerned. "How much?"

"You don't want to know."

"I have to," she insisted. "I'm the one paying for it."

He handed it to her.

Dinner for Two:

Insalata Dela Casa		$ 13.90
Spaghetti Alla Carbonara		$ 39.90
Dolce Ice Cream		$ 13.90
Chianti Vino		$ 24.95

		$ 92.65
State Tax	7.95%	$ 7.37

Sub-Total		$100.02
Gratuity	15%	$ 15.00
		=======
Total		$115.02

The figures had an instant sobering effect on her as she looked at the total amount. Never in her life had she been served a receipt this high. "Wow," was all April could say, but handed Greg the money. It was already past midnight when they left the restaurant.

Arriving at their home, the boat, both enjoyed the quietness of the night. Only the slight squeaking of rubber scraping against the dock could be heard as they set foot on the gangplank. April was chatty and giggling with happiness, closely following Greg as he stepped onto the boat. The glimmer of the light below deck caught his eyes. "Did you turn the light on before we left?"

"Don't think so," she said, pushing him below deck. She couldn't wait to get her hands around his body to consummate his earlier promise.

"Hatch's locked," Greg said, jiggling the lock a couple of times. He was slightly surprised because they had never locked the hatch before. At that moment a shot went off from the inside, aimed directly at Greg's chest. He died before his body landed on the deck.

April let out a scream into the night, never before heard in the yacht harbor until this moment, as she stared into the strange face of a bearded man holding a shotgun pointed at her, demanding, "What are you doing on my boat?"

Not understanding the events that had just taken place, she ignored his demands, stooping down to help Greg off the floor. When she realized that his body was lifeless, rage built up in her body for the first time in her life. Screaming, ignoring the shotgun pointed at her, she felt like killing the man staring down at her. "You killed him! You killed my friend."

What followed next was beyond April's comprehension. The man grabbed her by the collar of her jacket and tossed her over the rail, promptly followed by Greg's lifeless body. Watching them splash into the water below, the man's face clearly reflected his intentions, hoping they would drown in the cold Pacific waters.

SHATTERED HAPPINESS

The last image April's mind captured before blacking out in the cold water was her and Greg entering a tunnel. While she had heard about final images entering a person's mind when dying, she was overcome with fear. Fear, not because of her waning state of awareness, but fear because they had entered a state of darkness. Recalling stories about life after death, the individual was always enlightened by entering a brightly-lit sphere, a guiding invitation into the afterlife. Barely conscious, succumbing to the environment pulling her deeper into the water, she felt the cold chill pressing against her skin. It instantly brought her back to consciousness.

Along with the chill came fear for her life. Her autonomous body functions took over. She began to struggle. Never having had the pleasure of being in a pool or lake, April had never learned to swim. Short on breath and waning energy, she was able to grab a hold on a mooring rope struggling, in desperation pulling herself up to the surface screaming into the night, "Help! I'm drowning!"

Her shouts were heard in boats anchored nearby. Familiar with the environment of water, people knew it was a call for survival and began searching the surface with flashlights. Somebody shouted, "I see her," pointing at the water below. Minutes later April, in a semi-unconscious state, was hauled from the water and dragged into a nearby craft. When pressed for an explanation, April willingly complied. "He killed my friend."

Minutes later, after someone called 911, a police siren accompanied by an ambulance took over the quiet of night. "Over here," the people who'd rescued April shouted. It did not take long before the police took hold of the killer and in cuffs took him away after taking statements from witnesses, as well as from April with her promise to appear at the local precinct in the morning.

"You sure you don't want us to take you to the hospital?" the first responder asked. With lips blue from the cold and shivering, all she was able to do was shake her head.

By now, April had regained full consciousness. Aware of the reality of tonight's events, with Greg both killed and thrown overboard, she had already gone through enough trauma. All she wanted to do was crawl into a corner to die quietly. She desperately needed sleep. Willingly, she accepted an invitation to spend the night with the couple who had rescued her.

As promised, the following morning April appeared at the local precinct. Explaining her story about them being homeless and Greg and her seeking refuge on the craft, while the officer swiftly typed the information on paper, she was released without any charges. And that was it, the end of her life with Greg. While she had not been in love with him, she had become attached to him, especially after his promise of getting a job. That meant stability in their relationship with a possible future marriage bond. In today's world of uncertainty, with many young people living together without being married due to being minimum wage earners, her notion about a family might have been part of a past American tradition, but it was something she had wanted.

Thoughts like this reminded her of the job she presently held. Already late in the day, April realized that she had missed a day of work. Reporting now would be useless after her shift was already over. She would have to face the day manager tomorrow and explain. She knew that there was no exception to the store policy: "24 hours prior notice to schedule a day off."

"Sorry," her manager informed her the following morning. "I already hired a replacement."

"But I was detained at the police station all day," she said.

"You could have called. You know the company policy."

April was cast out, living on the streets again. There was one thing she had to do, which was getting her belongings from the boat. She headed for it.

"Can't have them," the police officer said, "not until the investigation is over."

"But," she insisted, "I need my things. How long will it take?"

"Don't know. Weeks, maybe months. All depends on when the magistrate can finalize your case in court. Low priority criminal cases take time."

That was the last April heard of it. Penniless and homeless again, all she could think was, "I need a drink." Where last night with Greg was the best she'd ever had, today that world had shattered forever. Feeling rage overtaking her senses, not only for all of her past failures in life and relationships, she decided to continue the uncertainty of the future on her own. Taking the initiative, her first step was in the direction of the nearest bar. "Whisky," she ordered, stepping up to the counter. Seconds later, she demanded, "Give me another," followed with "another" and more, until she stumbled onto the sidewalk hours later, smashed.

Evicted for not having enough cash to pay the final tab, April was not only homeless but penniless as well. In her present state of mind, she could not have cared less. Her legs only had enough strength to seek out the next vacant entryway, where she promptly fell asleep until awakened by the shop owner prodding her body. "Get up. It's time to go."

Dazed and confused, it took several minutes for her mind to clear enough for her to get up and head in the direction of the next public restroom. Feeling somewhat refreshed after splashing water on her face, her mind had cleared up enough to think again. Drowsy but sober, she left the facility but had nowhere to go. Feeling dejected, desperate, and directionless, yesterday's suppressed rage surfaced again but at a much greater force. She started cussing out life and the world with all of its letdowns, from dished out failures to unfulfilled promises.

There seemed to be no end to her misery. "I need a drink," was all her fogged-up mind could muster. It was a cycle that would repeat with each day for the weeks and months ahead. She lived the life of a bonafide homeless drunk, inheriting all of its side effects from hangovers to withdrawals. Fortunately for the victim, after saturating the body with alcohol day after day, hangovers gradually begin to wane. She was no exception. Without being plagued by aftereffects any longer she felt happy until the pangs of withdrawal took over her body. Where she had been able to control the headaches with pain killers, there was no cure for withdrawal pain other than a steady supply of alcohol.

Months into her misery, after people kept telling her to sober up, April realized she had become an alcoholic. Knowing the difference between being sober and coherent and drunk and in stupor, she realized that she needed help. With the support of another homeless woman in need of sobering up, one morning, both sought out a rehab clinic.

Her decision might have been a willing choice, but the treatment was pure misery. Subjected daily to strict instructions by the clinic's orderlies, her life became sheer torture. Withdrawal pains were miserable enough already, but enduring the endless sleepless nights that followed was even worse. It took six weeks of rehab, paid for by the state, to clean up her body from alcohol effects. April left the clinic in a sober state with the self-promise never to touch the stuff again. But, as was the case with many convictions, promises are there to be broken.

On the streets and roaming again, but currently sober, April had the opportunity to get to know what the city had become, a sewer for drifters and homeless. Although she had been drunk for most of the day just a few weeks ago, she still had been able to manage her personal hygiene at public restrooms.

Today, in a sober state, she saw what was really happening to the once-pristine environment. Not every neighborhood had been able to cling to the old traditions preserving a proud gold rush heritage, and many cultural changes had taken place since, such as the hippie movement in the '60s, gay liberation in the '70s, pop music in the '80s, hip hop during the '90s, followed by an economic recession and a Silicon Valley collapse, which certainly left their marks on the city.

Maybe it's time for a change of scenery, she thought with an immediate focus on her future. "But what should I do?"

She had no ready answer at the moment other than getting a job. Without it, she knew that it would only take a few penniless days for a relapse back into addictions and homelessness. April came to the realization why organized society was so important to many people. Where her comfort zone had been living on the streets for most of her life, trying to tackle the other side of society working and paying taxes were responsibilities she had never seriously considered. The thought alone made her feel extremely uncomfortable.

Evaluating pros and cons of a change in life, she could not come up with an answer. The hurdle, a major one, was always the same. "I can't afford to live in the city."

The reason was simple; she would have to earn an income to be able to afford the monthly rent for an apartment. Even a small place with only one living space would provide challenges not only for her but, as was the case already, for many workers with an established career. Apartment rents had skyrocketed in recent years. The result is clearly visible. Most places were occupied with multiple workers sharing the available limited living spaces.

With April having experienced her first job not long ago working at the café, she knew earning only minimum wage would not solve the problem. The revelation was a sobering one. She felt trapped again without an opportunity to make a living. After serious consideration, she came to a depressing conclusion: "I have to sell my body like Mom did or be homeless again. I'm screwed either way."

Drifting aimlessly around neighborhoods of the past, she begged again, but this time without the slightest desire and focus. "I have to get out of here," she thought. "But where?"

A thought struck her. *City Hall.*

"Why not?" she muttered, gladdened at the thought. "They'll help."

Her present situation reminded her of the time she and Eric were working for the mayor, trying to solve the homeless challenge. While their combined effort, due to city budget shortages, ended in failure, there was one chance for the homeless to change their life: a paid bus ticket to any desirable destination.

She recalled how the mayor's offer had triggered a homeless exodus to locations up north and to the east. Dozens of homeless took the opportunity and left for places they otherwise would never have had the chance to get to. Some went back to their hometown and families, while others sought out new venues in Oregon, Washington state, and the East Coast.

April, energized with renewed hope, went to City Hall as soon as she woke up in the morning. Her first stop was the local Salvation Army to get presentable attire to wear for the occasion. She realized that the clothes she wore were befitting for a bum only and needed a change. Browsing the personal wear section she selected a blouse, skirt, pair of new shoes and jacket she liked, and went on her way.

A brisk thirty-minute walk later she entered City Hall, heading for the mayor's office. "Good morning," the reception clerk welcomed her. "Long time, no see." She'd remembered April from the times before. "What brings you here?"

"I'd like to see the mayor."

The clerk seemed hesitant about April's direct approach and said, "The mayor is busy."

"I'll wait," she replied, taking a seat at the empty chair by the desk. Apparently uncomfortable with the unannounced visitor, the clerk left her desk to enter the mayor's office. She reappeared a minute later. "He'll see you now."

"Well, well," the mayor greeted with a smile upon her entrance. "How have you been? How's Eric?"

April returned a warm smile, stating, "He left the city for Canada. I never heard from him again."

"I'm sorry to hear that. But you know," the mayor explained, "I couldn't help him out any longer. Things with the homeless problem turned out really bad."

"I know that," April said. "I live it."

"What can I do for you?" he said with apparent concern.

"I remember an offer you extended us homeless several years back."

"What was it again? Please enlighten me."

"A free bus ticket anywhere."

"Is that why you are here?"

"It's the only thing I want."

"Well," he accommodated her with a smile, "the offer is always open. Where're you planning to move?"

"Some clean town. I can't deal with dirty cities and homeless mobs any longer. I need to change my life. I can't do it here. It's too expensive without a decent-paying job."

"Want some company?" he returned with a grin.

She was uncertain about his intentions. "I don't understand."

"I want to get out of this place too."

She understood. Both laughed loudly.

"I'll tell you what I can do. You give me a destination and I'll get you a voucher for the bus ticket. Fair enough?"

"I'll be grateful. Thank you."

"Stop by the desk clerk on the way out," he said, getting up from his chair. "She'll get you the voucher and you have a safe trip. You are a pretty lady. You'll do just fine. Bye," he said, shaking her hand. April took her exit.

The clerk was on the intercom, taking instructions from the mayor. She hung up. "Where do you want to go?"

April took notice of a U.S. map framed up on the wall. While she had seen and glanced at maps like it before, she had never been interested in any place other than San Francisco. Looking it over she seemed somewhat puzzled at the large empty spaces between the Pacific and Atlantic coasts, especially in the central regions. Her eyes were scanning for something familiar. Suddenly, she caught a familiar name that was standing out right in the middle of the map: "Colorado Springs." It was something she'd overheard other homeless mention as a place to relocate to. It seemed that San Francisco was getting too crowded even for the homeless. Why such a minor city located in the center of the country, she did not know, but figured it was her destiny calling.

"Colorado Springs," she happily announced to the clerk.

"Colorado Springs it is," she said, and handed April a voucher for the bus ticket.

She quickly left for the bus terminal so as not to miss the next departure.

COLORADO SPRINGS

April was seated at the back of the bus watching the country passing by, for once feeling adventurous and enjoying herself. Every seat was taken, occupied by individuals of various ages trying to get to their destination leisurely. After an initial fear of the uncertain future she had chosen, Colorado as the destination for a new beginning, April had settled in her seat for the two-day trip ahead. The bus, she learned on departure from San Francisco, took I-80 East all the way with a one-night stopover in Salt Lake City, her halfway point to Colorado.

For the most part of the first travel leg she kept to herself, since the seats near her were occupied by somewhat reserved individuals themselves. The travel was a relatively quiet affair with only subdued conversations drifting amid the steady hum of the bus engine. April, in-between naps, let her mind wander, wondering what her destination might have in store for her. She could not clearly remember why she had chosen Colorado as her destination, since most homeless would have chosen Washington state or Canada, especially after drug use had recently been legalized. It seemed that substance in abundance was the driving factor for the many displaced.

It was not until the overnight stop when she had a chance to meet other likeminded travelers her age during the evening dinner. There, she learned that two of those seated next to her in the restaurant were also headed for Colorado. A lively conversation took place for the rest of the evening with promises to keep in touch. The bus continued on its schedule early the next morning following a breakfast buffet. The remainder of the trip went by quickly while they enjoyed each other's company.

It was late in the afternoon when the city of Denver came into view, announced by the driver over the intercom. Following their exit from the bus, the two male companions remained in Denver while April changed busses to her final destination, Colorado Springs, arriving there an hour later.

On exiting the bus at her final station, Colorado Central Station in the middle of downtown, she asked the bus driver, "Where are the shelters?"

"You homeless?"

"Yes. It's my first time here."

"See that street?" he said with a gesture at Kiowa Avenue, fronting the bus terminal. "Turn left and go to the next corner, Tejon Street. You'll see a local location map on display. It'll indicate shelters nearby."

"Thank you."

"Good luck. Hope you'll find what you're looking for."

Facing a new location with a possible future, April found herself alone in the shadows of the sidewalk. Taking the direction indicated by the driver, although it was late in the evening, she could spot the street corner with the display case nearby. As she headed directly for it, she noticed something very familiar, a few homeless chatting at the corner of Kiowa and Tejon, seated by a flower patch encased by 2-foot concrete containment walls.

"How pretty," she muttered, admiring the well-kept city streets. Taking a few more steps brought her face to face with the homeless. Unsure of her initial approach, she faced the one talking. "Excuse me. Are all of you homeless?"

He shifted his focus and stared at her. "Who wants to know?" As usual, there was initial distrust when confronted by a stranger. The homeless, perhaps more so than local citizens, are in tune with the environment they occupy. It's their home. They get intricately familiar with places and passing people. Being idle most times, whether day or night, since they have no scheduled tasks, new faces are registered and categorized on a daily basis, a prospecting opportunity for receiving a donation.

"I'm homeless and just arrived on the bus from California. Can you help?"

"Well, well," he said, instantly adjusting his attitude. "Welcome to Colorado Springs." He introduced his fellow homeless and said, "What's your name?"

"April."

"Ben," he stated, giving her a once over. "These are my friends," he gestured. "Where's your luggage?"

"Don't have any. Lost everything I had. That's the reason I landed here."

"You came to the right place," he said, accompanied by prolific head nodding by his friends. "You need a place to stay?"

"Don't have any money. Besides," she explained, "I prefer to sleep out in the open."

"So do we," he said in agreement. "We usually spend the night sleeping at Acacia Park."

"How far is it?"

"Follow me," he readily offered, leading the way. "It's only a couple of blocks up the street." His friends followed, curious about the stranger. From their looks, they were rather cautious about her. It's an inherited habit most homeless display. They don't extend their friendship until they feel the person out for behavior and sincerity. Most are street-wise and can sense a person's intentions. Similar to animals in the wild, it was due to a need for survival.

Swiftly strolling along storefronts, Ben pointed out places to frequent and places to avoid by explaining the reasons. Minutes later they arrived at the far end of the current block, stopped by the traffic light. "See this?" he said with a gesture across the street ahead. "It's the park."

"Nice," April said, "but kind of small, isn't it?"

"Big enough," Ben said. "Not many of us stay in town. Most spend the night along the river nearby. Daytime," he explained, "we live in the city. It's got public facilities and several eating places right here." He gestured across the street.

"What about the Salvation Army? I need some things."

"Not to worry. There are several donation places in town. I'll take you there tomorrow."

They sat huddled together near a prominent tree growing on top of a small mound, smoking pot and passing around a bottle of whisky, telling about their past and what had brought them here. While she accepted some pot she declined the bottle. From their vantage point, they were able to observe traffic and pedestrians passing on streets and sidewalks below, dodging across the intersection with or without paying much attention to the changes of the traffic lights. It was something she had not seen in San Francisco. It seemed that local drivers have gotten used to the homeless crossing streets to their own tune.

"You have to understand," Ben explained. "This is a clean and small town we respect. Though it's recently been declared a sanctuary state, the illegal masses have not made it here yet. My friends and I," he indicated with a head nod at them, "see to it that it stays this way."

"What about the law?"

"That's the reason. We don't bother the cops and they don't bother us. It's a mutual respect."

April was impressed. "I think I'll like it here."

"It's getting late," Ben said, accompanied by a yawn. "I'm tired. Let me show you the public facility."

April jumped to her legs and followed. Again, she was impressed at the cleanliness of the restroom facility specifically built for the park. Worn out and tired from the long trip, she decided to defer body and hair washing until the morning after getting some personal items she'd need. She decided the same with eating, ignoring her hunger for now because she was penniless.

"Come," Ben said, leading the way back to the tree. "You can sleep with us. Here is a blanket for you."

April considered herself lucky having been received by this friendly bunch on top of sleeping out in the open without being confined to a dorm. She could see the stars and the Zodiac constellations Eric had taught her. How long had it been? She was too tired to remember. "Eric," she mourned with a silent sigh. "Where are you?" She promptly fell asleep.

Shaded by the tree, April and her new friends lay huddled in close proximity when she felt the sunshine warming her face. She opened her eyes to take in the daylight scene already on its way. She guessed the time of day by the position of the sun as most homeless did. Afraid she might have missed her friend's departure, she was content after identifying their faces close by.

"Morning," Ben said with a smile. "Looks like you slept well."

"I did. I must have passed out. Don't remember one thing."

"Catching up?"

"I certainly did."

"When's the last time you've eaten?"

"About 24 hours ago."

"Come." He helped her to her feet. "I'll buy you breakfast. Great eateries around here. This town was built by pioneers. They must have liked to eat. Servings are plentiful." April would learn that many of the restaurants in town were specialized in cooking serving the pioneering spirited residents, where others, visitors in town, provided ample diversities in fast and convenient food.

"I'm grateful," she said to Ben when he paid for her share. "Next meal is on me as soon as I earn some money."

"Don't worry about it. We all share our take with friends in need."

"How nice," she said but quietly thought, *What a difference,* when comparing this town with the City. She was not aware at the time that Colorado Springs had also been a city for many decades. Early in the previous century, there was a time when many towns applied for city permits to incorporate. Mostly forgotten now, the reason was simple. If the local people wanted the town and businesses to grow, the mayor had to incorporate, resulting in a number of departments to be staffed, mostly by influential and well-known citizens. Unfortunately for the ones trying to preserve inherited traditions, their lives would never be the same. Modernization and progress was quick to follow.

What preserved some of Colorado Spring's culture was its isolation from a mainstream industry, normally centered around rivers and shorelines. While today the city might still appear to be a Western town in flavor, it will not remain this way for long. Population growth will guarantee change is not far off.

It was thoughts like this that took April's attention while strolling leisurely along pristine and clean sidewalks. "I like it here. I think I'll stay."

"You won't be sorry," Ben said, smiling at her apparent innocence.

April took her time adjusting to the new environment, her new home. Though people carried a small town mentality, compared to San Francisco, the slow pace of living and leisure time made up for it. There was one thing April missed: the artistic entertainment presented and displayed by the homeless. But she considered it a fair trade-off when compared to the mess that came with the homeless crowds. There was not much entertainment for the homeless other than the daily gatherings at several spots, tolerated by city ordinance and accepted by the local population.

"Wait," April shouted, abruptly coming to a halt by the pedestrian crossing, alerting Ben. "Red light."

"Don't worry," he said, pulling her by the arm while stepping onto the street. "Cars will slow." Both kept crossing unhindered, directly headed for a place across the street displaying the sign indicating an eatery, Subway.

"My favorite place," April said on entering. Both took a seat by the counter, ordered a savory sandwich known for the place, while chatting about their past.

"I'm stuffed," April said, finishing up her plate while Ben paid the bill.

"What do you feel like doing," he asked her on the way out.

"How about the Salvation Army," she suggested. "I need a few things."

"I can take you there," he said.

"Just point me in the direction. I'll be a while getting some woman's needs."

He slightly hesitated but complied to her wishes giving directions to the place not far off.

April spent the next hour at the place selecting items she desperately need such as toothbrush and paste, hair brush, a pair of comfortable sneakers and shorts. "Excuse me," she muttered, bumping into another woman while reaching for a blanket.

"Don't mention it," the woman replied with a smile, giving her a once over. "You homeless?"

"Yes. I'm new in town."

The woman extended her hand, "Pixie."

"April," she said. "You live here?"

"Yes," was her reply. "Born here, live here, and probably die here."

"You must like it here," April suggested.

"Don't know anyplace else. Best place for skiing, hiking and biking, my life. Where're you from?"

"San Francisco."

"Wow," Pixie responded enthusiastically. "I always wanted to visit there. You must tell me about the place." Both finished up their purchases and together left the store.

"How come you shop at this place?" April was curious.

"I recently lost my job," she explained. "Don't have much money. Not many job opportunities in town. Needed a dress for an interview."

"What do you do?"

"Office secretary," she said with a hasted glance at her wrist watch. I've got to get going."

"Can we meet again," April asked, hoping they would.

"Sure. Where can I find you?"

"Acacia Park."

"Bye now," Pixie said while rushing off.

Ben showed up in the evening at the park. "You found what you needed," he asked after spotting her.

"I did." she said, inviting him to sit while brushing her hand over the comfort of the blanket, "care to join me." Sitting leisurely together, they watch the evening traffic while exchanging their day's activities. She sensed that he was preoccupied with something on his mind but ignored it. Getting ready to bed down for the night he finally approached her with, "You could sleep at my place."

And there it is," she thought. "The relationship offer." While she respected Ben's daytime presence and company, she was not ready for it. Though years had passed since his sudden departure, her mind was still tied to her past involvements, especially with Erik, her first love. She did not reject his friendly offer out of hand because she didn't wanted to spoil their friendship. Instead, she left the possibility open and stated, "I need to see the stars."

When he kept insisted, she held steadfast even after a police sergeant showed up on his evening round encouraging her to seek indoor shelter, or at least, "Get yourself a tent," he suggested.

"I will," she readily responded. It seemed that their homeless presence was tolerated during daytime but not for nighttime bedding down in a public park.

"You know where to find me if you change your mind," Ben offered on his departure.

"Thanks," she said, collecting her belongings and promptly set out on the quest of finding a more suitable location. It came in the form of a spot she'd noticed during her earlier stroll along the sidewalk two blocks to the south. "Cowboy's Nightclub," the building sign proclaimed.

"*Hmm,*" she thought after spotting the sign. "*Could be a place to earn some money.*

Night had fallen in the meantime with early customers arriving, as she watched from nearby their ID checking at the entrance. "That's the place," she'd decided.

"You can't stay here," the bouncer from the entrance ordered while approaching her presence, stating "this is a business place," and promptly chased her away.

She frowned, reluctantly backed off and walked away but not very far. She remembered the empty space at the next building entrance, an office complex. It was closed for the day and would remain so until the next morning, and longer on weekends. "Guess I'll stay here," she decided and folded out her blanked and pillow in front of the entrance. Since nobody from next door or otherwise bothered her, she decided to make it her place.

"Thanks," she muttered with a nod again and again, as departing patrons dropped dollar bills into her lap. It was two in the morning when the place finally closed for the night. Counting her earnings, $42, *"Not bad...not bad at all,"* she decided. "Think I'll stay." Since nobody ever complained it became her permanent spot.

For the first time since leaving California, she was content once more. April had found her new home.

Weeks later, one night she woke up, feeling a tickling on her face. With her eyes still closed, thinking it was a dog or cat licking her skin, her fingers touched something wet. On opening her eyes, she caught something new, something she had not seen before, little while clouds raining down on her. She thought she was dreaming, watching the beautiful scene illuminated by the street lights in its fullest splendor. She jumped up from her sleeping bag, stepped into the light and, with open arms, twirling her body, embraced the beauty of snowflakes touching her face. It was something new for April. It was the most exhilarating experience and joy she had ever felt and tasted. Her arms opened up wide to embrace the miracle of nature while twirling her body around and around, much like a child, laughing out loud. This experience alone was enough to keep her sleeping out in the open.

For April, one day was pretty much a repeat of the previous day, giving her time to recollect her past and her many failures in hope that the future would be kinder to her. And so, weeks had turned into months, until she noticed a permanent change in the season. Fall had set in and quickly followed with the cold of winter. It was here, waking up after a frosty night, when April realized what cold weather felt like on the body. "I've got to get some winter clothes," she muttered on waking up.

Where she was protected mostly from rain and heavy snow by the building entrance, winter cloths at times were not enough to keep the chill from her body. There were times on waking up when parts of her body were actually frozen. It was those days when she sought out a nearby shelter to defrost spending the coldest frostiest nights but always returned to her domicile next to the club.

Early one following spring day, April, after accepting the place as her permanent residence, easily adjusted to the town people's easy pace of life among the friends she'd made. Springtime was always a pleasure being awakened by the happy cheers of birds. It was a time to reminisce the past as well as planning out the year. Cuddled cozily under the blanket, daylight had just broken lacking street traffic, her mind was churning with opportunities in the quiet. "What should I do?" The question lingered on her mind for some time as she contemplated her options. "Should I stay here of move on?" The question was not at relocating to another spot in town. It was much bigger than that. Her concern was with the future. Where she has been in a comfort zone, earning enough money to make a living under the stars, and even accumulated enough earnings to carry her for months, she knew she had to change the course in direction but was reluctant to give up her acquired lifestyle.

"There you are," a voice interrupted her thoughts. "I thought it was you."

"What…who…", April stammered surprised, propping her body up on the elbow then recognized the face. "Pixie."

"I always wondered what happened to you. What are you doing here?"

"This is my home," she said with a grin. "I've been living here since we met."

"What. Out in the open. In the middle of town?"

"Yes," she said. "Don't you ever come downtown?"

"Not much since I started a new job. I work at an industrial park on the north end of town," Pixie informed her. "Let's have a Latte. I'm buying. We have some catching up to do."

It'd turned out to be a pleasant day for both. Getting ready to leave Starbuck's and hour later, "What do you feel like doing," Pixie asked.

"You lead on. I'll follow."

"Okay. The Mall it is." It had been months since April had been shopping at the Salvation Army. As for her personal possessions, she had the fundamental items deserving a homeless. As for anything else, it would hinder her mobility she'd object. Sure, there were the personal and incidentals every woman need such as toothpaste and brush, soap, comb, socks and pads, but these she could pick up at any convenient store in town.

She had not been to a Mall since her arrival, April completely enjoyed the place in the company of her friend. Whisking her in and out of the many shops, Pixie kept insisting her to get things but was declined with, "I don't have the space and where would I keep it."

The refusals made sense to Pixie but she seemed thrilled at having found her homeless friend. They spent the day together having drifted downtown into late evening. It was here when Pixie remarked, "Where are all the people coming from?"

"I know," April said, watching evening strollers crowding sidewalks and street crossings. "The same with the homeless.

It's getting crowded all around. Most come from the coast," she explained. "California is displacing many to other states. I hope it's not going to be a problem for the city. I'd hate having to give up my spot in town."

"You can always get a job," Pixie offered. "I'll help you find something when you decide."

"Really?" April was surprised. "It may just come to that." It would be an opportunity for April to think about in the quiet of night.

Since it was a Sunday with Pixie facing another work week she said, "I'll have to get some sleep now but promise to be back next week."

"I'm so glad you found me," April said. "I had a wonderful time and yes, I'll be right here. And thank you for all you did today." They parted with a hug.

Unfortunately, events would develop beyond their plans. Things would not remain this way. Since her arrival in the previous year, she, as well as her friends, had noticed changes pressing on their once-leisurely lifestyle. "Where're they all from?" she pondered, waiting for Ben's opinion as they walked along.

Their daily routine had mostly been the same since her arrival. Getting up late; cleaning up at the public place; seeking out a breakfast place, generally skipping lunch; taking a walk along Fountain Creek, a local river running along the town; napping noon hours away under some shaded tree; getting ready to 'work' the next hours, their expression for begging, an honorable trait; earning enough money for another night of social gathering; buying drugs or alcohol for the night; getting high on the substance until crashing into obliviousness—one after the other, repeated each day. For the time being, April maintained her promises to herself by staying clean of hard drugs and alcohol. Content for the most part, aside from a casual drag on a rolled joint, she did not feel the need to get drunk.

Already having lived here over a year, April considered herself seasoned to the town. Though Ben and she were seeing each other daily, with him bonding into a relationship but her considering friendship only with occasional sex, she could not push Eric from her thoughts. After all the years that had passed since he'd disappeared, she still loved him with all of her heart, but kept her emotions to herself. When the subject of love between her and Ben came up, she diverted any commitment to another time. The promise alone, though deferred, was enough for Ben to continue his casual relationship in favor of her needs.

Claiming stake next to the nightclub turned out to be the perfect location for her. During the daytime she stayed away from her spot so as to not interfere with the building's businesses, mostly occupied by legal offices. Once office hours were over, it was time for her to take possession, not over the entire building, only the front entrance. It was hers and everybody in the homeless community knew and respected it. Being a woman still held a preference over the homeless male population. Women were scarce among them and respected accordingly, much like during the frontier days.

The entrance to the building was not the only attraction for her nightly stay. More important was the place next door, a popular nightclub, Cowboys, frequented by thirsty patrons seeking to quench their needs. Watching the activities within from the outside, April wondered at times what went on within the club, but never had enough courage to enter. Although she mustered up enough courage a couple of times and approached club security at the entrance, she was told to stay out of the place, recognized as being homeless just by the clothes she wore, but they tolerated her evening presence lingering near the club entrance.

Her primary objective was to earn enough money from spent-happy patrons passing in and out through the evening and night. Aside from receiving personal attention from the customers she earned enough to pay for her daily needs.

To set pace with time, idle for the most part amidst likeminded friends who readily shared their substances, April eventually succumbed to drug use once more. Aware of her prior alcohol habit with subsequent rehab, she had vowed to stay clear of alcohol after her first arrival here. Drugs, she felt, were different from alcohol. Taking an occasional puff on a weed stick when offered, "I can manage and control the substance," she convinced herself. It took her some time to figure out the difference impacting her psyche. Where alcohol affected her mood in a negative way, making her angry and bad-tempered, drugs set her at ease and turned her happy. Though she'd noticed patrons chatting away cheerfully while getting drunk, alcohol affected her much like it had her mom, feeling miserable the following day.

She enjoyed her time in the company of Ben and his friends, habitual users to various drugs of individual preferences. For the time being, as long as the good times lasted, April was content, even though their lives were occasionally interrupted by firm, but friendly, police officers taking stock of the ever-increasing homeless population. Citizen complaints in the past year had become more frequent. To April's despair, more and more strangers were making their appearance, contributing to the negative connotation homeless places had acquired in recent years, and, in the process, adversely affecting the popularity of towns and cities.

While some homeless managed to preserve their personal appearances, others, mostly newcomers from the West Coast, succeeded in spoiling that image. Popular places for newly-arrived homeless were street corners and I-25 off-ramps, populated to entice drivers for a donation during a red light stop. To an observer, it became obvious that the homeless were tuned into a driver's motion seated behind the wheel, by reaching into a pocket or purse during the stop or remaining motionless. The notion might have been considered profiling in its own way, but it worked.

Regardless of the changes in time, as promised, Pixie kept in touch with April. As usually, they spent the day, not only with shopping but outings to nearby nature places as well. Her visits always brought joy into April's otherwise limited homeless existence.

HARSH REALITY

More time had passed at April's new location without so much as one personal incident. She could not be happier. Of course there was the occasional rebuff by a potential pedestrian when begging for money, but like all the other homeless after years in the community, she was hardened against rejections. The homeless did not take it personally, except perhaps a few hard-heads with an inflated ego and axe to grind with society and the government. It was only a natural response to let their frustrations out on the pedestrian with suppressed mutterings, such as a derogatory remark when rejected like, "Thanks, and come again," meant as an insult for not having a giving spirit.

Then, there were exceptions, as was the case within any society. There was the mentally disturbed, ranging from revenge to hate for anybody alive. This type was ready to pick a fight for a challenge when acknowledged. Fights were usually cut short by police stepping in because someone, a citizen, was always ready to inform the law with a 911 call. April, though familiar with smartphones, after watching passing visitors focused on the seemingly important and essential gadget, never understood how one's life and decisions could be directed by it. She was not aware, and had no interest in its entertainment aspect, as claimed by their owners, even though she became curious one early season after visitors arrived in troves, intently watching the screens, seemingly searching for something. Curious at first, she learned that they all were tuned into a game with purchase points earned, popular for a time.

For now, April was content within her chosen environment, celebrating a certain amount of recognition within her community. She had gained her respect some weeks ago when a homeless challenged her for her living quarters, the building entrance next to the nightclub. Patrons of the club were waiting in line by the entrance to get checked in. It was early evening when a stranger approached the space she occupied. "Can I join you?"

April appraised the stranger for a few seconds, then rejected his request. "There isn't enough space for two."

It must have set him off, being rejected by a woman. He stepped up craning down at her with the challenge, "Then one of us has to leave and it's not gonna be me."

Afraid she might lose her spot, she was on immediate alert. She deliberately stood up, shrugged off the overcoat slung over her shoulder, pushed back her shirt sleeves and faced him head on prepared for the fight leaning into his face. "Make me."

It was enough for him to lunge out and slap her face, but April was on guard. She blocked his arm. It startled him. It appeared that he had misjudged her. It had been some time since she had been forced into a fight. Generally, she tried to reject a fight with common sense and sound judgment. When that did not work, April allowed it to become a personal challenge. Depending on her mood, there had been times when she'd outright invited a fight. Such was the case here.

April waited for his reaction.

"I'll just have to teach you a lesson." He hauled an angry punch of his fist out at her face.

April quickly sidestepped and, in retaliation, delivered a powerful kick to his head. It was what fighters termed a roundhouse kick, in her case lethal enough to floor the opponent. Stunned and at a loss for words, he shook his head to clear his vision, faced her for another punch delivery, but missed his target again.

Pedestrians had gathered around the fighters, watching her skills while cheering her on: "Go get him" and "That's it, girl." Without any further words wasted on the now wholly-enraged homeless, April delivered another powerful kick, but this time to his gut. He sank to the sidewalk gasping for air. April was heralded for her skills in flooring what seemed to be a superior opponent in size as well as strength. When people realized that she was a homeless, they reached into their pockets and rewarded her with enough money to last her a few days. She extended her gratitude with a smile thanking *maybe I should turn professional.*

The homeless regained his strength and with some help from passing pedestrians quietly left into the night. Word about the fight got around quick to warn others in the homeless community. "Don't mess with her. She's a killer."
From that day on, April gained a deserving respect from her community of homeless. She had earned her black belt once more.

Today, April, in the company of Ben and friends, was seated at the Starbucks on Cascade Avenue, their favorite hangout for morning coffee. It was the first warm day in March after a long and cold winter. Winters for the homeless were especially harsh since most activities were restricted to indoors, contradictory to the free spirited culture of spending much of their lives outdoors. While many would seek shelter during nighttime, there were the diehard, weathering it out in the open no matter how frigid. Depending on the individual's coverage to keep the body warm, most would survive the cold while some perish in the process and others wound up in hospitals with frostbitten fingers and toes.

Spring was always welcomed as the beginning of a new year filled with promises, especially this year, 2020. There had been rumors in recent months about it being a special year in a mix of psychic predictions as well as biblical prophecies. In past years such predictions were mostly centered on end-of-the-world calamities, but this time around, they were focused more on a new world order uprising in the political arena, as well as enlightenment in the spiritual realm. It was today's discussion topic between April, Ben, and his friends.

Opinions were lively amidst the group, illustrating their personal knowledge on the subject in between taking sips of the richly-flavored Starbucks coffee. Cafes and convenience stores seemed to tolerate the homeless in town as long as they behaved orderly while at the place. Today, most were involved in discussing and defending their own opinions when April caught a news item on the TV scrolling across the screen. What got her attention was the header stating a "Breaking News" flash. What followed was a public warning about a new strain of virus sweeping the world. As she watched intently, the details that followed alarmed April. It specified the accidental release of a coronavirus, a deadly strain more lethal than those previously experienced.

"Listen up," she alerted the group, trying to get their attention. "Watch the screen." With the TV sound volume turned down, they had to strain their ears to understand all of the broadcast. Now intensely listening, most shrugged it off as an inflated news item, but April took it seriously. "This is not good."

"Forget it," Ben responded to her concerns. "Just another scare." As was the case with many homeless, the ones that could still comprehend had developed an innate distrust of the government and the news media alike. In their mindset, much of it was a conspiracy directed specifically at the homeless, trying to eradicate their independence lifestyle.

April remained quiet but vividly recalled the plight people suffered living through a couple of strains before several years ago. *What were they called?* she tried to remember. *Ah yes, MERS and SARS.* She decided to keep a close watch and not mix with strangers, knowing how vulnerable the homeless were to infections and viral diseases.

Finished with coffee and cupcakes, the group decided to make room for the daily lunch crowd to take over the space, heading for the creek. Their focus was a sought-out spot to spend much of the day in leisure. It was also a place to make new friends. What was not so pleasant was the filth some homeless left behind since many had put up their tents near the water. It was a convenient place to relieve themselves since they were too lazy to seek out public restrooms. While some homeless tried to care about the environment they occupied, other's did not. It was those that gave their culture a bad name.

April made it her mission to closely follow further news as the pandemic developed, newly specified as COVID-19. Starbucks became their morning gathering spot. She sensed that from here on that their lives, like all of the nation's, would change. Bombarded by government and health organizations with news that seemed to change daily from bad to worse, the homeless' living conditions were severely affected. First, there was the case of wearing a mask, mandated wherever one went. It might have been an inconvenience, but with masks bought up by health clinics, there were none available in stores for the public. As Ben and friends shrugged it off as mere hype, April looked everywhere, but shelves were emptied out. "What's going on?" she would inquire of the store clerk.

"Transportation stopped delivering," was the common reply.

When health organizations demanded the public wash hands multiple times daily, April would yell at the TV in frustration, "Don't tell me to wash my hands when you took all the soap supplies from us!" Where it affected mostly cleaning supplies, it got worse in the following weeks. Much worse. Shelves began to empty with all sorts of items from paper to groceries.

What made it bad was it affected food items, including snacks, a homeless' staple. Many went hungry, including April. It took weeks to set up enough soup kitchens to accommodate everybody. No matter what the city tried, nothing seemed to be enough. What rapidly followed had even greater impact on their survival: all stores and eateries closed with a mandatory COVID-19 lockdown.

It was not long after when the first homeless began to disappear from the scene. When April inquired about his or her whereabouts, "Oh," she was told. "They took them away." Her guess was as good as anybody's. It was either to the hospital or the morgue. Days later, one of Ben's friends was gone. Then another disappeared shortly after.

"What's going on?" April was stunned. "Are we going to be next?" she would lament to Ben. He was just as sympathetic after losing his friends. Soon it was only the two of them left from the group. The last TV news April caught at Starbucks before it closed permanently was the appearance of personal face masks. Since there were none available in the local stores, she proclaimed, "I'm gonna make us some."

There was enough material from the now deserted homeless tents to fashion masks. She made it her mission to use her acquired craft, though rudimentary, to supply others with masks made from scraps of materials they'd left behind. Homeless camps were ransacked by others to salvage whatever was usable, unaware that much of it had been infected by the virus. They too became victims at hospitals and morgues.

When April and Ben realized how easily and prolifically the virus was spreading, they went into hiding. The spot they found was a storage shed at one of the vacated stores on the south end of town.

"I wonder who could have abandoned the place," April said.

"Maybe they got scared and left town," Ben suggested. "Maybe the virus got them. I don't care. We just got lucky finding the place."

It proved to be a perfect hiding place since there were enough canned goods to last them weeks and maybe even months.

Days went by living in seclusion, then weeks without much change for them. "I wonder what's happening outside," April said, making conversation. Both took to making frequent comments and remarks like this throughout the day to keep their spirits and hope up for survival. With the country in lockdown condition with everybody confined to their home, April was afraid that it wouldn't take much for bad elements to emerge.

She proved right in her assumption. Fortunately, whoever owned the place had left the TV behind. To their surprise, utilities were still functional supplying power and water. They were able to catch the daily news warning citizens, first about break-ins and theft, quickly followed by looting. The bad news did not stop there. Riots had already started on the East Coast as well as out west. Before long, they escalated to taking over entire city blocks and migrating into smaller cities and towns as well. "I guess," April voiced her concerns, "we're the lucky ones."

"Why lucky?" Ben said, trying to reason out their own plight.

"We haven't had any riots yet. I guess people have more sense here. I wouldn't want to be trapped in a big city," April remarked. It was not the first time they had witnessed rioters destroying entire neighborhoods. Both followed the destruction of the country closely since there was not much else to do other than watch television. For the time being April and Ben felt safe. Though all of their friends were gone, dispersed or hospitalized, they kept their spirits alive with daily walks along the nearby river banks of Fountain Creek.

When exploring downtown, with police patrolling streets, they did not feel safe. "Looks like a ghost town," April said. "I wonder how long the government will keep us locked in."

"It doesn't look promising," Ben agreed. "Health organizations insist on one thing with the government claiming just the opposite. I guess they are as confused as we are."

"What do you think we should do," April pondered, "if this lasts much longer?" They had been confined for several weeks already without an end in sight.

"I think it's just the beginning of a long term from the Corona statistics on the news."

"I don't want to live like this," she complained.

"We've got no choice, do we? I'd rather stay here than being confined to a shelter," Ben declared, with rumors spreading about chaotic conditions of such places.

"Me too." Dialogue like this kept them in harmony.

"Besides," he added, "here we can do as we please. We couldn't sleep together in the shelter." He shot her a wink accompanied by a slight grin.

April remained silent. She wished he wouldn't bring up the subject of sex. She felt guilty about it because her love was still with Eric. Greg had also been an important part in her life, but, with time and distance, his memory had slowly been fading from her mind. She did not plan her involvement with Ben. It just happened one night after his friends were gone. Huddled together at the place they presently occupied, sleeping on the floor without blankets and chilled by the night's cold, it happened. Then they had sex again. While Ben seemed to enjoy it, she did not. To her it was more like a chore. Repeated almost nightly.

It's not what love should be, she thought in the quiet of night with Ben on top of her body, rapidly breathing into her ear. She hated herself for breaking the bond she still carried with Eric. *Why did you desert me?* her mind screamed into the nighttime silence, with tears trickling down her cheeks.

"What's the matter?" Ben said, surprised at her reaction. "Did I hurt you?"

"No. It's not you. I am feeling sorry for myself."

"But why?"

"The situation I'm in. I never thought I'd wind up living like a thief, hiding from one place to the next."

"Don't worry about it. It's only temporary."

"I meant for the rest of my life."

"I thought you liked living on the open."

"I do," she confided. "But not hidden inside a store."

"That'll change. I promise."

"How would you know? We could wind up living this way forever."

"Not a chance," he consoled her. "Corona will blow over like it did before. I've lived through several flu strains."

"You have?" It surprised her that he was still alive. "What about the hundred thousand deaths in this country alone and millions more worldwide?"

"Don't believe everything you hear on the news."

"Why shouldn't I?" She was puzzled at his boldness.

"It's mostly scare tactics and inflated statistics."

"You can't be serious. Why would the government do that?"

"It's pure political agenda."

"Could you explain it to me?"

"Okay," he said. "Rumors have it that it was supposed to be a Lab exercise, much like the war games scheduled with our allies on a periodic basis."

"But for what purpose?"

"There are several reasons much like in football. First, it practices battle strategies for winning in case of a war. Second, it'll identify shortages."

"Shortages in what?"

"Supply lines, ammo, proficiency in soldier performance, deficiencies in military preparedness, and many more flaws in the system."

"I get the picture, but what does it have to do with the virus?"

"Same thing," Ben explained. "Up to now, no country had an idea about how to effectively treat a Corona type virus. There has never been enough time to develop an effective immunization plan. They sweep the globe every few years, causing tens of thousands in human casualties."

"But there are already over one hundred thousand deaths in the U.S. alone," she said with a furrowed forehead. "I saw it in the latest news."

It became apparent to him that she feared for her life. Their lives.

"That's true. But," he explained, trying to calm her, "that's because health organizations are counting virus infections for the first time. It's never been done before."

"I don't understand the connection."

"It's like this," he said. "What you hear on mainstream media is just another Breaking News item. In today's world of instant information, everything is slated as breaking news."

"But why?"

"Good news doesn't sell. It's bad news people like to watch."

"That's terrible." April did not see it this way. "I like to watch nature shows and documentaries."

"Most people don't. They are tuned into CNN and FOX for a big part of the day."

"But why only watch the bad news?"

"It's a way of life now. Things used to be different when you were a kid growing up."

"I didn't watch TV. Mom wouldn't let me. Said it was not for children."

"I'm sorry about the way you grew up, but most children were able to enjoy family and childhood."

"How come you know so much?" April realized that she did not know anything about him.

"I was in the Army several years assigned to overseas."

"How did you wind up being homeless?"

"Got kicked out of the service for insubordination."

"But why?"

"For being AWOL."

"What does it mean?" She'd never heard about it.

"Absent without leave."

"Absent where?"

"It means that a soldier did not make it back to base on time before closing the gates or left the camp without permission." She understood. "Tell me more," April insisted, "about Corona. Will they ever develop a vaccine?"

"Science is working on it. As a matter of fact, they have been working on it for a hundred years."

"I don't understand."

"Ever since the Spanish Flu, each time a virus sweeps the globe, countries have been trying to develop an anti-serum against the specific strain. Unfortunately, the virus develops a resistance and morphs into another strain. The result is pretty much the same."

"What?"

"Vaccination trails behind the current strain and is not very effective."

"Yeah?"

"Medical science hasn't been able to predict a uniform morphed strain. Let's not dwell on the misery. I'm getting hungry. We got anything left to eat?"

More weeks and months slipped by April and Ben with them repeating pretty much the same daily routine. They slept in late, like many people did these days with privacy restrictions enforced. They took occasional strolls around downtown to check on the homeless and store situation but always returned with the same results, "Locked up and no homeless in sight."

Today, close to noon, it was time to get up anyway. "We're out of things," April reported after checking the canned goods locker.

"Let's take a trip to Safeway," Ben suggested. "I hear they reopened and are restocking."

"What about the lockdown?" April was always the cautious one.

"We'll see. Just get ready. We can use the restroom there to wash up."

Fifteen minutes later they entered the sliding door at the store. "Masks," the store clerk, seated by the entrance, ordered with a gesture at their faces. Both pulled their mask from their pockets and strapped them across the face. "Follow the arrows," the clerk directed. Their first trip was to the restroom. Cleaning was limited to only a quick splash in the face and washing hands because cleansing containers and paper dispensers were empty.

Since they had not been to the store in recent weeks, both were somewhat impressed at the orderly fashion in which shoppers proceeded. Following prominent arrows pasted to the floor to guide the shoppers, it was up one aisle and down the next, passing along partially-empty shelves. Though some items had been restocked, others, mostly toilet paper and many food products and disinfecting items, were still missing. "What should we do?" April said. "Try another place?"

"Let's just get whatever we can."

"How about the beans?"

"I've had beans to last me a lifetime," Ben said, looking around for more items just as a supply clerk appeared from the stockroom. "Is this all you have?" Ben queried with a gesture at the empty shelves.

"Whatever you see on shelves is all we've got," the clerk said, suppressing a sneeze then wiping his face on his jacket sleeve. He quickly disappeared again back into the stockroom.

"Beans again," Ben said, reaching for the few cans left with a wrinkled face. April grabbed a loaf of bread and some oranges on the way out, paying for the few items.

"Are you getting more stock?" April asked the cashier.

"Every week. Just keep checking," he replied.

"I don't understand something," April said while walking back to their place."

"What?"

"With the store almost empty of shoppers, how come there is no food?"

"Traders are hoarding," Ben replied, and truckers quit driving."

"You can't be serious."

"It's been done every time there's a disaster. Greed takes over the ones in charge."

"I don't believe it." April gasped. She could not believe how ignorant she was about worldly things.

"It's the traders, the merchants, the brokers waiting for opportunities like the one we're facing. They take control over the economy and let everybody suffer."

"It's not fair," April said with disgust.

"Ask yourself the question," he said. "Why am I homeless?"

"Now I understand."

Days later, April suggested, "Why don't we go into town and see what restaurants are open? I'm getting tired of eating beans only. I need a change."

"I'm tired," Ben said in-between coughing spells. "Besides, I don't feel well." He had been coughing and sniveling through the night. April checked him over and noticed his red nose and sore face. Since there was no paper to wipe, he'd been using his shirt sleeve to clear his face. "Do we have any aspirin?"

"Let me check." She did not find any.

Ben's condition got worse over the next several days. He'd developed a fever on top of having difficulty breathing. "You should see a doctor," April suggested several times, but he just shrugged it off with, "I'll get over it."

"What if it's the virus?"

"Not a chance. I'm healthy."

"You don't look it," she would reply, hoping he would respect her concerns.

"Let's go," she finally insisted.

"Where're we going?"

"The emergency clinic," she insisted the following day.

Ben's condition had turned from bad to worse in the last couple of days, with him too weak to resist. As April helped him along, he willingly followed to the nearest clinic. "He needs help," April told the masked orderly in charge.

"Wait a minute," the registrar, seated behind the desk, also wearing a mask, demanded. "I need an ID and insurance card."

"He doesn't have any," April said with a shrug of her shoulders.

"You can't come in," the woman insisted.

"He's homeless," April said, discouraged by the registrar's attitude. "He has to see a doctor."

Identifying as homeless triggered a response from an orderly nearby, who said, "I'll take care of him," and promptly disappeared down the hall. Seconds later he came back pushing a wheelchair. "You can't come back here," the orderly insisted when April tried to follow.

"When can I see him?"

"Check back tomorrow," he suggested, disappearing inside the double doors.

It was the last time April would see Ben. Though he was treated and strapped to a respirator, he never recovered.

She was informed days later when checking on him at the clinic, "He died from Corona infection."

April was shocked, not only because he was gone, but because she had developed similar symptoms a couple of days earlier. Though she tried to suppress her coughing spells while at the clinic, she was detained by the registrar. "I'll have to test you."

"Test me for what?" she objected, fearing the worst.

"Coronavirus."

Hearing that, she panicked and rushed to leave, but the orderly detained her. "Don't be afraid. We test everybody. It's better this way."

April, against her will, was detained at the clinic. Resisting a thorough examination, she tried to escape several times but, with additional aides, was restrained to a table. That day, after being administered medication, she succumbed to unconsciousness.

For the next three weeks, strapped to a respirator, heavily sedated, April was kept alive through life-saving equipment. Mostly incoherent, she went in and out of consciousness without being aware. When the medical staff decided that it was safe for her to be removed from the respirator, she went into convulsions.

"She stopped breathing," the medical aide, panic stricken, yelled out.

"Put it back," the lead physician quickly ordered the staff, who promptly reconnected the tubes. "She has to learn to breath on her own."

What happens when a patient is kept alive by the respirator is that the body's automatic motor functions for breathing stops. When the brain registers the change, it turns the function over to the equipment. When removed, the brain has to instruct the lungs to take over once more. This can only be accomplished by the patient himself forcing the initial breaths back into the lungs. However, it can be problematic if the patient's lungs, nerves, or muscle functions have been damaged, in which case surgery may become necessary before removing the respirator. In rare cases, when the patient may be too old to perform surgery, the respirator has to take over breathing for life.

"Breathe…breathe," the voice pressed on her brain as April regained consciousness. At first, she did not comprehend that the order was directed at her. The result was her suffocating and gasping for air again. It took several such attempts before her brain finally took control over her breathing function.

"Where am I?" April muttered at the medical staff surrounding the bed and monitors. She had just regained full consciousness and did not recognize her environment isolated within plastic sheets all around with the steady clicking of ventilator instruments turned silent.

"ICU," a voice stated.

"What am I doing here?" she demanded.

"Coronavirus attacked your body and damaged your lungs. We had to put you on equipment support."

"How long was I under?"

"Three weeks."

"Three weeks?" she shouted in disbelief.

Fully awake by now, something was pressing on her abdomen. She tried to get up with an urge for the bathroom.

"Not so fast," the physician attending to her said, pushing her back onto the bed. "Somebody get a pan."

Minutes later, April was coherent again but still shocked from the traumatic experience of suffocating. Though fading over time, the experience would remain with her for life. "Can I leave now?" she asked.

"Not yet," was the reply. "You're too weak to walk. We'll let you know."

April spent a couple more weeks in hospital recovery before she was strong enough to leave. On her way out, she was stopped by the checkout clerk. "I need to see your ID."

"I don't have any."

"How about your insurance card?"

"I don't have any."

"Who's going to pay the bill?" the clerk demanded.

"I'm homeless," April said. "Welfare, I guess."

"Have a seat." She was directed to a waiting section.

Minutes later an administrator showed up with a notepad and forms to fill out. She did as directed and was on her way thirty minutes later. The hospital had been her home for more than one month, but now she was out in the open again. This time, because she had no friends left, and she was penniless, hungry, and without a place to live, she felt the harsh reality more so than any time in her past.

April was at a loss. The hospital was miles up north at the fringes of town, too far for her to walk to the city. She went back inside the hospital and sought out an empty chair by the picturesque window facing the Rockies and sat there for the longest time while contemplating her next move. "Do I stay or move elsewhere?"

It was thoughts like this she tried to resolve. Other thoughts, not so pleasant, passed through her mind as well. There was Eric. Though distant, the connection was still real and alive.

Then there was Greg. Though she had not been in love with him, she still could not fathom the depth of psychological damage it had caused when he'd been so abruptly torn from her life, but she considered herself fortunate to be alive.

And last in her relationships there was Ben and his friends. All gone from Earth but still very vivid in her mind.

Too much time had already passed for her to clearly remember Kendo, her Japanese instructor, other than visualizing his excellent fighting skills.

With images like this skimming through her saddened mind, she became overwhelmed with uncertainties about what to do with herself. She even contemplated following her friends into the unknown. She called it the unknown because April had never learned about faith. Her mom, having been an atheist, had never taught her the sanctity of religion. She never learned the prayers of God, any god, to take her from life's miseries. Though she was aware of one certain deity, Krishna, found someplace in Earth's distant places and worshipped by some homeless, the fortunate ones having traveled there, she had never acquired its divine knowledge. Saddened even more at the lost opportunity, she realized that it could have saved her from complete misery.

Then, the thought struck to her, "I'm gonna follow my friends." It was a decision she knew would be a final one because nobody had ever returned from the abyss of death. She pulled herself together and approached the hospital pharmacy window. "I need some medication."

"Let me see the prescription," the clerk demanded.

"I don't have any. I'm homeless."

It seemed that was enough for the clerk to consider. "Who's your doctor?"

"I don't know. I was in a coma for the past month."

"Let me check. What's your name?"

April readily gave her the name and waited, hoping it would be enough information to satisfy the medical requirements to get the medication.

"What's the problem?" the clerk said.

"I have headaches that won't stop." Minutes later, she was handed a prescription. "Methadone," she read on the label. She'd heard from others addicted to the substance and knew it was a powerful opioid, enough to kill, if one chose to do so.

April left the pharmacy window, headed for the water dispenser, undecided what to do with it. She decided, "I'll take just one to see its effects."

"Time to go. Visitor hours are over," a voice prodded into her semi-unconscious state. Angered at the intrusion into her world of vivid dreams, she opened her eyes and rudely demanded, "What?"

"You must go now."

Staring at the uniformed guard, she knew it was time to leave if she did not want to wind up in jail. Back to full reality, she gathered enough energy to walk herself to the exit, driven by one thought: "What a shitty world."

The few hours under the influence of the opioid at the hospital was enough time to defer her initial thought about life and death. Sobered once more, she concluded, "I'll give life one more chance," to avoid taking on the responsibility herself. She lingered by the exit, undecided where to go next.

April managed to hitch a ride with one late visitor headed back to town. "Where you headed?" the driver wanted to know.

She thought for a minute, then said, "Drop me off at Kiowa and Tejon." Twenty minutes later they arrived. As she departed, the driver yelled after her, "Enjoy the clubs." There was no other place in the city April would consider. It was the hub of what limited nightlife there was in the city. "Home again," she muttered when she spotted a few familiar homeless faces gathered nearby at the intersection.

A popular intersection in the middle of downtown Colorado Springs, people still referred to the city as a town. The reason being, though the town had seen tremendous growth in recent years like many others across the states, the influx only occurred in the outlying suburbs. It was the core of the city, three to four city blocks of stores, clubs and restaurants, that attracted local citizens and visitors alike.

"Where have you been?" one in the group, who'd recognized her, said. "I thought you were dead. You know, Corona and all."

"I almost did die," she said. "Spent six weeks in the ICU."

"Welcome back. Glad you're alive. Want a fix?" he offered, reaching for a smoke.

"Yeah, thanks," she accepted. "What's new with the virus?" Having been dead to the world, she was curious about its state.

"Can't get into any place. Can't do anything. The whole country is locked up. People are ordered to stay home. All places are closed. Just take a look," he directed with a gesture up and down the intersection.

"Bummer," she admitted. "What about shelters and soup kitchens?"

"Still open. As a matter of fact," she was informed, "they're the only places open." Among her own kind again, the world did not appear as empty as she'd anticipated when leaving the hospital. "It would, could, be a new beginning," she thought with a glimmer of hope, pushing thoughts of her earlier despair from her mind.

TALE OF TWO CITIES

Having been permitted a new start in life after her bout with Corona, as despairing a life as it was, April had new hopes. Though only a glimmer, it was a start, nevertheless. It was this glimmer she'd build her future on. With the world on hold, due to the lingering pandemic, April had ample time to think about it. "What should I do next?" kept pressing on her mind, and "What could I do?" She suddenly realized how empty and useless her life had been, wasting away her adult years. The picture album she had started years ago was out of the question. All of her work and equipment had been lost to conditions beyond her control, with everybody dear to her lost under similar circumstances. She suddenly realized that, for her to go on, "I need something meaningful. It's got to be something to occupy my time other than just waiting for things to happen only compensated with a daily dose of drugs. But what?"

She realized, in order to come clean and remain that way, that it would take some disciplined effort on her part. A thought occurred to her. Why not write? In other words, she could record her past experience. It would have to be something meaningful other than just scribbles. "Why not write a book?"

Immediately discouraged at the thought, she realized she would not know how to even begin. She dropped the idea, but came up with a better one. "What about another journal?"

Only another failure, she thought. After contemplating alternatives she could not come up with one. "Journal it is," she decided with finality. It was the glimmer of hope April was counting on. It would become her mission again like years earlier. She'd plan to keep track of her daily life, as unworldly a life as it was, but with the inspiring thought of getting better, more motivating. Encouraged, her first trip the following day was to the Salvation Army. She located what she needed, a notepad and pen. April was set to begin her new journey. A journey into her mind.

With the Corona mask mandate just recently lifted outdoors, for the first time she was back at her favorite place she had claimed the previous year as hers, the spot on the storefront of the building next to Cowboys nightclub to spent nights, while seated at the base of her "Tree" at Arcadia Park most days.

Today, seated undecidedly, with the sun warming the grounds, she stared at the empty pages of her new journal. "What should I write? How do I begin?" Then it came to her. "Why not write the tale of two cities?" The thought gave her the stimulation she needed. Since she knew the intricacies of two cities, San Francisco and Colorado Springs, she could write about her own experiences in comparison by drawing similarities and contrasts from the homeless perspective, her perspective.

"But I don't have any material to start with." The thought dispirited her. But, minutes later, it came to her. "I'll start with the past. I've got ample material in my memory." April wrote in the diary, as the first entry, "What have I accomplished in life?"

"Nothing," she responded and scribbled an entry. Since she did not have the proper education every child deserved, she did not even know how to create a meaningful diary.

"Why not?" she questioned herself. After giving it some thought there was only one answer.

"Mom's fault." Though she did not want to shift blame onto the only family member she'd ever known, she could not see an alternative. In recollection, it seemed that she was dependent on her mom until age five. By the time she was old enough to talk, though only with limited vocabulary, it was enough to make sense to people. It was sufficient for her daily trot to the store and ordering things on credit. She did not know how and when the goods were paid for, even less where the money for the apartment rent came from.

"What have I learned in the process of growing up?" was her next entry. Groping for the answer, her mind remained a blank. Saddened, "I don't even know how to play children's games," was the thing that came to mind. "Too depressing," she muttered, deciding not to dwell on the early years pushing such thoughts from her mind.

"What do I know about life?" Other than knowing she was an expert in begging for money and drugs, and surviving on a bare minimum of food, her knowledge was very limited. Luxury to her was only a dream. She could not relate to the values it provided. "Okay then. What is left that I can write about?"

Her mind was already exhausted from groping for ideas. "I'll continue in the morning." Not happy with her progress, she closed the pad and tossed it into a shopping bag, along with the meager contents she had bought earlier in the day when a voice interrupted her, "where have you been? I thought you'd left town."

Surprised and curious she looked up into the smiling face of her friend, "Pixie!

April joyfully jumped to her feet and rushed close to embrace her friend stating, "You have no idea how happy I am to see you."

"I've been looking for you for weeks," apparently happy, Pixie states.

They hugged then spent the rest of the day reporting their personal experiences on how they had coped with the constant mandated changes by government and health institutions, in between breaks for lunch and later for dinner.

On departing, Pixie promised to get in touch with April when in town. The thought alone provided enough inspiration for April to start the journal and a new life.

ANOTHER JOURNAL

Today, early in the morning hours, April crouched, on her haunches with her back propped against the trunk of her Tree, at her favorite squatter spot. Newly energized after her friends visit, thoughts about her past flowed easily from her mind to the pages of the journal, touching on several more highlights from the past before a thought struck her. "My God, I only know one place." This created an anxiety she had not anticipated. "What am I going to write?" She counted the few lines she had managed to write and wondered how to fill in the blanks left staring back at her.

It triggered an inspirational thought she had not expected. "Write about your life from here on into the future." It was more of a command than a suggestion. "Thank you, Eric," she muttered, hoping it was his spirit that was directing her. Shifting her view from the blank page to her surroundings, for the first time she perceived a world filled with wonders. Though Colorado Springs was a small city, she realized that it contained a world of wonders on its own terms, waiting to be explored.

April suddenly become aware that the town had come alive while her mind was still anchored on the past. "It's the present I live in," she happily decided, looking at people passing in a new light. "Yeah."

With the awakening she'd just had, she hoped it would guide her from here on out. It would be her inspiration for facing an otherwise meaningless existence. She felt that her entire life had been wasted, but immediately replaced the thought with a happier one: "How else could I write about the past?" It put her mind at ease when recalling past highlights, including hardships as well as pleasant times, though a rare occasion.

"I wonder what he's up to," she thought while assessing a young, casually-dressed pedestrian approaching her. She suspected that he had spotted her further up the road since she'd noticed a dollar bill in his hand. "Here we go again," she thought, watching him drop the bill into her lap before briskly walking on before she could say a word. "I've got to change my appearance."

What she really wanted was to ask him a few questions for her journal. "How else can I learn about organized life?" Shy by nature, she knew she was not bold enough to approach anybody to take the initiative. For the time being, she was satisfied to just sit and watch people on approach. It gave her the time to formulate some ideas for her entries.

"Time to get going," she muttered, collecting her things. It was the homeless' strategy; if one spot did not pan out, "go and move on." This served two purposes. First, a walk provided some exercise for the day, and two, it changed the scene for other opportunities.

April had not come to grips yet about how to support herself in the midst of the pandemic. Having been granted a second chance at life after surviving the virus, she did not want to revert into the same boring trot of being a homeless. She felt that her mission was to be recognized for something other than just begging, something worth living for. She had to find something in the interim until her dream came through for publishing the book, still pending inspiration.

To fill her time, she stopped by Subway's, the place up the street, again frequented by most homeless in town. It was conveniently located across the street from Acadia Park, the nightly home for the homeless on dry days. Stepping up to the counter, she checked the menu on the wall, deciding what to buy for one dollar. "Five dollars," she muttered unhappily. "Everything is five dollars."

The counter server recognized her and said, "Hi. How can I help today?"

"You got anything for one dollar?"

"Only what's listed on the menu."

"I only have a dollar." Hungry and unhappy, April lingered for a second, then turned to exit the place. She heard the server call after her, "Wait. Here."

April stepped back to the counter. "I can't pay for it."

"Don't worry about it," the server said with a smile, handing her the lunch bag. "Enjoy."

"Thank you. I won't forget this." She left the store, happily heading for the park. This kind act gave her the idea to capture every incident of her daily passage through town for the journal. "I've got a purpose in life," she muttered, thankful for a new direction.

DRUG IMPACT ON APRIL

April, like most times after waking up in front of the building she had taken ownership of, began her daily routine with a trip to the public facilities at Acadia Park two blocks up on Bijou Street. As was the case today, she was awakened by the night watchman touching her gently on the shoulder. "Time to go."

Like many retirees working nights, he was complementing his meager social security earnings with additional income. On the job for three years already, nothing had ever happened to require his services other than a periodic round through the halls of the building. He wondered sometimes why building management kept him on the job. *Must be tradition,* he pondered, *but a welcome one.*

To keep from total boredom, after the club next door closed and street traffic quieted down, he usually spent some time with the homeless woman living at the building entrance. While management would not have allowed her to stay at the entrance, he had made a deal with her so she could spend nighttime hours there, as long as she did not cause any disturbances. It would surely cost him his job if there was a report.

April had made a similar arrangement with the police captain on night duty at their downtown precinct across the street, down one block on Tejon Street. In earlier days she would have been chased off and forced into one of the homeless shelters, but with the state's liberal political change, law enforcement had become more tolerant and understanding of the homeless' needs. She was grateful for it. For her daily personal hygienic needs, the public facility was only a couple of blocks away at Acadia park. It's where she was presently waiting to perform her morning chores. "Hi." April was greeted by a new face waiting for a stall at the restroom to be vacated. She gave him a quick once-over to assess his status. Since the facility was shared with the public, many common citizens, especially children using the playground, stepped in and out.

"Are you homeless?" she said, assuming his social status.

"What do you want to hear?" he said, not committing to anything.

"Why? What's the big deal?" she said, slightly irritated at his evasiveness. "Most of us are. It's nothing to be ashamed of."

"It's not that," he said, more accommodating. "I just got here and don't know anybody. I didn't want to come on strong. Sorry."

"You're forgiven," she said, reaching out with her hand.

He readily accepted hers and shook it. "I'm Aaron. What's your name?"

"April. Welcome to the Springs."

"Looks like a nice, quiet town," he said. "Where're you from?"

"California."

"Any special place?" he asked.

"San Francisco."

"Wow," he exclaimed. "I always wanted to go there. I hear it's beautiful. How come you left?"

"It used to be a beautiful city, but not anymore."

"Why? What happened?"

"There're too many of us. City council chased us out of town. They don't care about the homeless anymore."

"Tell me more," he insisted.

"I'll tell you what," she suggested. "Meet me at the knoll outside. I've got to go." One stall had just vacated and Aaron offered her the first chance. "Nice. Thank you." She stepped into the stall and locked it after her.

"See you there," she heard him say.

Sure enough, he was waiting for her when she walked up the knoll. Though it was only a short incline to her favorite resting place, a huge elm tree, her Tree, she referred to it as her knoll as well. Since April had established seniority among the homeless in town who knew her, most accepted her claim.

The knoll was about fifty feet distant, so she had a chance to study his persona. Slender and tall in build, pleasant looking face covered by an almost bronze tanned skin she casually approached him. She wondered about that; he must be an outdoors person. In contrast to his skin was a set of dark, well-groomed wavy hair. Though, ever since they had connected there was something that bothered her about him. She had gained enough wisdom, studying homeless come and go, to get a feel for their personalities. For some reason she could not explain, she thought, "His looks don't match his character."

From the personality perspective he seemed nice enough to be sociable. The problem she sensed was with his responses during their chats. For now, she put her concerns aside while facing him.

"So," April said, both seated on a nearby bench, "what brought you here?"

"Opportunities," he said.

"Business?" April said, trying to clarify. "Opportunity covers a wide range." While in her past she had accepted everything she was told, now, after having been educated somewhat by Eric and Greg, she had grown to be not only inquisitive but cautious as well.

"You may call it that." Since he did not provide any specifics, she left it as such for the time being. "I'd heard that this is the place to be for any business venture."

"Well," April corrected him, "that was before Corona. I'm not so sure about now. Many things have changed. I think it'll be some time before business, any business, picks up."

"Where there is a need there is a prospect, especially during hardship times. I'll find my calling."

"In what do you specialize?'

"Commodities."

"Stocks?"

"Anything people desire and need." Since he was rather evasive with her queries, she left it at that and waited for him to initiate the topic. Though she had developed an interest in other people, she was not a nosy person. *What was it called,* she tried to remember Eric educating her on meaningful conversation, *knowledge and wisdom. "Wisdom,"* she recollected, *"is still a long way off for me."*

"What?" He did not seem to understand.

"Nothing. I was just thinking."

"What's there to do in town?" he said, changing the topic.

"For now, nothing. Everything's still under lockdown."

"Then," he pried, "what do you do every day?"

"Don't have a plan yet. I just came out of the hospital."

"What's the problem?" He seemed to back off a distance.

"Coronavirus," she said. "I almost died but got immunized."

"Then," he said, "I don't have to worry about catching it." He might have been right in his assumption, or not. It all depended on how truthful the WHO and CDC[20] were about disclosures on the science and behavior of the virus.

"I think you're safe. I haven't infected anybody."

"Glad to hear it. I'd like us to be friends," he said. "Is there anything to do around here?" he queried again.

"We could go the creek. It's where most of the homeless hang out."

"What about you? You don't go there?"

"I try to stay away from drugs and alcohol. It's mostly what they do, smoke pot and tell stories."

"My kind of place," he said. "You coming?"

"I'd rather not," she said, disappointed at the revelation.

---

[20] WHO - The World Health Organization is a specialized agency of the United Nations responsible for international public health. The WHO Constitution, which establishes the agency's governing structure and principles, states its main objective as "the attainment by all peoples of the highest possible level of health."

CDC - The Centers for Disease Control and Prevention is a national public health institute in the United States. It is a United States federal agency, under the Department of Health and Human Services, and is headquartered in Atlanta, Georgia.

"At least you could show me the way." She agreed by picking up her backpack. It would give her some exercise, which she desperately needed. Being bedridden for almost two months had taken its toll on her body. "This way," she directed, leading the way.

"Why do you want to hook up with dopers?" she said, making conversation.

"My business sense," he explained. "Where there are people, there's an opportunity. You understand?"

She did and remained quiet for now. They came up on the narrow trail leading along Monument Creek. Since she had not been here for some time, April was unsure of where the homeless camps had been located. With mostly drifters inhabiting tent cities, they went up and were broken down by law enforcement quite frequently. Where one side was hoping for tents just to go away, the other side, the homeless, were hoping the state and city would accept them permanently as equal citizens. Unfortunately for the free spirited, it had not happened yet and perhaps never would.

Mostly walking in file on the narrow path, April kept leading the way while Aaron kept pace. "What are you going to do?" he wanted to now.

"You mean job wise?"

"Yes."

"I was a waitress in San Francisco. I can do it here once places are allowed to open again."

"I thought you said you were homeless."

"I am, but I can still hold a job."

"What about free spirit and tax free living?"

"I don't like begging. That's why I take on jobs."

"Actually," he agreed, "it's not a bad idea. I do the same, given a choice. There's only one difference between us. Where you like to work, I prefer dealing in business."

"You mean like a trader?"

"Exactly."

She may have had the wrong impression of Aaron. He seemed sincere about the business and she was willing to give him another chance at their friendship. April was surprised that they had not come across any tents or signs of homeless. She decided to call their walk quits and head back into town. "I don't understand why there's nobody by the creek. Let's head back," she informed him.

"What do you think happened?" he said, curious about the lack of homeless. It would greatly impact the business he planned to pursue.

"I don't know, but we'll find out." At this point she was as clueless as he. "Let's head for the shelter."

It might not have been common knowledge to most Colorado city dwellers, but there were officially a dozen facilities available to accommodate transients as well as permanent homeless needing assistance, with the most popular being the Springs Rescue Mission, located on 5 West Las Vegas St. Though all had to comply with commonly applied house rules, this was where April was headed.

Arriving at the location, it became obvious that the place was packed with homeless. Asking the shelter manager confirmed their assessment. "No place else to go," they were told.

"What about the other places in town?"

"Same as here."

"What do you suggest?" she said.

"Wait a couple of days," he stated. "We lose homeless to the virus every day."

April was suddenly reminded of her own interaction with the virus only days ago and turned to walk out. Aaron had been attentive to their conversation and understood. "What now?" he asked.

"Let's check with the Salvation Army. They should have something for you."

Sure enough, there was a variety in color and size of tents available, neatly stacked against one wall. One only had to pick the style of preference at no charge since they were donations from businesses and private owners. "What should I get?" Aaron said, checking with April.

"Whatever is comfortable for you."

"What about you?" Aaron said, selecting a fair-sized tent. "You're moving in with me?" It might have been wishful thinking on his part.

"I've got my own place," April said.

"You don't mean the building entrance?"

"That's my place and I wouldn't trade it for anything."

"You sure?" he said, hoping she would change her mind. His intentions became obvious to her. To argue further about it would not serve any purpose. She remained quiet.

"Where should I pitch tent?" he asked on the way out.

"Come," she said, pulling him back to the direction of the creek. A ten-minute walk brought them to the spot she had in mind. "Not bad," he proclaimed. "I can live with it."

She had taken him to Monument Valley Park, a wooded patch butted up against the Bijou Street bridge and vacant of homeless at this time. From the view one could see the Rocky Mountain range in its fullest splendor. As for entertainment, there was Monument Creek below within a short walk, the Santa Fe railway tracks and I-25 interstate running alongside the river, with periodic trains rumbling by at a unhurried pace of ten miles per hour. The speed was purposely kept slow to prevent collisions with deer crossing the tracks. While some trains increased their speed to 40 mph to keep transport time on schedule, it was only permissible during nighttime hours while residence dwellers living nearby were asleep. It did not work out for some of the people. Weekly complaints to the railway administration proved the facts because train operators were instructed to blow the whistles on bends, intersections, and deer crossings.

"See you in the morning," April said, departing for her domicile. The day had been a strain on her since she was still recovering from the virus.

After an invigorating rest, April appeared at Aaron's tent early. He was up already checking out the immediate environment. "Not bad a place," he said with an approving nod. "I like it."

"Do you feel like a run up the creek?"

"What do you mean?" It appeared he did not understand.

"You know, jogging on the path."

"I'm not used to working out. Haven't been running for years."

"Ever think of picking it up again?"

"Are you asking me?"

"I'd enjoy your company. Working out is much easier with a running partner. You should try it." She was impatiently hopping, warming up her legs for the track. "I'll keep the pace down."

"I did not think a homeless was into running," he said, somewhat surprised.

"I'm not your average homeless," she stated. "I learned from the medical staff at the hospital, while recovering from the virus, that exercising frequently is the best way to keep from getting sick. I've made it my daily practice and, so far, even with the recurring infections sweeping the land, I have not been sick again."

Running Monument Creek trail was a new experience for him and kept a relaxed pace, enabling them to talk.

"Where are you from?" April said, making conversation.

"Pueblo."

"The city south of here?"

"That's the one."

"Are there homeless like here? I've never been there."

"Used to be much like any place else. But not anymore."

"What happened?" She was curious because nobody here ever talked about the place.

"Bussing,[21]" he said. Their conversation was kept short while running.

"Is that how you got here?"

"Yes," he explained. "I'd just got off the bus when we met."

"Were you born there?"

"No. I'm an immigrant from El Salvador."

"I've heard about it, but don't know anything about the place. Where is it?" It explained the slight foreign accent she'd noticed.

"South of Mexico. Central America?"

"Is it nice there?"

"It's a beautiful place," he said.

"Then," she wanted to know, "why is everybody leaving?" April, while living in California, was aware of the problem. Everybody complained about it. That was the reason why the homeless population there had multiplied beyond the state's budget capability.

"Poverty you can't imagine unless you'd been there."

"What's the matter with your government? They don't take care of people?"

"They can't. Nobody has money. Nobody pays taxes. Politics is ineffective because they are all corrupt. Everybody is starving."

---

[21] PUEBLO, Colo., KRDO News, December 23, 2019 4:34 pm -- The city of Pueblo is recommitting $25,000 to bus homeless and the displaced out of the city. Pueblo Police will oversee the operation. The decision to reinstate the program came after an October city council vote. The program, in partnership with Greyhound Bus, is nearly identical to the bussing program back in 2017. During that first go around, the funds for bus tickets only lasted nine months.

During the first 9 months of the program, the Pueblo Police Department bussed more than 400 people, 166 of those that were bussed from Pueblo were children. A majority of the displaced and homeless went to Texas, Florida, and Mississippi.

"What about the economy? Don't you have any like everybody else in the world?"

"Sure we do, but it's all owned by land barons inherited from the Spanish way back when, and they don't share their wealth."

"I'm beginning to understand," April said, somehow bewildered at the revelation.

"Now you understand?"

"I feel sorry for you people."

"Don't feel sorry for me," Aaron said. "I'm going to make it."

Both were exhausted after their return and crashed in his tent. "Not bad," she admitted. "I think I'll come here to take my daytime naps. The knoll is getting too hot in the sun."

"You're welcome in my home anytime." Though in transit most times, many homeless consider the tent their permanent home.

"Thanks. I'll take you up on that." It appeared that both had found a partner they could live with. For April it was a blessing to have somebody likeminded in her life again. For Aaron, it seemed he enjoyed her company.

Both kept exploring each other's past experiences during their daily run.

"Have you ever had to defend yourself?" April was curious at his self-assurance.

"A number of times."

"Anybody ever get hurt during the fights?"

"It wasn't me, I assure you." He left it at that.

He seemed to be fit for anything. "I'm surprised at you," she admitted.

"About what?" They were taking a break to relax.

"Your confidence. How did you learn it?"

"I told you. I grew up in the ghettos. You learn to fight to survive."

There it is again, she thought, *character mismatch*. But she put the thought aside for now. April, while not educated in anything had learned people's behavior and responses, called street smart adaptation. Where she'd missed out on much of a scholastic education befitting to land a job, her education was much more useful living within her adopted homeless environment. Without realizing it, she had acquired the habit of profiling, usually reserved for investigative elements.

For now, since there was not much activity in town other than eating, drinking, and sleeping for the most part, Aaron and April took to daily bouts of jogging and running early in the mornings. They found it greatly helped their friendship as much as providing recreational pleasures, in addition to uplifting their otherwise downtrodden outlook during such difficult times.

Living daily in close proximity for most of their waking hours, it was only natural that April and Aaron developed more than just a friendship. With both being young adults at their peak, the daily workout only added to their testosterone and estrogen levels. It did not take much to get involved. While April still held on to her outdoor living under the stars, she spent the early hours of the night at Aaron's tent.

With her moving in part time, he made the effort to make her feel at home, hoping that someday she would move in permanently. While homelessness might appear to be a carefree and careless lifestyle to the outside world, many homeless still kept to organized social schedules. At a minimum, they followed the days of week, with most being aware when it was the weekend. Some even took the day to attend church service.

"What faith are you?" Aaron asked April one morning.

The question hit her unexpectedly. She thought a few seconds, then came up with, "I don't know. Why?"

"Because I am Catholic and feel like attending a service. How about it? Have you ever been to church?"

"Yeah. Looking around. I liked it but don't have any idea about their performances."

"Would you like to go?"

"Sure. I'm up for it. When?"

"I'll find out where and when they have a service. By the way," he said, "what do you believe in?"

"Religious wise?"

"Yes."

"I believe there is a God that created life and the universe, but don't know anything."

"Then," he suggested, "you're an deist."

"A what?" She'd never heard the word. "Sounds pretty nasty."

He chuckled at her ignorance but said, "Deism means the belief in a creator and that's it."

"What else is there?"

"Atheist."

"What's that?"

"Nonbeliever. It means there is no God and no Creator."

"Well," she volunteered. "Somebody had to create us and everything around us."

"Some people don't think so."

"It makes no sense."

"I agree," Aaron said. "You want to come along to find a church?"

"Sure." Like most times, she welcomed his suggestions. It provided them with an activity for another day in a stagnant world. Since it was early Sunday morning, they checked the schedule at the nearest church only a couple of blocks away, St. Mary's Cathedral on Kiowa Street. The first service was scheduled thirty minutes from now. "We'd better go back and get our masks," Aaron said after reading the sermon instructions.

"What a nuisance," April admitted. "I remember not having to wear these damned things. I hate it."

"You're not alone. Everybody does, but, for now, we don't have an option."

"I hope," she complained, "whoever started the Corona lockdown had a good reason. Otherwise there will be hell to pay for some."

"I agree."

The church sermon turned out to be a magnificent experience for April. She had never seen such festivity in her life. She could not believe that all of this was going on around the world each and every weekend. "How rich," she marveled.

"You like it?" he whispered during the service.

"Yes. I want to come back next week. Can we?"

"Of course we can. It's called High Mass."

April was thrilled at having found something so special. It would provide her the spiritual stability she needed in her difficult times ahead.

With her mind relatively at peace with the world, April woke up the next morning feeling affectionate. It might have been her church experience fueling her emotions for Aaron. Playfully, her finger traced along the contours of the strange tattoo permanently etched onto Aaron's shoulder. "What does MS-13[22] mean?"

"Oh. Nothing special."

"Then," she prodded, "why have it burned into your skin?" Tattoos were common among the homeless, but she could never understand why people did it. Not only did it appear painful, but from a logical perspective, she asked curiously, "What happens if you get tired of it?"

---

[22] MS-13, "Mara Salvatrucha," in English: "Roaring ants (friends protecting each other like ants) and "Salvatrucha" means (street smart Salvadorians)." Mara Salvatrucha, commonly known as MS-13, is an international criminal gang that originated in Los Angeles, California, in the 1970s and 1980s. Originally, the gang was set up to protect Salvadoran immigrants from other gangs in the Los Angeles area. Over time, the gang grew into a more traditional criminal organization. MS-13 is defined by its cruelty, and its rivalry with the 18th Street Gang.

"It's for life." He seemed conflicted.

"What does it do?"

"It's a club to protect people like me from getting hurt."

"But that was back in El Salvador. What about here in Colorado Springs? It doesn't mean anything, or does it?"

"I am spreading the word."

"What word?" It stirred a certain curiosity in April. She propped up on her elbow to watch his face.

"My business."

"You mean the trade?"

"Exactly." She left it as such, wondering what commodity he might want to pursue.

"Let's do something different today."

"What's on your mind?" she asked.

"Go for a ride."

"But," she objected, "we've got no car."

"Come," he said getting up from the sleeping bag. "I'll buy us a couple of bikes."

"Where did you get the money?" April was dumbfound at the revelation.

"I keep it in my money belt."

"I meant, how did you earn it?"

"Trading."

"Now I understand. You keep money matters very private," she volunteered.

"That I do. Nobody else's business."

"You can trust me. I respect other's private properties."

"I believe you. Now, let's get going."

It took a while to locate a bicycle shop that was open. Once they found one, April was surprised at the ease with which Aaron forked over the bills. The purchase was not exactly at the low end in price range. He seemed to be loaded with cash.

"I was wondering why we didn't go to the soup kitchen to eat."

"I don't like their cooking. Besides, I've got the money to pay for real food."

"We can't be choosy these days."

"You stick with me and your begging days are over."

"I appreciate the offer and am glad you mean it. But what about the business? There are no customers."

"Don't worry," he pacified her. "They'll come once word spreads. I've got plenty of cash to tide us over for the months ahead."

April was satisfied with his explanation and extremely happy she was not currently forced into begging.

BUSINESS VENTURE

Already one year into living through the constraints of the coronavirus had taken its toll on people throughout all ranks and social statuses. When word leaked out about COVID-19, it was thought to be just another flu season countries would have to deal with. But this turned out not to be the case. This was a strain expected to quickly morph into different forms, attacking not only China, but every country on Earth. What made it worse yet, was that it swept across the globe a number of times, taking with it thousands more in human casualties. On top of it all, there were conflicting casualty statistics released almost daily from governments and the World Health Organization (WHO) as well as the U.S. Department of Health & Human Services (HHS), completely confusing the public.

In addition, state governors and city mayors were given vague instructions and control over their respective territories, confusing the Corona issue even further. It did not take much for accusations and political finger-pointing to take hold in many states. The end result was clearly visible when demonstrations and protests took hold in many cities, quickly turning into riots followed by mass break-ins, lootings, and burning down entire neighborhoods. Everybody alive followed the events reaching out much like wildfire. On assessing the reason and cause, nobody was willing to take the blame. It appeared that people had lost their individual integrity, decency, and honesty on a grand cultural scale. To this day that question still remained: who was to blame for the criminal atrocities, perhaps committed by street thugs and hoodlums, but more likely by radical, organized factions.

Amidst all of the turmoil, one day, Aaron yelled, "April, you ready to do business?" Both had been attending local demonstrations, if only on a relatively small scale compared to reported national events.

"Sure. What do you have in mind?"

He lifted the backpack slung from his shoulder, opened it, and showed her its contents. "Sell these packets," he said, handing her a few samples. Stunned, April was sickened just by the thought of it. She knew immediately what their contents were. "Drugs!" she shouted. "You want me to sell drugs?"

"No need to shout," he pacified her. "It's easy pickings. Just look around and take your pick. They all want and need this stuff."

"But selling is illegal," she protested.

"Not anymore. You should know. This drug in Colorado has been legalized."

"But not the black markets," she insisted.

"Look," Aaron said, trying to talk sense into her. "If I don't sell it somebody else will make all the profits. You don't want to give up this great opportunity."

Why is it that every time somebody comes up with a great plan I feel guilty? she thought, but said, "You know I don't want anything to do with illegal dealings."

"I told you it's legal." She took his word. "Come on," he prodded her. "Take the bag."

"Let's do this," she suggested. "You handle the sale and I collect the money."

"Fair enough," he said, after giving it some thought. "Then, we are a team?"

"For now," she confirmed, but reluctantly.

"Fine. Now let's get to work." They sold out of their current drug supplies within the hour, taking orders for more from light to heavy drugs while April kept track of the supplies Aaron had to replenish.

"Where're you going to get your supplies?"

"Pueblo. Don't worry," he said. "They'll deliver.

And so, the stage was set for a successful business venture. Or was it?

Trouble began not long after in the form of competition. Rivalry was quick to take over. Bidding and underbidding became a standard practice. It was not long before profit margins began to suffer. Like many times before, the solution was annihilating competition. Gangs were formed, though on a smaller scale than in major cities, but damaging enough to cause casualties on both supplier and seller sides.

"Things have gone too far," April complained months later, when she realized that she had been tricked into something without an end. "I can't do this anymore."

"But we are a team," Aaron tried to reason with her.

"Sorry, but I'm out."

"Be reasonable. I need you. You are my backup. There are too many criminal elements to deal with by myself." This would not be the last time they had this argument. It came up every time somebody got killed. April had learned to love life too much for it be cut short over a mere drug sale. Not only was it the killings by gang members; what bothered her more was innocent people dying from overdosing.

"What are you so worried about? They know what they are doing," Aaron insisted when April pointed out the dangers.

"I didn't mind us selling simple drugs like dope and marijuana," she said. "It's all the other illegal and damaging drugs."

"Name one," he said.

"I can name you ten. You want to hear?"

"Go ahead. I'm listening."

"Painkillers – 191 million
  Inhalants – 22.9 millions
  Marijuana – 22.2 million
  Sedatives (Barbiturates) – 19 million
  Stimulants – 16 million
  Methamphetamines – 14.7 millions
  Alcohol – 14.4 million
  Cocaine (Crack) – 10 million
  Benzodiazepines – 4.1 million
  Heroin – 808,000."

Slightly irritated, "Where did you get that info?" Aaron wanted to know. "You're misinformed."

"Detox center I visited once. And no," she insisted, "I've seen firsthand how many addictions there were."

"You mean, place you were admitted to."

"Yes," she admitted. "But only once."

"That's one more than I have," Aaron stated with an evasive chuckle.

"Then," she said, "you don't use drugs?"

"Only recreational ones."

"Aren't they all?"

"It depends on the user. Some take it occasionally. Others are addicted for life."

"I'll make a deal with you."

"Fair enough. Let me hear it."

"You deal with your suppliers and I'll watch over you, but keep me from dealing with users."

"I promise. Now," he insisted, "can we get back to business?"

"It's all yours," she insisted.

Aside from their differences about his dealings, they generally got along more as friends than as a couple. It was tolerable for her as long as he abided by the law, which might have sounded like an oxymoron, contrasting between the dealers and law enforcement. Either way one looked at it, though legalized in many states and countries, it was a moral breach in society. It affected a nation's economic performance and productivity.

Colorado Springs, until now, might have been a city relatively clear of major criminal elements, but the current situation opened up new avenues for crime. According to historical statistics, economic depressions and recessions force an increase in crime rate. The reasons may be complicated, but can also be explained in simple terms: people have too much time on their hands. In any normal, organized condition, work is generally a gainfully-occupied individual's primary choice and function. When that incentive is removed, recreation takes over, directing much of one's daily life.

Where April was keenly aware of the economic changes Aaron's trading brought on, she also noticed the sudden increase in crime in the city. "I told you so," she would argue whenever the topic came up between them.

"Don't worry about it," he would say pacifying her, "we won't get involved."

When that was not enough, she forced herself to tolerate the influx of competing drug dealers into town. A prolific migration from nearby Pueblo to Colorado Springs followed, affecting the state of everybody's wellbeing. Crime rates went up and so did the tax burden on citizens in order to carry the city budget. Law enforcement needed additional manpower and transportation, businesses required security services which ate into their income, jails overflowed with criminal elements, citizens shifted blame onto city management and demanded resolution. It was a self-perpetuating cycle on an increase, not easily broken, eating into everybody's budget.

Once a peacefully-kept pioneering frontier town, the city was swept over with the prevalent state of affairs on the nationwide scale, propagated by the local media, leaving behind a simple news item to the continuous daily stream of "Breaking News."

One would think that drug dealers are under continuous watch and surveillance by law enforcement agents but that was not the case. While mostly conducting business during evening and nighttime hours, dealers are highly watchful of the environment, keeping a continuous guard within their dealing turf, mostly centered around common landmarks, easily known and spotted by potential buyers. Not much slips by their cunning senses. Every approaching face is carefully assessed as to whether they're friend or foe. Law enforcement knows it and so do customary buyers.

Where a deal may go bad is usually from competitive gangs and dealers infringing on one another's territories. Once encountered, the infraction will be snitched to the law to take action, mostly to eliminate the competition. Whether law enforcement is aware or ignorant of such conducted infringement acts is subject to conjecture but prevalent, nevertheless.

April more or less tolerated the changes Aaron's business brought on, but knew it was not what she wanted. "Is this how I want to live?" April contemplated on many occasions.

"Business is booming." Aaron would say when she brought up the topic. "Look at your life. We own a cozy home and automobile, you buy fashion items you desire, we can afford things we want. There is no reason to complain."

It was true, April had to admit. He'd bought them a home, small but affordable on Hancock Avenue just opposite Prospect Lake, had purchased a new Pickup truck, and had decorated their place with new furniture. "Why do I feel unhappy?"

"Don't complain," Aaron would say. "Just enjoy life. We've got it made."

A LIFE WITHOUT LOVE

For once, April was in a position of carefree living, but the same questions kept creeping up in her mind: "How long will it last?" and "Why can't I be happy like himself?" Her mind always came back to the same missing element, Eric. No matter how much she tried to erase him from her mind, his name and image kept popping up almost daily. "Why do I feel this way?" She tried to analyze but could not answer. "I should be happy in Aaron's company. I have no reason to complain. I've got everything a woman wants and needs." There was only one element missing, she realized, that could produce the state in her mind: "Love. Undivided love."

"What do you feel like doing?" a distant voice prodded her mind. It brought her back to reality. It was Aaron trying to get her attention. She pretended to still be sleeping and did not answer. *I should be happy and grateful for the life Aaron has provided.* It was a life way beyond her expectations when compared to the miserable existence she'd led for much of her young adult life. With her eyes closed she tried to imagine what kind of life it would be in the arms of Eric, her first love. She could only describe it as a blissful and heavenly, and how she longed for him.

"Eric, my love," she sighed.

"What?" the voice next to her ear said. She pretended to come out of sleep at the sound of Aaron's voice.

"I was dreaming," she said.

"Who's Eric?" Aaron demanded in a slightly irritated voice.

"Somebody I knew a long time ago," she said, justifying the faded notion she'd felt.

"Your first love?"

"You could say that," she said, trying to avoid further prodding.

"You still love him?" Aaron asked with a twinge of jealousy.

"It was a long time ago. I wouldn't know. I was dreaming." That ended further queries.

"What do you feel like doing today?" she said, getting up to avert further prodding. She realized that it was not fair to him, the way she felt about her past.

"We could hang out by the lake. We could take a ride. We could visit with friends or just stay in bed making love," he suggested with a chuckle.

"Let's take a ride up Pikes Peak. We haven't been there."

"Sounds fine with me," he agreed.

She should have been happy with his company and the life he provided, but she could not get her first love out of her mind. *What is this?* she questioned. *Am I this ungrateful or is it just personal lust?* She hoped not.

She thought of herself as a better person than to be obsessed by personal virtues. "We could stop by our favorite breakfast place."

"Sounds fine," he said, waiting for her to get ready. Since it was the weekend, he decided to put business aside until Monday. "Today it's only you and me," he declared, notwithstanding a potential business loss. Ever since he'd moved to the Springs and teamed up with April, his life had been nothing but success. A success beyond expectations, and he was grateful to her even though, at times, she did not appear to feel the same way. Although he sensed a certain distance between them, he attributed it to her earlier days living as homeless. The thought was enough not to prod her further. Though he realized that the element of complete dedication and undivided love was missing from their relationship, he valued everything she did for him. He was content.

"Did you bring a sweater?" April said on their way out. "I've heard it's cold on top of the Rockies."

"Don't have a sweater or jacket. Didn't need one in Pueblo. I'll tough it out." The day turned out as April had anticipated. Breakfast was ample like in most places in Colorado. Servings still seemed to be portioned out as they had in the frontier days.

The top of Pikes Peak turned out to be just as enjoyable. Aaron even displayed affections of which April hadn't thought he was capable. "I am really happy we met," he confessed. "You turned out to be a great partner for me."

"Only partner?" she said, somewhat disappointed.

"More than a partner," he corrected with a grin. "I think I'll keep you." Both had to laugh at his revelation. "I couldn't have done it without you."

"The business?"

"Not only the business. You give me moral support and take care of me. People are attracted to you and like you. I still can't believe you are a homeless."

"I was," she corrected. "Thanks to you."

"I think we make a good team. Don't you?"

"We sure do." They sealed the deal with a hug and a kiss.

April was relieved and reassured that this was the long-term relationship she had always wanted, even though the primary element of pure love was missing. For now, reassured by him, she was content.

The day was a happy one for the both. The sunset, when viewed from this altitude, was spectacular. In only minutes, darkness settles over the Rockies. Sundown can best be enjoyed from the tops of the mountains. People living on the flats below won't have this pleasure. Once the sun touches the peaks of the mountains it disappears within minutes. April, as much as Aaron, was impressed at the sheer size and diversity the country provided. Driving back was pleasurable as well. With a view provided into endless wheat fields to the east, and the Rockies and hilly planes to the west, they received a new awareness of their country.

"I think we found our home," Aaron declared. "Don't you?"

They ended today's escapade with dinner at their favorite steak house, celebrated with a bottle of fine imported wine from France. It appeared that in recent weeks the Corona lockdown had somehow been relaxed by the city mayor. More and more public dining places were permitted to reopen as long as the distance limits of approximately 6 feet were observed. For whatever reasons, health organizations determined that it would provide the public with a safety zone from further catching the virus.

To Aaron's surprise, April, as well as he, had acquired a taste for Cabernet wine. He seemed happy that she had her alcohol and drug addictions under control. It was bad practice for dealers to get involved with the products they pushed. He looked at her across the table. "You know," he declared. "You are a beautiful woman."

"And you," she rejoiced with a smile, "are a handsome man."

"Cheers." They sealed their relationship with a second bottle.

The short drive home was a happy one. Mellowed out by the wine, they settled in for the night. A life of hardship had finally paid off for April. "I can live like this," she thought, getting ready for bed. It was at this point when they heard the front door being smashed to pieces, followed by commanding shouts from that direction, repeated several times: "On the ground! Both of you."

A squad of hooded commandos rushed into the bedroom armed with assault rifles, thrashing their way to April and Aaron. In seconds both were handcuffed with nylon straps and forced onto their knees, being read the Miranda Act.[23]

April, in desperation, yelled out, "What's going on?" and "Please don't hurt me." Aaron remained silent, already

---

[23] In the United States, the Miranda warning is a type of notification customarily given by police to criminal suspects in police custody (or in a custodial interrogation) advising them of their right to silence; that is, their right to refuse to answer questions or provide information to law enforcement or other officials.

suspecting the reasons for the assault. His suspicions were confirmed.

"Both of you are under arrest for being members of MS-13."

April was devastated when she learned the full truth about the symbol tattooed on Aaron's shoulder. With their relationship abruptly cut short, they would never see each other again.

Aaron was detained in jail until his trial, after which he would serve a prison term followed with deportation back to his home country. Though he was not the hardened gang member most were, he had been caught up in the recent 2020 MS-13 roundup, initiated by law enforcement nationwide.

April was back on the streets, penniless again. She was not allowed to salvage any of her personal belongings from the home she had treasured so much since it was acquired with the money earned in partnership with a bona fide criminal.

It was here when she finally realized her predicament, enslaved to permanent homelessness. *No matter what I try. No matter what I plan,* she wailed in silence, *all is in vain. I'm doomed for failure.* All she had left from seemingly successful starts were the clothes she wore. Stepping out of the police headquarters in town after one night's detainment, her spirits were broken like so many times before, and she felt directionless.

"What can I do? What should I do?" She felt tired of begging for a living. She felt tired of adapting to relationships that never seem to last. She was completely disgusted with the way society treated her, even though she had nothing but good intentions. She felt inadequate to find and hold a job, especially in this time of economic recession and perpetual lockdown.

"Will it ever end?" she shouted into the air. "Mom, what did you do to me?"

The officer, inside the command center at the headquarters' reception area, watched April linger outside the door. Since she seemed like a nice person when he'd booked her the day before, he felt slightly compassionate. "What a shame," he muttered, leaving his glass-enclosed space, protected against the virus threat, and heading in her direction.

"What's the matter?" he said, touching her shoulder. "Waiting for a ride?"

Slightly startled, rubbing her eyes, April looked up. "I don't know what to do and where to go," she stated, teary eyed.

"Where do you live?"

"I used to have a home on Prospect Lake but my friend and I were evicted by the law."

"You have friends that could put you up?"

"No. I was homeless for most of my life."

"Then" he suggested, "why don't you check out the homeless shelter?"

"I guess so," she said and started walking in that direction.

"Hold up," he yelled after her. "I'll give you a ride."

She waited for the squad car and hopped in. "Why are you so nice to me?" she asked.

Pushing on the accelerator, he said, "I have a daughter your age. Just want to make sure you're headed in the right direction."

Drying her eyes, she looked at him with an unexpected sincerity. "She's very fortunate for having such a caring dad."

"Well," he said, "not always. The young sometimes neglect their parents. Probably what happened to you?" He glanced at her inquisitively.

"My mom died and left me stranded homeless at age ten."

They arrived at the shelter. He stopped, leaving her with one bit of advice: "Keep up your hope and stop by the station sometimes."

"Thank you for your kindness, and yes. I will."

FINAL CHAPTER

The year was coming to the end but not near enough to remove Corona from the once customary living. It was late in the fall when Pixie showed up at the park after spotting her friend, "Where have you been? I've been looking for you," embracing April with a heartwarming hug. They were sitting at the bench nearby warmed by the waning sun while catching up with past and current events. "I missed you," Pixie said in sincerity. "Don't you skip out on me again."

"I'm sorry," April replied, feeling guilty. It just dawned on her that she had completely ignored and forgotten about her friend ever since she'd met up with Aaron. "I didn't know where you lived."

Reaching into her purse, "Here," Pixies offered, handing her something. "My business card."

April studied it for a few seconds then pondered, "Administrative Assistant?"

"Yeah. I've been promoted."

"Is this your address?"

"Business place. Here," she said, taking the card and scribbled something on the back. "My home phone. You can call me anytime."

They sat for some time with April confessing to her unexpected involvement with Aaron, her drug associated business venture with him and sudden end, enforced by the law.

"How have you been," April wondered, giving her friend a chance to speak. "How are you coping with the Corona mandates?"

"It's not easy," she admitted. It seems that every week new orders are issued. I am totally confused."

"I know, but it doesn't affect me much. Us homeless live unsettled getting ordered and pushed around. It's our trade."

"Have you thought about getting a job again."

"I did after we met the last time but then I met Aaron. It forced me into a different direction than I had planned."

"I will help you if you want," Pixie offered.

"You will? I would very much appreciate it. I need help to break away from the misery of a homelessness. It's nothing but a troubled life. Both sat quietly for some time, April not sure if she could hold up her constitutional right for living in a government mandated society, with her friend's face reflecting similar thoughts about April's possible lack of commitment.

But, April thought in silence, *my life has been unsettling all along. So,* she conceded, *not much will change living within mandates.*

"I'm hungry," Pixie said. The sun was setting with evening breaking in. "Let's get something to eat. I'm buying. You know a place?"

"There is a Vietnamese place a couple of blocks away I always wanted to try."

"Getting tired of soup kitchens?" Pixie said with a grin.

"I crave something decent to eat for a change," April admitted.

"Me too. How about…" Pixie never finished the sentence. April's face suddenly shifted to the distance. She never heard the end of Pixie's sentence. Someone up the street had caught her attention. Her heart lurched, but "it couldn't be…but it was."

She suddenly jumped to her feet and ran away screaming in the direction of the stranger. "*Eric!*"

Pixie watched from the distance as April flung herself at him, both arms clutched around his neck, sobbing. Several minutes passed with her in that position, not letting him go, before she finally turned with a gesture in her friend's direction, pulling him along. Both walked up and April introduced him. "This is Eric, who I told you about."

"Pleased to meet you." Pixie greeted him with an extended arm but with mixed feelings. On the one hand, she was happy for April's good fortune but, on the other, she felt that she would be losing a new friend.

"We were about to get something to eat. Care to join us?" Pixie offered.

"I'd love to. I haven't eaten all day. Spent much of it around local homeless shelters looking for April here." He gestured at her with a smile.

"Well," reluctantly, Pixie said. "You found her," and promptly led the way to the restaurant nearby, the Saigon Café.

The evening was a pleasant affair for all. Pixie could sense that April was ecstatic to have Eric back in her life again. He seemed elated as well. After placing their dining orders, Pixie mostly sat by, quietly listening and watching them through the evening.

The first explanation April demanded from him was, "Where have you been all these years? You have no idea how much I missed you. Right?" she said with a gesture at Pixie.

"All she ever talked about was you, Eric," she agreed.

He described his journey into the Canadian wilderness, how he staked out his piece of land, built a log cabin, hunted for food, fought off aggressive animals, weathered out extreme seasons, and wished he had company. "I thought about you all the time," he said, reaching for April's hand.

"So did I," she replied, absorbing all of his presence. "Why didn't you let me know? You promised to keep in touch."

"I wanted to create a home for us."

"But," April protested, "it's so isolated up there in the wilderness, isn't it?"

"It doesn't have to be," Eric said. "Word spread. Friends quickly followed. Before I knew it, I had a town on my hands."

April mulled it over in silence. "I still want to enjoy the world."

"So do I. But not until we'll have a home to come back to."

"Well," Pixie said, apparently getting sleepy suppressing a yawn. It was close to ten o'clock in the evening. "This place is getting ready to close. Curfew, you know."

Sure enough, April was served the bill. Erik quickly retrieved it. "My treat," he insisted. "It's been too long that I've neglected you."

With April close to tears, overwhelmed with happiness at having Erik back in her life but saddened about losing her friend Pixie, she offered, "Why don't you come with us?"

"What? Canada?"

"Sure," Erik said. "We have plenty of eager guys in the community only too happy to accommodate you."

"Give me some time to think about it," she replied. "Maybe I will." They exchanged addresses. Although the homeless are drifters without permanent social ties, many have a point of contact such as a shelter, local friend, or even the local post office, just in case.

"Will I see you again?" Pixie said in tears. Both women hugged for a final goodbye.

"I don't know. It depends on Eric here. What have you planned?" April asked, teary eyed.

"I'm here to take you home," he said, addressing her, with a slight gesture of apology in Pixie's direction.

It did not seem to make her happy, and rightly so, to possibly lose April from her life but she had to deal with it. She seemed deeply saddened that from here on out she would be walking downtown alone again.

"I want to thank you for taking care of April," Eric said, reaching out to shake Pixie's hand. "If it wasn't for you, she probably would not have been here. Thanks to you she is still alive and healthy. Right?" With a smile on the face, he looked at April for approval.

April had become quiet. Turning to her friend, she said, tears clouding her visions, "I will never forget you." She leaned out and kissed her cheek. Sobbing freely now, she took Eric by the hand and turned to leave.

"I am so happy for you, April. I'll write you to keep in touch."

Watching both disappear around the next corner, closely clutching each other, Pixie abruptly turned and left, saddened in one way and happy for her in another. She deserved a better life than being trapped into homelessness. "But so do I," she muttered into her emptiness. "Canada? Maybe. Sounds inviting. "Weeks later, Pixie received a letter, informing her that April had taken possession of Erik's home in the Canadian wilderness. But there was more. While it was their permanent home, she also indicated that Eric had bought a motor home which they took on frequent trips around parks and even explored some of the surrounding wilderness. Pixie felt envious and felt sorry for herself. Where April's dream had become reality, Pixie's was still very much the same, entrapped into the small frontier's town.

April's life had taken a turn she had always longed for but could never achieve on her own. With Erik by her side now, her lifelong misery was slowly fading from her mind. Each day was a new adventure for her. First, there was the community Erik had created, followed by getting to know the town's inhabitants.

Dreams she used to harbor, to her pleasure, had finally become reality. She couldn't be happier with Erik by her side. Sometimes, when waking up in the morning, she would pinch her arm to make sure that it was not just a dream.

"Erik," she said one of those mornings.

"What, sweetie?"

"I want you to know that I am really happy being by your side."

"What's the matter?" Once more, much like during their past relationship, a caution flag went up. *Here comes the first complaint,* he thought.

"I hope you feel the same. There is only one request I have for you. Please, never…never leave me again. I would not survive another emptiness in life."

"I promise. I felt guilty the whole time after I left you."

There was one thing she felt would make up for his deserting her. She felt that she'd deserved it.

"When this Corona misery is over, could we take the trip to France, and Italy? Mom always talked about places she wanted to visit but never had the chance." She silently prayed that he would agree.

Erik took his time to respond. She thought he was unsure about following through with her desire, but he was already calculating the cost and if they could afford such a trip.

"How soon," was all he said while watching a possible dream for her come true.

April was thrilled at the possibility for her lifelong dream to materializing into something she'd never dreamed possible, but for now could settle into a normal way of life.

On their return from another weekend outing, there was yet another surprise waiting.

"Pixie," April yelled out and rushed into her friend's arms who apparently had decided to visit them at their Canadian community and surprised both with her presence.

"Now," April cheered, with her friend close by, "I am content. My life is wholesome."

Erik, on hearing her revelation, could not be happier. His silent thoughts were, *Maybe there is hope for a fulfilling relationship after all.*

PROPOSED SOLUTION

"Where there is a need, there is a solution," has been my personal motto in career, as well as personal life. Where the career was filled with challenges throughout many projects and tasks, my acquired knowledge through prolific reading and historical research, has always paid off. The solution is there, sometimes visible, at other times hidden and dormant. One just has to recognize the need. And the need with this writing is to find a workable solution for homelessness.

I am not the first person challenged with this solution and am not going to be the last but will certainly try my best to come up with something that should work for both factions, the homeless culture, as well as a disciplined society.

The question becomes: "What do the homeless want?"

It may be a complete and selfish notion by the homeless to demand everything from the government and organized tax payer, without contributing some of their energy and time to the cause. But, that is the nature of the economically deprived and selfishly demanding individual forcing the homeless issue.

I feel humbled, as well as challenged, in pitting my brain against the thousands of concerned individuals from within government agencies and organized social groups that have tried to come up with an answer, but certainly will try my best to address the elements required to satisfy, or at least accommodate some of the needs. Following are major highlights to consider and evaluate:

    a. Reserved piece of land near populated areas
    b. Easy access with free transportation to cities
    c. No confinement unless desired
    d. Structured, but flexile-elected management
    e. Collective communal spirit
    f. Local collective counseling
    g. Promote skilled applications to provide: shelter, homes, town facilities, gathering places, etc.
    h. Opportunity for job skill training

    i.   No taxation – principle of homelessness
    j.   No political and governmental demands

SPECIFICS

A) To preserve the homeless culture in its entity as desired and demanded by the homeless: "Reserved piece of land near populated areas," may need state or federal government interventions. No matter what county or state will be involved in providing sufficient settlement space, there is always some empty or unsettled piece of land available. Resettlement is nothing new. It provided workable solutions in past cultural endeavors with American Natives, Religious and other groups seeking separation from the general public to suit their privacy cause and needs.

I should point out an important factor. My practical approach to a homeless solution does not consider cost and budgets needed by authorities to fund my suggestions. However, I have read enough studies and proposals on the homeless situation to realize that in the long run, the immediate solution will offset the initial expenses by multiple factors, in turn, saving millions of wasted dollars, on trial by error accommodations, when implemented.

B) The main consideration for: "Easy access with free transportation to cities," is another important factor linking to section A. Where American Natives and Religious groups may have been satisfied being isolated from organized society, the homeless are not. They demand and seek out ready access to commerce, shopping, and entertainment facilities when needed and desired. The reason is obvious. They do not contribute to industry and commerce and are wholly dependent on support provided by the government and reliant on organized society, meaning us citizens.

But more importantly, the city is a best source for their daily supplies of drugs and alcohol. Without ready access to the substances, we might as well forget the entire settlement effort. That leaves easy access to transportation.

"How can one obtain ready access to transportation without paying for it?"

Taxies such as Yellow Cab are out of the question and so are Lyft and other privately held companies. What remains is the Bus. Bussing would probably be the best suitable transport for their purpose and least expensive for the tax payer to fund and government to regulate. However, there would be strings attached in the form of regulated travel times, much like in an organized society. Busses will run scheduled from morning to late night with mandatory closing time during night time hours. Whoever misses the last bus will be subjected to local ordinances, enforced by police.

There will be no concession or special accommodation for the homeless when trying to bunk on the streets or parks. There will be no exception. They will be subjected to the same rules and regulations as mandated for the general public, unless one desires to spent the night in the city individually paying for hotel, motel, apartment, hostel or other accommodation.

C) What makes homelessness distinct from American Natives and Religious groups as identified above is: "No confinement unless desired." Where the two groups identified above are bonded by their common heritage, race or faith, the homeless are not. They are thrown together from various levels of society generally accepting their diversified back grounds. What matters most is to gather enough substance and sustenance to survive another day and night without confinement and authority control.

I must point out that over the past decades many forms of housing solutions, from neighborhood projects to communal living, have been tried without much success. Some, mostly the economically deprived, after having been evicted of dwellings and individual privacy, welcomed the opportunity for being accommodated with housing and government support. Many welcomed the housing initiatives to enable them a new and productive life in the social environment of their inherited or acquired lives.

Unfortunately, a problem as a permanent solution in all cases gradually surfaced. It was the lack of sustainable support. Overburdened with taxes, cost of living increase, inflation and economic recessions, most housing projects rapidly collapsed, leaving occupants without heat in winter and air conditioning during the hot season without an alternative for support, ending their new start in life in a very short time, leaving the destitute to fend for themselves.

D) Whereas structured living for the homeless has also been tried numerous times, it has always ended in failure. The main reason for failure was due to multitude causes with the major reason being: "Missing structured and flexible-elected management."

"What is the major cause for homelessness?"

"Lack of discipline."

It used to be, where every child knew the meaning of discipline. It was an inherited cultural means for parents to teach their children the meaning of life, "If you don't behave, you'll be punished." Depending on severity, punishment may have ranged from negligent to severe but nevertheless, leaving a lasting impression on the child. Unfortunately, it is not the case with today's many homeless. Where they, the grown-ups, in many instances behave like children demanding everything their addicted minds desire or crave, they have either forgotten or completely lost the notion of discipline. It is this notion that must be reestablished once more.

"How can that be possible with the adult?"

"Through firm, but understanding parenting."

The homeless has to learn and respect the environment they chose to make a living. There cannot be an exception. It is either comply or get booted out. A hardcore drug addict may need to have a sober moment to comprehend the ruling but it's a necessity for communal living. And, communal it will be, but with accommodations for individual needs, as well as provided opportunities.

Opportunities will come in the form of communal directions and management provided for by capable individuals trained in managing people and affairs, volunteered from within the homeless' own ranks. Recruitment does not stop there. Skills for creating and implementing the various needs for a community will be elected from within and by the respective communal resources to first, construct needed housing followed with the necessary utilities and provisions from gardening produce to raising livestock with initial tools and skills provided by county, state or local businesses. Regardless of acquired habit and addiction, everybody capable of work will get involved. Rules and regulations will be curtailed to a bare minimum to make the community work.

Those are the rules to obey by. There is no hurry for building a new home for the individual or family. Tents and portable toilets provided by local government and stores will be used as temporary housing and facilities. The question remains:

"Who will pay for it now and into the future."

"Tax payer for now and community member in the future."

Once the initial settlement is created, it can easily be sustained and supported by communal members. After initial settlements are established and proven worthy and successful, the homeless' mindset will accept the required responsibility and limited discipline for having guaranteed shelter, support, and freedom of living away from the general society a homeless desires.

E) I assure the reader, once such a community is built, the "collective communal spirit" will follow. A homeless, regardless of background and acquired plight, though destined for outdoor living, will not accept personal isolation. They have the need to mingle among their own kind within a personally acquired environment. It is the relentless demands and orders from local or federal governments, established business and concerned citizens that they despise. Once demands and orders are removed, their homeless spirits will take productive roots, to enjoy the fruits of individual participation and achievement.

Of course, there has to be peace and order among the community. Where minor infractions will have to be solved by communal management through deserving penalties, more severe cases will have to be dealt with by city and county authorities. Crime, no matter created by whom, needs to be punished. Otherwise, we will experience more terrorized situations we have witnessed with rioting in cities and towns, lootings of businesses, burnings of neighborhoods, vehicle vandalism, personal assaults and killings in recent upheaval and lawlessness created by criminals during the Coronavirus lockdowns.

F) "Local collective counseling," as is the case with any community, large and small, there will be individual needs for personal counseling in mental and medical health, as well as for physical wellbeing. Again, it will be a service provided locally, if minor in nature or for more severe cases, from professional services provided by the city or county. Where living in an organized society mental imbalance may occur at a minimum during normal times, a homeless community will experience it to a much greater extent due to the prolific use of alcohol and drugs.

Due to the inherited distrust for the homeless towards law enforcement in general, self-policing will become a major factor, again, enforced by communal members. The mere mention of, "Police" and "Jail," will be enough to reconsider any criminal intent on the individual for not getting cast into the hands of disciplines society. Perhaps over time, the inherited fear, along with rejection, may well diminish with second generation communal members. After all, it will become the choice of the individual to remain at the community or move into organized society. It's been done all the time in native reservations.

G) Another factor, perhaps the most important one is for: "Promoting skilled applications," for providing shelter, dwellings, town related facilities, gathering places and whatever else services are necessary and desired to manage a well-developed community. Well-developed for the homeless may be an oxymoron just by the notion in itself. We all have experienced the mess and disorder found within tent cities, in today's homeless community.

I should point out again that it is not entirely the homeless' fault for living in a shambled environment. Governments, at times, have seen similar conditions as a result of conflicts and wars where both sides have been fighting prolonged years without meaningful incentives. Over time, initial enthusiasm and energy gradually wane, resulting in stagnation from the initial cause. Likewise, conditions can also change within the political and economic wellness state, affecting a specific nation's leadership. Consequently, conditions have to be periodically assessed and monitored with occasional interaction between any given community and local government.

H) Amidst all of the considerations stated above for providing a future life, not only for the homeless that pioneered in creating the community but more importantly, for next generations, there is another important factor to consider: "Opportunity for job skill training."

It may be a notion not considered by the current residences, but will become important to their offspring. The thought alone may be something foreign to the homeless itself, but should be consider for their children growing up within the community.

I'm talking about one of my favorite subject: "Discipline."

"It is discipline that must be taught to a child from birth on."

"Discipline," may be a harsh and offending label to many in today's lifestyle, but is still necessary to maintain law and order. Without it, just another homeless drifter will grow up in a place created by former drifters. Agreed, not every offspring will have virtues instilled while growing up to fit into an organized society. There are always exceptions passed along, much like inherited habits such as drugs and alcohol. It will be up to the individual parents to decide what should become of their children. It is the reason the community was created on first place, bringing likeminded people together to try and live in peace and harmony, suitable to their taste and habits.

But that reason was reserved for the original pioneers. Every growing-up child must be provided with an opportunity equally extended to the common citizen living in the organized society. It's up to the parent to provide such chances, if they want their child to flourish in a country providing endless opportunities such as the United States, the foundation of "equality and freedom for all."

Where the child may have experienced a sense of "freedom" extended by birthright form within a community, "opportunity" must be provided in the form of education and discipline. Consequently, much like with public teachings, a communal school becomes the focal point for every child living within the community.

I) The second most despised notion within the homeless community is "taxation," the principle reason for isolating themselves from organized society.

"Taxes?" Their response when the word is brought up.

"Not for me."

"Never."

"Not ever."

These are some of the responses one will receive when the subject of taxation is mentioned. It is the very reason why the homeless wind up in the gutters. The word, equal to poison itself, must have been forever instilled in the homeless' brain. The thought alone will bring on a violent reaction in many. Where, for the most part, most of us citizens grow up with the purpose of becoming a productive part in the nation's organized society, there are the exceptions to the general rule.

I say "for the most part," purposely for the following reason.

I've never thought it possible that the once most revered and respected nation on the globe, the United States of America, will fall into the realm of a "third nation." And here we landed, in the "Year 2021," much like life in a homeless "tent city" environment, subjected to chaotic conditions in many sectors of the country. To get a better and unbiased objective on our prevalent chaotic state of affairs, daily, I tune into foreign news broadcasts. I must say, whatever individual or sector in our government created the mess we live in today, it is viewed with disgust by other nations.

Not only did we create an out-of-control-condition of lawlessness, being terrorized from within the country from our own people, we are setting trends carried around the globe to the rest of the world.

"Who's fault was it to create such chaotic conditions" many of us ponder.

"It wasn't the homeless' fault."

"Then, who's responsibility is it," the question remains.

"Us Citizens," or our leader's in government, the "Politicians?"

The facts were slow to surface, but they are now out in the open as for who created the uncontrollable conditions we all have to endure at this time. I don't want to dwell on Coronavirus and prevalent state of national affairs because the very thought brings on a reaction of total disgust. But, there is consolation to it all. The political pendulum will swing to the opposite side soon to balance out the state of national affairs. It did in the past and, once more, will happen in the future to preserve the country's safety and wellbeing, protecting its citizens and constitution, to carry us safely into a future with endless opportunities, once more.

J) This brings us to the last article on my list of homeless demands: "No political and governmental interference." The proposed article in my list of "Homeless grievances," by no means cover all of the possibilities for making a community work. However, as stated, they are articles of importance to all members trying to create their own environment, political and economic. It may be easier said than done when considering the acquisition of needed land owned by the government.

Notwithstanding all of the many objectionable elements involved in creating not only one community, spread throughout out every state, county and city in the nation, but places as demanded by the culture. It may seem an impossible task when considering many failed endeavors of this nature in the past, but an attempt must be made since there is no alternative, aside from incarcerating the homeless within tent cities, county jails and federal prisons, forever dependent on social support managed by the authorities and funded by tax payers.

"What are the driving factors for success," one may ponder.

"There are numerous," is the obvious answer.

Let's look at the most important ones that, on a much smaller scale can equally be applied to the community of any size. Following are examples of elements viewed from a national and global perspective but equally important and applicable to the communal life. Once the community is organized and accepted by society, it can flourish on its own or become part of the local environment. The incentives to achieve success will be created through the common bond originated from the once meaningless lives of the homeless, motivated through the aid of:

a) Law and Order
b) Wealth and Prosperity
c) Trade and Economics
d) Industrial and Technology
e) Domestic and foreign Policies
f) Current and future Expansion

It all comes down to factors of healthy lifestyle for all within the security of the nation as well as the community.

"Will it end there?"
"Of course not."
Let's analyze the individual factors.

A) Law and Order – As we all have recently experienced, 2019 through the present date, to preserve global status and citizen wellbeing in the country, law and order are primary instruments for creating and maintaining a safe and secure environment for its population and leadership alike. If it cannot be achieved, the country will face anarchy. In mentioning the state of anarchy, I must admit that the general American citizen is not well informed of this tumultuous condition the nation could experience. Being born and raised within turmoil, following the collapse of Germany after WWII, I can project such condition at first hand.

Living within a state that lacks law and order, one must take an interest in foreign news broadcasts, projected by unbiased and uncensored events as they occurred in another country. There are numerous places in the world where people are ordered to accept chaotic condition created by selfish leadership considered Dictator, or nation run by extremists considered Fascists, or worse yet, entrapped into decades of war and conflicts to places such as Iraq, Afghanistan, Somalia and many more fueled by industrial giants, such as us.

It is not to say that countries such as the United States, Russia and China are intentionally forcing chaotic conditions on less fortunate nations, smaller in geographic size without developed status and economically limited industries. Such is mostly based on political ambition and/or allied an nation asking us for protection. Help to another nation is how we became involved in the past, where after the conflict was resolved, we pulled our troops out of the war zone without expecting a "Thank you," or receiving any restitution for precious lives lost and hardship endured, at times over many decades.

On a smaller and local scale, the state, city, and county, situations can get out of hand and just as bad, as we have recently experienced firsthand with domestic terrorism taking over, if we let it happen. One may want to ask:

"Who is to blame for such lawlessness?"

"Who ordered the national guards to stand down?"

"Where was the police force during the chaotic condition?"

"What about politicians, national defense, administrative leadership with many federal, city, and county administrations in hiding?"

"What about our president and his administration?"

I can assure you, the chaotic conditions were promoted from the top on down through all ranks. Our leadership must not think much of us citizens to create a national crisis not seen for two hundred years affecting each and every one of us economically, industrially, socially and personally, primarily using the Coronavirus as an excuse.

"How can the nation's people fix such atrocity when the government won't." There is only one solution:

"Voting the right people into office."

"People, wake up from your dazed comfort zone!"

B) Wealth and Prosperity – These are two major virtues that will only be achieved through a healthy economy supported by a sound judicial system enforced by law and order. I can only pose one question:

"Whatever happened to the American Dream, the quality that brought people like myself to this once powerful nation?"

To create a healthy nation that can enjoy a long-term prosperity is not created overnight. It takes decades, and sometimes even longer. Being prosperous means you have a life worth living, achieved through financial success. Prosperity should be everybody's aspiration and enjoyment, whether rich, middle class or poor. It should be an opportunity to strive for not only by the individual, but more importantly, as a nation. It is the nation that will provide and sustain the security for its individually acquired wealth.

Moreover, prosperity should be all of our goals. Being prosperous means you have a life worth living. It means you are making the world a better place and helping others prosper as well.

This country not only enjoyed a "Rich prosperity." In the period of 1947 through 1979, it created what was considered a time of the "Great prosperity." Everybody in the nation benefited from the success. Business promoted more earnings for the wealthy. The industry supported the middle class where every able-body worker could have a home, automobile and conveniences to support the entire family. The poor, disproportionate, and needy received ample support from state and federal government. Our society was booming.

"What happened," I ponder many times.

"Success is not everlasting," is the answer.

Unfortunately, the good times will never last long. Prosperity, as a result promotes ambition, which brings along desires for more, turning into greed by many. It does not stop there. Greed is not enough for some successful individuals. What follows is power and control. Those who excel in it develop a great urge to dominate the masses which affects everybody and everything else, including the very nature of our culture. Once corruption sets in and becomes prevalent, it is the beginning of the end of the good times. People born in the 50s, and before, have experienced this cycle with its downward trends several times over in past decades.

There is not much the consciences individual can due other than continue with your effort and wait it out. It seems that every other generation faces the same or similar cycle from success to failure of a nation. Personally, I have come to accept the trends as part of an economic cycle as proven and projected through history. It's not only this country that gained great success, many nations before us experienced the same cycle of success followed by the ultimate collapse. It's the collapse that will spur on a new cycle for the capable nation. Others may never succeed again.

C) Trade and Economy

To explain trade, it is a basic economic concept involving the buying and selling of goods and services, with compensation paid by a buyer to a seller. The exchange of goods or services between parties equally falls into the same category. Trade can take place within an economy between producers and consumers, or could extend internationally to allows countries to expand markets for both goods and services that otherwise may not have been available. It is the reason why an American consumer can pick between a Japanese, German, or American automobile. As a result of international trade, the market contains greater competition and therefore, more competitive prices, which brings a more affordable product home to the consumer.

Trade does not stop there. It also affects the financial system and stock exchange. Trading globally, between nations, allows consumers and countries to select goods and services not available in their own countries. Almost every kind of product can be found on the international markets from food, clothes, spare parts, oil, jewelry, wine, stocks, currencies, to many more products. Services are also traded with tourism, banking, consulting, and transportation when in demand.

It does not stop there when trade goes global. Again, success does not last once Comparative Advantage takes over and becomes the norm. Global trade, in theory, allows wealthy countries to use their resources in labor, technology, or capital more effectively. Because countries are endowed with different assets and natural resources in land, labor, capital, and technology, some countries may produce the same goods more efficiently and therefore sell it more cheaply than other countries. If a country cannot efficiently produce an item, it can obtain the item by trading with another country that can.

D) Industrial and Technology
Technology, as a whole, is comprised of many industry sectors with the major ones being Internet, Ecommerce, Consumer Electronics, AI, Robotics, Outsourcing, Information Security, Health, Media, Marketing, Education, Finance, Insurance,

Stock Exchange, Science, Space, Energy, Transportation and more.

To get an understanding for technology, one must look at the industry as a whole. The technology sector is often the most attractive investment goal in any economy. The U.S. technology sector, for instance, boasts of companies like Google, Amazon, Facebook, Apple, Netflix, IBM, and Microsoft being leaders in the industry. These companies have been created and benefitted with rapid growth and expansion from technology.

Where the technology sector was initially anchored in semiconductors, computing hardware, and communications equipment, once catching root in the U.S. industry, rapidly extended their tenacles into many other business sectors. Soon, more space was needed for Internet companies, which flooded during the initial Internet boom through the 90s. It did not stop there.

Technology has replaced other industries that once were directing our economic growth. Take for instance the leader in previous centuries with the Industrial Revolution being a success, initially for the U.S., quickly followed by other countries with equal successes. Looking at today's outlook into the future, it is technology that will drive commerce, services, production, transport, deliveries, energy, to mention some. Where these expansions may be earth bound, much greater technological challenges are awaiting us such as space exploration pending budget allocation, artificial intelligence AI, and new technologies experimented with in laboratories, eventually making their way into mainstream society.

E) Domestic and foreign Policies

To get a true picture of policies, domestic policy are administrative decisions that are directly related to all issues and activities within a state's borders. It differs from foreign policy, which refers to the means a government advances its interests in external politics. More specifically, domestic policies are broad and can cover various issues important to society covering just about every social issue for abortion, capital punishment, domestic violence, human trafficking, homelessness, illegal drugs and more. Domestic policies help to solve issues by putting forth plans, laws, or even programs to make improvements within society.

In contrast to domestic policy, localized to the interior of the country, foreign policy is for promoting freedom and democracy in the protecting of human rights around the world. Specifics and values captured in the "Universal Declaration of Human Rights" and in other global and regional commitments are consistent with the values with which the United States was founded centuries ago.

F) Current and future Expansion

With regards to the proposed communal life, it is assured that there will come the time and need to expand the community, facilities, and/or location once it has outgrown its present space. Depending on population density, it may present a challenge for the authorities to either increase the settlement's present size or to allocate new space. It would not be the first time a settlement demanded more space.

Alternatively, it could also be a case where the settlement could be terminated because the settlers moved on or merged into mainstream society. However, it may take generations for that to happen. But by that time, sentiments and demands between citizens and the homeless may have resolved itself on its own merits accepting government and political policies extended by the authorities to the once homeless society.

APPENDIX A – Articles on Collaborative Objectives

This Appendix is Eric's Articles on Collaborative Objectives, that he'd developed for the Mayor of San Francisco to help the city with the growing homeless problem in response to the Federal outlined "Home Together" program.

Objective 1.1 – Collaboratively Build Lasting Systems "With regards to you homeless, this means ending homelessness. Leaders from all levels of government come together to provide a roadmap to success for homeless communities across the country. This common vision allows them to coordinate activities, policies, and priorities through regional, state, and local working groups, councils, and other processes to achieve progress. Bringing together areas of the government reduces duplicative or contradictory activities to ensure the most effective use of public resources."

"What exactly does that mean?" one attendee broke in.

"It means exactly what it says," Eric patiently explained. "Building homeless communities and supporting them." Regardless of his diligence and patience, there continued to be interruptions with every article that followed. He allowed their interruptions after he realized that, while the articles might have been written and clearly understood by government officials in political terms, they were subject to interpretation by the homeless.

Objective 1.2 – Prevent Housing Crises and Homelessness, "means balanced living quarters at your preference. Reduce the prevalence of risk of housing crises. To make inroads in reducing the risk of housing crises, communitywide action is needed to address the wide range of policies contributing to the availability of, and access to, an adequate supply of safe and affordable housing; health and behavioral health resources; education and meaningful and gainful employment; opportunities for economic mobility; affordable child care; and legal assistance."

"What is 'balanced living quarters'?" another caller demanded. "I can speak for all of us."

"It means you can chose whether to live in an organized and paid-for apartment, or you can remain in the homeless community," Eric explained.

Objective 2.1 – Identify and Engage All People, "what about it?"

"It means," Eric explained, "You'll be subjected to census and counted. It's important to quickly identify and engage individuals and families when they do fall into homelessness—including sheltered and unsheltered homelessness in locations such as cars, parks, abandoned buildings, encampments, or on the street."

"Here we go," was the next complaint. "Herded and tagged like sheep."

"It doesn't mean that at all," Eric protested on behalf of the government. "It is necessary to establish a budget for your growing culture."

"What culture?"

"Homeless culture."

"So," one wanted clarified, "we are a culture now?"

"If you want to remain homeless, you'll be considered a culture because that's your ultimate objective. Isn't it?" Eric challenged him.

There was a silent pause while the revelation needed to be digested. It was something the homeless had not considered and from the many positive signs, it appeared they approved of the unity and terms.

Objective 2.2 – Access to Low-Barrier Emergency Shelter, "means emergency shelter, other temporary accommodations, and other crisis services are the critical front line of communities' responses to homelessness, helping people meet basic survival needs for shelter, food, clothing, and personal hygiene, while also helping them resolve crises and swiftly secure permanent housing opportunities."

Objective 2.3 – Coordinated Entry to Standardize Assessment and Prioritization Processes, "means accounting for and taking into account the unique needs of different populations, including parents, infants and young children, youth, people with disabilities, people living with HIV/AIDS, survivors of domestic violence, and populations that are disproportionately represented among people experiencing homelessness."

Objective 2.4 – Assist People to Move Swiftly into Permanent Housing, "means to end homelessness as quickly and efficiently as possible. Communities must focus on streamlining connections to permanent housing and providing people with the appropriate level of services to support their long-term housing stability."

Objective 3.1 – Prevent Returns to Homelessness, "means ensuring that individuals and families do not fall back into homelessness. It will be necessary to strengthen partnerships with, and connections to, a larger array of federal, state, local, and private programs that serve low-income households, including programs that: advance education and employment opportunities and support upward economic mobility; provide connections to health and behavioral health care services; and link people to a range of other programs and systems that support strong and thriving communities, such as quality child care, schools, family support networks, and other resources as stated in 'Home Together.'"

Objective 4.1 – Sustain Practices and Systems at a Scale, "means communities across the country are demonstrating that ending homelessness is not just a worthy ambition, but a measurable, achievable goal. In order to sustain those successes, communities will need to monitor outcomes and returns to homelessness, to ensure that adequate investments into the crisis response system and into permanent housing interventions are sustained to address future needs, and to continue to refine projections to address changing needs and ensure the maximum impact of investments over time."

APPENDIX B – Addictions & Users

10 Most Common Addictions & Users in the U.S. in 2021.

Painkillers – 191 million
Drugs like codeine, Vicodin, and Oxycontin are commonly prescribed to treat pain. Painkillers' prescription status does not mean they aren't addictive. Addiction to painkillers can develop from seemingly harmless levels of use. Most patients who become addicted to prescription painkillers don't notice they have a problem until they try to stop use. Painkillers are also abused without a prescription, which can also lead to an addiction.

Inhalants – 22.9 million
Inhalant addiction is particularly dangerous because inhalants are volatile toxic substances. The effects of these substances—gasoline, household cleaning products, aerosols—are intense and can have immediate consequences including hospitalization or death. Chemicals prevalent in inhalants can linger in the body and brain long after stopping use, making complete recovery more difficult.

Marijuana – 22.2 million
The legalization of marijuana in some states has made the drug's use more socially acceptable. This trend can distract people from marijuana's addictive potential. Rates of marijuana addiction might also be growing due to increasing potency (over 60 percent) over the past decade.

Sedatives (Barbiturates) – 19 million
Millions of Americans are prescribed barbiturate sedatives, commonly known as sleeping pills, to treat tension and sleep disorders. Every year, thousands of prescription users build a tolerance—and ensuing addiction—to drugs like Lunesta and Ambien. Sleeping pills can produce mind-altering effects that lead to continued abuse.

Stimulants – 16 million

Stimulants range from prescription drugs, such as Adderall or Ritalin, to illicit substances like meth. These drugs are highly addictive, and intense withdrawal symptoms make quitting difficult. Stimulant users can quickly build a tolerance to the drug's euphoric "high," leading to increased use and risk of overdose.

Methamphetamines – 14.7 million
Methamphetamine is a central nervous system stimulant. It affects chemicals in the brain and nerves that contribute to hyperactivity and impulse control. Methamphetamine is used to treat attention deficit hyperactivity disorder (ADHD). Methamphetamine is also used to treat obesity in people who have not lost weight with diets or other treatments.

Alcohol – 14.4 million
The social acceptance of drinking can make alcohol addiction hard to spot. Despite its legal status, alcohol's potential for abuse opens users up to many health risks and possible addiction. Alcohol abuse has numerous negative consequences. In addition to deaths from liver disease and alcohol overdose, drunk driving claims thousands of lives every year.

Cocaine (Crack) – 10 million
Rates of cocaine addiction in the United States are dropping. Crack cocaine, which is cheaper and more intense than regular cocaine, is responsible for many crippling addictions and ruined lives.

Benzodiazepines – 4.1 million
"Benzos"—such as Valium, Xanax, Diazepam, and Klonopin—are prescribed as mood-regulating drugs to manage conditions like anxiety and stress. Those developing an addiction to these drugs oftentimes aren't aware until they can't function normally without the substance. Benzodiazepines are especially dangerous because of their powerful impact on the brain's chemical makeup. Withdrawals can be deadly without medical assistance during detox.

Heroin – 808,000

Heroin's severe withdrawal symptoms make beating a heroin addiction a difficult task. Treating heroin addiction typically requires a combination of therapy and medications to help manage symptoms of withdrawal and cravings. Heroin abuse has been growing in the United States, particularly among young women. There is growing concern over heroin users contracting and spreading diseases like HIV and AIDS by sharing needles for injection.

APPENDIX C – April's Journal Accounts...Continued

Intrusions by Others

After a couple of days, with both resting at home while continuing to make entries in the journal, April illustrated some of her own accounts. Intrusions were something April had experienced first-hand. She did not have to ask anybody else about how it feels to be invaded.

"No matter what the conditions are living on the streets, there is always somebody out to get you."

"It used to never be this way but in recent years, with the influx of drug addiction, the homeless culture has changed dramatically."

"If it's not for money they want or need to get another fix, they'll steal you blind of things worth a few dollars at a pawnshop, if you let them get away with it."

"You learn to protect your property and fight for your subsistence, the little you have."

"It's a constant struggle to get through another day, week, and month only to realize you wasted another year."

"Life passes by so quickly before you know wasted time went by without a change."

"You really don't mind as long as you're healthy. But, once you get sick, the struggle for survival takes over, but there's a problem: you are totally subjected to the person treating and helping you."

"What it means is that you only get pity and sympathy sometimes from the individual helping you. Most of the times it's dislike and disgust people display."

Lack of Privacy

One of her most memorable moments was talking with a female soldier who never could fit back into structured society after her return from Afghanistan. When she told her story, tears came into April's eyes.

"I had really bad post-traumatic stress disorder (PTSD) after returning home," she insisted.

"Without a family and goals, and no meaningful job prospects, I wound up homeless. Being a woman and young, even though I was part of a platoon and had been in the company of men and other women sharing bathroom facilities, what bothered me most was the complete lack of privacy. You'd think it wouldn't bother me but it did. I sought out places to hide but never really felt comfortable and safe."

"How did this impact you in the long run?" April asked, feeling a deep compassion for the woman.

"The constant vulnerability just seemed to build up to a state of mind where I lost complete sense of reality in behaving like a normal person.

"I became short-fused, intolerable to everybody, angry at the slightest confrontation, ready to pick a fight.

"Being a trained combat fighter, I was fearless to begin with, but without getting reprimanded by a superior, as is the case in the military, I built up an aggressive behavior beyond my control. It did not take long for me to land in jail, not only once but a number of times."

"How do you feel now, today?" April said, wondering if there would ever be a chance for the woman to adjust.

"I still don't know what to do with my life. I'm addicted to drugs just to contain my inner rage, without any change in sight. I need help but can't break away from this life."

It was enough for April. She felt depressed at the lack of willingness and strength for the woman ever to have a prospect or opportunity to better her miserable life. She had heard of PTSD but could not associate with it. While she thought she'd had a tough life, it did not even compare with others. She'd had enough for today, maybe even for good.

Learning to Survive
Glancing over her journal notes, April noticed there were a couple more topics on the list. Since they were important issues for any homeless, she needed to address them. The next time April wandered into homeless territory, she approached a fairly

clean-looking young man who was seemingly assessing her while she passed him on the sidewalk. "What are you doing here?" he asked.

"Taking pictures for the paper. May I take some?" she politely asked.

"Go ahead."

"I'm actually more interested in what a day is like for you, living on the street."

He readily complied to her request. "While a day may start out promising, most days end up with a struggle, mostly emotionally but sometimes ending physically. The weird thing about being homeless after a day's struggle," he explained, "is as soon as you crawl into your sleeping bag, it makes you feel relatively safe. It's like a kid's security blanket that shuts everything out for the night until the next morning, when the first shopper kicks you in the ribs—Hey, get up—or a store owner demands, 'Get off of my property.' What amazes me most is how quickly I adapted to the environment and daily routine, begging to survive another day."

"Is that all you want from life?" April said, prodding for more.

"It's good enough for now. I don't care much for planning out my future. The whole world is upside down, if you ask me. Nobody gives a damn about one poor homeless slob living on the sidewalk. I am not complaining as long as I can keep fending for myself."

"I wish you luck for the future. Take care." April turned and went on her way without looking back.

Rejected from Home and Family

"I was kicked out of the house by my mom after we had another of many arguments," a homeless complained.

"What did you do?" April said, feeling compassion for the young woman.

"I could not do anything right for her by standing up for my rights. At sixteen, I wasn't a child anymore and was attending college. Luckily, I had a car to sleep in for the months that followed. I got a job so I could afford to buy food, but it affected my school grades. I flunked tests and was disqualified from attending the next semester."

"I can sympathize with you," April admitted.

"What scared me the most was having to sleep in public parking lots, but there was a problem. I got chased by security from lots many nights and had to find another location. At times, the police got involved, creating a police record for vagrancy. That was the first step that forced me into homeless living.

"What bothered me most was the nightly crime conducted in the city. I felt unsafe and frightened to a point where I cried myself to sleep. With drug addicts, alcoholics, and psychopaths roaming the streets, you never knew when you were going to be attacked and robbed. I tried to return home but my mom refused to take me back, saying, 'I can't trust you.'

"The police are supposed to protect you, but that isn't the case. There were many times I was pulled from my car, tested for alcohol and drugs, handcuffed and thrown into the back of a patrol car, winding up in jail for the night. Next morning, I would return to my car and find it torn apart from searches for drugs and weapons. I was always afraid of losing my car which was my home. Without it, I would be forced to sleep on the ground somewhere just like other homeless. I don't know what my future would look like other than being homeless bound for the rest of my life."

Feeling sorry for the unfortunate, what else could April do but console the young girl? "Stay safe and keep up your spirits."

"Are you coming back to visit me again?" the girl asked.

"You can count on it."

Searching for a Sleeping Spot
Walking another district and street, April stumbled across one of many makeshift spots homeless called their home. It was a

pitiful sight, its inhabitants meaninglessly loitering in the gutter. As expected, after getting close enough to talk, filth could be seen everywhere, with evil smells seeping up from every corner of the sidewalk. For April, living on The Hill in a pristine environment, the mere presence was revolting to the point of almost getting her sick. She turned to leave and bumped into a young woman her age loaded down with an oversized backpack almost too large to fit her frame.

"Sorry," the woman muttered, moving on.

"Wait up," April called after her. "I'd like to talk to you."

The woman turned to see. "What?"

"Can I talk with you?"

"Why?" There was a definite defiance in the woman's attitude. It sounded like trouble to April, but she stood her ground.

"You've got a minute? Just want to talk."

The woman eyed her curiously, then challenged, "I don't talk to strangers."

"I used to be a homeless," April claimed, watching the other woman's attitude change from defiance to curiosity.

"How did you get out of it?"

"Can we sit somewhere? How about some ice cream?"

"You serious?" It was obvious that nobody had ever made such an offer. It even produced a warming smile.

"Yes, I'm serious. You know a place?"

It was enough for the woman to get going. "Follow me. I know a place around the corner."

April picked up the conversation as they went. "I want you to know that I'm not nosy. I just want to take a couple of pictures."

The woman halted in her tracks. "I don't like it. I don't want to wind up in some magazine or paper."

For whatever personal reasons she had, April respected that. "Okay. We'll just talk."

It was immediately apparent that the woman had not had an ice cream treat for some time. She greatly enjoyed it. "This is too much. Nobody has ever treated me this way. You sure you are a homeless?"

"Several years. I started living on the streets in this area."

"Really? How did you get out of it?" April had her attention. At least for as long as her treat lasted.

"I got lucky. Collided with a biker on an intersection. We became friends and live together now."

"Sounds like a fairytale. Wish it'd happen to me."

"It is," April assured her.

"How do you feel living a normal life again?"

"It took some time to adjust to disciplined society but my friend helped me a lot. I am much indebted to him, but also love him."

"You are one fortunate chick. Tell me more."

April was pleased that she'd captured the woman's mind and could make time to tell her story for the first time, only because somebody had asked her. "Later. I want to learn about you. Tell me how you wound up here."

"I want you to know, I didn't plan on becoming homeless," the woman insisted.

"Nobody does, I assure you," April consoled her.

"I became homeless at age 16 after finishing high school. I left home for the city, not knowing what to expect. Practically penniless, I had high hopes of finding a job. It took several days to orient my senses amidst the bustle of trolley cars, streams of car traffic, speeding pickup trucks, and sidewalk pedestrians bumping into me. I became overwhelmed. In the bustle of things I failed to locate a hostel cheap enough for the night and wound up sleeping in a boat anchored by the bay. And so, days and weeks went by, searching for a job, eating a free meal in a soup kitchen, honestly begging for money to live another day and seeking out a quiet spot to bed down, only to wake up at sunrise praying today would be the day I'd land a job."

"I know the feeling," April said. "I went through it."

"So, one day followed another with the same routine. It wasn't what I had expected from life in the city but I didn't have complaints since it was only temporary, I thought. In the meantime, I met new faces almost daily, advising me to do this and do that and sometimes I got invited to stay overnight at their place. Unfortunately, it was a place and time plagued with unemployment and nobody was hiring. Even fast food places had a waiting list of job seekers.

"I survived the winter by begging people for quarters daily and by bunking at a crowded homeless shelter. It was a long winter and I could hardly wait for spring to get back out in the open again. Regardless of my meager lifestyle and measly begging, it's here where I feel at home now. What about you?"

April felt it was her turn to tell her story now, but wanted to move from the sidewalk, which was getting busy with pedestrians rushing home from the office to catch the cable car. It was getting late in the afternoon and she felt parched from talking. "Can I get you something to drink?"

"You buying?"

"Of course. It's the least I can do for you after taking your time."

"I've got nowhere else to go. Okay."

"How about a shake?"

"That'd be great." They spent more time together within the cheerful atmosphere of a Ben & Jerry's, with a promise to meet up again soon.